The Others

Blood on the Stars XIII

Jay Allan

ISBN: 978-1-946451-15-6

Books by Jay Allan

Flames of Rebellion Series
(Published by Harper Voyager)
Flames of Rebellion
Rebellion's Fury

The Crimson Worlds Series
Marines
The Cost of Victory
A Little Rebellion
The First Imperium
The Line Must Hold
To Hell's Heart
The Shadow Legions
Even Legends Die
The Fall

Crimson Worlds Refugees Series
Into the Darkness
Shadows of the Gods
Revenge of the Ancients
Winds of Vengeance
Storm of Vengeance

Crimson Worlds Successors Trilogy
MERCS
The Prisoner of Eldaron
The Black Flag

Crimson Worlds Prequels
Tombstone
Bitter Glory
The Gates of Hell
Red Team Alpha

Join my email list
at www.jayallanbooks.com

List members get publication announcements and special bonuses throughout the year (email addresses are never shared or used for any other purpose). Please feel free to email me with any questions at jayallanwrites@gmail.com. I answer all reader emails

For all things Sci-Fi,
join my interactive Reader Group here:

facebook.com/groups/JayAllanReaders

Follow me on Twitter @jayallanwrites

Follow my blog at www.jayallanwrites.com

www.jayallanbooks.com
www.crimsonworlds.com

Books by Jay Allan

Blood on the Stars Series
Duel in the Dark
Call to Arms
Ruins of Empire
Echoes of Glory
Cauldron of Fire
Dauntless
The White Fleet
Black Dawn
Invasion
Nightfall
The Grand Alliance
The Colossus
The Others

Andromeda Chronicles
(Blood on the Stars Adventure Series)
Andromeda Rising

The Far Stars Series
Shadow of Empire
Enemy in the Dark
Funeral Games

Far Stars Legends Series
Blackhawk
The Wolf's Claw

Portal Wars Trilogy
Gehenna Dawn
The Ten Thousand
Homefront

Also by Jay Allan – The Dragon's Banner

Chapter One

HWS Effestius
Venta Traconis System
Year of Renewal 267 (322 AC)

The beam sliced through the vast expanse of dark and frozen space, an electric blue spear, speckled along its vast length with bits of swirling black and dark gray. There was an eerie aspect to it, a feeling of coldness despite the massive amounts of energy that drove it and it brought death in its wake.

The extraordinary energy lance was a thing of sinister beauty, possessed of a magnificence that provoked wonder and astonishment for a passing instant, at least, before those emotions turned quickly to darkness and terror. The deadly beam continued its way across hundreds of thousands of kilometers of emptiness and then through the heavily armored hull of the Hegemony monitor, cutting through deck after deck and leaving fire and death behind it. Heavy alloy plating seemed to offer no more resistance to the weapon immense power than had the vast emptiness of space.

Effestius's scanners were going wild, their feedback a flow of indecipherable nonsense, as every attempt to analyze the deadly weapon, to identify the massive energy even then slamming into the ship, was stymied by the indecipherable...*strangeness*...of the thing. It *was* energy, that much was clear, and it put out some kind of radiation as well, but only two conclusions were truly clear in those terrifying moments. First, it was something utterly unlike the weapons the Hegemony's ships carried...or anything else the monitor's crew—or its AIs and their vast petabytes of records and data—had ever encountered.

Second, it was the deadliest and most powerful destructive force anyone on *Effestius,* or anywhere in the rest of the Hegemony fleet, had ever seen, vastly surpassing the power even of the battleships' great railguns.

The beam, no more than twenty centimeters in diameter, cut through the hardened hyper-steel hull of the great battleship, and sliced more than a kilometer and a half through, before emerging from the other side, leaving a second gaping wound in the hull. Inside, all along the deadly beam's path, decks were torn open, systems damaged and destroyed, and hundreds of Kriegeri crew were killed, sliced apart by the beam itself, incinerated as secondary explosions tore through the guts of the vessel, or taken by the deadly cold and vacuum in compromised compartments, killed before they could even shut helmets or activate emergency life support systems.

"Scanner command, I need something better than you don't know. That thing just tore through the entire ship. What the hell was it?" Kel sat stone still in the center of the monitor's massive bridge, exerting all his will—backed up by the pompous self-grandeur he'd always accorded himself as a Master of the Hegemony—to remain calm, to do what he could—what little he could—to staunch the wave of fear spreading through his flagship.

Spreading through the entire fleet...

Through his own transfixed mind, too, though he struggled to deny that last fact, even to himself.

"The AIs have no answer, Megaron. The energy readings

we're getting…they *can't* be correct."

"Why can't they? Because it's more powerful than anything you've seen before? Have you witnessed everything in the universe, Kiloron?" Kel despised sloppy thinking and flawed logic. He was arrogant, some might even call him insufferable, but at his core he was a creature of intellect. The beam had cut through one of the Hegemony's grandest and strongest vessels of war with a strength that defied imagining. But it was still only an energy weapon. It could be explained…his people and their machines simply didn't know how.

Yet.

"Damage reports, all decks." Kel almost disciplined the officer for his careless and shoddy logic, but there wasn't time, not then. He had to save his ship.

Save his fleet. If there were more enemy ships out there—and he still hadn't been able to get a precise location on any of them—his entire advance force was doomed. His orders were to hold in the system, and to send a report back to Calpharon if any enemy were contacted. His flagship was gutted—that was certainly contact—and he knew his first and foremost duty.

He turned toward the comm station, even before he got a response on the damage reports. "All courier ships are to depart at once, at maximum thrust. The high command *has* to know about this. Transmit all available data to the ships before they enter the tube." Kel's voice was still strong, but it was an illusion. His thoughts were becoming more erratic, the realization that he was very likely facing his death in the coming hours, if not minutes, chipping away at his resolve.

"Courier ships acknowledge, Megaron."

"Damage reports on your screen, Commander."

The two responses were almost simultaneous, and it took a second or two for his mind to process both. Then, his eyes dropped to his screen, moving slowly over the scrolling reports. He expected the worst…but what he saw was even more terrible. The damage to *Effestius* was vast, probably mortal if his damage control teams didn't pull off a miracle in the next few minutes.

Something was still holding *Effestius* together, amid the internal explosions and rolling power failures, his own continued existence confirmed that. But it wasn't much. His ship was critically damaged, three of its reactors knocked out completely, along with half the transmission lines leading from the fourth. There were widespread malfunctions throughout the ship, and every weapons array he had was down. As if to emphasize the dire nature of the situation, the bridge lights flickered twice and then a few seconds later, they went out for good.

The emergency units kicked in almost immediately, not exactly replacing all of the lost illumination, but providing enough light for his officers to run the ship. What was left of it, at least. The battery power would last for a few hours, four or five at most. But Kel knew, deep in his mind, and in his rapidly beating heart, that *Effestius*'s backup power systems would never get the chance to burn through their charge.

Kel stared at the readings coming in, and as he did, a thought slowly began to take shape, a conclusion that stripped him of the last of his courage. His ship was as good as dead, one of the grandest warships of the Hegemony, gutted by a shingle shot from the enemy ships still defying his efforts to precisely locate them. He was there to fight, to defend Hegemony space, but none of that mattered anymore. It was over, save perhaps, for the technicality of actual death, at least for him, and for the fleet's flagship.

He didn't have to wait long for that verdict to become official. Even as he sat there, transfixed for a moment in the cold shock of his conclusion, he felt the shadow of death closing in around him.

He could hear explosions all throughout the massive vessel, and moving closer. The air was caustic, tinged with fumes from the fires and the sharp smells of chemicals released from compromised storage facilities. He imagined the hell on the ship's lower decks, the heat and intense radiation, the Kriegeri, Hegemony warriors all—*his* warriors—dying, choking to death as the air became increasingly toxic.

Kel was no coward, but in that instant, he felt his resolve drain away, his eyes watering as he struggled to deny the death he knew had come for him. He clawed out for hope, anything, even self-delusion was preferable to the dark fear and misery overcoming him.

But there was nothing…nothing but a yawning black pit in front of him, the great cold hands of death reaching for him, taking hold.

He snapped down the visor of his helmet, feeling an instant's relief as cool, pure air flowed into his lungs. But the respite was short-lived.

A moment later, the containment on *Effestius*'s last reactor ruptured, and the great ship vanished in an instant, transformed for a brief few seconds into something almost like a new star…before it slowly disappeared, leaving only radiation and residual energy readings to show that a six-kilometer long warship had once been there.

If Kel had been aware, if he'd been granted a few second's more sentience, he might have considered it a merciful end, a less painful way death than fire or suffocation offered…and an escape from a war that could only bring obliteration and despair.

But there had been no time, no realization. One instant, he was battling against his fear, and then…he was gone.

* * *

"All units, full thrust. Active scanners on maximum power. I want a complete report immediately. I want to know what's going on up there!" Ilius sat in the command chair of the

Hegemony flagship, the position occupied until recently by Chronos, his friend and immediate superior. Number Eight was still the fleet's overall commander, and the Hegemony's effective military leader, but he'd been stuck on Calpharon for weeks, immersed in emergency sessions of the Council. *Talk*, Ilius thought with caustic derision. *Pointless prattle.*

Between the politically-charged inquiries about the failure of the Rim absorption campaign and the likely tsunami of fear-driven arguments and debates about the Others and how to meet the possible invasion, he suspected Chronos already missed the relative simplicity of the stress and danger of battle.

And we can upgrade that invasion status from 'possible' *to* 'actual'…

Chronos was a true leader, and Ilius missed his superior's presence. Despite the failures in the just concluded war, there was no one Ilius trusted more with the top command than Chronos, and in the absence of his friend, the responsibility weighed heavily on him.

There was enough blame to go around about the results of the war on the Rim. Chronos had failed, certainly, as Ilius himself had. The millions of Kriegeri committed to the war had as well, and the Council on Calpharon, too, which had prevaricated on sending resources to the Rim. Mostly, perhaps, they had all underestimated the humans on the Rim—their numbers, their industry, their capability—and the whole thing had fallen into a deadly cycle. The more the Rimdwellers proved their capabilities and their worth, the more essential it became to make them a part of the Hegemony. The greater the losses suffered, the more pressure to show gain for it all, to add the rich industry of the Rim to the Hegemony's economic base. The Rim worlds had suffered from the Great Death, certainly, but far less severely than those systems coreward. Underestimating them had been understandable enough, especially when comparing their worlds to the irradiated and damaged planets the Hegemony had already reclaimed, but that didn't change reality.

None of that mattered now. The Others had come, and they had to be faced, with whatever force remained, the Rim forces alongside the Hegemony's, if Carmetia could somehow achieve that seemingly impossible bit of diplomacy, or without if need be.

Chronos had welcomed Ilius warmly on the commander's return from Confederation captivity. That had been friendship, to a point, but Ilius knew it had been more, that it had come from a place of desperate need, too. Chronos had been desperate for someone to fill his chair, someone he could trust with the fleet, all that remained of ready Hegemony military power after the losses suffered on the Rim, as it moved to face the coming onslaught. Someone capable and trustworthy to face the enemy coming from without, while Chronos addressed the fractures and weaknesses from within.

Ilius knew Chronos had faith in him, but he had also seen something in his commander's eyes, the doubt about leaving the fleet himself on what seemed likely to be the start of the Hegemony's greatest challenge. Chronos had always despised the political maneuverings so prevalent on the Council, but both he and Ilius had realized immediately, there was no choice. The Hegemony faced the greatest threat in its history, and no one—not the Council, not the military, not the legions of highly-ranked Masters in the elite think tanks—seemed to know just what to do. More than a century of fear, of preparedness, of shouted warnings, were all for naught. The Hegemony was in dire peril, weaker than it had been in generations, and the only people it could look to for help had been turned into inveterate enemies by its own actions.

The war on the Rim had been a failure, but now Ilius began to see the true scope of the disaster his people had suffered there. He had questioned the order to surrender

Colossus, and he'd ached to fight on, to take whatever chance had remained to retake control of the great vessel. He'd been ready to send his Kriegeri against the boarders in a last mad assault, struggling to take the explosives before the Confeds could detonate them. But then Chronos had told him why he'd issued the order, passing on the latest intel he'd received from Akella.

Ilius could still remember the feeling, like a cold hand gripping his spine. The Others. They *were* real, and by all accounts, hey lived up to the descriptions Ilius had long discounted as exaggeration. They were a deadly danger, validating the fears long fanned by legend and rumor.

And they had returned.

No doubt remained, no refuge for hope that Armageddon could be averted. Ilius didn't know what he faced, but his concise intellect stripped him of the ability to grasp for pointless shreds of hope. With *Colossus*, with the power of the Rim aligned alongside the Hegemony's own, he dared imagine there would be a real chance of victory against the terrible foe. But his people had lost both of those things. The Rim viewed the Hegemony as a hated enemy, and *Colossus* had been surrendered and left behind. The Hegemony had gambled on gaining control of the Rim, and it had lost. It stood alone.

Ilius didn't expect the Rimdwellers to return *Colossus* any time in the foreseeable future, but the fact that the great ship still survived was something. At least he tried to tell himself that.

Colossus might still return and join the fight, though only in the seemingly unlikely eventuality the Rim nations could be turned from enemies to allies, convinced to leave behind their rage and their thirst for vengeance for the losses they had suffered and join with the Hegemony against the greater enemy.

That task lays heavy on Carmetia's shoulders…

Ilius knew Carmetia. She was a Master, and a

distinguished one, though her rank was considerably lower that his own. He considered her to be reasonably competent, if a bit too strident and annoying for his tastes, but he wondered if she was up to the enormous task that had befallen her.

If she realized her success or failure might very well determine the future—the survival—of the Hegemony itself.

The Rimdwellers are stubborn...

Part of Ilius wanted to look down on his recent adversaries on the Rim, to view them as something just the near side of barbarians, and to despise them anew for allowing petty grudges to blind them to the deadly danger they all faced, the Rim no less than the Hegemony, if the Others could not be stopped.

Then, he questioned how *he* would feel, if, for all his prized intelligence, he could so easily reverse his attitudes, to embrace an invader as an ally. To forgive millions of deaths, to allow the possibility of trusting those you'd just fought desperately against. Yes, there was danger coming, and a fate far worse than absorption into the Hegemony, but how could he expect them to believe that? The Rim lacked any recent experience with the Others. The Rimdwellers had no reason to fear the Others, or to realize that their recent enemies were now their only possible allies. The only hope they had. To them, the dark menace even then moving toward Ilius's fleet, would seem a phantom, or more likely, a lie told by those seeking to undermine them.

"Commander, we are receiving a transmission from *Alpina*."

Alpina? Effestius *is the fleet flagship...*

His stomach went cold, tense.

"On my link, Kiloron. At once."

"Yes, Commander."

A moment later, a voice poured into Ilius's ears. It was familiar. Megaron Helas was Ilius's colleague, not just a comrade, but one among the minuscule group the normally reclusive Master called friends.

And the fleet's second in command…

Ilius could hear the stress in the officer's voice. No, it was more than stress. It was stark terror.

"Ilius…they came out of nowhere. We couldn't even detect them, not until they were right on top of us. We picked up strange readings, spatial anomalies, but nothing useful for targeting. *Effestius*…destroyed. Commander Kel and the entire crew…dead. *Jellas* and *Cormacen*, too. We're trying to pull back, but…"

Ilius winced as Helas's voice was drowned out by the sounds of explosions. *Alpina* was a massive ship, one of the Hegemony's monitors, the largest warships known, save only for *Colossus* itself. The great battleships had been built to face the Others, and they'd remained in place on the coreward border, even through the war on the Rim. Ilius tried to tell himself he was hearing a transient explosion, a random case of energy feedback, but he'd never been very good at ignoring reality. *Alpina* was in trouble, bad trouble if the ship's deeply-located and heavily-armored bridge was taking damage. Monitors had been built for war, and they were designed to be as close to impervious to damage as possible.

But as he watched, Ilius knew, that wasn't close enough.

"Helas, full thrust, all ships. Get the hell out of there. Get your fleet back to the tube." It was precisely the kind of pointless speech Ilius despised when he heard it from others. Helas's ships were clearly already at full thrust, or as close as the damaged vessels could manage, and just as obviously, it wasn't going to be enough. *Hegemony's Glory*'s scanners were struggling even to detect the attacking ships, but what little data they'd gathered was clear. The immense dark cloud on the display was advancing relentlessly. It was an image of blackness and danger, one that seemed almost to pull his courage and his will from his body as he stared at it. Whatever force was out there, it was pursuing Helas, and it was going to catch her battered fleet. Not a ship would escape.

Ilius knew, deep in his gut, he was about to watch his friend die. He was about to witness the utter destruction of an entire Hegemony fleet.

Unless he did something at once.

He couldn't stop the disaster unfolding before him, but perhaps he could mitigate its effects. Every urge in his body, every wild thought in his mind, screamed out to advance, to plunge into the fight without hesitation, to save Helas and the thousands of Kriegeri serving in her fleet.

Or to die trying.

But Ilius did nothing. He said nothing. His discipline slammed down into place, hard, immovable. Helas's forces were valuable, important to the Hegemony's combat-readiness.

But the fleet he led was vital. It was essential. It represented the bulk of the Hegemony's remaining military strength massed together. If it was destroyed, the war was essentially over, almost before it began.

If he allowed his fleet to be crushed, the Hegemony would fall almost immediately, and any chance, however remote, of coaxing the Rimdwellers to enter the war in time, would be lost.

The nightmare so long feared had proven to be real, worse even than darkest whispers had made it out to be. Ilius knew his duty. Even if it meant watching thousands of comrades—and one of his closest friends—die. Even if it meant abandoning Hegemony worlds, and their vast populations to slavery and even genocide. The war just beginning would be fought for nothing less than the survival of humanity itself, and no price would be too high to pay for such a victory.

That all made sense. He knew running immediately would be the smart thing, the tactically correct option. But he just couldn't leave Helas and all her ships and crews. This was not the place for a decisive battle, for the inevitable all-out effort to halt the enemy advance. That would come later.

He was going to have to retreat, soon, to pull back before his entire force was trapped. But before that, he was damned sure going t do whatever he had to do to get Helas's ships—some of them, at least—out with him.

"All vessels, maintain forward thrust, but reduce to thirty percent. Prepare to arm weapons arrays."

Chapter Two

Confederation Naval HQ
Troyus City
Megara, Olyus III
Year 322 AC

"Congratulations, both of you. I'm sure it sometimes felt like every force in the galaxy was trying to separate you, but in the end, you beat them all. We've had some desperate struggles, all of us. Almost certainly, we'll have challenges tomorrow, more war and hardship, no doubt, and probably a host of things we couldn't predict, but for today, for a few weeks together, try to forget it all. You both made it here, so savor that, and enjoy each other. No two people deserve happiness more. And you know that's sincere, that I'm not one for pointless platitudes." Gary Holsten stood a meter in front of the wall, wearing an impeccable suit, the gray material so soft, so fine, it served as a de facto reminder that he was one of the wealthiest men in the Confederation as well as the head of Confed Intelligence. His posture communicated a seemingly contradictory combination of rigid respect and the casual nonchalance of a wealthy and lovable rogue.

Tyler Barron smiled, mostly in gratitude and respect for his friend—and perhaps a bit because he'd heard Holsten

deliver a few platitudes when it served his needs. He didn't
have much doubt the magnate and spy had detested such
utterances, even as they'd come out of his mouth, but he
was damned good at them, nevertheless. Still, Barron knew
the words he'd just heard were sincere. He was just about to
respond when Andi beat him to it.

"Thank you, Gary. I'd wager we might get a few
weeks…but I doubt it will be much more than that. There's
just too much work to do." Andi Lafarge wore a long and
magnificent dress, crafted from a fabric that seemed almost
alive with various shades of blue coming to life as the angles
of light shifted with her movements. It was an indulgence,
more expensive even than Holsten's suit, but then Andi *was*
one of the Confederation's wealthiest women—something
that still felt very unreal to her. There was more than a little
of the orphan prowling the streets of the Gut searching for
food left in her, and while she found many of her oldest
memories painful, she never lost sight of the fact that those
very trials had forged her into what she'd become. She owed
everything to that skinny little child, crawling through the
refuse—human and otherwise—in that miserable industrial
hell, and she'd vowed never to forget.

"I just *might* pull off a disappearing act if I tried. Almost
certainly, I could. But this guy would be missed in about ten
seconds. And since I'm stuck with him now, I'll have to
make some effort to master that *admiral's wife* thing."
Holsten knew Andi was joking, but he also caught the
anxiety in her voice. She loved Tyler Barron, he was sure of
that…and Barron was utterly devoted to her. But the
admiral was from the same world he'd come from, that of
privilege and power and prestige. Tyler Barron's trust funds
and naval commission had practically been waiting for him
in the delivery room, while Andi's mother had been
fortunate to find a dark corner in an abandoned warehouse
to give birth to her daughter. Andi was immensely charming
when she wanted to be, and she'd picked up a considerable

education over the years, but Holsten suspected part of her always felt like an outsider.

Barron knew all about Andi's past, of course, but Holsten doubted his friend could truly understand what it had been like for her in those days...any more than he could. Andi Lafarge was a force of nature, one who tended to attack problems head on, usually with considerable aggression. But he knew her role alongside Tyler Barron— *the* Tyler Barron—had always intimidated her on some level, even back to the earliest days of their infatuation.

"Andi, you are magnificent, almost as a supernova standing next to this grim and drab warrior. That is all the more amazing, perhaps, since I know that you are no less the fighter. I find it hard to believe you would go anywhere *entirely* unarmed...and yet, I am at a loss to imagine where, in that astonishing gown, you've stashed a weapon." The voice was a new one, distinct, loud, and brimming with confidence. Vian Tulus was not just a military officer and a dear friend, he was the Imperator of the Palatian Alliance, the head of state of the Confederation's most important ally.

Holsten liked to think his intelligence networks had paved the way for the development of Confederation and Alliance cooperation, but in the end, he had to admit, even to himself, that Tyler Barron had carried that load almost alone, beginning with the famous duel between *Dauntless*— the first *Dauntless*—and Katrine Rigellus's *Invictus*. The two captains had been enemies then, deadly adversaries, and only Barron of the two had survived the fight. Effective diplomacy was rarely based on such encounters, but the Palatian culture was unique in many ways, and even amid calls for vengeance and reprisal, there had always been a respect among the Palatians, an inner voice that no doubt called to most of them, saying, 'this man defeated one of your best...respect him.'

"You are too kind, Imperator Tulus." Andi smiled sweetly, playing her role perfectly, save perhaps for a slight discomfort detectable to those who truly knew her. Holsten had been born to vast wealth, and he'd never known a moment of deprivation. He'd tried to imagine the desperate poverty that had spawned a young Andi, but he knew he would never truly understand.

"Imperator Tulus? Surely, we can do better than that for a comrade of such duration and distinction, not to mention a sister, the wife now of my own blood brother. I am Vian to you, Andi…always."

"Thank you again, Vian."

"We are honored that you have come so far, my brother, and so soon after returning home to, what I can only imagine, is voluminous work." Tyler Barron turned and nodded gently to the Palatian ruler.

"Such things can always wait, Tyler my brother, when more important things call. I would not have missed this for any reason. Indeed, I was nearly astonished when I got word that you were finally moving forward. I have watched with some amusement for years now, as you both executed your intricate dance together, weaving a veil of nonchalance over a relationship all who knew you well could see was resolute and unbreakable."

A look of surprise came over Andi's face, but only for an instant. Then, she regained her control. "Well, Vian, this one…" She leaned in against Barron's shoulder. "…he grows on you given enough time."

The Imperator of the Palatian Alliance stood unmoving for an instant. Then, he let out a loud and raucous laugh. "Yes, Andi, my sister…I must absolutely agree with you on that. He truly does."

* * *

Tyler Barron lay in bed, looking out through the gauzy curtains, his eyes catching the first hints of dawn sunlight. The room was beautiful enough, though it bore the signs of hasty repairs. The war was over, at least for the time being, but the work of recovery had just begun. Megara had been invaded and then liberated, two vast campaigns that had left the shining jewel of the Confederation in smoldering ruins. It would be many years, lifetimes perhaps, before the Confederation capital returned to its former glory.

That time period would be shortened, at least, by the fact that only rebuilding was needed. The Hegemony forces were powerful, and they had fought like madmen…but they had exercised restraint. If they had *truly* bombarded Megara— and the other worlds they'd occupied—there would be decades of radiation cleansing ahead, before talk of new construction could even begin.

That was unequivocally a good thing, but it nagged at Barron, too. He'd allowed himself to despise the enemy, with good reason. He'd lost friends in the war, as well as millions of spacers and Marines serving under him. The Hegemony had been an invader, and that was enough to inflame the warrior's rage inside him. But he also knew, with the Hegemony's technological superiority, if they'd have been willing to conduct nuclear bombardments or biological attacks instead of protracted and resource hogging invasions, they almost certainly could have broken the Confederation. How many billions of deaths could even the most stubborn of government officials, the most intransigent of his officer and spacers, have endured before they had surrendered?

How many could *he* have endured? He liked to consider himself determined—many called it stubborn—but how much death could he stand? A billion? Ten billion? 'Never surrender' was an easy thing to say, but at some point, it would have been nothing more than pure evil to allow so many to die with no hope of victory.

The Hegemony had been driven from the Rim, but only because *they* had held back, declined to use the power that could have given them victory. As much as he despised their culture and hated them for the carnage of the war, some part of his mind told him, a truly evil enemy would not have acted in such a way. There was honor, of a sort, in the way they had conducted themselves, and it grated on Barron. He wanted only to wallow in righteous rage and hatred, and the denial of that simple viewpoint only inflamed the raw wounds in his psyche.

"We have to talk, husband dear. You may have too many years of military service under your belt to *truly* appreciate the decadence and grandeur of sleeping late, but I do not. You're going to have to meet me halfway, at least. I'm not sure just where that is, but it's not dawn, I can tell you that much."

He rolled over and pushed the thoughts of Hegemony motivations from his mind. He even managed a smile of sorts. "No, no…you're not laying this one on me. I've been lying here, awake I'll admit, but barely moving, totally silent. If you woke up, that's *your* deal. If you want to relax and sleep until eleven, you're going to have to stop plunging into places like Dannith, or picking fights with opponents like Ricard Lille. That kind of baggage isn't the best sleep aid."

"Well, maybe you're right…at least a little bit." She smiled. "But, with the war over, we should get some quiet, some calm. Those old ghosts will fade away." Barron could see that she'd tried her best, but also that she didn't believe what she'd said any more than he did. The Hegemony had been on the verge of victory, even without *Colossus*. No doubt, risking Rogan's Marines' destroying the great ship would have been difficult…but just maybe they'd have retaken the occupied compartments in time, and killed all the boarders before they'd been able to detonate their explosives. And, even if *Colossus* had been lost, Barron was sure the Hegemony could have won if they'd pushed hard enough.

So, what made them retreat? Why were they so concerned about Colossus *surviving, concerned enough to surrender the big ship to us, their enemy, rather than seeing risking an attempt to retake it?*

Barron didn't make a habit of believing things his enemies said, but there was a growing knot in his stomach, a fear that there *was* another danger, perhaps yet another enemy. As detestable as it was to imagine allying with the Hegemony, something inside him—strategic sense, gut instinct...something—was telling him he couldn't ignore the possibility.

"So, what should we do today? How do you want to pretend your mind isn't almost entirely on the Hegemony, and on why they did what they did?" Sometimes he was sure she could read his mind.

He smiled at her. He loved her, respected her...but sometimes, he just forgot how damned smart she was. She knew everything as well as he did, and she no doubt harbored the same concerns.

"I don't think there is anything to do, at least as far as the Hegemony goes. I'm worried, yes, but I'm not ready to believe them yet either, and even less so to send our forces coreward to help people we were just fighting. Yes, *maybe* there is a new threat. Or maybe it's all some kind of trap. Perhaps they hoped to lure us in, to win an easier victory...and save *Colossus* in along the way. I think we'll just have to wait and see what happens."

He reached out and embraced her. He *was* happy, on some level, more than he'd ever been. But the coldness was there, too, an emptiness draining away the joy that should have been unrestrained. He'd tried to focus on Andi, on his relief that she had survived her mission on Dannith, that even as her impulsive and aggressive nature had put her in grave danger, fortune's grace—and her remarkable collection of skills—had seen her through it once again. He *was* happy about that, of course, and deeply grateful to have her back, but as he lay there, all he could think of was the danger lurking out in the shadows...and those he wished were there who weren't.

Van Striker, Sara Eaton...so many friends and comrades lost over the years of war. He was concerned about the danger that might be coming, certainly, but there was something more this time.

He wondered just how much more he could endure—the pain, the death, the suffering. He was only a man, and he knew he had a limit. Even his grandfather's wars, as brutal as they had been, ended. But Barron seemed stuck in an endless series of conflicts, of disasters and blood-soaked battles, one coming right after another. Was that where they were? Not truly at the dawn of peace, but only in a brief respite before more killing, more struggle?

He didn't have an answer, but he knew he would push forward, fight for all he held dear, and for the duty that drove him...but he knew he couldn't face the fire forever.

No one could.

Chapter Three

HWS Hegemony's Glory
Venta Traconis System
Year of Renewal 267 (322 AC)

"The portside line will engage thrust at thirty percent deceleration."

"Yes, Megaron."

Ilius was still, like a seated figure on some grand statue. He was a Master of the Hegemony, a megaron, a veteran warrior, and he kept reminding himself of all that, and of the obligation he had to lead the Kriegeri and other lesser humans, to set the example with his insight and courage. It was a way to hold back the fear, if not an enormously successful one. Nevertheless, despite his greatest efforts, he couldn't push aside the realization that he was facing a mysterious enemy, one about which he knew almost nothing.

One whose power had already been demonstrated with stunning effectiveness.

"Get Helas on my channel." Ilius had watched as the advance fleet—the one he'd come to save, the one Helas now commanded after the death of Kel, its original leader—pulled back in a controlled retreat. In his desperate attempt to latch onto anything positive from what he saw, he grasped at the discipline the fleet displayed, even as disaster overtook them. They had fought grimly all the way as they pulled back, engaging the enemy ships the best they could, even if that had been utterly ineffectively.

But whatever he told himself, one thing was utterly clear. The mighty Hegemony was facing a far superior enemy...and Ilius had no idea how to defeat them.

Any thoughts he'd nursed of fighting it out in Venta Traconis were gone. He'd hesitated giving up, resisted for a while consulting the AI to confirm the population numbers on the system's two planets. But reality had asserted itself with merciless finality. Fighting in Venta Traconis would mean only the almost complete destruction of Hegemony military power. He'd watched Helas's ships struggling to establish scanner locks, to hit the enemy ships that were savaging their formations. For all their efforts, the technology that had long been a source of pride to the Hegemony, there were no confirmed hits. None. And, certainly no kills. The Hegemony fleet wasn't outmatched...it was virtually helpless. All Ilius could do was see that as many ships as possible escaped, to bring back the data they'd collected, in the hopes the combined brains of the Hegemony's best could devise a way to meet the invaders on something closer to even terms next time.

The population numbers—the people he would be leaving behind—were upsetting, and if a fair proportion of the roughly three hundred million in the system consisted of Defekts and low-level Arbeiter—a not uncommon breakdown so far coreward, where the radiation and biological exchanges during the Great Death had been the most vicious—there were at least sixty million of reasonable rankings...not to mention over a thousand Masters in supervisory positions. Ilius didn't know how the Others would deal with captured planets and populations, but what he'd gleaned from the old accounts was far from reassuring.

You won't save one of them if you let the fleet be destroyed here…you'll just condemn billions more you might otherwise find a way to defend…

His resolve was like iron, but that didn't completely stop the doubts. He could hold his fleet in place, waiting for Helas's retreating ships to make good their escape, only so long before it was too badly damaged, before its own way out was cut off. He would have to run—soon—and any ships that hadn't managed to complete their pullbacks would be left to the enemy's mercy, just as the two inhabited worlds.

Ilius was struggling to adapt to the reality unfolding around him. The war on the Rim had been bloody, brutal, and it had worn heavily on all those who'd fought in it. But the Hegemony had been the invader there, and in almost every instance, the superior force. Now, he had to adjust to being the weaker side, to watching the stronger enemy advance. He had to think first of preserving his forces, of avoiding total disaster while he probed for any weaknesses, used what advantages his people had. He now held the position the Rimdwellers had, worse even, since the enemy overmatched his forces by a far greater margin than the Hegemony had enjoyed over the Rim navies. He *had* to find ways to counter the deadly threat, to focus on his fleet's strengths, even as those he'd recently fought against had so effectively utilized their bomber wings.

The only problem was, so far, Ilius hadn't come up with any advantages. His ships could barely track the attackers, and while he couldn't be sure some of Helas's vessels hadn't scored hits, he had no hard data, no detailed damage reports. No way to make reasonable tactical decisions.

No way to even know if a single Hegemony ship had done meaningful damage to one of the enemy vessels.

"Megaron Helas on your channel, Commander."

He tapped the headset, activating the comm unit.

"Helas…you've got to get your ships back faster. We're running out of time." It was blunt, direct…and nothing more than the simple truth. "No excuses," he added almost immediately, though he knew Helas wasn't the type to shift blame. Anything that doesn't make it into the tube in time is…" He paused for a second, fairly certain he didn't have to finish what he'd been about to say. "I don't care if you need to overload your reactors, burn your engines to cinders, or what, but do *something*."

Ilius had seen what the Rimdwellers had managed to do by torturing their equipment, pushing their systems to the brink. He'd also seen them suffer the consequences, ships damaged, even destroyed as systems were pushed too far. He was only halfway to full realization that his people were now in the same situation their former enemies had been in…that they were going to have to take wild risks, think out of the box.

Or they were going to lose the war. Badly.

And quickly. He had to find a way, *some* way, to stop the enemy, or at least delay them. Or they'd be at Calpharon in a matter of weeks.

"We've got a lot of damaged hulls, Commander. If we push the engines and reactors too hard…"

"And if you don't, you're all dead." It was brutal, after a fashion, but it was true. And there was no time to argue.

"Yes, Commander. I will do all I can."

"See that you do." It was harder edged than he liked, especially for an officer he respected as much as he did Helas, but it was what she needed to hear then. "And, Helas…I want your ships to transmit all your scanner results onto the fleetnet at once…and continue to do so as more data comes in." Ilius knew Helas understood his purpose at once. The most important thing the fleet would bring away from the lost battle was data. Petabytes of information that would hopefully allow the analysts back at fleet command to improve on tracking and tactics, to develop ways to more effectively fight the enemy. Because if the Hegemony fleet had to face the Others with no better targeting than it was managing in Venta Traconis…they were finished already.

*   *   *

"Commander Tragus, engineering reports all batteries back online and ready to fire at full power."

"Very well, Hectoron. Tie in with most recent scans, and open fire." Tragus was a Kriegeri of high rank, and *Avia*'s commander-in-chief. The cruiser was a mid-level vessel, almost insignificant next to the massive monitors and the battleships of the line. But he was young to command her—very young—and he drew immense pride from his position. His career promised great advancement to come.

If you get out of this, that is…

The bridge lights dimmed for an instant as the guns fired. He'd cranked all his weapons to maximum power, even beyond maximum. He didn't have any authorization for such an action, and technically, he was violating regulations, but one look at the display made it clear enough just how dire a spot the fleet was in. He'd served on the Rim, and he'd seen the enemy there make good use of overpowering weapons. He'd seen the downsides, as well, on the Rim, and again moments before, when a burnout shut down *Avia*'s entire weapons array. For a few minutes, he feared he had knocked his ship out of the fight, but then he got lucky. He'd felt the relief physically as the report came back to the bridge. The damage was repairable. His engineers had promised him full power in five minutes, and in fact, they'd delivered it in less than three.

He would see they received the deserved commendations…again, if any of them made it out of Venta Traconis.

His eyes moved back to the display, anxious for the usual readings, news of any hits, or even confirmations that *Avia*'s shots had missed their targets. But there was nothing but the same confusing mashup, signals that appeared to be enemy ships, zoning in one instant, and out the next…and his own vessel's shots seemingly vanishing as they entered the inner zone around the ghostly and mysterious ships.

He'd faced danger before, and fear. Even defeat, but the frustration of not even knowing if he was striking against the enemy was almost unbearable.

You do know…we're not hitting a thing.

Tragus was enough of a veteran to understand the complexities of targeting at the ranges typical in space combat. There was no way his people—or any of the gunnery teams in the fleet—were hitting those ships, not without precise and sustainable scanner locks. The chance of scoring a random hit from more than a hundred thousands kilometers was so miniscule as to be nearly mathematically indistinguishable from zero.

We have to figure out how to get precise locations on these things…

His mind raced, even as *Avia's* guns fired again, almost certainly missing.

They're antimatter-powered, almost certainly. That's got to be useful in some way…

He realized it was, but not at the immense range between the two forces. *If* he could get within ten thousand kilometers, and *if* the enemy didn't have some kind of impenetrable shielding, he *might* be able to track them that way, get his scanners locked on the radiation signature of their antimatter fuel.

Of course, every ship in the fleet, battleships and monitors as surely as a cruiser like his own, would be blasted to plasma before they got anywhere near that close.

"Hectoron, I want all scanner arrays programmed to detect any signs of antimatter usage or storage." He could feel the officer about to respond, and he added, "Yes, I know we're out too far, but let's see if we can find anything at all."

"Yes, Commander."

"In fact, I want a complete analysis of *all* detectable

radiation coming from those ships. I'm talking about every known form, however rare. We might not understand it, but that doesn't mean we can't track it." He felt off balance, as though he was grasping around for any ideas at all. Which was exactly what he was doing. But then he realized, if the Hegemony did manage to secure the knowledge to successfully target the Others, that was exactly how it would happen. It would be a brilliant discovery…and an accident.

He sat for a moment, watching the data moving across his screen. Then, he saw something.

He reached out for his controls, to replay what had just come through. But his executive officer beat him to it.

"Commander, we're detecting radiation levels outside the usual spectrum. The signals are weak, but they're steady. The scanners wouldn't even detect it normally, not this range. But our full band search caught something. Barely."

"Intensify the scan, and localize it. Target those signals exclusively. I want a complete analysis, Hectoron. Now! From both the AI and the science teams." He winced as the main display showed a bright flash, an incoming shot from the enemy. For an instant, he was ready to pat himself on the back for the evasive routine he'd ordered, the maneuver he told himself has saved his ship. But then he saw *Farsalus* disappear from the screen. The battleship had been positioned almost directly behind *Avia*. Whatever his evasion tactics had accomplished, he realized he owed his ship's survival more to its lower status on the enemy's target priority list. The Others were going to destroy all the monitors and battleships they could before they started worrying about light cruisers and escorts.

"Commander…we have a tentative match. Not a direct one, but a ninety-four point one six overlay."

That was damned close…but Tragus didn't know if it was close enough. There were a lot of forces and types of energy in the universe, and not even Hegemony science knew them all.

"What is the match, Hectoron?" Tragus was an experienced commander, but he was would be the first to agree that his knowledge of radiation types and intricacies was limited.

"It's a Sigma-9 wave, Commander. Or close to one."

"Sigma-9? That's not a normal space pattern, Hectoron, it's…" His voice slipped into silence, and he paused.

"One of the background radiation readings from inside the transit tubes, Commander. But we're detecting it in normal space…which may account for the minor variance from standard readings. The AI confirms there are no recorded instances of such a radiation pattern in normal space."

Until now…

Tragus felt a wave of excitement…and one of foreboding. Just maybe, identifying the radiation type would allow him to reprogram *Avia*'s scanners, to tighten his ship's target locks.

But just how advanced are the Others? We barely understand how to use the tubes, and they're harnessing energies from alternate space?

He tried to disregard the fear, but the coldness in his stomach defied being completely ignored.

Tragus didn't know much about the history of the great tubes that made interstellar travel possible, whether they'd been built by those who had founded the empire, or if even those ancients had simply found them, the bounty of some advanced race that had come before. General consensus held they were imperial creations, but Tragus had never heard any real evidence to support such a claim.

If the Others understand the tubes…at least enough to harness the same type of energy used…

"Hectoron…I want the scanner suite reprogrammed to track the Sigma-9 signals. Full power to all dishes…and launch a spread of probes as well, maximum dispersion and one ten power on their scans. Let's see if we're really onto something here."

"Yes, Commander."

Tragus sat quietly, his eyes locked on the data scrolling across his screen, first from the ship's scanners, and a few minutes later from the probes. The Sigma-9 pattern—*the Sigma-9 like pattern*—was there, stronger than it had been in the earlier scans.

And right where he expected the closest enemy ship to be.

"Hectoron, I want all targeting parameters wiped. Reprogram all batteries to lock onto the new energy wave. One percent dispersal pattern, maximum rate of fire."

"Yes, Commander."

Tragus turned toward the main display, watching, watching to see what *Avia*'s scanners continued to detect. Seconds passed by, each one agonizing, almost like a small eternity. He barked out an acknowledgement when the hectoron reported the targeting routines had been revised. He saw the status lights appear along the top of the screen, too, further confirmation that his new parameters were in place. Then, there was nothing, just continued vague and intermittent contacts. Tragus felt disappointment, renewed despair. It had been a guess, he told himself, a flailing effort to find some way to track the deadly enemy.

Then he saw it.

A reading, fleeting, tenuous at first, but growing in strength as the AI adjusted the scanner wavelengths at a speed no human mind could comprehend. He saw the strange wave appear on the display, growing stronger, and before he even had the chance to order it, his exec added the overlay, a standard Sigma-9 pattern from one of *Avia*'s transits.

They *were* almost identical, he realized, a few seconds before the AI's calculation appeared. Ninety-five point two. It was close, close enough perhaps to decide he *was* seeing some kind of Sigma-9 pattern. But Tragus realized that didn't matter. The science teams could analyze the radiation, decide just what to call it. He was a warrior, not a researcher. He only cared about one thing. Whatever it was, it was damned sure manmade, and he could track it.

"Hectoron, gunnery is to target that signal. I want maximum rate of fire, full dispersal pattern." He'd found a way to target the enemy ships—maybe—but it was still rough. Even with a burst of shots, it was going to take some luck. But if it worked…"

"All batteries redirecting fire, Commander…"

Tragus was tense, his body tight, eyes focused on the display. He could see the flashes, his ship's relatively small guns firing at the only contact in range. It *was* an enemy ship, Tragus was sure of it, even though his rational mind still called it a guess. The target was on a course right past *Avia*, toward a cluster of battleships and monitors behind. Tragus felt a flash of anger, of wounded pride that the enemy didn't appear to consider his vessel enough of a threat to attack.

That's what let us get close enough…

He saw more flashes, all around the AI's best guess at the enemy position…and then something different, something that looked very much like one of *Avia*'s shots had connected.

Was it possible? Had his ship scored a hit? He stared at the display, waiting for the AI's analysis to answer his question.

But the enemy answered it first.

Tragus watched in horror as the contact, the enemy vessel he suddenly realized without doubt *Avia had* hit, changed its thrust vector immediately. The ship was altering its course, and even before the AI recalculated the projected new vector, Tragus knew with cold certainty.

His people *had* scored a hit on their target.

And the enemy ship was realigning its course in response. It was repositioning, coming right at *Avia*.

He'd done it. He and his people had managed to successfully target one of the Others' ships.

And now they were going to die for that.

Chapter Four

Colossus
Lyra System
Year 322 AC

"Commodore Fritz, the surveying teams have been working twelve hour shifts for two weeks now. We've simply got to reduce the intensity of the schedule, or we're going to see more accidents...if not a full-scale revolt. It's a miracle we haven't had any fatalities yet, but at this pace, it's only a matter of time." Antoine Dennis was about two meters from Anya Fritz, standing up to the fearsome engineer with an intensity that told officers who'd served with her that the civilian was utterly fearless.

Or that he simply had no idea who he was dealing with.

Most likely, the latter.

"Mr. Dennis, I appreciate your efforts, and those of your engineering teams, but I can assure you, this is *not* a breakneck pace. Compared to damage control efforts in battle, this is a picnic we've been on, one on a nice sunny day right next to the lake." Fritz's tone was calm, but to those who'd served at her side, the beginnings of the gathering storm were no doubt clearly recognizable.

"Need I remind you, Commodore, that we are not in battle right now, and neither is the Confederation at war.

This is a peacetime operation, and it should be run like one."

"What do you know of war and peace, Mr. Dennis? What, exactly, is 'peace?' Were we at war before the Hegemony invaded our space, without warning or formal declaration? What security should we read into the enemy's withdrawal? Do you have some guarantee I do not understand, some assurance from the spirits of the universe that the Hegemony will not return? That the Union will not strike us while we are still recovering from the last war? You rely heavily on peace to justify a reduction in workload, but you have never seen war yourself, have you? Nor considered the price warriors pay when we begin a conflict unprepared. What value do you think I and my people place—*can* place—on your opinion on such matters? What price are you prepared to pay if we waste time, and find ourselves unready for the next struggle when it comes? Will you step forward, be the first to die? Will I look down on your burned and mangled corpse, as I have those of so many of my comrades?"

Anya Fritz knew she should try to hold back, especially with the civilian officials and contractors, but the war was too recent, the losses too fresh. She was stuck there in the Lyra system, too, far from a proper base or facilities. She'd forgone any real leave since the end of the war. She'd even missed Tyler Barron and Andi Lafarge's wedding. The fact that she'd been invited had touched her deeply, hitting at emotions most of her engineers would be surprised to learn she possessed. Declining had been like nothing she could easily remember, a painful and melancholy choice that had been no choice at all. Her work on *Colossus* was simply too vital, and the great ship too far from Megara to justify the time a round trip would have taken.

And, by God, if I could miss that, this…engineer…and his lazy-ass crews can keep the hell up with my veterans…

It wasn't entirely fair, she knew on some level, to

compare Dennis's engineers to her hardened crews. But she
didn't care.

She shook her head, and her eyes met his, almost daring
him to counter her response. The workload *had* been heavy,
but *Colossus* was one of the greatest pieces of technology
ever to fall into Confederation hands, and there was no time
to waste in deciphering its secrets. She imagined one day
revamping the entire lexicon of Confed tech, upgrading
warships, factories, information processing…taking the
Confederation's civilization centuries forward in a matter of
years. All from what her people gleaned from *Colossus* and
its systems.

But for the moment, all her efforts, and those of the
thousands of engineers and technicians working with her,
had failed even to allow the great ship to make a single
transit. Colossus was all-powerful…and helpless and
vulnerable as well. As long as the ship was so close to
immobile, it was vulnerable to a Hegemony raid to retake it.
Hell, even the Union could have a go at it, if their intel had
discovered anything material about the great ship.

The first six months had been spent almost exclusively
on checking and maintaining the antimatter storage systems,
the very part of *Colossus* her team had boarded nearly a year
before to destroy. The ship used antimatter for power, and
the vessel's tanks stored more of the precious material than
the Confederation had produced in its entire history.

More by orders of magnitude.

That was one area where the Hegemony had outpaced
Confed technology. The Rim nations all knew *how* to
produce antimatter. That was basic science. The problem
was producing the energy the operation required, the vast,
unimaginable amounts of energy. Antimatter was still largely
an experimental substance in the Confederation, available in
minute quantities, useful for research, but not for mass
application in drives and weapons systems.

The Hegemony railguns used antimatter charges,

relatively small ones, but still dwarfing any amount the Confederation could produce. But Fritz could only imagine the immense efforts that had been required to produce the quantities of antimatter *Colossus* utilized. Even for the Hegemony, she knew it had to have been a nationwide project.

Dennis had remained silent for a moment, clearly intimidated by the fierce engineer. But finally, he worked up enough courage to continue his argument. "Commodore Fritz, my people are far from home, and they volunteered to come here, to help with your project. But, I'm…"

"Help? Were my people 'helping' yours when they were fighting the Hegemony forces, struggling to protect as much of the Confederation as they could? Are your engineers not being paid—and *well* paid—to be here? Listen to me, Mr. Dennis, and listen carefully. I am in charge of this operation, and it will run on the schedule I dictate. Anyone who cannot keep up will suffer the consequences."

"Is that a threat, Commodore?" There was anger in Dennis's tone, and astonishment…but mostly fear.

"Yes, Mr. Dennis, that's precisely what it was."

* * *

"Up the flow rate…but slowly. I think we might have it figured out, but this thing still gives me the shakes." Eric Kalmut was sitting on the massive conduit, a three-meter-wide pipe stretching across the huge open chamber. Kalmut shifted himself slightly, trying to adjust his balance. He was a veteran, one of Commodore Fritz's top engineers, but he had one weakness, and it was eating away at him as he mounted his perch thirty meters above the deck.

He was scared of heights.

Kalmut was usually fearless, the first one to crawl into a damaged compartment, or to brave radiation, fire, or any other danger he encountered in his work. He was no coward, not by any measure.

At least, not when his feet were on the ground.

"We're already at eight point three gigawatts, Commander. And the feed is only open thirty percent."

Kalmut nodded. He was as amazed as any of his team at the sheer amount of energy that coursed through the power arteries of *Colossus*'s systems. He was beyond impressed at the massive ship's technology, and he'd had a dozen epiphanies in the months he'd been prowling around the vast depths of its engineering sections. *Colossus* was a massive technological windfall, unlike any that had come before, and Kalmut was sure it would advance Confederation science a century or more. As soon as he and his people were able to truly figure it out.

They'd made some progress, certainly. And, they'd hit walls, too. Antimatter was one of those. The awesome power of the high-tech fuel was no surprise, and *Colossus* held massive stores of it. But producing usable quantities was still a capability out of reach of Confederation technology and engineering, and for all the great ship offered, that mystery wasn't one of them.

Materials in general were a problem. Kalmut's edginess came from his acrophobia certainly, but the fact that he was sitting atop and energy flow powerful enough to fry a dozen cities to ashes wasn't helping. He reached down and put his hand on the metal of the conduit. It was cool, no sign of the massive power a few centimeters inside.

The insulation capacity of the conduit was incredible, and while he could discern the effects of the strange alloy, he couldn't begin to understand how to produce it. That would take time, and probably a lot of it. And a better research facility than three dozen ships parked out in interplanetary space, all protected by a massive task force there to defend the Confederation's bounty against any who might try to seize it.

That's why we're here, to figure all this stuff out.

Kalmut pulled his thoughts from antimatter and advanced alloys to the situation at hand. His job was to test every centimeter of conduit, to measure—to the maximum ability of his instruments—stress levels, and to ensure that when Anya Fritz gave the orders to fire up the monster ship's engines, everything would go as planned.

He would do his best, but in the end, he knew it would come down to a guess. An educated one, perhaps, tweaked linguistically to something more reassuring, like 'estimate' or 'projection,' but a guess nevertheless.

Kalmut glanced down at the scanner in his hand, trying without much success to ignore the glimpse he caught of the edge of the conduit, and the drop below. The readings were perfect, spot on. There were no leaks, no detectable seepage, nowhere in the whole section of power line. Just like the other three hundred kilometers of primary conduit he and his team had inspected. That was an immense workload, and it exhausted him even thinking about it, and the days, weeks, months of grueling work it had all entailed.

It also put his people somewhere close to halfway through.

* * *

"Admiral…before I begin, I just wanted to express my sincere gratitude at the invitation to your wedding, and express my sorrow at not being able to attend. As we discussed, we simply cannot be sure the peace with the Hegemony will hold, and *Colossus*'s current position leaves the vessel vulnerable…even to Union aggression, at least until we are able to resume full operation of the defense grids. I simply didn't think the project could endure the delay my traveling to and from Megara would have entailed. Please accept my very best wishes to both you and Captain Lafarge."

Anya Fritz sat at the small desk in her quarters, leaning

slightly to bring her mouth closer to the comm unit. It wasn't necessary, not really. The equipment was highly sensitive, and the AI would clean up any noise or interference in the signal. Still, it was an affectation she'd long allowed herself.

Or a good excuse to allow her fatigue to erode her normally ramrod straight posture.

Fritz was a relentless taskmaster, a reputation she'd both earned by deeds and by a little targeted self-promotion wherever possible. It had served her well, and she fancied it had saved her life more than once, not to mention the lives of the thousands of spacers on the ships on which she'd served. She wasn't about to let her engineers get the slightest glimpse at her own exhaustion, to see that the nonstop workload had come close to getting the better of her no less than it had all of them. Endless battle and technologically superior enemies were bad enough, but allowing a chink in her carefully-constructed armor was unthinkable.

"My teams have made considerable progress, but virtually every system in *Colossus* requires extensive research before we can even attempt operation. We have basic power systems and life support operating reliably, as well as some minor, mostly-positioning thrusters, but it will require considerable work before we can safely operate the main engines or navigation systems…and even longer before I would feel comfortable activating the weapons grid. There is no question in my mind *Colossus* is adapted imperial technology, probably an ancient hull the Hegemony found and restored, replacing defective systems with their own. The Hegemony technology is easy to spot, and far simpler to master, though it still exceeds our own in complexity. The old imperial systems are extremely sophisticated, and I am hesitant to move too quickly in evaluating and activating them."

Fritz straightened up, more to stretch her back than to resume her normally-upright posture. She let out a long sigh, a luxury she allowed herself only in the complete solitude of her quarters. She'd intended to ask Barron for the time she needed to move slowly and methodically through the study of *Colossus*, but her own doubts began to force their way in.

"A decision has to be made, one regarding the time sensitivity of the project. A slower pace will unquestionably allow us to proceed more safely, taking fewer chances with poorly understood technology." She hesitated. "But I must tell you, sir, I am troubled by the manner in which the war ended, and we obtained control of *Colossus*. I do not trust the Hegemony, and I am far from comfortable that, whatever their ambassadors may state, they will not return and renew hostilities. If that is their intention, they would almost certainly take action to regain control of *Colossus*. The fleet deployed to guard the ship is substantial, but a strong and focused Hegemony effort would almost certainly succeed."

She took another deep breath, holding it for a moment, steeling herself as she prepared to release her *real* fear.

"And, even if the enemy maintains the peace...I am deeply troubled by whatever caused them to suddenly sue for peace and surrender *Colossus* to us. They have never been dissuaded by heavy casualties, and while it would no doubt have been a blow for the great ship to be destroyed, it is lost to them anyway. What could have put that kind of scare into them? Of more concern, perhaps, do they really believe we will come to their aid, that surrendering *Colossus* allowed the vessel to survive to join whatever fight they face? That seems exceedingly unlikely to me, and it makes me wonder about their true agenda. Perhaps they do plan to launch a raid, to seek to retake *Colossus*."

The thoughts pouring from her mind were terrifying. Fritz hated the Hegemony, as much as nearly every other officer on the Rim. But it was simplistic to make sweeping declarations about never fighting alongside the Masters and their genetically ordered minions. She would never have imagined Union ships lined up alongside the Confederation's vessels either, but Admiral Denisov's forces battled with distinction.

And, if there *was* something out there, some deadly threat that remained a mystery, did they really have time to waste in restoring *Colossus* to operational status at a slow and steady pace?

"I can continue as I have been, or I can accelerate our efforts. That will involve some level of increased risk, and perhaps worse, I am not sure I can give you a reasonable estimate of how much that will be. Whether it is worth the additional danger and uncertainty is largely a strategic and tactical decision, and as such, it is yours to make, Admiral. Should I continue at the current pace, or should I increase our pace? And, if your decision is to accelerate the project, should that be a moderate increase...or do you want me to push forward as quickly as possible, regardless of the risk?"

She didn't like that last option at all...but she liked even less the prospect of some deadly new danger emerging while *Colossus* was still stuck in space, useless. And she had a pretty good idea that Tyler Barron would agree. She had a good bet what the admiral's answer would be, and even though she agreed with him, it roiled her insides to think about it.

Chapter Five

HWS Hegemony's Glory
Venta Traconis System
Year of Renewal 267 (322 AC)

"Commander Ilius!"

Ilius's head snapped around, his eyes focusing on his chief aide. The officer was usually calm, a cold and grim block of granite on the bridge, even in the heat of battle. But excitement had slipped into his normally even tone. Fear.

"Yes, Kiloron?"

"We have rough scanner contacts on what we believe are three enemy vessels." There were icons all across the massive display, at least a hundred contacts, every one of them the AI's guess an enemy ship was located somewhere in that general area. It was all unreliable, terribly inaccurate, and utterly useless for something precise like targeting. Ilius had no idea what was notable about three of those guesses at ship locations compared to the others, and he almost expressed his doubts on the usefulness of the entire report.

But he'd come to respect the officer's opinion too much to doubt him out of hand.

"There are over a hundred possible contacts out there, Kiloron. What is it about these three?"

"They appear to executing complimentary vector modifications, Commander. It appears they're all moving on a single target."

Ilius shook his head. It didn't seem like the Others needed to mass their ships to obliterate even his most powerful monitors, but three of them attacking a single target didn't strike him as particularly noteworthy. "I fail to see the relevance of…"

"They're moving on a single light cruiser, Commander." The officer had never interrupted him before, but any anger Ilius might have felt at the mild offense was gone in an instant.

Why would three of those ship be moving on a glorified escort?

The enemy had been mostly ignoring all the lighter Hegemony vessels, going after the monitors and battleships, cutting away at the fleet's real fighting power. *So, what's different about this ship?*

"Identify target vessel."

"It's the light cruiser, *Avia*, Commander. Under the flag of Kiloron Tragus."

Ilius's eyes dropped to his screen, even as the specs for *Avia* appeared. He scanned the data, hesitating for a moment when he saw Tragus's genetic rating. *Very high Kriegeri range…almost Master level.* Tragus was a capable officer to command such a small vessel. Then, Ilius saw the commission date. The command was the officer's first, and no doubt the precursor to greater assignments to come.

No doubt at all if he's figured some way to cause concern to the Others…

Ilius's eyes moved toward the coordinates posted on the side of the screen.

If he lives to get a higher command…

Avia was still fairly deep within the system, and with enemy ships closing…

He's never going to get out.

Ilius worked his controls, pulling back recorded data on

Avia, on the ship's activities just before the enemy targeted it. He watched, silent, almost ignoring the back and forth across *Hegemony's Glory*'s bridge as he focused on a series of weapons blasts. The cruiser had opened fire, its shots clearly directed toward a specific area. The targeted fire continued for a few seconds, and then a bright flash filled the screen.

A hit?

It took a few seconds for the reality to sink in, and then Ilius knew.

Avia had been able to target the enemy ship. Somehow. They had tracked a vessel and managed to establish a firelock, a feat that had eluded every other ship in the fleet.

His fingers moved quickly over the controls, bringing his screen back to a real time feed centered on *Avia*. His stomach tightened.

The small vessel was conducting wild evasive maneuvers, an impressive display of navigational and piloting skill. But with three enemy ships on its tail, Ilius knew it was only a matter of time.

He also knew, the only officers and spacers in the fleet who knew how to target the Others' ships were in that beleaguered cruiser.

"All units within five hundred thousand kilometers of HWS *Avia* are to adjust thrust vectors immediately and close to support range. Repeat…all ships within five hundred thousand kilometers are to support *Avia*." A short pause. "At all costs."

He didn't know if he could save the cruiser and its crew…but he knew deep in his gut he had to try. He knew they were the key to learning how to fight the Others.

* * *

"Continue evasion pattern three for one more minute, Hectoron. Then adjust to pattern four." Tragus was struggling to remain calm. He was a veteran, and he'd fought in some of the fiercest battles on the Rim. The Rimdwellers had been tough opponents, deadly and stubborn, but they were just an enemy, not so unlike his own Kriegeri. They lacked the distinctly *different* nature of the Others. The enemy from beyond the coreward reaches of the old empire seemed to drain away the courage of an adversary, almost as a dampener absorbing g forces. The Confeds and their allies on the Rim were dangerous fighters, but the Others were like some kind of nightmare conjured from one's deepest fears.

And three of their deadly ships were on *Avia's* tail.

They were all in range, of course, deeply within range. That only made the evasion efforts more essential. The enemy targeting was precise, and their weapons deadly. One mistake, one move executed fractions of a second too late, and *Avia* would be a floating cloud of plasma.

"Evasion pattern four executing, Commander."

Tragus glanced over at the main display. He was doing the best he could to confuse his pursuers without adding too much time to *Avia's* arrival time at the tube. He was grateful the AI lacked sufficient data on the enemy to calculate a percentage chance of escape. There wasn't a question in his mind if such a number was available, it would be a depressingly low number—if not a fraction— and seeing it would serve no purpose at all, neither to him nor to his crew.

"Maintain fire, all batteries." Tragus knew one thing. If he was going to lose his first command, if he and his people were going to die in Venta Traconis, they were absolutely going to go down fighting. He'd scored one hit already, he was sure of that…and a few seconds later, the flashes on his screen told him his batteries had connected again.

He felt a brief rush of excitement, a few seconds of satisfaction that were quickly washed away by two stark realizations. First, his people's life expectancies were likely measured in minutes, if not seconds.

Second, even their success, the hits they had scored on the elusive enemy, were ultimately pointless. He didn't know if the enemy hulls were made of imperial alloy, or of some other advanced hardened material, but he was pretty sure neither of the hits his small ship had managed would matter. *Avia*'s guns were just too light, too weak. He couldn't imagine them doing more than superficial damage to one of the Others' ships.

And that seemed like a poor trade for loss of his entire crew.

"Commander, we've got more ships adjusting vectors. They appear to be modifying thrust to move toward us."

Tragus shook his head. *Such pointless excess. They've got us already, surely they know that…*

"Queue up navigation pattern five, Hectoron. Prepare to implement when new enemy ships are…"

"No, Commander…the new contacts are not enemy vessels. Our own ships are adjusting course. I've got a minimum of twelve battleships and four monitors, sir…and they're definitely heading toward our position."

Tragus was silent for a moment, stunned. *The fleet was trying to escape, to save as many of the heavy ships as possible. Why would they be moving toward us, risking heavy units to save a cruiser?*

"Sir, I have Megaron Ilius on the line."

The words hung in the air for a second before Tragus could fully comprehend what his officer had just said. Then he slapped the side of his headset immediately. "Megaron…"

"Listen to me, Kiloron Tragus, very carefully. Am I correct that you figured out how to target those…*things*?"

"Yes, Commander…or at least I believe so. They seem to emit…"

"Not now, Kiloron. I've got half the fleet closing on your position. You just keep those evasive maneuvers going and get that ship back to the tube. Stay alive, Kiloron, stay alive. *Avia* has just become the most important ship in the fleet."

"Yes, Megaron." The words made sense, and then, in some ways, they didn't. Tragus understood the tactical importance of the data and tactics his people had compiled for targeting the enemy, but the whole thing still seemed somehow unreal. And, no matter what Ilius ordered him to do, he was far from certain he could keep up his evasive moves going long enough to escape. It wouldn't take more than one direct hit to obliterate his cruiser. He could be right fifty times, and wrong once, and he and his people would still die short of the tube.

He sucked in a deep breath. He'd created the evasion plans before the fight, a bit of preparedness that had proven prescient, and had bought his people as much time as they'd had so far. But he was far from sure that would be enough, that he would be able to direct his hunted ship to safety.

He saw a flash on the display, an enemy shot coming close—too close. A stark reminder that death was stalking his small band of Kriegeri and their ship.

He took a deep breath and did what he could to center himself. "Shift piloting control to my station, Hectoron." If anybody was going to try to fly *Avia* out of the desperate danger on its tail, it was going to be him.

"Yes, Commander."

Tragus stared directly at his screen, even as his hands gripped the controls. The pre-programmed plans were heavily random, and they'd proven to be quite successful so far. But if *Avia* was going to make it to the end of its desperate run, it was going to take more, something extra.

He flipped a series of switches, activating his manual controls.

Let's see if we can mix this up a little more...

* * *

"All ships, I want *Avia* surrounded by barrages. We may not be able to get hard firelocks on those ships, but we can do something to distract them, get their attention off Tragus's cruiser.

"Yes, Commander." A pause. "We lost *Gessalon*, sir. And *Moltara*."

Ilius didn't react to the news of two more monitors destroyed, though his mind held all the details, the lengths of the ships, the immense tonnages, the thousands of Kriegeri crew aboard.

The years of construction required to build a ship of that size…

He'd been struggling to save the fleet, to get away with the Hegemony's main battle forces still more or less intact. He'd been on the verge of success with that…until he'd watched *Avia* score a direct hit—perhaps the only one any of his vessels had managed. The war was as good as over if the Hegemony forces couldn't effectively target their enemies, and the only way he knew for sure to preserve the secret to whatever success Tragus and *Avia* had achieved was to get the ship out of the system, intact, or as close to intact as possible.

However many heavier ships it cost. However many Kriegeri died in the hopeless fight.

Hegemony's Glory shook hard, and a shower of sparks cascaded down from one of the large ceiling conduits. For an instant, Ilius thought he was going to die, that his flagship had been crippled. But a series of preliminary damage reports confirmed that the hit had been a superficial one. In a relative sense, at least. A quick glance at his screen told him his ship had taken as much damage as it would have from a direct hit from a Confed primary battery. But the reactors were still in decent shape, and the engines were online.

"All operational guns, maintain fire. We need everything we can get right now." That wasn't strictly speaking true. Ilius had more than forty ships of the line converging, covering the space behind *Avia*. Still, the enemy vessels had maintained their single-minded pursuit of the cruiser. Only Tragus's skillful evasive moves had stymied their efforts to take the ship down.

The small group of enemy ships had advanced well in front of their main formation, and Ilius's vessels were almost within point blank range. Still, his gunners were unable to get precise locks, and their shots lanced all through space, coming within ten or twenty thousand kilometers of the enemy vessels, and sometimes much closer, but failing to score a single verifiable hit.

For a time, perhaps four or five minutes, his battleships and monitors fired without stop, without a single return shot from their targets. Then, suddenly, all at once, the enemy ships veered off from their pursuit of *Avia*.

Ilius was flooded with relief. For perhaps a second. Then, he watched at the Others engaged their thrusters again, altering their vectors…and coming around on the large group of battleships and monitors he'd assembled.

He tapped his headset, even as he felt his blood run cold. "Tragus…get that ship the hell out of here, now! I don't care if you have to burn your engines to smoking ruins." He closed the line before the officer could reply, and he watched as a great beam lanced out from the closest of the enemy ships, slicing completely through one of his battleships—*Sallinia*, he realized almost immediately. The great vessel shook hard, and then its thrust dropped to less than ten percent. The scanners reported internal explosions wracking the ship, and half a dozen spots where fluids and gasses were leaking, pouring out in great gouts and freezing almost instantly in the black coldness of space.

Ilius thought for a moment the ship would blow, but it remained on the screen, desperately wounded, its interior almost certainly a nightmare of fires and radiation and death. He wanted to feel relief that the ship had survived the hit, but his mind was too focused, too clear for that. *Sallinia* was still there, but the battleship had no chance of getting out of the system. None.

And, unless its crew figured out how to target enemy ships in the next few minutes, whatever Kriegeri remained alive in that tortured hull could not expect the same treatment Tragus and his people were getting. In the frigid terms of war, they were expendable next to their colleagues who possessed vital tactical information.

"Commander, *Avia* is beginning its final approach to the tube."

Ilius moved his eyes to the side of the main display, grateful for something to look at beyond *Sallinia*'s continuing death struggle. The enemy had indeed given up its efforts to stop *Avia*. That was good, the result he'd hoped for when he'd sent so many ships in to run interference for the cruiser.

Now, all he had to do was get those heavy units out...and that was going to be much more difficult than it had seemed twenty minutes earlier.

Whatever Tragus's people did...I hope it's worth it. We're paying for their escape in blood...

And even as the thought went through his mind, his eyes caught a bright flare on the display. *Bellophon*, a monitor. The immense vessel suffered a far quicker, and much more spectacular death than the one stalking *Sallinia*. One instant the ship had been there, firing its massive broadside...and a few seconds later it was gone, nothing remaining but a roiling inferno of nuclear fusion and annihilating antimatter.

Chapter Six

Hall of the People
Liberte City
Planet Montmirail, Ghassara IV
Union Year 225 (321 AC)

"You're on your own with all of this, Sandrine. I have exceeded my authority already. I can't risk involving the Confederation any more directly in this...change of government." Kerevsky was an ambassador, but at heart he was a spy. He longed to provide more assistance to Sandrine Ciara's coup, to strike against a Union government that had been his people's enemy since before he was born.

He wasn't naïve. He knew enough of Union culture to assume Ciara was no less power hungry than Villieneuve. A successful coup wouldn't replace a communist dictatorship with a democratic government. It would probably change very little...save that the new First Citizen would be indebted to the Confederation. He didn't expect friendship to replace a century of enmity, but he would be happy enough if functional cooperation between neighbors replaced an endless series of conflicts, separated by tense stretches of cold war.

"Your assistance, both financial and otherwise, has been invaluable. I thank you again for all you have done, and I repeat my promise that the new Union government will be a far better neighbor to the Confederation."

Kerevsky nodded, and he looked over at her with a friendly smile. He could hear the tension in her voice, the slight variance in her normally cold and even tone. *How could she not be scared?*

He knew only too well how Gaston Villieneuve dealt with traitors, and no one could face the possibility of such consequences without *some* trepidation. Hell, he was scared himself. He had no direct involvement, nothing official at least, but he didn't doubt the Sector Nine interrogators would quickly draw what they needed from any captured conspirators, and trace how much of the financing had come from Confederation Intelligence's discretionary funds. Diplomatic immunity, and perhaps more reliably, Villieneuve's desire to avoid the risk of war with a Confederation now free of the Hegemony threat, would *probably* protect him, even if suspicion turned his way. And, if that wasn't enough, he had escape routes, or at least places to hide if he needed them. But none of that completely banished the knot in his stomach.

The two remained silent for a moment. Kerevsky was usually a cold-blooded professional, but he'd developed an affection for Ciara. They'd posed as lovers for months— indeed, they had *been* lovers—but from his professional position, she was also an asset, at best a temporary ally. He'd made his own plans for damage control in the event her coup failed, but he'd mostly tried not to think about the prospect of stepping back and covering his own tracks, while she was captured, and tortured and killed. There wasn't much he could likely do to intervene in such a situation, but he'd begun to realize just how difficult it would be for him to sit back and not even try.

You can't involve the Confederation any deeper in the whole mess. You've already gone far beyond your mandate. You'll be lucky if you don't end up in the stockade when you get back home. Or worse.

"Good luck, Sandrine," he said softly, with no intention of anything more. But then he leaned forward and embraced her.

"Thank you again, Alex…we'll celebrate when this is all over." She stepped back and looked at him for a few seconds, and he could see the true magnitude of the fear she was struggling to control. Then she turned and walked out the door.

* * *

"You all know what to do. The instant we get word that Villieneuve…that the first phase is complete…we need to gain control of the key strategic objectives. Gavrin, you and your people will seize the broadcast center. Victorine, your target is the main city utility control. Jean, you and your security forces are to occupy and hold the main approaches into the city center. The Foudre Rouge will likely accept orders from any government authority that seems legitimate. So, we've got to lock down control of the capital. We need a fait accompli, and we need it fast. Otherwise, we may end up fighting half a million Foudre Rouge who start taking orders from someone else."

The dozen or so men and women assembled were the prime movers in the coup about to commence. She'd gathered them together by a variety of means, exploiting animosity toward Gaston Villieneuve, liberally spreading Confederation cash around the group, promising plum positions to those who joined her. It had been deadly and dangerous work, and she'd approached them all with great care. One ill-fated recruiting attempt could easily have blown the whole effort, with unthinkable consequences for her. But she'd held her group together, a conclusion confirmed by the lack of Sector Nine death squads showing up at her door.

Now it's finally time…

Kerevsky had helped her buy time as well, feeding her just enough Confederation secrets to keep Villieneuve satisfied. She'd despaired more than once of bringing the plan to fruition, but somehow, she'd managed it. A few more hours, and it would be done. Gaston Villieneuve would be dead, and she would be the new First Citizen.

"Your teams should be moving to the rendezvous points even now. We're ninety-five minutes from zero hour. The plans are set, and success depends on everybody doing his or her job. We've planned and planned this. Now, it's time to do it. We all know what's at stake." She paused and took a deep breath. "In a few hours, we will have saved the Union. And each of you will be at the very center of power. Let's get it done."

* * *

The steward walked slowly down the corridor, struggling to hold the small tray steady. He'd delivered the tray, and others like it, a hundred times, but tonight was completely different. He was doing more than bringing tea this time, and it took all he could muster to push back against the barely controlled fear and to steady himself as he took the final steps to his destination.

He knew the deadly danger of what he did. If the plot failed, if the intended victim survived the poisoning attempt, the consequences would be unthinkable. He'd worked in the Hall of the People for years, and even as he'd strived to remain in the background, almost as part of the furniture, he'd seen his share of nightmares. He didn't know exactly what happened to those unfortunates Sector Nine dragged from the premises, but his guesses were vivid enough to keep the sweat pouring down his back.

Elise...and the children. This is for them...

He reminded himself yet again why he was taking such a terrible risk. Sandrine Ciara had approached him, but it had been the Confederation ambassador, Kerevsky, who'd finally lured him in. The price had been a simple one. His family would be smuggled out of the Union and resettled in the Confederation. His children, and one day his grandchildren, would know opportunity and freedom he could never imagine. It was a reward worth any risk, and of course, all the discussions had spoken of him joining his wife and children. That was a pleasant hope—or fantasy, depending on how much optimism he could muster in any given moment—but in his heart, he knew he was sacrificing himself for all of them, to get them out of the hell that imprisoned the Union's working classes.

But a plot against the First Citizen…

The consequences of failure were beyond the limits of imagining. But he doubted even success would save him. He'd be lucky, perhaps, if the guards simply shot him on sight. A quick death ranked disturbingly high on his list of desirable outcomes.

They will remember you…they will live lives they never could have here…

He'd negotiated hard, secured guarantees not only of asylum, but of a considerable stipend as well. His family would live in comfort, his children would gain top quality educations. It was a fair deal, even worth the consequences if things went bad.

He took a deep breath, and he realized he'd been at the door for several seconds. He drew on all his strength and will to steady himself. Gaston Villieneuve rarely gave him so much as a second glance. The First Citizen wouldn't notice his evening steward was a bit sweatier than usual, his hands a little shakier than they normally were.

Would he?

* * *

"So, it is confirmed. The Confederation, and its allies, have made peace with the Hegemony. That is quite disappointing, even if we have strongly suspected it for some months now. The Confeds have suffered considerable losses, certainly, but we might have hoped for them to be rendered rather weaker by the conflict before it ended. Our own reconstruction continues apace, but after the losses we suffered when the traitor, Denisov, defected, any hope of resuming hostilities to take advantage of the weakened Confederation fleet is out of the question, at least for the time being." Gaston Villieneuve leaned back in his chair and sighed. The Hegemony had been a threat to the Union as well, of course, and their apparent withdrawal from the entire Rim was good news of a sort as well. But his hatred of the Confederation made it difficult for him to truly understand and appreciate that fact. Villieneuve had been measured and deliberative in his younger days, if always cruel and power hungry, but in recent years he had found himself ever more hotly obsessed with the idea of avenging past defeats on the Confederation.

"Unfortunately, First Citizen, I am compelled to agree with you, especially in light of the seeming endurance of the Confederation-Alliance treaty. If we must be prepared to face both powers—and that seems likely, certainly as long as Vian Tulus holds the Imperator's chair—we will have to increase ship production, even from the current accelerated levels, and we will need at least three years to bring the fleet to sufficient strength, and very likely longer. Unless, of course, the Confederation again becomes engaged with the Hegemony." A pause. "I am aware that past efforts to forge an alliance with hat power were not successful, but perhaps..."

"Unlikely, Admiral. The Hegemony was clearly not interested in any alliances, and I find it hard to imagine that has changed. We will have to do this ourselves, and that means increasing production levels...fifty percent?"

"Is that even possible, First Citizen? The economy is

already on the brink of…"

"It will require considerable austerity measures, Admiral, and some reduction in ration levels on most planets, but the people of the Union will endure what they must so our great nation can prevail. You see to the proposed roster of new ships, and leave finding the resources to me." Villieneuve paused and glanced down at his chronometer. "If you will excuse me, Admiral, I'm afraid we both have other business pending." Villieneuve stood up, and the admiral darted to his feet immediately after. "Yes, First Citizen, of course. I have executed all of your directives regarding the…other matter. Everything is in place, just as you ordered."

Villieneuve smiled. "That is good news, Admiral. Very good news indeed."

Chapter Seven

HWS Hegemony's Glory
Venta Traconis System
Year of Renewal 267 (322 AC)

"All ships in attack group, maintain full fire. We may not be able to hit them, but it looks like the volume of fire is at least distracting them. All vessels not in the immediate firing line are to withdraw on the tube at once and begin transit operations." Ilius watched the display as it became clearer and clearer that the enemy ships that had been pursuing *Avia* had altered their vectors to face the force of battleships and monitors he'd brought in to cover the cruiser's escape.

They're making a mistake...giving us a chance...

It was a tactical error, or at least it seemed like one to Ilius. He was surprised his attack had succeeded in its purpose. He hadn't expected his adversaries to bite, especially since they'd seemed so intent on hunting down the fleeing cruiser.

The enemy were not fools, that was clear. They'd immediately seen the danger in the fact that a Hegemony vessel had apparently managed to target and hit one of their ships. Their initial reaction, to destroy the offending vessel, had been tactically correct. It was a misstep, Ilius was sure, to give up on chasing down the cruiser so they could face a phalanx of battleships that were unable to effectively target them. Was it arrogance, the belief that whatever *Avia*'s crew had figured out, it wouldn't really matter?

Perhaps...but don't make the enemy a favor of your own hubris. They may not have full information. They may believe that Tragus and his people have already shared their targeting secrets with the rest of the fleet, with the heavier units. That those battleships and monitors will be able to aim their weapons effectively. Perhaps that is why they have altered their attack vector.

Ilius's satisfaction at the success of his diversion quickly faded in the blinding reality that the enemy was coming right at him, too.

"Yes, Commander. All battle line units acknowledge. All other ships heading for the tube at maximum thrust." The report pulled his attention back to the bridge, to the main display. He'd acted on impulse, placed a large number of his ships in extreme danger to try to rescue a cruiser whose crew *might* have something useful the rest of the fleet could use to face the enemy next time. It was a wild gamble, and even if Tragus's people *had* developed a way to lock onto the enemy ships, if he lost enough of his combat strength, it still wouldn't matter.

He turned back to his screen, twitching his nose as he did, trying to ward off the caustic smell in the air. *Hegemony's Glory* had taken a hit, no more than a glancing blow, really, but even a seemingly minor strike from the enemy's terrible weapons had caused significant damage. Ilius was just grateful the power systems and the engines remained more or less intact, but the flagship's weapons array was down by about thirty percent. He tried not to think of what a direct hit might have done.

Might still do...we're far from out of this fight.

His eyes moved to the edge of the display, to the small blip that signified *Avia*'s location. The cruiser, at least, was out of the fight, or almost. He looked down at his own screen, his fingers moving across, enlarging the small figures next to the ship's icon. Three minutes to transit. Three minutes, and the small cruiser, the only ship that had managed to hit one of the enemy vessels, would be through to relative safety. And, in the quarter hour after that, a good portion of the fleet would transit, too, as close to a wild scramble to escape as Ilius thought possible without destroying morale or exposing his ships' vulnerable rear sections to unfettered enemy attack.

Many of those ships would escape without further damage, including a good portion of his initial battle line. But the monitors and battleships covering the retreat, including *Hegemony's Glory*, faced a far more desperate outcome. Some would escape, at least it was likely they would. But losses were going to be heavy, and there was more than a small chance the flagship—along with the fleet commander—would among the vessels lost.

Ilius had never been a coward, but he'd also spent most of his career commanding in a position of considerable superiority. Even on the Rim, where the enemy had been fierce and intractable, the Hegemony forces had always held the technological advantage. Now, they were the underdogs in every measurable way, and Ilius struggled to adapt to that reality. Dying in the war was a grim enough prospect, but facing his end in the first battle, before his people had endured the true challenge ahead, shook his normal resolve.

A bright flash caught his eye, a near miss, one of the brilliant blue beams ripping by less than five hundred meters from *Hegemony's Glory*. It had been close enough to short out some scanner antennae on the ship's port side and to light up Ilius's board with a series of damage control reports, mostly shorts and burnouts in the outer sections.

It was also enough to batter further at the veteran commander's crumbling resistance. In the terms of space combat, that shot had been as close as a miss came, and he knew his ship—and he and his crew—had escaped death by the merest slightest of fate. It was a stark realization, even for a hardened warrior, and Ilius could feel the sweat matting his uniform to his hot and slick flesh.

"Double cycle the rate of evasive patterns." The order snapped out of his mouth, almost without conscious thought. The increase would make *Hegemony's Glory* even harder to track and hit, but it would burn through the available sequences twice as fast. When the preset random patterns were gone, the ship would either repeat them in a different order or it would rely on the AI's imperfect random number generation subroutine. Either way, there would be some kind of discernible, trackable pattern, one Ilius was sure the enemy's AIs would quickly analyze. He'd just set a definite countdown on *Hegemony's Glory*'s survival, and that of the other ships in the line, but even after he'd abruptly issued the command, he nodded, reaffirming his intent. He was worried about surviving after the next twenty minutes, but his primary concern just then was getting *to* twenty minutes later.

"Yes, Commander. Nav routine updated per your command." A few seconds' pause. "Megaron, *Avia* is about to transit."

Ilius turned and looked over at the main display, watching as the small dot representing the light cruiser, such an unlikely great hope for the Hegemony, moving into the final approach. Ilius didn't know if he would survive the battle in progress, or if his fleet would be mortally crippled by the time it had completed its withdrawal. But Tragus and his people would escape to show their comrades just how they had managed to establish a target lock on one of the enemy ships. That was the closest thing Ilius was likely to get to a victory in what was otherwise turning into a crippling defeat.

He wasn't sure that made all that much sense, but he chose to embrace it as such.

* * *

"Twenty seconds to transit, Commander." *Avia*'s bridge was almost eerily silent, save for the sound of the officer's voice reporting its approach to the transit tube. The crew was focused, disciplined, but their growing relief at the prospect of escaping Venta Traconis hung over the chamber, almost palpable in its essence.

Tragus sat stone still in his chair, in the center of his command crew, his eyes fixed on the main display, a single number in the forefront of his mind.

Seven.

That's how many battleships and monitors he'd seen destroyed. Not in the battle as a whole…just in the group that had intervened to allow his small vessel to escape. Seven vast ships, behemoths that took years to construct, crewed by thousands of highly-trained Kriegeri. All gone. It had been an appalling trade for *Avia* in terms of tonnage and lives lost, and he was feeling the pressure inside him grow with each passing second.

His people *had* managed to hit an enemy ship, there was no question about that, and it appeared they were the only vessel in the fleet that had achieved that milestone. Still, he was far from sure his tracking method was reliable, that the hit had been more than a fluke. Each passing instant, with every great Hegemony warship with its thousands of Kriegeri crew added to the butcher's bill, only increased the pressure, the grinding need, that what his people had discovered indeed make a difference.

"Ten seconds, Commander."

Tragus remained silent, even as a flash on the display increased the fateful number of sacrificed ships to eight. Procedure specified an acknowledgement to each report his officers issued, but there was no need. His crew was well-trained, capable. They understood what was happening, even as he did, and they knew he'd heard their words. They were veterans, warriors of great ability, and they would serve well in whatever struggle had come upon the Hegemony.

How they would deal with the fact that thousands had traded their own lives to save them would be a personal matter for each to face, as likely as not, alone in the dark.

"Five seconds."

Tragus took a deep breath, and through the guilt and the pressure, another feeling forced its way out, one almost primal in its nature.

Relief.

He'd long considered himself a courageous warrior, one ready to make whatever sacrifices were required of him. He'd faced danger before, even thought he was going to die once out on the Rim. But now, he wanted to live, a fact he'd tried to set aside, a realization that seemed somewhat at odds with his creed of service, to the end if necessary.

The war had just begun, and any reasonable analysis offered little hope of victory, or even survival. The Hegemony faced by far its most desperate moment, and even if his people had indeed developed a way to target the deadly enemy ships, that wasn't even close to evening the score. The enemy was superior in every way, its ships faster, more powerful. He couldn't imagine a scenario where he would survive the war. Yet, escaping from the ongoing fight, fleeing from the current system, buying even a few more days, weeks, months, of life…it filled him with a sort of energy, a drive to put all he had left into getting out of the system. He let out a long exhale as *Avia* slipped into the tube and began its transit.

Began the escape that so many thousands had died to provide.

* * *

Ilius sat quietly, something he found far more difficult in the current situation than shouting out a series of rapid fire orders. His silence was an admission of helplessness, of his inability to do anything to increase the chances that his ship, or the others still in the system, would escape.

The enemy ships were in pursuit, their weapons lancing out, deadly shafts of still-mysterious energy, bringing destruction and death to any ship they struck. The enemy seemed almost godlike in its power, invincible, unstoppable. But Ilius's mind, the part of it clinging to cold logic and rationality, came to a different conclusion, one devoid of the fear and foreboding closing in on him elsewhere. The enemy *was* awesomely powerful, and a deadly adversary, perhaps one that would destroy the entire Hegemony. But they weren't invincible. Their targeting, for one thing…it was accurate and sophisticated, but it wasn't prescient. The enemy gunners or AIs or whatever system was controlling those deadly beams, still struggled to overcome random evasion patterns. Their beams were deadly, powerful enough to cripple a battleship with a single well-placed shot, but most of the enemy fire ripped harmlessly through empty space. Ilius didn't doubt the enemy targeting was superior to the Hegemony's, but the difference there was marginal.

Of more concern was the inability of the Hegemony vessels to effectively hit the enemy ships. Ilius's gamble, his sacrifice of a dozen ships of the line to allow the escape of one cruiser, had been directed at that problem. Maybe, just maybe, Tragus and his people could lead their comrades closer to parity with the enemy.

Ilius winced slightly as he saw one of the beams rip by *Hegemony's Glory*. He almost looked down at his own screen to see just how close the shot had come, but he stopped himself. There was nothing to be gained by knowing.

He did check another distance, the range to the tube. The flagship was about two thirds of the way back, and even as he reviewed the remaining distance, the ships of his rearguard were already transiting. He had tried to maintain as much order in the formation as possible, but his sub-units all had explicit orders. Blast across the next system at full thrust. Ilius didn't know if the enemy would pursue closely or not. Such maneuvers tended to be difficult, since the pursuers still in the current system had no idea what thrust increases and vector changes the already-transited vessels might have initiated. A well-executed transit could usually be turned into an effective escape…though Ilius was well aware he had very little hard data on the Others' maximum thrust capacities.

Even as he was still staring at the display, another of his ships vanished. *Melachon*, a monitor. He'd lost dozens of ships and tens of thousands of veteran Kriegeri already, but seeing one of his largest vessels obliterated less than one hundred thousand kilometers from the transit tube was like a hard punch to the gut. He'd rushed to Venta Traconis to save the advance fleet, but by the time the last of his ships escaped, there was a good chance he'd have lost more vessels than those he'd originally come to rescue. All for nothing.

Or perhaps not nothing, not if *Avia*'s data, the secret to Commander Tragus's targeting, proved to be worth it all.

Chapter Eight

Hall of the People
Liberte City
Planet Montmirail, Ghassara IV
Union Year 225 (321 AC)

"Let's go...stay quiet and keep it moving." Victorine Lechamps squinted, staring as far as she could down the dimly-lit corridor. Her people were security troopers, mostly her own, and all carefully selected for reliability. They were risking their lives, every one of them, and one misstep could bring a world of hurt down on them in minutes.

"We're almost there," she added, her eyes moving down the small column of armed men and women. The hallway was used mostly for maintenance and repairs, and it was perfect for slipping her people into the utility control center unnoticed. Almost thirty armed soldiers would be noticed immediately anywhere in the open, and they would, at the very least, attract scrutiny. Lechamps didn't know how Ciara had managed to get the access codes to the hidden corridor, but she felt a small burst of relief, a realization that the leader of the coup even then underway had been careful, and had planned everything well.

In a few minutes, we'll control the city's water and electrical power...

She had a precise list, conduits she had to cut, areas of the city that were to be plunged into darkness, even as the other groups struck their targets all around the Union's capital. The broadcast center was near the top of that list, along with every main communications nexus. No word was to get into or out of the capital, not until the announcement of the new government was broadcast.

"Everybody, check your weapons." The entrance to the utility control complex was less than a hundred meters ahead. There would be guards inside—six according to the most recent data Ciara had been able to obtain—though Lechamps knew it was dangerous to rely too heavily on that. Her people shouldn't have any real trouble with a force that size, or even one a bit larger, but combat was always an uncertainty. There was no time for mistakes, or for less than total preparedness. Errors, carelessness, delays…they all killed.

She reached around her back, sliding her own rifle around and holding it out in front of her. She'd read the schematics, checked the plans again and again. The access door would let her people out just down the hallway from the main control center. Her people would be out, and a quick five or six meter jog later, into the main workspace.

Inflict minimal casualties. That was her directive. At least among the civilian staff. Ciara wanted as many of the people in that room back at their jobs come morning, not bleeding to death on the floor or cursing the new order for slaughtering their friends and coworkers. Union politics was usually about raw force and terror, but Ciara was trying a kinder and gentler application, at least in a relative sense. The rationale made sense to Lechamps, but then she only knew the old status quo, and there was still some uncertainty in her mind, some question as to whether she wouldn't be better off if her people opened fire indiscriminately, and made it clear they would tolerate no resistance.

She stopped at a large square hatch and turned back toward her people. She nodded, and then she whispered, barley audibly, to the front row, "I'll go 5, 4, 3, 2, 1." She held up her hand as she spoke, dropping one finger as she spoke each number. "Then we go in. No talk, no more noise than necessary. Just through the hatch and down the hall to the control center. Armed guards are to be shot on sight, but nobody else, not unless they make a threatening move."

She turned back, waiting perhaps half a minute as her people relayed her orders. Then she held her hand out, all five fingers extended.

She pulled back her thumb, then another finger.

Then a third, a fourth. She reached out her other hand, twisting the controls for the hatch as she dropped the last finger.

The door slid to the side, and she reached up, grabbing hold of a metal bar stretching across the top and pulling herself through. She took three steps, and then she turned, making sure her people were behind her. Then she extended the rifle forward and strode quickly down the hall toward the control room. She took a few more steps, and then pushed through the door into the large main area, her mouth open, ready to shout out instructions to all those present. Her eyes were darting all around, searching for any guards.

Then, she stopped suddenly, and her stomach shriveled into a knot.

*   *   *

"Your tea, First Citizen." The steward had been nervous out in the hall, but he'd somehow found the strength to hold it together as he stepped into the room. He'd set the tray down, without, he believed, any obvious signs of fear or tension, at least no more than that normal for those who served the often-unpredictable Villieneuve. "Is there anything else I can do for you, sir?" He turned slightly as he spoke, half driven by his burning desire to get out of the room, and half by muscle memory from the hundreds of times Villieneuve had said 'no.'

"Yes, Steward. It's Rillet, isn't it?"

The steward felt a coldness in his body. Gaston Villieneuve had hardly noticed him before, much less his name.

Something was wrong.

"You have brought me my tea for what, over a year now?" Villieneuve's voice was cool, non-committal. "Yet, we have never taken the time to speak, to get to know each other."

The steward could feel the sweat pooling up along the back of his neck, the long rivulets breaking free, sliding down his back. He wanted to turn and run, but that would be suicide. So, he just stood where he was, trying to hide the shaking, and to keep his voice steady as he replied. "Yes, First Citizen. It was a year last month."

He remained silent for a few seconds, as long as his growing panic would allow. Then, he added, "If that is all, First..."

"I told you that was not all, didn't I?" Villieneuve's tone hardened just a bit. "Stay for a moment. I should make more effort to appreciate those who provide services to me. The affairs of state can sometimes be...overwhelming...but that is no excuse. I am never to busy to inquire as to how those on my staff are faring, wouldn't you agree?"

Villieneuve was staring with a cold intensity, and Rillet's courage and discipline were melting like ice in a blast furnace. "First...Citizen...I understand you are...very busy. I...I...I really should be going. I know you have much...to do."

"Like drink this tea you brought me, Rillet? No doubt it is perfect, as always, just the amount of sugar I like, perfectly brewed…or perhaps there is something different this time, something new in the mix?"

Rillet was shaking uncontrollably, but he still tried to respond, to force out intelligible words. "I…I…don't know…what…"

"Sure, you do, my loyal steward." Villieneuve stepped forward, scooping up the cup of tea as he did. Even as the First Citizen moved toward him, Rillet could hear something behind him, the sounds of boots on the hardwood floor.

"First Citizen…please…I must go…" The words were mixed with sobs, and Rillet could feel the tears streaming down his face.

"I would offer you some of this…" Villieneuve held the cup in front of him. "…but I'm afraid that might impair your ability to answer questions, and we wouldn't want that, would we? My people at Sector Nine are quite good at asking questions, my dear Rillet."

The steward sunk to his knees, as whatever shreds of hope had remained to him failed. The Confederation ambassador had promised to take care of his family whether the coup succeeded or not, but now his own fear was joined by panic over what would happen to his wife and children if they weren't able to escape.

"Please…First Citizen…"

"Am I right, then, Rillet? Would you be less than excited at the prospect of sharing my tea? The tea you just brought me?" Villieneuve stepped closer, even as two pairs of arms grabbed the steward from behind and held him like a vice. "Why, Rillet? Why would you betray me? Do you think me a fool?"

"Please…no…please…" Most of the words from the steward's mouth were coming out close to indecipherable gibberish.

"My sources are more reliable than your cohorts might have hoped, Rillet. Certainly, my people in the kitchens were on to your mischief. Such mischief is best left to those trained for it, and not an ignorant fool who delivers food and tea, wouldn't you agree? Now, you're going to tell me everything I don't already know, and you're going to do it now...before I have your family brought in here—yes, they are already in custody—and fed to wild dogs in front of you as you watch. Then, you will find out just why Sector Nine is so...well-regarded...for its efficiency and skill."

Rillet lost all control, and he slumped to the ground. He lay on his side, quivering in abject terror, even as Villieneuve's voice continued. "Don't worry, my dear Rillet...you will not be the reason all your allies die. We already know much of the plan, and I can assure you, we have taken the necessary precautions to defeat this treacherous coup attempt."

* * *

Lechamps could hear her people coming up behind her, even as her hopes escaped her and her courage slipped away. She'd expected perhaps half a dozen guards. Instead, there were at least forty armed soldiers in the room, with more pouring in from doorways on both sides. They looked like Foudre Rouge, almost, but there was something different about them. Their uniforms, certainly. They wore black tunics and trousers, and they carried small automatic weapons.

She turned, thinking for an instant to make a run back to the maintenance corridor. But there was no point. She'd never make it, and even if she did, the soldiers would just follow. She was dead, she knew it with a cold certainty. The only question was, would it be right there and then, or later, after the worst a Sector Nine interrogation team could offer?

She knew she had to fight, that her people had to fight...and die. It was the only option, considering what awaited her if she allowed herself to be captured. The logic was ironclad, but she still wavered. It was one thing to decide to die, to accept there was no alternative.

It was entirely another to do it, to actually move forward, to face the final seconds of her life.

Thoughts ripped through her mind, seductive notions of later escape, of talking her way out of the situation. But that was all nonsense. She'd been caught, weapon in hand, co-conspirators at her back. She was dead, as coldly and certainly as if she'd already had a bullet in her brain. All that remained was to determine how much pain, how much agony she endured first.

How much dignity she retained before death took her.

She reached down, half ignoring the memories, the images of her life, even then pouring out into her consciousness. She brought the gun to bear as she lunged forward, and she shouted to her people to follow. She knew some would hesitate, some would surrender…and they would suffer torment unimaginable. In another place, another time, she would have wept for them, for those who'd followed her and lacked the presence, the control, to seek a quick death. But her thoughts were awash with her own fear, her sorrow for herself. Her regret for allowing herself to be drawn into such a dangerous plan.

She felt her legs moving forward, her fingers tightening on the trigger, even as part of her screamed at herself to stop, to throw her hands in the air, to drop to her knees and beg for mercy. But there would be no mercy, she knew that, and a few more days of life would come only at a staggering cost in suffering and torment.

Better to die here, now…

She fired her rifle, and then again, as she ran forward.

She felt something, and then again. There was no pain, but her eyes dropped down, and she saw the blood pooling out into two large circles on her tunic. She was still moving forward, but she felt as though her legs were hardening, turning to cement.

The room moved, flipping all around, and then she was down, on her knees, her rifle on the floor in front of her, and one hand extended, holding her body up in a prone position. There was still no pain, but she could feel the weakness, the sensation of all her strength draining away.

She waited for the final shots, the killing attack, but nothing happened. Her thoughts were jumbled, her mind fuzzy, confused. But she saw her rifle, and some last bit of discipline took charge. The soldiers would take her prisoner, drag her to some Sector Nine torture chamber.

Unless they had to kill her.

She gathered what remained of her strength, and she lunged forward, her hands reaching for her rifle, even as the soldiers closest to her reacted, opening fire.

A dozen or more shots hit her, and this time she *did* feel the pain, the burning agony of the projectiles tearing through her flesh. But her face held only a strange smile, born of the realization that her pain how would be brief, short-lived…and it would spare her torment beyond description.

She felt the cool hardness of the floor under her, the warm wetness, the blood pooling all around. She slipped away, hoping as she did that her people followed her lead, that they embraced a merciful death, and not the hell that awaited those who were taken alive.

Chapter Nine

Restored Senate Hall
Troyus City
Megara, Olyus III
Year 322 AC

Tyler Barron walked through the soaring masonry arch, a polished marble edifice boasting to all who passed through of the power and glory of the Confederation, and even more so, of the Senate that governed it. The effect was lost Barron, though, and he only frowned as he stepped under it, trying to ignore the loud tap of his boots on the polished marble floor.

All around, for kilometers in every direction, Troyus City, and the rest of Megara, lay mostly in ruins. There was construction everywhere, and in every city, every inhabited area on the planet, roads, hospitals, emergency housing, were all in desperate need of repair and rebuilding. It turned Barron's stomach to see that the politicians had poured such a vast amount of the still-limited resources available to their own glorification, when so many millions still huddled together in vast tent cities, clustering around portable heaters and eating whatever, often inadequate, supplies reached them.

Barron had long been troubled by the corruption and

arrogance he saw in the Confederation's government classes, but the stark imagery of so much suffering so close to the opulence on display in the Senate Compound was particularly upsetting. He carried images with him as he walked through the second of the series of restored great arches, views of his spacers and Marines, of course, so many dead in the vicious fighting that had saved the Confederation, but others as well. Above them all, however, at that moment, was the face of a young girl, no older than five or six. He'd seen wandering through the rubble, calling out piteously for her mother, who was nowhere to be found. He'd given the child all the coins he'd had with him, but even as he was reaching into his pockets, he cursed himself for the miserable inadequacy of the gesture. There was little food to buy, and almost no medicine, and even as he'd walked toward the Compound, and the appearance he'd been commanded to make, he couldn't stop himself from calculating that little girl's chance of survival.

A coin toss...

Tyler Barron was a veteran, a stone cold professional at the art of war, but he despised the losses and suffering so endemic to humanity's favorite pursuit. And as much as he'd long endured the pain of seeing his military comrades killed and maimed, he found the devastation and suffering of the people in general even more difficult to endure.

"Admiral Barron, welcome to the restored Senate Hall. My name is Alison Davies...please call me Alison. Speaker Landry sent me to wait for you, and to guide you to the meeting." The young woman was pleasant, almost irritatingly so, and she was dressed in the flawless attire of a Senatorial aide. Barron tried not to frown as he glanced at the quasi-uniform—clearly brand new and quite expensive—but he felt his hands tightening, aching to form fists, as he wondered if there was any luxury, any pointless piece of self-aggrandizing nonsense, the Senators had failed to waste scarce resources upon.

"Thank you, Alison. I'm afraid I just got back to Troyus City, and if I'm not late, I suspect I am close to it."

Barron managed something he hoped resembled a smile. Well, maybe 'hope' was a strong word, given how little he gave a shit for Senatorial pomp. Still, the young woman was not the target of his ire, at least not yet. She might one day rise to that level, but if she was a young politician in the making, if she'd been staring into her mirror every day for years, practicing giving speeches to cheering crowds, he had no proof. She deserved the benefit of the doubt, and Tyler Barron gave it to her.

Emmet Flandry, however, was another matter. The Flandrys were rich, richer even than the Barrons, if not quite as immensely wealthy as the Holstens, and Emmet had skillfully used the confusion and tumult of the war, and the forced relocations of the Senate, to blaze a trail from the upper middle of the pack to the Speakership itself. It had been an impressive move, even for a man with nearly limitless financial resources, and Barron knew he should respect the achievement, at least on some level. He didn't like Flandry, didn't respect the man any more than he did most corrupt politicians, and the politician's money-paved route to the top repelled him.

Still, he hoped he might be able to work with the Senate's new leader. Like it or not, Emmet Flandry was one of the two or three most powerful politicians in the Confederation, and Barron, as the newly minted commander-in-chief of the navy, was going to have to learn how to coexist with him.

"Not at all, Admiral. The Speaker advised that you would be coming directly from the shuttle dock." A pause. "Congratulations on your marriage, Admiral. The entire Confederation rejoices with you." It was the same tone as before, flawlessly polite, with just enough seemingly genuine emotion to make the whole thing sound like staged bullshit.

Barron felt his smile slipping away. The aide was pleasant

enough, but he couldn't escape the growing certainty that her entire demeanor was utterly fake. Maybe she was closer than he thought to becoming the full-fledged political animal she clearly sought to be.

"Thank you again. Now, perhaps we should get to the meeting. I wouldn't want to hold things up."

She nodded, and then she turned sharply. "Right this way, Admiral Barron." She walked across the vast expanse of the outer hall and down a corridor only slightly less ornate. Barron's head turned from one side to the other, and with every view of the opulence of the building, he became just a bit angrier.

Finally, they reached a double door. The aide stepped inside and introduced him. "Admiral Tyler Barron, Commander-in-Chief of the Confederation navy." She stepped to the side, and she stared at Barron with a sickly smile. The admiral held back a sigh, and he walked into the room.

"Speaker Flandry, Senators…I am sorry if I am late."

"No worries, Admiral." Emmet Flandry had an unkempt look to him, uncommon for a politician of his current stature. He was clad in an immensely expensive suit, but it was so rumpled, he looked as though he'd just rolled out of bed. He spoke with an almost insane Philophoran drawl, which surprised Barron every time he heard it. The disheveled old politician hadn't been back to his dreary homeworld in two decades at least. His political machine was so all-powerful, so dominant on that relatively poor and backwards planet, he'd never had to trouble himself to return home to campaign, or to meet any of his constituents. They were little more than votes to him, and ones he didn't have to work too hard to gather. "It is a great honor to have the hero of the Confederation here with us." The words were gracious and respectful, but there was something about the tone and the delivery that made it all sound dirty to Barron.

"Of course, Speaker Landry." Barron turned toward a woman standing along the opposite wall. "Ambassador Carmetia." He nodded his greeting. He'd been practicing his manners around Hegemony personnel, but the scars of war were slow to heal. Part of him wanted to pull his pistol from its holster and turn the Hegemony's ambassador into a stain on the shining marble of the wall.

"Admiral Barron. I am quite pleased to see you here. I have much to discuss with this committee, and I believe you will understand most of it quite clearly." She hesitated, just for a few seconds, but something about the edginess in her mannerisms struck Barron. He had come prepared to ignore or disbelieve anything Carmetia said, but as his eyes focused on her face, on the rigid tension in her shoulders, realization slowly dawned.

She is scared.

Carmetia continued, maintaining her composure, but unable to completely hide the fear Barron suddenly believed was very real. "I am here to speak of an enemy we call the Others, an adversary who is not only deadly dangerous to the Hegemony, but also a dire threat to the Rim, and all humanity wherever it exists."

It was an almost wild claim, a lie so daring, so exaggerated, it wouldn't fool a child. There was only one problem, and it weighed on Barron like chains.

He didn't think it wasn't a lie.

He prided himself on reading people, which most of the time meant disbelieving what he was told. But now his eyes were fixed, and his attention was on the Hegemony Master, even as pieces began to assemble in his mind, most prominently, the explanation Carmetia's claim offered for the Hegemony's sudden abandonment of their invasion, and perhaps even more for their stunning surrender of *Colossus*.

"That is quite a claim, Ambassador. In the bayous of Philophoria, we've got a saying. When somebody tells you they ran into a swamp lizard, cut the size in half."

Barron's eyes shifted to the politician. His first thought was to deride the man, to wonder how he could miss what he himself perceived so clearly as sincerity in Carmetia's statement. But then he realized. *He* does *believe her, or at least he suspects there is truth to what he says. He's working her, trying to see how she reacts.*

He stared at Flandry, and his read on the politician changed. The Speaker still disgusted him in many ways, but there was a new respect growing. Or, at least, something like respect.

Don't underestimate this man…

"Speaker Flandry, I assure you I am telling nothing but the truth. Our recent…withdrawal…from the Rim is a testament to the danger. The Hegemony has never failed to absorb a human population, never in its history before the cessation of the recent war. It was the appearance of the Others that prompted our actions, and whatever differences and bad feelings remain between our peoples, I can assure you most earnestly, that the Others are a deadly threat not only to my nation, but to yours. If we of the Hegemony are defeated, the Rim will fall in its turn. I have come to warn you of this threat, and I have brought evidence with me. I urge you all to review it, to understand the magnitude of the threat, and when you have, my government has instructed me to…"

Carmetia paused, and for the first time she seemed visibly uncomfortable. "They have instructed me to request a treaty with the Confederation, and with its allies." Another pause. "I am here to ask for an Alliance, for the Rim powers to stand with us against the Others. To contribute your armed forces to the fight against the Others."

The room was silent, even Speaker Flandry apparently lost for words. Barron looked around the room, struggling at first to get a read on the Senators present. Then, slowly, he began to see their doubts, even anger. Carmetia's words hadn't swayed them.

But they had convinced him. He was still trying to fight it off, to argue with himself, but deep down, he believed she was telling the truth, that there *was* a deadly threat out there.

And he suddenly realized, he'd been concerned about something of the sort for months, ever since the war's sudden end.

Barron feared the idea of a deadly new enemy, of leading his exhausted and depleted warriors into a new fight, a deadlier fight. But perhaps most of all, he dreaded having to stand beside the enemy that had hurt his people so badly. He wasn't proud of his hatred, but he also knew it had helped him deal with the losses, the pain. He wasn't sure he could let it go.

He wasn't sure he could survive without it.

"By all means, Ambassador, you have been granted an audience with the Senate's leadership committee...show us your evidence. But I warn you, whatever you have brought will have to be compelling to overcome my doubts, and I suspect those of my colleagues as well." Barron watched as Flandry spoke, and for all the Speaker's evident skepticism, he became more certain with each passing second that the politician was at least concerned.

He had been standing since he'd arrived, but he sat down as Carmetia proceed to lay out the supporting evidence she'd brought with her. By the time she was finished, Barron felt fear, worry, foreboding. But one thought rose above them all, one realization he found most daunting.

How am I going to tell my spacers and Marines they have to fight another war...as allies of the Hegemony?

* * *

"I'm going to be blunt, Admiral. I know you don't like me. You don't like any politicians. That's okay, I don't much like most of the officers who prance around with chests full of medals, feeling superior to the rest of us, as if fighting a few battles is all it takes to run the Confederation. So, let's make an agreement, just between us. We'll both cut the carnosoid crap. I like to think I can smell a load from a kilometer away, and my read on you is that you can too."

Barron didn't like the politician, but his quasi-respect for the man's intellect was growing. He'd been surprised when the Speaker had requested—requested, not ordered—that Barron come to a private meeting. The whole thing felt a little like climbing into some kind of mudpit, but he needed to find out just what the Speaker thought of Carmetia's request, and he figured there was at least a chance of honesty and straight talk if no one else was around.

And that sounded like straight talk to me.

Barron couldn't remember the last time someone had begun a conversation with a declaration of mutual dislike. He found it strangely refreshing. Flandry was still vermin, his thoughts on that hadn't changed. But he was smart vermin…and just maybe, that made him useful as well.

"I like to think I have a reasonable nose for it, Speaker. Though, I've never seen a carnosoid, I'm afraid. We don't have anything like that where I'm from. Just some good size birds of prey…wing spans of three, three and a half meters." Barron almost continued, but he decided to let Flandry take the lead.

"I'm certain of that, Admiral, your nose, I mean. As to the matchup of a flock of giant birds against a carnosoid, we'll just have to leave that with a big question mark on it."

Flandry paused, and a crooked line appeared on his face, something quasi-disturbing that Barron guessed was a smile. "So, let's do each other a favor. I won't congratulate you on your wedding, and you don't tell me how wonderful you think it is that I gained the Speakership. Neither one of us cares. But I do think we both care about keeping the Confederation safe. Whether that comes from some high principle of patriotism, or simply a realization of vulnerability emphasized by the debris spread across Megara and the other costs of the last war, is irrelevant. We have been forced to stare into the face of our exposure, and I feel confident that neither of us wants to see Megara occupied once again by an enemy…any enemy."

Barron listened quietly, and then he nodded. "I believe we can agree on that, Speaker. We have too often allowed confidence to turn into pride, even hubris. And we paid a terrible price for it. I, for one, do not feel we can ignore *any* threat, proven or not. The White Fleet was a noble effort." Barron paused. It *had* been noble to his view, but he hadn't been oblivious to the fact that it had also been a way for the Senate to get rid of a military officer who'd become a bit *too* popular.

"Then, we are agreed. Despite the Committee's rejection of Ambassador Carmetia's request, I do not think we can simply ignore this potential danger. And yet, neither do I believe we can simply join forces with the Hegemony. For one, what guarantees do we have that they will not simply continue their attempt to conquer the Rim after we help them defeat their enemy?"

Barron was surprised at Flandry's words. They went against much of what he'd come to expect from politicians and their short-sightedness.

"You are realizing I'm not the same kind of political animal you've dealt with before, Admiral. Oh, by all means, let's continue our agreement not to dance around each other. I'm as much of a politician as any you've ever met. But I'm a practical man, as well, born on a bayou rice plantation that made enough in a good year to feed us all, and maybe fix a leak in the roof. I don't believe my own bullshit, at least not entirely. I know you blame past Senates for the lack of preparedness for the Union wars, and I can't argue with you about that. You're right. It's understandable enough. Senators from places like Ulion or Craydon have their hands full often enough just maintaining their grip, but they're generally for more military spending to keep the factories running. But it takes a lot more to grease the population of a core world like Ulion that a few big orders for guns or ships…at least it did before the Hegemony War. Fortunately for me, Philophoria is a putrid, bloodfly-infested pit, whose people don't have the vision to see much beyond a Confederation-funded flood control project or two. It's cheap and easy to maintain my base, Admiral, and I don't need to raid military budgets to fund a lot of crowd-pleasing foolishness. You may look at me and see a corrupt politician, but I'm also one free enough from the need to buy my next reelection to actually try to decide what's best for the Confederation."

Barron listened to every word with growing surprise. He'd never heard a politician speak quite so…honestly. He found it refreshing, but also unnerving.

"I appreciate your candor, Speaker. It is quite…unexpected."

"It's not something you're likely to hear outside the walls of this office, Admiral, but I think we understand each other. You're an idealist in some ways, or at least enough of one that I don't think you harbor images of making yourself a dictator or emperor. You've had chances before…ones I suspect I might have taken myself. So, if I don't have to worry about you as a rival power—not too much, at least— then I can work with you, and take advantage of your unquestioned military skills."

The room was silent for perhaps half a minute, Barron was trying to wrap his mind around what he was hearing, and Flandry was giving him the time he needed. Finally, the Speaker spoke again. "So, Admiral, assuming your silence signifies some type of tentative agreement, perhaps we can discuss a course of action. Simply put—straight from the swamp as we put it back home—what should we do next?"

Chapter Ten

Hall of the People
Liberte City
Planet Montmirail, Ghassara IV
Union Year 225 (321 AC)

There was no way to deny it, no time for pointless hopes or prayers for a miracle. The coup had failed, and it had failed badly.

Gaston Villieneuve was a sociopath, a man utterly without conscience, without regret for any of his actions, however vicious and violent. But he wasn't a fool. Quite the contrary, he was a genius in his own right, a brilliant, if twisted intellect.

Kerevsky suddenly knew, the realization hitting him like the first shaft of dawn light. It was over. Any chance of overturning the Union's government, of whatever faint and fragile hopes he'd had that Sandrine Ciara might prove to be a less despotic leader—or at least one less hostile to the Confederation—were gone. All he could do now was try to mitigate the damage.

He'd covered his own tracks fairly well, at least he thought he had. But suddenly, he was plagued with doubts. Was he underestimating Villieneuve *again*?

He turned and snapped off a series of orders to his aide.

He had to assume the worst, and that meant staying in the shadows, at least until he had a better sense of what was happening. He considered himself tough, and he'd seen his share of pain, but he was also experienced enough to dispense with false confidence. If Sector Nine came for him, if Villieneuve was prepared to risk provoking the Confederation by torturing its ambassador, he was certain he would tell them everything he knew. Not quickly, perhaps—he still liked to think he could maintain his defiance for a good while—but Sector Nine was expert at breaking people, and they would eventually wear him down.

No, you can't let them take you...

He would kill himself before he let that happen. But he wasn't one to give up easily, and he had another alternative. He could lay low. Even hide, if he had to.

His first thought was to get to his ship, but that was pointless. If Villieneuve was prepared to throw the Confederation's ambassador into a torture cell, he'd be ready to open up Montmirail's defensive batteries and blast one lone Confed cruiser to dust.

There were other options, preparations no normal ambassador would have made. Kerevsky was a spy himself, and the foot in that camp had always been more securely planted than the one in the diplomatic world. He had safe houses, stashes of currency and weapons, all sorts of resources in place for just the eventuality he faced. Sector Nine could find all of those, too, of course, if they looked hard enough. But not immediately. And with the failure of the coup, all he could do was play for time.

"Destroy the records, Kyle...and get the staff ready. We're going to activate one of the safehouses...now. Just in case."

"Yes, Ambassador." Kyle Corbin had always looked even more uncomfortable in his role as a diplomat's assistant than Kerevksy had been as ambassador. Corbin was a spy, too, and a damned good one.

Kerevsky paused, Sandrine Ciara pushing her way into this thoughts. Doctrine was clear regarding the handling of burned assets, but he was having trouble writing her off so quickly. If she was even still alive somewhere.

He told himself they'd been using each other, that they'd become lovers for practical reasons, to work each other the best they could, and not out of any emotional nonsense. Sex had always been a prominent part of espionage toolkit, and the fact that each of them had been employing the same tactic on the other didn't change the basic facts.

But the thought of her in a Sector Nine cell, screaming in agony until her throat and vocal cords were reduced to bloody ruin, troubled him. He cursed himself, berated his lack of discipline, his weakness in allowing himself to care what happened to someone he should just have been using. Worse, perhaps, Ciara had failed, and her value and utility had plummeted along with the prospects of her coup. She was a liability, even if he could find her. Trying to save her would be exceedingly dangerous, and even if he pulled it off, having the prime perpetrator of the coup remain at large would only inflame Villieneuve's paranoia, and eliminate any chance of things blowing over.

But then he saw her face again, smiling, lying next to him at first, but then morphing into a screaming, tormented nightmare.

"Get everything ready...I'll be right back." It was stupid, insane, and every bit of his training and experience cried out to stop him. But it all failed, sense, tradecraft, the cold, analytical way he normally approached problems. He just couldn't leave her, not to the fate Villieneuve would inflict on her, and he knew she'd never escape on her own. Not without his help.

He put up his hand, stifling his Corbin's objection. "I know, Kyle, I know. Just do what I asked." He exchanged a quick glance with his aide, and then he slipped out the door, heading toward the door…and into the wild tumult of a dying coup, and a city gripped in its deadly aftermath.

* * *

Sandrine Ciara raced down the street. It was more of an alley, really, lightly traveled and out of the way. If anyone spotted her there, they'd be suspicious at once, but at least she had a chance to avoid contact. If she ventured out onto one of the main avenues, she expected her lifespan would be measured in minutes. Her image was everywhere, and she hadn't had the time or place to even make an effort at a disguise.

No, they won't kill you. Villieneuve wants you alive. He wants to show you what happens to those who betray him…

She felt a chill, and her body shook uncontrollably. She was operating on adrenalin, her intellect and cunning subverted almost entirely to an animalistic desperation to survive. There was no place for critical thought, for detailed analysis. Such pursuits could only verify the hopelessness threatening to overtake her.

Even as she ran, as her instincts led her, random thoughts drifted through her mind. It was strange, she mused, that she should feel such terror. She'd killed her share of people, even sent many to the very torturers that awaited her. It seemed that one who had done such things, committed such cruel acts, should be ready to face their own fate with at least some sort of composure. But she was as coldly terrified as her victims had ever been, as much consumed by mindless panic as any target she had killed or tortured.

It was worse, perhaps. She had a much clearer idea of what awaited her than most of Sector Nine's victims.

She turned a corner, her already knotted guts tightening further, until her eyes confirmed the alley ahead of her was still clear. She sucked in a deep breath, struggling to hold back the contents of her tortured stomach…and failing as she leaned forward and retched up a small bit of foam and bile.

She knew she should keep going, that there was no time for rest. But she could feel her resolve fading, and even as her will to live flared up, screaming from inside for her to keep running, another realization formed.

It's over…there's no way out. And you can't let them capture you…

There'd been a certain kind of courage in launching her coup, but she began to sense that much of it had been delusion, false confidence of success fending off the terror of the consequences of defeat. Now, she faced a grim conclusion. She had to kill herself. There were no other options.

She'd taken lives before, many of them, yet the thought of killing *herself*, of plunging her knife into her own chest, seemed impossible. She knew she'd endure an end a thousand times slower and more painful if she didn't, but as she faced the reality, it seemed an impossible thing to do.

You have to…you know what the alternative is…

Her mind was dark, filled with shadows, the distorted faces of people she'd killed, laughing at her, tormenting her, as she faced the same black fate she'd inflicted on them. They were spies, traitors, she told herself. They'd deserved death. But she knew that was only partially true. She'd killed innocents too, and no small number of them. Guilt and innocence were largely irrelevant concepts in the Union, and suspicion alone was enough to mandate a death sentence. But she had gone beyond even such casual brutality. She'd tortured and killed people to influence others, murdered husbands, wives, children of those who resisted her demands.

She'd never considered herself evil. She'd simply done what was necessary, to preserve the Union, and to advance her own position. But now that she faced the same end she'd inflicted on so many others, she felt almost as though she was torn in two. Part of her wanted to survive, to find some way to escape. But there was a voice in the depths of her mind, growing in intensity, a dark shout that she deserved death and torture, that her current situation was nothing more than simple justice. Would there be redemption in enduring what she'd inflicted on so many others? She didn't have the answer, but whatever it was, she knew with grim certainty, she didn't have the courage.

She pulled out the knife, the last weapon she had, and she held it in front of her. She paused, wondering with almost absurd detail how to do it. Should she plunge it into her chest? Or cut her own throat? What would be quickest, the least painful. For an instant, her fear ebbed, as the analysis became almost clinical, removed from her in some way.

Then, reality reasserted its dominance. She held the knife in front of her, the razor-sharp point pressing against her clothing. She increased the pressure, feeling resistance from her jacket. Her arms loosened, and she pulled the knife away, her other hand moving about the jacket, slipping the garment off. Then she pulled at her shirt, tugging at the material, exposing the flesh below. She pressed the knife against her again, and she recoiled at the coolness of the blade on her skin.

Do it...do it now...

He thoughts battled inside her, waging a war in her head, her rational mind pushing her to finish things, to escape the terrible torment that awaited her. But the fear pressed back, the will to live struggling to hold her hand, to keep the blade back...to live, even if only for a few more minutes.

There's no other way. You know what will happen if they catch you...

She could feel her teeth grinding, her body wracked by chills, even as the sweat poured down her back in torrents. Pain, too, as a fleeting bit of courage gave her the strength to push hard enough on the blade to draw blood. But she couldn't finish, couldn't bring herself to make that last push.

She felt stark panic at what would happen to her if she was captured...but she couldn't kill herself, at least not with only a simple blade. She had to do something, find a way to escape. She didn't know how that was possible, or who could help her, but she had to try.

Who *would* even help her? Whatever allies she had were either dead—or in Sector Nine cells—or they were doing everything possible to distance themselves from her and her planned coup. She had used people her entire life, done terrible things to gain power and position. She had no friends, no real relationships. No one would help her when she had nothing to offer in return.

She stood for a moment, her mind grasping for something, anything. Then, a single thought materialized.

No, why would he help you? You used him, just as you have everyone else.

Alexander Kerevsky had been an asset, certainly, but as she stood there, fighting off the panic trying to take control, she realized there had been something more there.

But you used him anyway. Why would he care? Why would he risk himself to save you?

She was shaking her head, trying to push the idea away. Kerevsky was just one more acquaintance else she'd mistreated, a tool that had served a purpose.

But he was something more. There *had* been a connection there. She had felt it, and she suspected he had, too. It was tenuous, a sparse and frayed hope that the Confederation ambassador would—could—help her.

But there was no point in deeper analysis of whether Kerevsky would help. He was her only option. And through her fear, the blind panic gradually turning her intellect to pure instinct, she realized the alley where she stood led to the Confederation embassy, or close to it.

This is stupid. He won't help you, and even if he wanted to, what could he do?

It didn't make sense, it was pointless. She tried again to bring the knife to her chest, to gather the strength for one final thrust. But it just wasn't there.

Kerevsky was all she had…assuming she could even get to him.

Chapter Eleven

Planet Calpharon
Sigma Nordlin IV
Year of Renewal 267 (322 AC)

"I am relieved beyond words to see you, old friend."
Chronos stepped forward and embraced Ilius. It was an
oddly expressive gesture, and far more emotional than
Number Eight's usual demeanor. But Ilius understood.
There would be a certain amount of delusion among the
members of the Council and the Hegemony's senior
Masters, calls for his head, accusations that his
incompetence, and not some overpowering enemy, had
been the cause of the disaster at Venta Traconis. But
Chronos knew and trusted him. His friend was a longtime
skeptic of the legends of the Others, as he himself had been,
but Chronos was nothing if not a realist. With over a
hundred ships lost—and Ilius's own admission that his fleet
had not destroyed a single enemy vessel—there were no
other conclusions to reach. None based on analysis and not
on unfocused arrogance and pride.

The Hegemony had met its match, and possibly its
doom. Ilius knew that, and he'd spent the trip back to
Calpharon trying to find a way to meet the threat, and to
overcome whatever dithering overtook the Council. He'd

been confident on one thing, at least, that Chronos would be rational.

"It is good to see you, Number Eight." Ilius knew Chronos well enough to call the Master by his name. The use of his ranking title was a desperate reminder to himself of his friend's rank and power, and whatever meager hopes he could draw from that. "I came right back here to report, though no doubt, word has already reached the Council, if not the general public."

"The Council, yes, but not beyond. The vote to impose secrecy was unanimous." Ilius could tell from Chronos's tone, his friend didn't approve of withholding such news. Whether he'd voted with the others out of political maneuvering—there was no gain in being the sole vote against—or because, as much as he disliked the classification of such important information, he still believed it was the best option, was still uncertain. Chronos was generally straightforward and direct, but Ilius knew his comrade was not above 'playing the game' when he had to.

The two men were silent for a few seconds. Then Ilius reached out and put his hand on his friend's arm. "Chronos…my report is not *all* doom and despair…" That was only partially true. His report—and his own outlook—were pretty damned close to hopeless. But there was a scarp of good news, and that was better than nothing. "We were unable to track the enemy with sufficient accuracy to establish target locks. All except for one ship, a cruiser. Captain Tragus, the commander of *Avia*, insists his ship was able to establish a usable lock…and that they scored a hit on one of the enemy vessels. I questioned the report at first, but there is substantial evidence to support his claim. Scanner reports, from *Avia* and from other vessels positioned nearby, back up Kiloron Tragus's claims. It appears *Avia did* score a hit on one of the enemy vessels."

Chronos looked back for a moment, a thoughtful expression on his face. Then, he said, "That is certainly worth looking into, but can we be sure Kiloron Tragus developed some way to target the enemy? Perhaps it was a fluke, a lucky shot, or even something that exploited an enemy malfunction or mistake. It must be repeatable to be of use."

"I thought the same thing, Chronos. Until I reviewed the data. I am convinced Kiloron Tragus found a way to track the enemy's ships...with sufficient accuracy to support dynamic targeting. I have reviewed his theory and methodology, and I believe it offers us hope of being able to adapt, to meet the enemy next time with at least the ability to inflict damage on them. We may not have the accuracy we'd like, and our weapons are certainly less powerful than theirs, but I believe Tragus's scanning protocols *will* work. We're still outmatched, perhaps hopelessly so, but at least next time, we might be able to do some damage to them."

Chronos looked back, silent for half a minute, with an expression that made it clear he would have disbelieved utterly what he'd just been told had it come from someone less reliable than Ilius. Finally, the Master said, in a tone that combined equal amounts of hope and skepticism, "Well, then the first order of business is to sit down with Kiloron Tragus, and have a hard look at what he's come up with." He paused again, looking around. "And we will keep this to ourselves for now, Ilius. The Council has descended into politics and infighting, no doubt powered mostly by fear. I will assemble my own research team to review Tragus's data. That way we can be sure nothing interferes. And, for the moment, I think fear is our ally, at least in keeping the Council in line. Let us not offer unsubstantiated hope just yet."

* * *

Ajia read the words from the screen, her voice a bit wobbly, perhaps, but executing the entire effort with a skill that belied her tender age. The little girl had long wisps of hair hanging down to her shoulders, the color a cross between blonde and light brown that defied simple categorization.

She was also perfect, at least to Chronos's biased eyes.

"Very good, Ajia, my sweet." Chronos knelt down and put his hands on the girl's shoulders. He looked back toward the only other person in the room. "She is amazing, Akella." Chronos knew it was unseemly for one of his rank to be so taken by a mere child, even his own. But Ajia had quickly gained a hold on her father, and she hadn't let go.

"She is quite the terror, too. I can assure you of that." Akella smiled, as her eyes moved back to the girl. "Her half-brother was nowhere close to the handful she is."

"That is a sign of extreme intelligence, you know." Chronos was the eighth most genetically perfect human being known to the Hegemony, and he was fully aware how absurd his dotage was. He just didn't care.

"Is it now?" Akella smiled at Chronos, half the warmth due a longtime friend...and half looking very much like something else. Hegemony culture did not promote—or even allow—permanent relationships, and certainly nothing like the paired couplings prevalent in the Confederation, and some of the other Rim nations. And certainly not among the Master class. The Hegemony existed to pull humanity away from the abyss, and monogamy, particularly among those possessing the strongest genetics, was an impediment to advancing the foundational quality of the human stock. A Master was expected to have multiple children, ideally each with a different partner. Chronos believed fully in that policy, in theory, at least, but in his moments of true clarity, he realized he had also allowed his affection for Akella to grow into something...inconvenient...in Hegemony society.

And the look he'd caught on her face told him she felt at least somewhat the same way.

Akella turned and gestured toward a woman standing in the doorway. "It is time for Ajia's nap, Cassis."

"Yes, Number One." The governess walked across the room and reached out to take the child's hand. Ajia objected immediately, and she lunged quickly to escape and to run toward Chronos. The Master smiled again—and on a deeply hidden level, the child's iron grip on him tightened. "Go, my sweet. It is time for your nap. I will come to see you again before I leave." Chronos always found it difficult to leave the girl, but Hegemony culture—and law—was adamant that children lived with the genetically-superior parent. His other offspring lived with him, as befitted Number Eight of the Hegemony, but Akella's ranking exceeded even his own lofty designation. Ajia's mother was nothing less than the most genetically perfect human being known.

She was also the Hegemony's effective ruler, though she shared power with the other members of the Council. Despite her rank, and her immense roster of responsibilities, she found considerable time to spend with both of her children, something else that set her apart from many of her peers. And fed Chronos's ever-growing feelings for her.

The two stood quietly while the governess carried the girl out of the room. Then, Akella spoke, the happiness so recently evident in her voice gone. "Your message mentioned something hopeful, some new tactic? Anything other than despair would be most welcome right now." Akella had seemed cheerful when Ajia was in the room, but now Chronos got a serious look at just how heavily the stress and tension had worn on her. The Council was largely full of narcissists who delighted in every bit of power and privilege they could gather to themselves, but Akella had always been different. She'd accepted the responsibilities and workload her genetics had destined her to endure, but she'd always seemed like she longed for a quiet and simple existence, something Chronos knew she realized she could never have.

None of us will have anything if we don't find a way to win this fight...

His mind's discipline failed for an instant, and an image of Akella—and Ajia—flashed through. Not smiling and happy as they'd been moments before, but dead and bloody, lying under the ruins of Calpharon.

No…I won't let that happen. Whatever I have to do.

But Chronos knew the words were empty, even as they came out of the depths of his mind.

"I have begun researching Kiloron Tragus's data. *Avia*'s entire crew has been transferred to the project and sequestered." A pause. "I thought this was best kept quiet, at least at first." By 'quiet,' he meant hidden from the Council and the meddling of the other senior Masters, and he had no doubt Akella understood him perfectly. He was less sure, though, that she'd support something that would only cause more problems if it was discovered.

She frowned for a few seconds, but then her face resumed its neutral expression. "It will be unpleasant if word leaks out, or even when we finally have to report the findings…but I agree with your decision. The Council is simply too divided, and this is life or death."

"That was what I thought. I am sorry I didn't tell you sooner. I wasn't sure…"

"You weren't sure I would agree with you?"

"No, well not entirely. But I didn't think you needed more bearing down on you."

"So, why tell me now? You could have hidden it a bit longer."

"Because we have made some progress. We believe we have verified Tragus's tracking method."

"Tell me about it…but remember, it has been some time since my days in the lab." Chronos pushed aside a passing thought, a concern about Hegemony society taking a mind as strong as Akella's, and filling its time mostly with political bullshit. Chronos believed in the Hegemony's sacred purpose, and he was proud of his own genetics and ranking…but sometimes he wondered if his people didn't go off course sometimes.

"Kiloron Tragus—and if this turns out to actually work, we're going to have to promote him, Kriegeri or not—guessed that the enemy ships emitted a strange band of radiation, one that does not exist in normal space."

"Where does it exist, then?"

"In the transit tubes. In the alternate space inside the pathways between systems."

Akella was silent for a moment, but the shock was evident on her face. Hegemony science had come a significant part of the way back to the greatness of the old empire, but the tubes were still a complete mystery. No one even knew if the empire had created them long ago, during its vibrant initial period of growth, or if they had simply been found, the inheritance from some older, now lost civilization. But one thing was certain. Any civilization that could utilize, let alone master, the technology of the tubes was going to be enormously difficult to face in battle.

"If that's true…"

"I know." Chronos looked down for a few seconds before his eyes returned to Akella. "But whatever the implications for the enemy's technology, it is also a way to track them. At least we have reason to hope it is."

Akella nodded, still clearly shaken by the revelation. "What practicalities has the research produced? Do we have revised scanners ready for deployment?" A pause, and a deep sigh. "I don't even know how we're going to make modifications to the entire fleet quickly enough, with the Others advancing against us." Chronos looked down again. He knew how they were going to find that time, and he suspected Akella did, too. By abandoning more worlds to the enemy. By pulling back, waiting to fight again until the fleet was ready.

No matter how many billions that left at the enemy's mercy.

"We will have to find a way. We can't defend anyone if

we can't target the enemy ships." Chronos didn't push harder. He knew Akella understood the price the Hegemony would pay for the time it needed, and he saw no reason to discuss it further.

"How far are you from something workable?"

"That depends…" They'd come to the part about which Chronos was deeply uncertain. He didn't like pushing off a momentous decision on Akella, of adding even more to her burden…but he was going to do it anyway. "We have something we *think* will work right now, but it's completely untested. Ideally, I'd prefer to send a small task force to find the enemy and test the whole thing."

"Send a group of ships to almost certain destruction in the hopes that they are able to get data back via drone or courier ships hovering near the tube?" Akella's description was grimmer than the one in Chronos's mind. It was also spot on.

"Yes," Chronos said reluctantly. "But it would be extremely helpful to have solid operational data before we undertake a refit of the entire fleet. Even at such a…cost."

"You're right, it would. If we had the time. Which we don't."

Chronos was silent again. Akella was right, and he knew it. But he also knew they would be betting the survival of the Hegemony on a wild guess that a single cruiser's commander had developed a way to target the enemy ships. Without operational testing, without more data…the whole thing was insane.

But as Chronos stood there, he knew it was their only choice, and Akella obviously did, too.

Chapter Twelve

Grand Palais Hotel
Troyus City
Megara, Olyus III
Year 322 AC

"You *can't* be serious." Andi stood along the wall of the plush hotel suite, staring at Barron with an expression that mixed anger and fear, with just a touch of horror thrown in. "I knew this 'admiral's wife' thing was going to be difficult, but we've been married for what, six weeks? And, you want to take off for Hegemony space…and you don't want me to come?"

Barron looked across the room. The exceedingly luxurious hotel was another structure that had been hastily rebuilt, probably as much to provide a place for Senators to host their assignations and secret meetings as for the stated purpose of accommodating foreign dignitaries. Whatever the rationale, it made Barron uncomfortable, but there wasn't much choice in terms of lodgings. The Barrons had long maintained a sizable manner house in Troyus City, but that stately old building was now little more than shattered stone and twisted metal, and it hadn't even occurred to him to do something about that. He'd rebuild it, he was sure of that, but he would wait until the millions rendered homeless by the war had roofs over their heads.

"Andi, I don't *want* to go. Be reasonable. You can't play the role of some naïve innocent. You understand strategy and tactics—and the dangers we face—pretty damned well, probably better than I do sometimes. You know the Hegemony didn't surrender *Colossus* and end the war for no reason. Either they're up to something we don't know about…or there is one hell of a threat out there, one that is a total mystery to us. Either way, don't you think we have to know?"

"Of course we have to know. But why you? Why does it always have to be you?"

"I'd try to explain that to you, but you already know. Why did you lead *Pegasus* into every dangerous corner of the Badlands? Why did you go after Ricard Lille? How about your trip to Hegemony-occupied Dannith? Neither one of us shies away from our duties, Andi. You know that."

"But if the Hegemony *is* planning something, you'll be putting yourself at their mercy."

"Not exactly. I'll be taking a sizable task force with me."

"Into the heart of the Hegemony? And what good will that do if they turn on you? A few extra spacers to die with you?" There was something in Andi's tone, something different. Barron had argued with her before, legendary rows that seemed inevitable when two people of nearly infinite stubbornness were thrust together. But there was something there he hadn't heard before, something…new.

"Andi…yes, it's possible the Hegemony's surrender of *Colossus* was some kind of trap, but you know that's not very likely. They could have beaten us in a straight out fight if they'd continued, with or without *Colossus*." Barron hesitated. "There's some kind of threat out there, I'm almost certain."

"The Hegemony isn't exactly our ally. Maybe their enemy is a potential friend."

"That's certainly possible, but how can we know if we

don't go out there and investigate?"

"So, somebody has to go. I'll repeat my question. Why you?"

"Who else? Who can I send out there? Who can handle whatever happens, negotiate with the Hegemony—or their enemy—and make decisions on the spot? Who has that kind of authority?"

"No one...not you, either. At least, I'd bet the Senate doesn't think you do."

"That may be true, but I'm the closest we've got, and you know that. I can get away with more than anyone else."

"You mean you can mutiny if it serves your purpose...and have a decent chance of squirming out of trouble. And if that doesn't work, I can just come visit you in the stockade."

Barron didn't respond right away. There was something about the way Andi was arguing that was different from her normal controlled obstinance. *And, she's the last one who should be lecturing anyone about following the rules...*

"I'm sorry, Tyler..." Her voice softened, and she moved toward him, sliding her arms under his. "We've just had so many separations, so much time apart."

Barron had been on the verge of getting angry, of lashing back at her with all the times she'd insisted on doing something crazy, leaving him behind to worry. But her touch, and the soft sobbing he could hear as she pressed her face into his shoulder, drained his anger away. He was awash in guilt and regret, and he'd have declared his intention to remain on Megara with her then and there...if so much of his reason for going hadn't revolved around the fear of some deadly new enemy coming to the Rim and killing millions.

Killing Andi...

He didn't say anything, he just put his arms around her and pulled her even closer. He didn't want to leave her anymore than she wanted him to go. But he didn't have any choice. He had to defend the Confederation.

He had to defend Andi.

*　*　*

"I could go coreward, you know, and you could stay here and deal with the defense of the Confederation." Clint Winters stood no more than a meter from Barron, staring at his comrade with cold eyes.

"Thank you, Clint, I appreciate that, but no. I've got Senatorial authorization to investigate, and to treat with the Hegemony authorities, and my rank as navy commander gives me more latitude to…make spot decisions."

"Yeah, I can exceed my orders as well as you can. I think you know that."

Barron was in no mood for laughter, but that didn't stop a small chuckle from forcing its way out. "Yes, I do know that, only too well. But I think it's got to be me, for a number of reasons. I don't want to go, but I feel I have to, and that means you have to keep things under control here…and be ready for whatever happens if I don't…" His voice slipped to silence. He didn't need to finish. He knew Winters understood.

"I'll watch the home fires, Ty." Winters still looked like he was on the verge of resuming his argument, but he remained silent.

"I know you will."

"And, make sure *Colossus* is as well-protected as possible until we're able to move her deeper into Confederation space. I authorized Anya Fritz to accelerate her efforts to get the thing mobile, which is a risk…but in Anya's hands, one I thought worth taking."

"I have to agree. If it was anyone else, I might think differently, but your old engineer from *Dauntless* is nothing short of a wizard in the guts of a ship."

"That she is." A pause, then: "There's one other thing,

Clint. I recorded a communiqué, and I'd like you to get it to Vian Tulus on Palatia…without going through official channels." The Alliance's Imperator had returned to his homeworld just after the wedding, but Barron wanted his blood brother fully apprised. If some unknown enemy did threaten the Rim, he had no doubt Tulus would lead his forces into the fight without hesitation. But launching massive fleets for war took time and preparation, and Barron was going to see Tulus got just those very things.

"You mean without the Senate knowing about it?"

"You know that's what I mean, old friend." Barron looked around, more an involuntary impulse than any real concern that he and Winters weren't alone. He wasn't looking to cause any trouble with the reconstituted Senate, but he didn't intend to risk them sending some watered-down communiqué to Tulus either. The Imperator would take Barron's words seriously, and that meant he'd have his forces ready if they were needed.

And Barron's gut told him they would be needed.

"Consider it done. I'll get a thrill from slipping one by those chattering fools." Winters had, if possible, even less respect for politicians than Barron did.

"Thank you. And keep a close eye out. With a chunk of the fleet coming with me, a task force defending *Colossus*, and a ton of ships assisting the rebuilding efforts on and in orbit around Megara and Ulion, your free forces will be a little sparse. If anything unexpected happens, get word to Tulus. My communiqué asks him to take anything from you as if from my mouth."

"I'll keep watch, Ty. And I'll ask Tulus for help if I need it."

Barron was silent for a moment, a grim look coming over his face. "I do have one more favor to ask, Clint. A personal one." A brief silence. "If something…happens…to me…will you look after Andi?"

Winters nodded gently. "Of course, Ty…though I'm not

sure I know anybody more capable of taking care of herself than Andi."

Barron sighed softly. He hadn't been able to get Andi off his mind. He'd been prepared for a massive fight, a no holds barred battle to keep her on Megara, to prevent her from coming with him. He wanted her safe, and he'd been determined to hold his ground this time. But after the first few moments of argument, she hadn't even suggested coming. Of all the eventualities that had rattled around in his head, that one had never occurred to him.

And it had unnerved him.

"Yes, that's true, but there's something different this time. She tried to get me to stay, but she didn't...well, it was just different. It would really put my mind at ease if I knew you were keeping an eye on her."

"Say no more. I'd do whatever I could for you, Ty, and Andi's a friend, too. Whatever you run into out there, whatever scrapes you get into, you don't have to worry about her.

Barron nodded appreciatively. It helped a lot to know Winters would be there, and he realized Andi *could* take care of herself. He didn't have to worry about her.

But he *was* worried, so much that if anything less than the safety of the Rim was at stake, he wouldn't have gone.

* * *

Andi stared out, gazing through the clear wall, her eyes moving in half a minute from moist to an outpouring of tears streaming down her face. She was worried about Barron, certainly, and sad about what promised to be a lengthy separation. They'd been torn apart so many times, and with the end of the war and their marriage, she'd finally let herself believe they'd have some time together.

But there was more to it than that, a concern greater than separation. It was something she'd wrestled with telling him, and almost had. But in the end, she'd decided to keep it secret. She didn't want him distracted, worried about her…especially not when he might very well be going into a life and death situation.

She stood in the observation area, looking out through the gray fog and light rain toward the shuttle. The doors had closed, almost indistinguishable from the gleaming white hull. She'd only caught a passing glimpse of him, and he hadn't even been aware she was there.

She and Tyler had already said their goodbyes—again—at the hotel, but she'd decided to come to the spaceport and watch until his shuttle launched. The temporary facility was nothing compared to the vast complex destroyed during the fighting, and without internal launch hangers, Barron and his staff had been forced to walk across the wet tarmac to enter the shuttle. She'd watched as he stepped up the small ladder, and climbed inside. She struggled to remain positive and optimistic, but her cold view of things compelled her to think what she'd tried so hard not to.

Is that the last time I will see him?

She remained where she was, unable to see Barron anymore, but willing to accept a view of the ship that carried him as an alternative to nothing. Her thoughts drifted back, across space and time, to the day she'd met then-Captain Tyler Barron. She remembered her first impression as though it had been yesterday. It had been far from love at first sight. In fact, he'd irritated the hell out of her. *Pegasus* and its tiny crew hadn't had any real chance to gain control over the planetkiller and get it back to Confederation space, and if *Dauntless* hadn't intervened, she and all her people would almost certainly have been killed by the Sector Nine operatives also trying to seize the giant artifact. But at the time, those plainly obvious facts hadn't prevented her from blaming *Dauntless*'s captain for keeping her from her prize…and for his ultimately destruction of the greatest treasure she had ever seen.

That hadn't been her only impression, of course. As much as he drove her crazy, she couldn't lie to herself, not well enough to be convincing, at least. She had been attracted to him from the start, and as much as she'd despised naval officers and uniforms in those days, she had to admit, he'd looked *good* in his.

She watched as a cloud of steam enveloped the shuttle, the small craft's engines igniting and vaporizing the water glistening on the hull and pooling all around. A few seconds later, she could see the blast, the flames pouring out from the thrusters as the shuttle moved, slowly at first, and then more rapidly, into the sky.

She watched the ship ascend, for as long as she could see it in the gray, hazy morning, and then, almost in an instant, it was gone.

Tyler was gone.

She stayed where she was for another moment, and then she heard a voice, her own, the words coming out almost involuntarily.

She spoke softly, and what she said was meant only for herself. "You *have* to come back, Tyler, my love...you *have* to." She sniffled, a failed attempt to clear away her tears. "I need you, I have always needed you. *We* need you." She stared out at the blackened, empty stretch of the launch pad, still partially obscured by billowing clouds of white steam, the spot that had held Barron's shuttle until a moment before.

"You have to come back because I'm pregnant..."

Chapter Thirteen

Hall of the People
Liberte City
Planet Montmirail, Ghassara IV
Union Year 225 (321 AC)

"I want her found immediately! Is that understood?" Gaston Villieneuve slammed his hand down hard on his desk, the pain resulting from the overly zealous move only adding to his fury. "Do you know what I spend, what the Union government spends? On Sector Nine, on police, on Foudre Rouge? On surveillance and computational assets? And none of you have been able to find *one* woman, a traitor, on the run, who has to be hiding in some rathole somewhere. Find her...or I'm going to start suspecting that some of you were in on the whole coup attempt." The malevolence, the dark, sinister threat in that last sentence hung over the room like death itself.

"Yes, First Citizen...I have Foudre Rouge platoons sweeping the city. All transit in and out of the capital have been suspended. She may be hiding somewhere, but she won't escape. There's no way out for her." The military officer was maintaining his calm best among those present, but that also only stoked Villieneuve's anger. Foudre Rouge always gave him the flops, something about the clone soldiers he'd never been able to precisely pinpoint.

"We have captured over a dozen co-conspirators, though many more committed suicide before we could restrain them." That was no surprise. Many of Ciara's plotters were Sector Nine themselves, and they knew all too well what awaited them if they were captured. Villieneuve scowled at the section chief, but secretly he was actually impressed that Sector Nine had managed to catch so many alive. "They are even now being interrogated, First Citizen. I am confident they will supply the intelligence we need to track down…"

"You are confident, Lusette? Confident? *I* was confident my intelligence services were watching for potential treason. I was confident your people would find Sandrine Ciara immediately. That was days ago, and all you bring me are excuses, and increasingly worthless promises. Clearly, my confidence was misplaced. So tell, me Sector Chief, General…are you merely incompetent, or are you traitors, too?"

Villieneuve often used threats and the appearance of rage to motivate his people. It was the way of the Union, and he knew no motivator was quite as powerful as pure, stark terror. But this time it was no act, no display designed to get his aides' attention. He was overcome with fury…and he was scared too, at least a little. Sandrine Ciara was a capable operative, more than a match for the idiots standing in his office trying to placate him. He'd known that all along, of course, and he'd even indulged himself that she might one day replace Ricard Lille as his senior operative. Perhaps more tellingly, she'd managed to plan and execute her coup without raising any suspicions, at least not until the last minute. The plot was in ruins, most of its participants dead, or in Sector Nine cells wishing they'd been fortunate enough to be killed. But it had been a nearer run thing than it appeared. Gaston Villieneuve was a sociopath and a paranoid, but he wasn't a fool. He knew he'd gotten lucky, and it was more than his need to take revenge on those who'd betrayed him driving his wild fury. It was the fear that if he gave Ciara another chance, she very well might succeed.

"Go," he shouted, banging his hand down again, this time with a bit more care. "Get back to your work. Find Sandrine Ciara, or the next meeting we have will be far less pleasant than this one.

The assembled personnel, all bullies and tyrants in their own right, scrambled out toward the door, amid a cacophony of verbal acknowledgements and a heavy cloud of fear. Villieneuve watched as the last of them slipped through the door, and then he leaned back in his chair, letting out a deep breath and putting his hand to his face. He'd allowed his people to see only his anger, the rage that would produce the fear he needed. The fear that would drive them. But he felt some of his own fear, as well. Villieneuve had never been timid, nor one to shy away from a plan because of the risk. But the coup had unnerved him. He'd uncovered a hundred plots against him over the years, but never one that had come so close, that had been so well planned and funded.

Funding…where did Ciara get the money she used?

Villieneuve knew all his people, certainly those at Ciara's level, had slush funds, corrupt stashes of money used for a variety of purposes. But that didn't explain the sheer volume of coin she'd clearly distributed in the thwarted coup. His first suspicion had been Kerevsky. The Confed ambassador didn't seem the type to get involved in anything like a coup attempt…but then, Ciara *had* been playing him, working him for information, using, among other things, her considerable sexual charms. Perhaps the Confederation ambassador *had* provided funding for her abortive revolution. He'd already ordered Kerevsky's ship searched, and he'd been surprised when the Confeds had quickly assented, allowing Sector Nine teams to scour their vessel's every deck and compartment.

There had been nothing suspicious.

He hadn't demanded access to the embassy yet. The Confederation was, and always would be, his enemy, but he wasn't ready to commit an act of war, not yet. Not when it appeared very much like the Hegemony had withdrawn from the Rim, leaving the Confed navy entirely uncommitted. Besides, the building was already riddled with surveillance devices, more than a few of which had long escaped detection efforts.

Still, he hadn't come up with any other ideas on where Ciara had obtained the funds to launch her coup. He'd recouped large sums from those she'd bribed—and he'd been amused at how many of the captured revolutionaries gave up their comrades far more quickly under torture than they had their stashed funds. There had been no electronic transfers, nothing but untraceable platinum coins. Union currency. But where had she gotten so much?

He shook his head. Villieneuve was an intelligent man, one accustomed to figuring things out. But he was getting more and more frustrated with each passing hour. He needed Ciara. He needed her to ensure there was no renewed attempt to depose or assassinate him…and he needed her to determine if there had been any Confederation involvement. Ciara was tough. She wouldn't fold quickly or easily.

But she *would* fold. Everyone could be broken, and Sector Nine had spent two centuries mastering the art.

* * *

"Why did you help me?" Ciara sat at the small table, a rickety wooden thing that looked more like garbage than furniture. There was a small plate in front of her, full of food she hadn't touched. Her mood had shifted over the past hour from despondent to angry, and then back again.

The room was a mess, half a dozen holes in the walls,

and chipped and peeling paint everywhere else. The Confederation Intelligence safe house was tucked away in one of the poorest industrial neighborhoods surrounding Troyus City, and it looked every bit the part. It wasn't comfortable, not by any measure, but it was one of thousands, almost indistinguishable from each other in their sameness, and far less conspicuous than anything more luxurious would have been.

"Sometimes, it's best to simply accept help, Sandrine. Does the 'why' matter that much? You're here, and not dead in the street, or in a Sector Nine cell somewhere. Isn't that enough?"

"Of course, but how long will that last? Gaston Villieneuve will never stop looking, and if you are caught helping me…"

"The First Citizen is a formidable individual, there is no question of that, but he is not omniscient. I authorized his people to search my ship in orbit, and I have taken steps to ensure there is no incriminating evidence in the embassy. My people are aware of a number of the surveillance devices Villieneuve's people have planted in the compound, though no doubt there are others we have not found. That is why you are here, in this rather disreputable neighborhood. I am confident, as much as I can be about anything, that Confederation Intelligence's acquisition of this property is untraceable."

"I am relieved, of course…and grateful. But where do we go from here? I have no real data, but I suspect many of my co-conspirators have been killed or captured."

"Most of them, unfortunately. Many were killed in the initial raids, but at least fourteen have been taken to Sector Nine interrogation facilities. As far as my information goes, it appears everyone with any knowledge of my support for your operation, save of course, the two of us and a few of my top agents, has been killed. That's a lucky break for us." Kerevsky paused for a few seconds. Ciara understood what he'd meant by 'lucky,' and she also realized why he'd felt uncomfortable about his words. Her people had died, or they soon would die, quickly in the street, or in torment in Sector Nine's cellar, but the fact that no one with truly vital knowledge had survived to be the subject to such interrogations, was, in its way, a good thing.

"So, we remain hidden for a while. What good does that do? What hope is there? The coup lies in ruins, those we so carefully lined up to participate dead or telling Villieneuve's inquisitors everything they know. There is no way to put the thing back together, and in the aftermath of Villieneuve's inevitable crackdown, no way to recruit new participants. It is not possible to mount a serious effort to gain control of the government, nor will it be for years to come."

"I believe you are correct, Sandrine, at least in a direct sense. However, if there is a way to cause a sufficient level of confusion and discord, perhaps a more modest operation, one simpler to plan and organize, could serve that purpose."

"And, how do you propose we achieve that, what did you say, confusion and discord?"

Kerevsky stared right at her, his face as impassive as stone. "By ignoring the effort to seize government installations, to secure the support of generals and other powerful functionaries, at least at first. By focusing on a single, difficult but attainable goal." He was silent for ten seconds, perhaps twenty before he finished, before he spoke the words that made Ciara's insides spasm.

"By assassinating Gaston Villieneuve."

Chapter Fourteen

CFS Dauntless
Two Transits into the Badlands
Year 322 AC

Tyler Barron sat behind the large desk, staring at the display on the wall, but seeing nothing except his own thoughts. He'd bumped Atara from her rightful place yet again. Travis finally wore the admiral's stars she'd long deserved, and she was technically the commander of the task force even then blasting through the Badlands toward Hegemony space. He was there as the Confederation's representative, an amorphous position that made him part lofty military officer, part diplomat, and part something else. He expected he'd fill in that blank before too long. There wasn't a doubt in his mind that whatever lay ahead, it would be full of the unexpected and difficult to handle.

He leaned back in the chair, the admiral's chair. *Atara's chair*, he reminded himself. *Dauntless*, the most recent ship to carry the name at least, had been built from the start as a flagship. *And that flag is Atara's, and yet here you are, in her seat.*

Dauntless had VIP quarters, of course, facilities ready for any dignitaries the ship had cause to carry from one place to another, but only the two offices, one for the ship's captain and the other for the fleet's admiral, were fully linked into the tactical suite. Atara still served as *Dauntless*'s skipper, of course, and she'd merely yielded the larger room and set up shop in the captain's office, but Barron still wondered how she dealt so well with constantly living under his shadow. She'd been his first officer, the captain of his flagship, and now she held an admiral's post that could never be truly real as long as the navy's fighting commander was there. He'd often thought about how fortunate he'd been to have a comrade with Atara's intelligence, her tactical cunning, her courage. Now, he added another attribute to that list, the somewhat freeform concept that she seemed to excel working at his side, and never showed the slightest signs of resentment at how he soaked up all the light and air in the room.

Still, for all the displays and scanner feeds, the AI relays and tactical assessment assets at his disposal, Tyler Barron's mind was hundreds of lightyears away, back on Megara.

He'd expected a fight from Andi, a bared teeth brawl over coming with him to Hegemony space. But after a weak effort to convince him not to go at all, there had been nothing. Nothing save acquiescence. That was what nagged at him the most. In ten years, he'd seen Andi argue with desperate passion, fight like a Quillian deathfang, stand firm against every bit of pressure the universe could throw at her.

But he'd never seen her give up meekly. And that scared the hell out of him.

He was edgy about the mission, too, caught between mistrust of the Hegemony and the growing confidence there was, in fact, something dangerous out there. Something that scared the hell out of the Masters and their forces that had almost conquered the Rim—that *would* have conquered the Rim if they hadn't pulled back. He'd tried to get off Megara with as few restrictions from the Senate as possible, but Flandry had proven to be as frustrating a rival as he'd been useful as an ally. Barron's mandate was broad in terms of gathering information, but he didn't have the power to agree to any alliances with the Hegemony or any other power, and he was forbidden to engage in combat unless his own forces were expressly targeted and fired upon.

Barron had always tried to maintain a calm focus on duty. His steadiness in desperate situations had been the rock on which his career had been built. But that strength was failing him. *Dauntless* and the rest of the task force were still more than twenty transits from Hegemony space, and he felt almost as though the next jump would plunge his fleet into a hopeless battle. He was edgy, uncomfortable, having trouble holding his focus.

He was scared.

The uncertainty of what lay ahead came at him from one direction, and his concerns about Andi, the questions about what he'd left behind, hit him from another. He had to regain his focus, to stay sharp when *Dauntless* reached Hegemony space. He would have to rely on his judgment, probably on the fly, without the data he needed to make proper decisions.

"Admiral Travis is at the door, sir." The AI's voice startled him, as it had half a dozen times on the trip. He hadn't reprogrammed Atara's parameters. That just seemed like too much on top of taking her workspace. But he'd had the same voice on his AIs for more than a decade, and the one Travis had chosen was considerably different in tone and volume.

"Show her in."

The door slid to the side, and Atara Travis walked into the room. "I just wanted to check on you, Ty." Greeting a superior, and especially the Confederation's naval C in C and chief envoy to the Hegemony by his first name, not to mention a shortening of that name, was extremely inappropriate, at least by normal standards of the service. But Atara Travis was as close to Barron as any sister could have been, closer even, since they'd shared crises and dangers together so many times.

"I think you just miss your office." Barron glanced up, grateful for the distraction. "Like I said before, *you* should work out of here. The captain's setup is more than I need."

"Yeah, you don't think I know part of you wishes you were still *Dauntless*'s captain? The old *Dauntless*, of course. Though as much as I loved and miss her, she was a bucket of bolts compared to her replacement."

Barron ignored the comment about his old ship. It was a hundred percent accurate, but it just wasn't in him to remember anything but a romanticized version of his first battleship command. "I guess we all remember certain times, but our lives pay no mind to them. Duty is a fierce mistress, and when she calls, how can we say no?"

"We can't." A pause. "But don't worry about the office, at least. The captain's suite is more than enough for me, and if you end up having to meet any Hegemony big shots in here, I think the plusher room will be useful. They all think they're genetically superior already. Let's not do them the favor of inflating those outsized egos anymore."

Barron nodded. "You should be the diplomat."

"No way. I didn't work my way out of the industrial pits to spend my time trading lies with a bunch of pompous fools. Duty led you to that terrible pass, my old friend, not me...and it made a discriminating choice. You hate it, but you can do it. I'd hate it too, but I think I'd make a wreck of the whole thing."

"You like to underestimate yourself, but don't waste your time trying it with me. I've seen you in action, and in too many other tough spots. And, don't forget, if anything happens to me, you're next in line here. You'll be the Confederation's emissary to the Hegemony."

"That's the best reason I've ever heard to keep you alive. Conveniently, that very task is the core of my own duty at present." She smiled, but it only held for a few seconds. Then she sat quietly for a while before she continued, "Seriously, Ty, do you really think we can work with the

Hegemony, be their allies? The whole idea makes my stomach clench like a fist…and I suspect it would be even harder on the spacers. How much blood did the Hegemony spill? How many of us held dying friends in our arms or spent months in infirmary beds?"

"We had this conversation before, Atara…when Andrei Denisov showed up with his fleet. And, our hatred for the Union is a lot older than that for the Hegemony. How many people died fighting their forces? My grandfather was killed in the third war, his shuttle tracked down and blasted to atoms. But we fought alongside Denisov's spacers, and I suspect they were the margin of survival more than once."

"This is different."

"I know you want to feel that way, I do too. But how is it *really* different?"

"The Union is a despotism, and their leaders are evil, certainly. But the Hegemony Masters consider us all…inferiors. How do we treat with them as allies, as equals, knowing every minute they think we should all be their slaves?"

"I have as much angst toward the Hegemony as anyone, you know that. But let's not let ourselves wallow in self-indulgence. I find their society as repugnant as you do, but don't tell me you don't see the logic in it. They're far coreward from the Rim. The worlds they encountered early in their recovery were far more damaged by the Cataclysm than those farther out. They dealt with severely degraded populations, with people whose scarred DNA threatened their very survival. The Kriegeri and Arbeiter are definitely second-class citizens compared to the Masters, but I don't think it's really accurate to call them 'slaves.'"

Atara looked over at Barron. "Maybe you *are* ready to deal with them."

"Stop that…you know I have the same feelings you do. But that doesn't mean we should indulge in exaggeration. Look at Denisov's people…do you still consider them enemies? How about the Union itself? This kind of thing is complicated, and if there is an enemy out there worse than the Hegemony—possibly *much* worse—what will you do? Let the Hegemony be destroyed out of spite...before we are right after them? Or join forces and try to stop whatever threatens us all?"

A defiant look flashed across Atara's face, but it quickly faded. "I know you're right, Ty, but I'm still worried. I'm worried about how I'll handle it, and I'm worried about the spacers, too."

Barron returned his friend's gaze, silent for a few seconds. Then he said, "If you want to worry, worry about whether there really is something out there, something we can't defeat, even alongside the Hegemony. We're heading to meet with our old enemies, to see what they are facing. But what if we're plunging toward a hopeless fight, one all the forces of the Hegemony and the Rim together can't match. What if we're heading to our doom?"

* * *

"Alright, let's do one more sweep, and then we'll head back to base." Jake Stockton had always felt at home in the cockpit of a fighter. It was natural to him in many ways, as though that's where he'd been born to be. But now he was edgy, distracted, and it came through in his flying. He'd have given himself a good dressing down if he'd been one of his pilots, and maybe even a few weeks' grounding to give some time to think about paying attention. That was one challenge that plagued the top of the pyramid. There was no one to keep you on track, to slap you down when you got out of line.

And Stockton didn't doubt he needed that from time to time, just like any other pilot.

There were no enemies on the screen, no contacts at all. That wasn't a surprise, though Stockton's combat sensibilities treated it as one. There hadn't been anything since the task force left Confederation space, not even a Badlands rogue trader or two flitting about.

That was the result of the war, he knew. With Dannith in Hegemony hands for so long, and the Badlands enemy-occupied territory, the trade in old tech prospecting had pretty much dried up. It would return, he suspected, if any extended period of peace was maintained, but just then, that dead section of imperial space was even more haunted than it had been before.

He brought his ship around, toward a nearby planet. He was close enough to see it with his eyes, and he sat for a few seconds and just stared. It was beautiful, vibrant blue with three hazy white rings around it. Stockton had been a warrior his entire adult life, and he'd come to see the universe as a battlefield, scarred by endless fighting and death. It was easy to forget the magnificence on display, the stunning beauty present out in the depths of space when one looked out past a screen, and directly into the hypnotic depths.

That blue glow is pretty, but it's just a bunch of toxic gasses, the atmosphere of a planet so cold it would be a race to see if it poisoned or froze you to death the fastest.

Stockton had come to appreciate some things more than he had when he'd been younger, but he was still a cynic at heart. There was only one thing he knew with absolute certainty, something he believed as iron-hard fact. One day he would die in his fighter. He didn't know when his end would come, but he'd always known how it would.

"Alright, I think that's enough." He was still looking at his scanner as he spoke into the comm. "The system looks clear." Unsurprisingly, Stockton was a huge believer in supplementing capital ship scans with scouting flights, but he was enough of a veteran to realize that if the Hegemony—or anyone else—wanted to hide badly enough, his people could fly right past without picking them up.

Solar systems had too many gas clouds and asteroids and planets to hide behind, too much radiation and particulate matter to allow complete confidence in any scanning or scouting effort.

He listened as the acknowledgements came in, six in total. Half a dozen squadrons was a far larger force than he'd needed for the mission, but he was doing all he could to keep his people sharp, to get them out into their fighters before their combat reflexes atrophied entirely. Stockton had craved peace his entire life, part of him had, at least. The other side saw it mostly as a mirage, a deception that eroded his pilots' readiness, and left them unprepared for the inevitable resumption of hostilities. Stockton could imagine a universe without war—as a fantasy—but he didn't believe it was possible.

There was something else bothering him, eating away, something he hadn't even shared with Stara. Most of the fleet's spacers were edgy, concerned to some extent that they were heading into a Hegemony trap, or perhaps worse, that their recent enemies *did* have a new adversary, one that threatened the Rim as well. But Stockton had gone beyond mere jitters. He was utterly certain the task force was heading into battle. He wasn't sure who the enemy would be. He didn't discount Hegemony treachery…but he didn't expect it either. The enemy's actions, especially their surrender of *Colossus*, had mostly convinced him of the legitimacy of the unknown threat. He was grim enough at the prospect of throwing his squadrons back into the meatgrinder against the Hegemony.

The thought of sending them against an enemy that outmatched—that *terrified*—the Hegemony, made his stomach heave.

Chapter Fifteen

Planet Calpharon
Sigma Nordlin IV
Year of Renewal 267 (322 AC)

"No, not you. I'm going to send someone…"

"More expendable?" Ilius interrupted Chronos. The two were close friends, but Ilius usually showed the higher-ranked Master and superior officer the formality his position demanded, certainly when discussing military matters. But this time he disagreed with his friend, and he was determined to fight it out until Chronos saw it his way.

"Yes," Chronos snapped back, after a short pause. "If you must put it that way, I can't lose you now, not with the fight that is coming."

"But we need to test the new scanners, and we need reliable data."

"Surely, you are not suggesting you're the only capable officer in the navy?"

"No, of course not. But this isn't a normal mission. It's…"

"Suicide?" Chronos took his turn interrupting.

"Dangerous."

Chronos stared at Ilius. "What battle isn't dangerous? This is more than that, and you know it. We can't afford to risk any more ships than necessary, just enough to close and get off a number of volleys...to see if Tragus's theory is valid. How many of those ships do you think will escape?"

Ilius didn't answer.

"Exactly. Helas volunteered as well, and I refused her, too. We're going to have a fight, my friend, a big one, and at long odds, even if these scanners work. That will be somewhere near here...it may even *be here*, at Calpharon. It will be a battle we cannot lose, and when it comes, I will need you there. I will need Helas, too."

"So, you're going to send someone you *don't* need to determine if the new scanners work?"

"Stop it. I understand why you want to go, why you feel you have to go. Why Helas felt she had to go. But there is no place now for guilt, for wild gestures. This isn't the war on the Rim. We're fighting for our lives here, for the existence of the Hegemony. For the very survival of humanity. You're a Hegemony Master, one of the most capable people ever born. Act like it."

Ilius was surprised at just how hard-hitting Chronos's words had been. They were nothing but pure truth, but the part of him that rebelled against his hard intellect, against cold analysis, still craved to go, to see the deed done himself. To face the enemy that had killed so many of his people.

"I'll take your lack of a response as acquiescence." A pause. "I considered sending Tragus—he volunteered as well—but I don't think it's wise to risk an officer who may very well be the first true hero of the war. So, I decided to send Krellos."

"Krellos?" There was surprise in Ilius's voice, bordering on shock. "But he's been retired since before the Rim war began. He's nearly..."

"Yes, he's old...and he's been inactive for a considerable time. But his career record is spotless, and he volunteered, most forcefully, to return to service."

"I don't doubt his abilities, Chronos, but..." The words tailed off. Ilius wanted to go, felt he *had* to go...but that was all emotional nonsense, and his intellect was slowly reasserting itself. He didn't have the right to get himself killed before the Hegemony mounted a real effort to stop the enemy. If he'd developed a deathwish of some kind, he had no doubt the Others would accommodate him wherever he faced them. His duty was clear. He knew he couldn't lead the expedition. But that didn't quiet the voices inside.

"Krellos is well aware of the danger, of the...difficulties the force will face to escape. He is near the end of his lifespan, and he knows he has neither the strength nor the endurance to command forces is a protracted conflict. He is prepared to accept the sacrifice if that is his fate, and sending him allows us both to entrust the vital mission to a reliable commander and not to risk an officer we need in the war." There was a cold, brutal logic to Chronos's words, and Ilius found himself nodding. Logic was almost sacred in the Hegemony, the victory of intellect over pointless emotion.

Such things had always made sense to him, but sending an old man, one who had served the Hegemony well, to his death, left him feeling...something he had never felt before. Lost? Uncertain? He wasn't sure. But he slammed back, driving it all someplace deep in his mind. Nothing mattered but defeating the Others.

Nothing.

He'd just pushed aside his doubts, for the moment, when a voice blared through the comm unit.

Master Chronos, Master Ilius...the scanners at the system's outer marker have detected incoming ships, approximately sixty in number.

Ilius felt a tightness inside, and he struggled to suck in his next breath. For a brief, terrifying few seconds, he believed the Others had come, that somehow they had already reached Calpharon. That was impossible, he knew, but that knowledge did nothing to stop the fear.

Until the voice on the comm continued.

"They are broadcasting identification beacons and a communiqué. They are Confederation vessels, Commander, and they are requesting permission to approach Calpharon."

* * *

Tyler Barron sat on *Dauntless*'s bridge, silent at his station next to Travis's. He'd commanded the White Fleet, been on the bridge when that force had plunged forward into previously uncharted space and discovered the unexpected existence of humans far from the Rim.

It had discovered the Hegemony. With tragic consequences.

But now, he'd come farther than any Confederation fleet ever had. Farther than anyone on the Rim had ventured in more than three centuries. To the very heart of the Hegemony.

He looked up at the brilliant blue and white sphere, the world that had birthed the Hegemony and its Masters more than two hundred years before. Calpharon was coreward enough that Barron knew almost certainly it had been reduced to a scarred ruin during the Cataclysm. The idyllic globe he saw now was no doubt the result of massive rehabilitation efforts...another reminder that the Hegemony, so recently the enemy, was well beyond the Confederation in most areas of technology.

"Admiral, we're receiving a reply. She identifies herself as Akella, First of the Hegemony, President of the Ruling Council."

"On speaker, Commander." Barron knew he should take the comm privately. He had no idea what the Hegemony's ruler would say, and caution seemed well advised. But his people had come with him, farther than even the White

Fleet had gone. If they'd made that journey for no reason—
or if it had all been a trap—they deserved to know
immediately.

"I understand I am speaking to Admiral Barron...the
famous Admiral Barron. Welcome. I am Akella. I regret that
circumstances have, until recently, made us enemies, but I
can assure you I have always respected your abilities and
accomplishments, even when we were at war."

Barron always hated such diplomatic prattle, but Akella's
tone was different from most he'd heard before. Against his
better judgment, he found himself believing she was sincere.
Barron almost replied, but he stopped himself. *Dauntless* was
lighthours from Calpharon, and the words he was hearing
had been spoken nearly one hundred eighty minutes before.
He'd expected to hear from some duty officer, presumably
authorizing *Dauntless*, at least, if not the whole task force, to
approach. He was surprised the first response had come
from no one less than the Hegemony's head of state.

Was it a show of respect? Or part of the trap?

"Your ships may approach, Admiral, at your
convenience. All system defense forces have been notified
of this authorization. I must request that your fleet remain
five million kilometers from Calpharon, but *Dauntless* may
enter planetary orbit."

Barron felt a sharp reaction, a resentment at Akella's
request—demand?—that the rest of his task force remain
some distance from the planet. But it quickly passed.
Calpharon *was* the Hegemony capital, and the two powers
had been at war for some time. Barron's anger flared briefly,
the voices in his own head declaring, with some venom, that
the Hegemony had started the war. But that faded as well.
He didn't believe the Hegemony had concocted the entire
scheme—and surrendered *Colossus*—just to lure him to
Calpharon to kill or capture him. If it *had* been a trap, there
would have been massive Hegemony forces waiting on alert,
and his whole fleet, not just *Dauntless*, would have been

destroyed. Though, a quick glance toward Atara's station told him she was less convinced.

"Hold comm playback." Barron's eyes moved from the communication officer to Atara. "Admiral Travis, the fleet is to advance to a position five million kilometers from Calpharon. Minimum travel time."

"Yes, Admiral." There was a pause, and Barron knew some part of Atara was waiting for him to order the fleet to battlestations, or at least red alert. Just in case. But he was going to disappoint her. He hadn't come so far just to start another war with the Hegemony.

He almost followed up that *Dauntless* would continue alone to Calpharon orbit, but he held his tongue. It would take nearly ten hours for his task force to reach the five million kilometer mark, and he was content to wait until the last minute to invite every officer on the bridge to stare at him with concerned glances.

* * *

"You are most welcome, Admiral Barron. Please accept my thanks on behalf of the entire Hegemony." Barron stood silently as Akella spoke, his thoughts wandering despite his best efforts to focus.

So, this is the most 'genetically perfect' human being in the galaxy? Akella was attractive, though not astonishingly so. Her features *were* all quite close to generally accepted ideals, and she had a patrician elegance to her mannerisms. Whatever his true thoughts about the Hegemony's genetic rating system—and he wasn't quite sure what they were—Barron had no doubt at all about Akella's intellect. She was smart, there was no question about that. He wondered if she was truly more intelligent than some of his own comrades.

"Thank you…Number One?" Barron wasn't sure of the appropriate protocol, and once again his revulsion for the pomp and pointless nonsense that so infected diplomacy reared its head. To his surprise, his counterpart responded in kind.

"Yes, Admiral, that *is* the correct form of address, but let us dispense with it, shall we? We each know something of the other's culture, but far from everything. Let us scandalize those of ambassadorial inclinations who surround both of us. Please call me Akella."

Barron was stunned. He'd hated the Hegemony for years, despised the Masters as something very much like evil overlords. But he found himself liking this Akella, despite the fact that she was the highest-ranking of all the Masters. She was certainly the least pompous head of state he'd ever met, though he wasn't sure that was quite a fair comparison where Vian Tulus was concerned. The Imperator *was* Palatian, after all, and certain allowances had to be made, at least for wild boasting about past battles.

"Thank you, Akella...and I am Tyler." He felt somehow...dirty...for being familiar with her, for seeing her as a human being, for liking her. There were just too many ghosts for him to allow for such thoughts, at least not without a healthy shot of guilt. *Don't forget...whatever she seems like, this woman had to approve the invasion. The Hegemony's forces could not have attacked without her consent...*

"Thank you, Tyler." A pause, brief but noticeable. Then, she waved her arms toward the various assembled Hegemony officials, and almost immediately after, to the line of Kriegeri guards standing three meters behind her. "Go, please, all of you. I would speak with Admiral Barron alone." There was some hesitation, among the most pompous looking of the dignitaries, and even more the Kriegeri. But Akella gestured again, with a level of aggression that surprised Barron, given the pleasant nature she'd displayed to that point. The others began to disperse, filing out through the three doors on the far wall. Finally, the Kriegeri followed, clearly reluctant to leave their leader unprotected in the presence of what they no doubt still perceived as an enemy, but even more unwilling to directly disobey her.

Barron turned toward his two aides. He'd almost gotten into a rare shouting match with Atara over his refusal to bring a Marine escort with him. She'd had a full platoon, armed and armored and ready to go, but he'd sent them away. He understood her impulse, and her concern for his safety, but he'd seen the absurdity of it, too. He'd been about to shuttle down to the enemy's capital city. No forty Marines ever made could have done a thing to save him if the Hegemony authorities wanted him dead. They could only have increased tensions.

"Wait for me outside," he said softly to the two aides. They looked as reluctant as Akella's Kriegeri had…and as unwilling to refuse their leader's order. They followed the Hegemony personnel out.

When the doors closed, Akella gestured toward two chairs facing each other at angles. "Please, Tyler, have a seat."

Barron walked toward the chairs, and he sat in one, watching as Akella took the other. There was a silence, not all that protracted, though it felt long to Barron. Then Akella spoke. "Tyler, I believe you are a direct man, and I like to think I am not one to pointlessly waste time, nor to shy from difficult subjects. It is only natural that you mistrust me…all of my people, that you likely despise we of the Hegemony and all we stand for. Such is an inevitable side effect of war. I could spend hours trying to explain my people, our creed and our sacred purpose, but that would be to no avail. Let us simply acknowledge that for all the loss and sacrifice of the recent conflict, it should be evident that we sought, where possible, to minimize civilian losses. We were an invader to you, Tyler, but we did not come to destroy your people, nor, as I doubt you yet fully believe, to enslave them. Our system is different from yours, born perhaps of our proximity to a section of the galaxy far more severely damaged in the Great Death, what your people call the Cataclysm. Our duty, as we see it, at least, is to unite all humanity, and to protect them…from the mistakes that have been made in the past, from the rule of deeply flawed and dishonest leaders. That is what we sought to bring to the Rim, and though I know you will not agree or accept my explanation, I felt you should at least hear it from me."

Barron took a deep breath, as much to keep himself from lashing out with any rash or unhelpful remarks as anything. "Akella, you are correct that our peoples see many things, the recent war included, from sharply divergent points of view. To us, nothing is as precious as our independence." Barron knew that was only partially true. It was certainly how *he* felt, but he didn't want to guess at what percentage of the Confederation's population would readily trade their freedom for shaky promises of safety and a modicum of prosperity. "I will, however, accede to your points about the limited nature of the war that was conducted. Our military forces suffered grievously, but save for Megara and the other places that saw protracted ground fighting, damage to planetary surfaces was minimal, and losses among the populations restrained." He found it difficult to speak the words, though he knew they were true. The losses he'd suffered—friends and comrades killed, many while carrying out his orders—were too fresh, still far too painful to be washed away by some amorphous gratitude that billions of civilians hadn't been nuked into oblivion as well.

Barron thought he caught an uncomfortable look on Akella's face, but it vanished before he could get a good read. Had it been regret, guilt? He didn't know. The Hegemony's leader was proving to possess impressive self-discipline. In spite of his anger and resentment, Barron found himself liking her more and more.

"I could try to convince you of the utility of our cause, the reasons why we have endeavored to…absorb…other human populations into the Hegemony. I could allow you to speak with Arbeiter and Kriegeri who would attest to the improvements in their cultures and living standards since they were brought into the Hegemony. But I do not believe such efforts would materially change your mind, certainly not in a reasonable period of time. My read is you are a stubborn man, Tyler, close to immovable when you truly believe something. I do not ask you to agree with my beliefs, with those of my people. I simply ask you to see that the goal, safeguarding humanity's remnants, is not an evil one at its core, and to allow that others, myself included, are as resolute as you in such things."

"Would you be able to bring in Defekts as well to speak on the Hegemony's behalf along with the offered Arbeiter and Kriegeri? Or are they all in mines somewhere, digging for radioactive ore until they drop to the ground and die?" Barron cursed himself the instant the words escaped his lips. Such provocations were not likely to be productive in any way, but he'd never been able to forget what he'd seen years before when the White Fleet had first ventured into Hegemony space, the way the Defekts were treated, how they were used as expendable labor.

"We can trade barbs, Tyler, though I suspect that will come to no productive purpose. I can only state that you on the Rim have not carried the burden of dealing with such populations, millions of people with DNA so badly scarred, they are barely human."

Barron could hear discomfort in Akella's voice as she offered up a defense of her people. *She doesn't approve of it either...at least she has doubts...*

After a long pause, Akella continued, "I do not deny that many of my people have behaved badly toward the Defekts, and certainly the most...inferior among their numbers. Such attitudes are born of the degraded nature of the Defekts, in part, yet I would also say to you that such conduct is not commendable. It is not the Defekts' fault their ancestors

were damaged by radiation and biological warfare, yet is
their place in Hegemony society so different than that of the
many impoverished workers on your Iron Belt worlds?"
There was no accusatory tone in her words, simply calm
rationality. Perhaps we can agree that both our cultures have
their faults, as well as their strengths. Surely, you can
acknowledge that our commitment to preventing a repeat of
the Great Death, and our efforts to reintroduce technology
and modern methods of medicine food production to
worlds reduced to virtual savagery, have had some positive
effects."

Barron winced at the jab at the Iron Belt's lower classes.
Those worlds were the pride of the Confederation's
economy...and the shame of its pretensions to be an
enlightened power that valued freedom. Still, he barely
managed to hold back the angry response that formed
almost reflexively. "All cultures have their positives and
negatives, Akella...but the fact remains that your people *were*
the invaders, the aggressors. The White Fleet that first
encountered the Hegemony was an instrument of
exploration, not conquest. Had you not attacked us, we
would have withdrawn voluntarily and respected your
borders."

"I have no doubt, Tyler, but allow me to ask you one
question. Your people know far less than mine about what
you call the Cataclysm. You see yourselves as rising up from
its effects, rebuilding civilization and prosperity. But what if
all your achievement on the Rim is no more than a
momentary blip. What if the downfall is still underway, if all
your people built will be swept away in another wave of
decline? Would our attempts to bring your people into the
Hegemony be justified if we were able to prevent that?
Would the deaths of some millions of spacers and soldiers
be too great a price to pay to save the billions on the Rim
from a dark age thousands of years long?"

Barron was becoming more impressed with each passing

moment. He wasn't sure he believed Akella's premises, but he didn't have the slightest doubt about her intelligence…and he was beginning to believe in her honesty as well. He still despised the Hegemony, but if he *had* to work with them, he thought he could tolerate Akella. At least from what he'd seen so far.

"You draw conclusions that far outstrip the evidence. You may state that the Cataclysm is still, in effect, underway, that all we view as a rebound is merely a temporary respite in the slide. Perhaps that is true…but it is a lot to accept without proof."

"I will show you proof, Tyler Barron, or at least substantial evidence. I will share with you all my people know of the events that destroyed the empire, and you can decide for yourself. And I will also allow you to view all my people know of the Others, including footage of our recent engagement with them. You may still harbor reservations, even profound disagreements with Hegemony ways and culture, as well as the current status of decay in human civilization, but I do not believe you will retain the slightest doubt that the Others are a grave threat, both to the Hegemony, and to every man and woman on the Rim."

Barron nodded. Part of him wanted to argue, and he was far from accepting Akella's position that the Hegemony's aggression had merely been part of an effort to arrest the decline of civilization. It was too convenient, too cleansing of the guilt the Hegemony bore for so many deaths and so much destruction. But he believed her warning about those she called the 'Others.' He'd believed it before she'd said a word, before the meeting had even begun. Perhaps not fully in his mind, but totally and without doubt in his gut.

"Perhaps, then, that is the place to begin. As intriguing as I suspect I will find your imperial histories and archeological reports, it certainly seems this enemy—the Others, as you call them—is the matter of paramount importance. I would very much like to see the documentation of your recent encounter."

Chapter Sixteen

Colossus
Lyra System
Year 322 AC

"Slowly, Commander, slowly...push that thing too hard and..." Fritz didn't finish the sentence. She didn't have to. Eric Kalmut knew only too well what would happen if the antimatter containment failed even the slightest bit. He found the whole business unnerving, though he was grateful, at least, to have his boots on solid ground, or, more accurately, solid deck. He'd spent about as much time as he could manage crawling over narrow catwalks and shimmying along conduits suspended twenty meters up.

"We're moving up a tenth of a percent a second, Commodore, and we've got it capped at a five percent flow rate. I don't know how much slower we can go." Kalmut had a good sense for the immense power flowing through the conduit, even at the restricted rate. Antimatter was an incredible fuel, by far the most powerful known to human science. But it was beyond volatile, and any contact whatsoever with ordinary matter would have the most unfortunate consequences.

Kalmut watched as Fritz looked down at the small scanning device in her hands. She was searching for leaks, he knew, but he also wondered if there was any real purpose in that. It wasn't like normal radiation, where catching the contamination early would allow the area to be evacuated or the leak to be plugged. By the time Fritz could detect loose antimatter particles, it would likely be far to late to salvage the situation. Confederation ships didn't use antimatter, first and foremost because Rim technology had not developed ways to economically produce the precious substance. But there was another reason, one that hung like a cloud over efforts to restore *Colossus* to fully operational status. Confederation safeguards and control systems lacked the advanced shielding and backups required to effectively deploy antimatter. A microsecond's leak in any system was almost certain to result in catastrophe, and Kalmut had watched Fritz check out every safety and backup system what seemed like a hundred times. By normal standards, work on *Colossus* appeared to move at a snail's pace, but measured against the reality that one serious malfunction could destroy the entire vessel and everyone aboard, operations had proceeded swiftly enough.

"We're up to fifty percent flow rate, Commodore. All systems appear fully operational. All shielding one hundred percent functional."

"I'm not picking up any leaks, either. You may be right, Commander. We may have things working, at least here." A pause, then Fritz continued. "But antimatter is cantankerous. I know we're getting more pressure to finish here, but I'm not going to rush any work, at least not on the power systems. I want everything checked and rechecked...and then checked again. I'll push the engineers—our own and the contractors—working on all the other systems, but the engines and reactors will remain the sole domain of the staff I handpicked. I don't want anyone in here except people who served with us in the wars. Antimatter is dangerous to anyone, but it's new for us to be using it on this operational scale, and not only that, but once we've exhausted what's in the storage units, *Colossus* will he helpless. It might make a nice museum or something, but it won't be a warship anymore. The Confederation couldn't produce enough antimatter in a millennium to refuel this thing. We might rig some fusion reactors to move it—slowly—but that's about all we could manage for the foreseeable future. And the work would probably take years."

Kalmut nodded, silent for a moment. He'd been thinking about everything Fritz had just said, and the realization that no matter how well they adapted *Colossus* to their operations, the best they could hope for was to move the great ship to some permanent location. Deployment to any kind of active operations was out of the question, at least until a way could be found to refuel the vessel. That reality had hung like a pall over the entire effort.

"It's a shame, Commodore. We've got something this powerful, and we really can't use it. Could you imagine the thing running out of fuel in a war zone?" Kalmut's tone and his easy reference to battlefronts exhibited the somber assessment Fritz and most of the Confederation's veterans shared. After two brutal wars—and for those left from the old *Dauntless*'s crew, the desperate fight against *Invictus* that had preceded them both—peace seemed a vague and implausible concept. The Hegemony hadn't been defeated, they'd just offered a truce and pulled back. Anyone looking for a bet that peace had finally come wouldn't find many takers in the fleet.

"It is, Commander. No question. I've even wondered if we wouldn't be better off tearing the thing apart and studying its tech. I'd wager we could push our science forward a century or more, and probably fairly quickly. Otherwise, *Colossus* is going to be an immobile hulk, studied, of course, but nowhere as effectively as it we really tore into it. I don't know when we'll be able to produce kilograms of antimatter, much less the vast quantities this ship uses. That could be more than a century from now, maybe even a millennium. It's not just the tech, that's the easy part. It's the energy requirement. Until we can built vast energy collectors around stars or harness an entire planet's geothermal activity, we're going to be stuck producing grams of antimatter...nothing that's going to send *Colossus* back into battle.

The room was silent for a moment, and then Fritz looked back down at the scanner. Everything still showed clear. But before she could turn back and tell Kalmut, her comm buzzed.

She tapped the small device on her collar. "Fritz here."

"Commodore..." The officer on the line was clearly hesitant to continue. "...Mr. Dennis is...demanding a meeting with you immediately." It was painfully clear the young lieutenant on the line would rather have cut off a finger or two than relay that particular message to an officer as legendary in the navy as Anya Fritz...not to mention one famous for unloading on those who upset her with a fury that was the talk of the fleet.

Fritz felt the wave of anger building. She almost snapped back, but some part of her, probably grown of age and wisdom, reminded her the officer on the comm hadn't done anything. She was just an unfortunate pawn, stuck in the middle of a storm.

She would save her rage for Dennis. He wanted a meeting? She would give him a meeting, though she suspected he would get a lot more than he'd bargained for.

"Conference room three, Lieutenant. Fifteen minutes. Please advise Mr. Dennis that means fifteen. If he is so much as thirty seconds late, I have him thrown out of one of the airlocks." She shut the line before the officer could respond.

Before she'd *had* to respond. It had been an act of mercy to a junior member of her staff.

Antoine Dennis could expect nothing of the kind. She'd

spent as much time as she cared to arguing with the fool. She was going to explain the facts of life to the self-appointed representative for the civilian contractors working on *Colossus*, and she was going to do it in a way that allowed no chance he could misunderstand.

She gestured to Kalmut and told him to continue, and then she stomped out of the room, her boots clanging hard on the smooth metal deck.

She decided not to stop by her cabin to get her sidearm.

Barely.

* * *

Andi stepped out of the shuttle, reaching out and grabbing the small handhold. She was used to being agile, sure on her feet, but she'd been a bit off the last few weeks. The nausea had been the worst, and she'd spent no small amount of time revisiting anything she'd dared to eat, but she also found the dizziness off putting. It wasn't severe by any measure, but for someone accustomed to her old level of activity, it was annoying.

She looked across the deck, the scowl on her face vanishing almost immediately as she saw Anya Fritz standing along the wall about ten meters away. The engineer started moving toward her almost immediately, and Andi matched her friend's pace. Andi had known Fritz as long as she had Tyler, and while they hadn't spent an enormous amount of time together, they shared the camaraderie of those who had fought and struggled side by side. They were members of the same group, and they were connected through the battles they had fought, and the people they loved and respected. And, with Tyler gone, Andi was excited to see anyone who felt like a connection to him.

"Andi, it's so good to see you." The normally cool and grim engineer threw open her arms and embraced the new arrival. Andi appreciated the gesture, though the pressure of

Fritz's tight embrace made her stomach flop a little. She was grateful her face was over Fritz's shoulder, facing away. She'd told almost no one about her pregnancy, and she intended to keep it that way until she had no choice. That would be soon enough, she knew, but it wouldn't be right there, in one of *Colossus*'s landing bays.

"It's good to see you, too, Anya. I'm sure they've kept you busy out here. My God, this thing is incredible."

"Yes, it's been one thing after another. I'm afraid we've just begun to scratch the surface." A pause. "By the way, I'm sorry I couldn't make it back for the wedding. I would have loved to be there, but there is a lot of pressure to get *Colossus* moved somewhere more secure. The admiral told me to proceed at my own pace, but I know he was worried about making at least some progress quickly."

"No worries at all. I can't imagine how crazed your schedule has been. And, you're right, Tyler never said so specifically, but I know he was worried about the whole situation with the Hegemony, and even the Union. Getting *Colossus* someplace we don't need a whole fleet to guard it will make a lot of people's minds rest easier, I suspect." Barron's concern for the great ship was one of the reasons she had come. She didn't imagine she could offer anything substantive to aid Fritz's operation—though she was, or had been, somewhat of a practical expert on old tech—but checking on things, and perhaps most importantly, confirming that Anya Fritz had been free to operate without interference or harassment, seemed like the best she could do for Tyler just then.

It was also just about the last chance she'd have to get away from Megara, at least until the baby was born. Andi didn't have the slightest doubt about Tyler or being married to him, but she'd been a wanderer all her life, and the thought of settling down, of living in one place for years and years, scared he hell out of her. And another few months, and transit point travel would be out of the question, at least until after she gave birth.

"I'd love to catch up, Anya, but business first. I'm mostly here for Tyler, to make sure that you've been allowed to run the operation as you see fit. You know how important it is to safeguard this ship, and to glean from it what we can. I'm not the fleet admiral, but I think I can pull some of the same strings while he's gone. And, I've got a few connections of my own." Not the least of those was Gary Holsten. The head of Confederation Intelligence was one of Tyler Barron's closest friends and allies, but Andi had actually worked as one of Holsten's agents. Perhaps more importantly, she'd been captured and tortured by Sector Nine, and she still had some play in milking the guilt Holsten felt for sending her to Dannith in the first place.

"So far, we've been left alone." A pause. "The civilian contractors have become somewhat of a pain. They've got a representative now who thinks he can negotiate working conditions with me...but all he's going to manage to do is negotiate his way to an all expenses paid tour of *Colossus*'s exterior, straight from the airlock without a suit."

Andi smiled. "I might be able to help you with that particular problem. I had some similar...challenges...on Craydon, though more from the oligarchs than the workers. I suspect your particular gang of troublemakers will be easier to...reason with."

Easier to scare...

Chapter Seventeen

6,000,000,000 Kilometers from Planet Eliason
Upsilon Vega System
Year of Renewal 267 (322 AC)

Ilius sat quietly, part of him regretting the fact that he'd pushed Chronos until his friend and superior had consented to his posting with what was being called, optimistically, the Verification Force. He was as hopeful as Chronos, and everyone else involved, that the scanner mods would actually work, that they would allow the outgunned Hegemony ships to at least fight back in a material way against their deadly enemies. But he found his confidence wavering.

It wasn't fear feeding Ilius's uncertainty. He'd come beyond that, accepted his fate. For all his efforts to focus on the war and ways to win it, at his core he'd given in to hopelessness. He'd been at the one large battle the Hegemony had fought against the invader, he'd watched vast monitors, the greatest and most powerful ships known, save only for *Colossus*, stand utterly helpless, unable to even strike at their attackers, even as the enormous hulls were split open by the Others' deadly beams.

Some part of him, a spark in the depths of his mind perhaps, watched with some shred of anticipation, to see if

Avia's crew had indeed discovered a way to target the enemy's ships. But his grim attitude came from other places, too. He'd seen the fleet savaged, thousands of helpless Kriegeri, and the Masters leading the fleet, killed. He'd watched the might of the Hegemony, and the great polity's pride in its power and place in the galaxy shattered in a matter of hours. But he'd escaped the misery of seeing just what the Others did to a captured system, how they handled worlds full of Arbeiter and Kriegeri—and Masters, too.

He was positioned right in front of the tube, a place he was mandated to remain, not just by Chronos's order, but also those of the entire Council, including Akella herself. He had been authorized to go, but only to observe, to gather the needed data, and to return to Calpharon before any enemy forces could engage his small cluster of ships.

The rest of the small fleet would not be so lucky, he realized. Some of the ships might escape, at least part of him wanted to believe that, but a lot of his people were going to die in the next few hours. He dreaded watching more of his Kriegeri sacrificed in a hopeless struggle, and more, the planet Eliason had over half a billion inhabitants. His people weren't even pretending to try to defend it. The system layout mandated the position of his fleet, a location that allowed unimpeded communications from the fighting ships to the small group of vessels waiting to bring the data back to Calpharon.

A position well back from Eliason, leaving the planet exposed along the expected enemy approach vector.

Ilius had tried not to think about what had happened to the inhabited words in Venta Traconis, an exercise that, altogether, had not been particularly successful. The records about the first incursion by the Others were sparse on details of the treatment of captured populations. The Hegemony was younger then, its expanse smaller, its planets far less populated. Ilius tried to tell himself the hundreds of millions on Venta Traconis's two inhabited planets, and the millions more in other systems that had simply been abandoned to the enemy advance, were being held in some kind of humane captivity. But he didn't believe it.

"The Verification Force reports multiple contacts, Commander."

Ilius heard the officer's words, and he pulled himself from his dark thoughts. Duty still came first.

"Very well, Hectoron. Let's keep a close watch on what is happening. All comm receivers on maximum. Any incoming data feeds go right to the AI, understood?" The fact that the Others had ships there was information any of his people could understand. But the petabytes of data that would be coming in, every detail of every scanner reading from more than three dozen ships, defied examination by any human mind, Master or not. If he had to watch forty ships sacrificed to the enemy, he intended at least to come away with usable data, every detail of what worked and what didn't. He'd been sent there simply to determine if what had been informally dubbed the '*Avia* Method' actually worked, but he wanted more. If the scanner program *did* allow effective targeting of the enemy, he wanted more than confirmation…he wanted every detail that could allow the system to be refined, improved.

"The lead ships of the Verification Force are closing into projected enemy fire range."

Ilius sighed softly, doing all he could to keep it to himself. This was the moment, the ten or twenty minutes that would determine the mission's success or failure. If Krellos's ships were blasted to atoms before they reached their own firing ranges, all his warriors would all die for nothing. Ilius and the crews of his monitoring ships would transit, and run back to Calpharon, defeated and empty handed.

But if the evasion routines worked well enough, if Krellos had some of the old magic left in that ancient mind and body, maybe—just maybe—Ilius would return with word that Kiloron Tragus's firing solutions worked, that the next time a Hegemony fleet met the Others in battle, the fight would be at least a bit more even.

*   *   *

"All ships, continue forward." Krellos sat in *Hetaria*'s command chair, his eyes still bright, attentive, despite his advanced age. His flagship was almost as old as he was, as were most of the vessels in his cobbled together force. The deployment of the fleet's oldest and most obsolete ships to the desperately dangerous expedition—Krellos felt he owed it to his crews not to call it a suicide mission—had been his suggestion. It had required some crash retrofitting to bring the scanning suites up to snuff, and upgrades of the weapons arrays to allow the small force to truly test out their new targeting algorithms, but it preserved the most battleworthy vessels for the fight Krellos knew was coming, the struggle that would ultimately determine if the Hegemony survived.

"All units acknowledge, Commander."

Krellos was resolved to his likely fate, and while he longed on one level to be there when the Hegemony fought the ultimate battle for the future, he had lived a long and productive life. He relished the chance to return to the colors, to serve the Hegemony one last time, to die as he had lived, as a Master and a protector of humanity. His greatest regret was that most of those who would die with him were far younger than he was, that many would lose long and productive decades that otherwise would have lain before them. The loss of so many useful lives would be a tragedy, though one that seemed insignificant compared to the magnitude of all that was at stake.

"Commander, we're picking up energy readings from the enemy formation. AI analysis suggests weapons systems being activated."

Krellos remained still, though he could feel his hands shaking. It wasn't fear, just the tremors he always endured, the result of the nerve damage spreading through his aged and failing body. He was old, even by the standards of humanity's genetic elite, but he had not escaped all of time's ravages.

"All ships, engage pre-programmed evasive routines." He had done all he could to ensure his small force was prepared to complete its mission, whatever the cost. The enemy's weapons outranged his own, and that meant his fleet would have to endure—and survive—incoming fire while it continued to close. When—if—his ships reached their own firing range, they could complete their mission, determine with some level of certainty whether or not the radiation detection routine enabled effective targeting of enemy vessels.

If the algorithms worked, if his people were able to score a certain number of verified hits—ten was the number in his mind—he could give the retreat order…and every ship in his small command would be free to make a run for it, to try to escape, however unlikely such a result might be.

His eyes were fixed on the display. The massive, 3D setup was another new addition to *Hetaria*'s otherwise simple and dingy bridge. There were tiny flashes, a few at first, and then dozens, as the lead formations of the enemy fleet opened fire. His ships were already into their defensive routines, and Krellos nodded silently, an expression of gratitude that whatever technological advantages the Others possessed, they did not appear to include the ability to negate random, chaos-driven evasive maneuvers. That was no guarantee of survival for any of his vessels—a fact emphasized by the disappearance of one of his ships from the display, the first casualty of the battle—but it did offer hope, at least, that his people who died would not do so in vain.

He winced as one of the flashes zipped right past *Hetaria*, coming, he guessed, within two or three kilometers of the battleship. *One point two*, he silently acknowledged, as the AI streamed the data onto his screen.

His recollections of space combat were many and varied, but the forces he'd led had always been superior, and death and defeat, if they came at all, had been slow, gradual. He remembered ships being damaged, battered by hit after hit until finally, some critical system or another failed and triggered an epic explosion. Or vessels were simply pummeled into lifeless hulks. But he knew well from reviewing the data from Venta Traconis, that the enemy's main guns could cripple a Hegemony battleship with a single shot, and even destroy one outright. It was a different feeling, one harder to control, as he looked into the display, knowing any second could be his last, that he and his flagship's crew, so far untouched by the enemy's fire, might die at any moment, without the slightest warning.

He watched as three more of his ships were hit, two suffering severe damage, and the third vanishing in an instant of thermonuclear fury. He known when he volunteered, that his force would suffer terribly closing to combat range, but it had been many years since he'd seen his comrades dying in such numbers, and he found it harder to endure than he'd expected. However ready he'd believed he was, he realized there were some things one could never fully prepare for. He'd prepared himself for heavy losses, even to die himself…but now he began to imagine a total failure, the loss of all his ships before they closed enough to test their new target locks.

He opened his mouth, as if to give a command, but he remained silent. He'd been about to order his ships to alter their evasion routines, but he realized that would be a waste of time at best, and harmful at worst. The programs had been devised in as random a pattern as possible. The losses he'd suffered so far were the result of the Others' targeting prowess and high-tech scanners, not any failure of the routines. If he ordered his commanders to take control themselves, to engage in their own programs, the loss rate would almost certainly spike.

Krellos was a veteran of more than two-thirds of a century of service, a hardened warrior who had faced countless dangers. But even he felt overwhelmed, held almost in awe by the mysterious ships moving steadily toward his fleet, the eerie blue beams of their weapons slicing through space, and when one connected, inflicting catastrophic damage on the ships he commanded.

His eyes darted to his screen, to the range display. Fifty thousand kilometers until his lead ships could open fire. The range would still be long, and shots fired from such a distance would provide weak and confusing data regarding the efficacy of the fire locks. He knew he had to get at least some of his ships in close, near enough to overcome the enemy's own evasion tactics, and determine with some sense of certainty whether the new scanner programs truly worked.

His mind ran calculations, evaluating the losses to date, and extrapolating those he was likely to suffer the rest of the way in. The enemy's hit rates would climb as the distance diminished, though how much was probably more guesswork than calculation. He decided to call it an estimate, and he finished his analysis. Some of his ships would get close enough, assuming the enemy hit rates didn't soar as the range dropped. He tried to cut off the line of thought before it moved to the inevitable next calculation. A projection on how many of his ships might survive long enough to make escape attempts…and how many had even a remote chance of making it back to the tube. The effort failed. He didn't have an exact analysis, but he didn't need one to know that none of his people—not one—was going to make it out of Upsilon Vega.

Perhaps our deaths can continue to serve. No doubt Ilius would record everything happening in the system. The enemy targeting data, their accuracy percentages at different ranges, to median damage caused by hits at various distances...it was all useful tactical data, a bit more coin, perhaps, paid in return for the lives of eighteen thousand Kriegeri and nine Masters.

And one very old fleet commander, perhaps just a bit less useless than people had thought...

* * *

"Megaron Krellos's ships are opening fire, Commander." Ilius's crew was disciplined and focused, as were most Kriegeri forces. And *all* of those who served under the veteran megaron's command.

But discipline and experience proved inadequate to hide the tension and excitement in the officer's voice. Ilius might have scolded the Hectoron, but he knew the Kriegeri was as aware as he was—as every officer and rank and file warrior in the small armada was—that the next moments would reveal whether the Hegemony fleet had a chance in the war, or at least the ability to hurt the enemy, to make them pay for their gains. There were reasonable standards, even ones that were very tough and strict...and then there was expecting human beings to behave as machines.

Besides, Ilius was far from sure his own tone and demeanor were hiding the anxiety gnawing at him.

He watched silently, his tension growing with every sudden flash on the screen. Krellos's ships were indeed firing...and they were missing. Ilius watched a dozen shots, and not one came close to any of the enemy ships, at least as far as he could tell at his own vessel's extreme range. Even as he sat there, he realized how much he'd allowed hope to penetrate his usual grim and skeptical psyche. He could feel the sense of promise slipping away, the now unwelcome hope being driven from his mind.

Krellos's force had lost half its strength, but the

surviving ships were still pressing on, moving forward with as much thrust as sometimes-damaged engines could produce. The output, and the resulting acceleration, had fallen, of course, when the vessels had been compelled to divert energy to weapons arrays, but the fleet was pressing on with what Ilius realized was suicidal bravery. He'd never been one to allow emotions to slip into his assessment of war, but years of seeing the often selfless sacrifice of the Rim warriors, the desperate determination they had displayed in the face of overwhelming odds, had shaken him from his almost robotic expectations. He understood heroism in ways he never had, and he realized he was watching it in action.

Another pair of ships blinked from his screen, another thousand Kriegeri lost. But the rest of Krellos's fleet continued on, blasting away at their maximum rate of fire.

Then he saw it. A shot from *Hetaria*'s main battery. A hit.

Ilius closed his eyes for a second and then reopened them, focusing again on what he'd seen. He was about to request confirmation from the AI when three more shots hit enemy targets in rapid succession. The hit rate was still poor, no more than four or five percent. But there was no doubt the targeting was working. The chances of four random hits were so unimaginable as to be almost indistinguishable from zero.

Ilius felt a wave of excitement, one that almost slipped past his efforts to remain calm. He'd seen an entire battlefleet, one vastly larger than Krellos's beleaguered force, fight a protracted battle without scoring a single hit, save only for *Avia*'s one focused shot. Now, a dozen remaining vessels, some of them damaged and leaving trails of instantly refreezing atmosphere and fluids behind them, had scored no less than four hits.

Five...

Ilius turned his head, looking toward the scanner contacts, the enemy ships now engaged in something far more like an actual battle. He could see their reactions, an increase in evasive maneuvers, and a few seconds later, after two more of Krellos's shots connected, something new.

Energy readings, radiation. One of the enemy ships was showing signs of detectable damage.

Ilius's head snapped around as his bridge crew erupted in a ragged wave of shouts and applause. It was the kind of outburst he rarely tolerated. But this time, he just looked around the bridge, and he added his own acclamation to that of his people. It was a victory, small, fleeting, far from decisive, but a triumph nevertheless, a light in the darkness of defeat that had plagued his people since the Others had arrived.

He felt as close to unrestrained joy as he could ever remember, and he dared to imagine a route, a long and bloody one for certain, but a path nevertheless, to survival. To victory.

His excitement was short-lived, however, as cold reality reasserted itself with brutal force. He was staring right at the display when the small blue symbol, the icon representing *Hetaria* disappeared. For an instant, he tried to imagine it was a scanner error, a failure of the display mechanism. But he knew with cold certainty that the old battleship was gone, and with it Krellos.

The Hegemony had lost a hero...but the old man had died as he had lived. In combat, and in victory.

Ilius glanced over the display one more time, confirming to himself that none of the handful of vessels remaining in Krellos's force had any chance at all of escaping. It hurt to leave them, but he knew his duty. Krellos was gone, and soon, thousands of his warriors would join him. It was a dark and somber end to the mission, but it had not been in vain. Kiloron Tragus's theory had been confirmed, his targeting tactics validated. Ilius's ships clustered around the tube had collected petabyte upon petabyte of detailed data, and their duty was now clear.

The Hegemony was still outgunned and outclassed, but at least it could fight back now. That was no guarantee of victory, or even survival, but it was a chance…and that was the best Ilius could have hoped for.

"Hectoron, all ships are to initiate maximum thrust, all vectors toward the transit tube. We've got the data we came for, and now we've got to get it back to Calpharon."

"Yes, Megaron."

Ilius glanced one last time at Krellos's survivors, now no more than half a dozen battered ships bracketed by multiple enemies. It was almost over, and when the final vessel was destroyed, it would be nothing but a mercy. It was painful, and thoughts of his old commander and mentor drifted through his mind. But those spacers still fighting, out there battling through their last moments—and Krellos who had led them there, the hero who had already passed on to legend—had at least not been sacrificed for nothing. Millions of their comrades would use the knowledge they had provided. They would fight to avenge the losses suffered in Upsilon Vega, and at Venta Traconis. They would fight to save the Hegemony.

To save humanity.

And the heroes lost there would never be forgotten, not if the Hegemony endured.

He leaned back as he felt this ship's engines firing, driving the vessel, along with its companions, toward the transit tube.

Toward the way home.

Chapter Eighteen

Planet Calpharon
Sigma Nordlin IV
Year of Renewal 267 (322 AC)

"No, that is not going to happen. First, I could never convince the Confederation Senate to approve it, even if I was willing." Barron stared at Akella, his eyes cold. "Which, I must emphasize without doubt or reservation, I most certainly am not." Against all odds, Barron had actually warmed to his Hegemony hosts. He'd been treated with courtesy and respect, and he'd come to accept them, if in a halting, irregular sort of way. Moments of respect had been interspersed with sudden memories of the war, of the terrible losses the Hegemony invasion had inflicted on his warriors. His head was spinning, the confusion struggling to overtake his rational thought, to lead him one way and then abruptly, to shove him off in another direction.

But when Akella suggested—gently and diplomatically—that the two sides attempt to negotiate a return of *Colossus* to Hegemony control, Barron had no doubt whatsoever how he felt.

"I understand your point of view, Admiral, I truly do, and no doubt I would feel the very same way were I in your shoes." Barron had been stunned at how charming Akella was, and how calm and reasoned. He'd come to see the Hegemony as brutal conquerors, and while he was still far from forgiveness for all that had happened, he was beginning to see the other side. Bits and pieces, at least. Certainly, the humans living coreward of the Rim had suffered vastly more in the Cataclysm, and as much as he bristled at the idea of another power conquering him 'for his own good,' he couldn't help but understand to an extent what drove the Hegemony and its leaders.

Still, Akella had devoted enormous amounts of her time to private discussions with him, as well as meetings between the two of them and Chronos. He acknowledged her devotion, but it told him something more, something unintended. Akella was trying to keep him away from the rest of the Council as much as possible. He believed the Hegemony's Number One was a true believer, that her only concerns were saving humanity from a repeat of the disasters of the past. But Barron didn't have the slightest doubt many of her colleagues, while playing lip service to such lofty ideals, were simply arrogant and defensive of their prerogatives as highly-ranked Masters.

"You would very likely feel the same way…and I wonder how you would respond to a request by your, hopefully former, enemies to return the very superweapon they had deployed against you."

"I cannot say, Tyler. I will not insult your intelligence with answers drawn from the scripts of diplomacy. What I ask, I ask not because I consider it fair, nor because I am sure I would consent myself, but rather because it is so vitally important to defeat the Others. Though you may not yet fully believe me, that is as crucially important for your own people as for mine. *Colossus* is a great weapon, the manifestation of pre-fall imperial might. Since it was found, and my people restored it to functional status, it has served as the core of our defensive forces, waiting in silent watch for the Others to return."

"And yet, you detached it from that purpose and sent it to the Rim. To fight my people." Barron had managed to check most of his resentment, but he could hear a bit of it slip out, resurgent in his words.

"My people are loathe to admit their faults and errors, Tyler, and the Masters above all. I am no exception. The invasion of the Rim could not have occurred without my approval, so I bear the guilt for all that happened. Such action was our way, all we have known, and however many perished in the fighting, understand that orders of magnitude more would have—will—die if the Great Death returns, if we live now, not in a period of recovery as some would believe, but in a mere pause of a far longer decline. I do not make excuses, nor do I ask for pardon, but I beg you to consider that there is much your people do not know, of the galaxy and its history. Can you say, for all your love of independence and your defiant courage, that you are sure your people do *not* face a continuation of you Cataclysm? Does the Rim and its history over the past two centuries seem like a return to the Pax Imperia, to centuries, no millennia, of peace and prosperity? Your Confederation, barely one hundred years old, has fought, what, four wars with the Union? Your Palatian allies endured a century of enslavement, did they not? And, they used their independence to ensure they were never again conquered...by instead subjugating their neighbors. Indeed, for all the clear camaraderie your warriors exhibited in the recent fighting, my understanding is you yourself fought a bitter conflict with a Palatian vessel. The Rim is torn with strife and plagued by almost constant war. Can you really say to me, Tyler Barron, that your people, not just of the Confederation, but all the humans on the Rim, have truly evolved out of the dark age that followed the imperial fall, that your are not still in that decline, still sinking into barbarism and despair?"

Akella's words hit Barron like a club. She'd started by

admitting her own people's faults, and that had disarmed him, tamped down on his angry response. He felt the urge to answer her questions, to state with unwavering certainty that the Rim was indeed rising from the darkness and not descending back into it. But her arguments were cutting, and he had no replies, none that didn't leave him full of doubts. He was the grandson of the Confederation's great hero, an officer who had cut his teeth in one war, led his forces to victory in another desperate conflict…and lived to die in a third one. His father had been lost in battle as well, and his own career, as he looked back on it, seemed like nothing so much as a continuation of that trend. He could resent the Hegemony, rage against Akella for allowing her forces to invade his home, but he couldn't question her intelligence…and now that he'd spent time with her, he couldn't portray her any longer as a murderous monster bent on conquest. Things were indeed far more complex than he might have imagined, and whatever he felt about the Hegemony as an enemy, he had no difficulty imaging even worse adversaries out there. He retched at the idea of sending Confederation warriors to fight and die to save Hegemony worlds, but the cold shadow standing behind him whispered the same question to him again and again.

If Akella's people are destroyed, what will happen to the Rim?

"It is too much, Akella. I can believe much of what you say, and yet the most recent enemy, and the one who inflicted the worst damage on my people, is still the Hegemony. We can talk of the Cataclysm, of civilization rising and falling, of terrifying enemies approaching. But the only incontrovertible fact I can draw upon is that little more than one year ago, your people were killing mine." Barron's words held a firmer line than his thoughts. He'd seen footage of the force Akella called the Others, and while he was well aware such things could be doctored and manufactured outright, his blood had still run cold while he'd watched. He couldn't prove any of it was accurate, but he believed it was…and that made the walls close in on him. He couldn't imagine sending the massed Confederation fleets past the Badlands to Hegemony space, to fight alongside their recent enemies. But the idea of simply waiting, of the Confederation leadership burying their heads in the sand, while this new enemy crushed the Hegemony, and then came for the Rim, was no less unthinkable.

"I can apologize for the invasion if you wish, Tyler, though I would not wish to do so, as you are an intelligent man, and you would know it was not entirely sincere. I am sorry so many were killed, that so much suffering resulted, and I obviously regret the destruction of so much combat power on what turned out to be the eve of the Others' return. But I will not disrespect you by claiming I do not believe your people would be better off as part of the Hegemony, that I am not convinced we all face an inexorable decline into a dark age thousands of years long if we cannot find away to avoid the mistakes of the past. I do not wish ill to your people, Tyler Barron, quite the contrary, though this may seem a difficult thing to comprehend from your point of view, as one who fought my warriors. As one who lost friends in the war."

Barron was struck again by Akella's apparent reason and her calm assessments. Again, he didn't agree with everything she said…but he wasn't sure he quite disagreed either.

Does it really matter? Even if she convinces you, can you get the Senate to consent to send the bulk of the fleet to Hegemony space…

"Very well, Akella, you have convinced me of one thing. We must put bad feelings from the war aside, and the vast differences in our cultures and beliefs. Whatever happens with…the Others, as you call them…I would strive for a future of peace between our peoples. Yet, the Hegemony's basic directive gives you no choice, does it?. If my people, if all the Rim, were to join in your fight, help you defeat the Others, what guarantee do we have that you would not immediately renew your efforts to subjugate us? Your initial reasons would remain, the crusade that has defined the Hegemony since its founding. I have no desire to become one of your Kriegeri warriors, Akella, and I believe I can speak for all of my comrades in that regard."

"There is no question in my mind, Tyler, no discernible doubt that you would achieve Master status if you submitted to the Test. Indeed, the Rim suffered far less than our own worlds in terms of genetic degradation during the Great Death. Many of your people would place very highly. It is possible, even, that a new Number One would emerge from one of your worlds. If that happened, you would see that I am no hypocrite, when I stepped aside and turned the Hegemony over to a Rimdweller." She paused. "Excuse me for that tangent. To answer your question more directly, you would have my word, Tyler Barron. If your people aid us, there will be no renewed invasion of the Rim. The Hegemony will abandon its core directive with regard to the Rim. We will seek to remain allies with your people, not to absorb them into the Hegemony."

Barron almost scowled, but he didn't. It seemed absurd that he would believe the leader of his recent, bitter enemies…but he realized he *did* believe her. Still, he knew it wasn't enough. "I do not question your integrity, Akella. Yet, what assurance is there in your word? You can be replaced any year, any time the Test reveals one of your people with a higher rating than yours. And, of course, there are myriad other ways power could change hands. You may feel the Hegemony is above such things as coups and civil wars, but I cannot afford to make so casual an assumption. You are still asking me to convince my people to risk all in a battle they almost certainly will not see as their fight, to save an enemy who may very well turn around and attack them again. Unlike you, I am not the sole leader of my people, and I do not believe, however convinced *I* may be, that I can persuade them to such a course."

Akella sat quietly, her face impassive. Then she opened

her mouth…but the words she'd intended never came out.

The comm unit on the table buzzed. She nodded to Barron, and she tapped the unit. "I requested that I not be disturbed, Kiloron."

"Many pardons, Number One, but Megaron Ilius has returned. The Verification Force has engaged the enemy…and they were successful. They were able to score multiple hits on the Others' ships. The *Avia* plan works, Number One."

Akella remained remarkably unemotional, considering the import of what she'd just heard. "Call the Council to assembly, Kiloron…by my command. In one hour." She tapped the comm, closing the line. She sat for a moment, silent. Then she stood up. "I must go, Tyler. I must address the Council."

"I understand. I can wait for you here."

"No."

Barron turned, startled.

"You will accompany me…if you are willing. I must convince you I am trustworthy, and keeping you from my peers, from the Council and the rest of the high command, will not achieve that goal. I ask only that you keep in mind that we, too, have difficulties among each other, even as I perceive considerable friction between you and your Senate. Many on the Council are recklessly proud. Many have lost their way. But by showing you all of this, I hope to convince you that I, at least, am true to my ideals, and to my word."

Barron nodded, all he could manage at first through the surprise that hit him. He'd wanted to hate Akella when he'd first arrived, but now he found that impossible. She was admirable, almost familiar, and he knew she would have fit in well with the group of his closest comrades.

And yet, she is—was?—my enemy.

Chapter Nineteen

Confederation Intelligence Safe House
Liberte City – Petrusca Ghetto
Planet Montmirail, Ghassara IV
Union Year 225 (321 AC)

"How do you think I can possibly kill Villieneuve?" Sandrine Ciara was still stunned at the words that had come from Kerevsky's mouth. They'd been discussing the subject for weeks now, and the shock was still as potent as it had been the first time. "How could I even get near him? And, if I *was* able to get close enough to make an attempt, how could I get away?" She paused. "Or, I guess my getting away is not a crucial element of the plan. Ridding you—and the Confederation—of Villieneuve would be a substantial service. Even in the desperate power struggle that would almost certainly follow his death, it's hard to imagine anyone worse prevailing and taking control. A major change in policy is unlikely, but even stasis would be a victory of sorts for the Confederation. We both know Villieneuve will renew hostilities as soon as he believes he has a chance at victory." Another brief silence. "I understand now how you expect me to repay my debt. Certainly, it is not unreasonable, not after all you've done for me. I'd be dead, or worse, if you hadn't helped me, and likely face down in the gutter somewhere rather than striking back, taking my enemy with me."

"Sandrine, please...you know that is not what I mean." A lie, or at least partly so. He *had* been conflicted, a war waging in his head between his feelings for Ciara and his duty as a Confederation Intelligence operative. He wasn't quite able to acknowledge he was suggesting a tactic that was very likely to send Ciara to her death, but he was sure he couldn't pass up any chance to get rid of Villieneuve. As long as the sociopathic ruler controlled the Union, another war was a virtual certainty. And the universe had become far more complex since the last Confederation-Union conflict. The Confederation could easily find itself facing both the Union and a renewed conflict with the Hegemony at the same time. Killing Villieneuve wouldn't guarantee peace, but it would greatly increase the chances, at least for the foreseeable future. The Union dictator had a pathological hatred for the Confederation, blaming it for all his past failures. A sustainable peace between the two powers was impossible unless Villieneuve was...removed from the equation.

Concern for Ciara wasn't the only issue he was struggling with. His motivations were pure enough, to safeguard the Confederation, to protect it from future dangers. But he hadn't been sent to Montmirail to orchestrate a coup. He'd already greatly exceeded his mandate, so far to no gain. If he *could* eliminate Villieneuve, he'd have something to show for straying so far from his orders. But could he really justify extending the magnitude of his...improvisations...to assassination with the argument that he'd failed so far, but another try might ultimately be worthwhile?

He knew his concerns should have rested exclusively on that last issue, that sacrificing a Union asset to attain a desirable end should not hinder his choices. But could he really send his lover to her doom? Ciara had been a tool, and nothing more, or at least Kerevsky knew that was what she *should* have been. He could hear Gary Holsten's words echoing in his head, shouting at him to keep all relationships with assets cold, impersonal. He'd failed in that, though part of him was still arguing that Ciara was nothing more than a tool, that the feelings he'd developed for her were simply facets of his deep cover and tradecraft.

The question remained, could he pull himself back, act with coldblooded rationality? Or would he fail in his duty once again, and tie himself to someone who'd become, in every way and form, save her possible utility in an assassination plan, a liability?

"You wished to seize power, did you not? Your coup may have failed, but with Villieneuve...out of the picture...you may yet have an opportunity to salvage parts of your plan." He didn't really believe she would escape even a successful assassination attempt, but it was all he had. And he was trying to convince himself as much as her.

"We both know that will not happen, Alexander, my lover. We are realists, you and I, both veterans in our field of endeavor. Ask me to die for you, to repay you for saving me in the aftermath of the coup. But don't lie to me. Don't ask me to believe that I will survive the plan you are proposing. I will be fortunate enough to reach Villieneuve, to get a significant chance of killing him. But I know well, as I suspect you do, the realities of this plan. The First Citizen has always been quite adept at cultivating loyalty—or an effective facsimile—among his guards. To survive, I would not only have to get in unnoticed, I would have to get back out before anyone discovered the body. That is possible, perhaps, but far from likely."

She paused, Kerevsky standing silently, still wrestling with his thoughts. Duty would win the fight for his soul, he knew, but he would never forgive himself for sending Ciara to her death.

"I will do as you ask, Alexander. Not because I believe I can survive the attempt, or even succeed for that matter, and not because I owe you for saving my life." She took a step toward him and extended her arm, her hand touching his cheek softly. "I will do it for you if you ask me to…but you have to ask."

Kerevsky felt an instant of satisfaction at the thought of removing Gaston Villieneuve from the equation. But the feel of Ciara's soft hand on his face shook his resolve. He tried again to convince himself he wasn't sending her to her death, with no more success than he'd achieved moments before.

He looked at her, his eyes meeting hers. She was right in front of him, so close he could hear her breath. She was a killer, he knew, cold blooded, with a trail of victims behind her he didn't dare to imagine. She was Sector Nine, and for all of his professional life, she had been an enemy. She deserved death, he suspected, as much as anyone did, and he imagined a whole crowd of ghostly faces, clamoring for him to send her to her well-deserved end. But even as he began to speak the words, the pain hit him. She was what she was, and he didn't lie to himself, try to mold his knowledge of her into some kind of palatable lie. Deserving or not, evil or not, he had feelings for her. And he had to ignore them. He had to let her go…no, he had to send her. However much it hurt.

"I'm asking you, Sandrine…please work with me on this. Please try to kill Gaston Villieneuve."

* * *

"We have searched the Confederation vessel again, First Citizen. The crew gave us unrestricted access. There is no way Minister, that the fugitive, Ciara, is on that vessel." The officer seemed a bit nervous, at least as much as Foudre Rouge ever got. Gaston Villieneuve had always been an unnerving presence, but since the coup attempt, he'd been a force of nature. He'd ordered thousands of executions, anyone involved in the coup attempt and those he imagined to be part of the cabal, too. No small number of innocents had met their ends in the weeks since Sandrine Ciara's attempt to seize power, friends of those involved, families, household staff. And there were no signs the killings were going to stop anytime soon.

Not while Ciara herself remained at large.

"I am revoking the Confederation embassy's credentials, effective one week from today. You will lead a detachment there to inform Ambassador Kerevsky personally that he is to be prepared to board his ship and leave Montmirail at that time. He will be escorted to the border by a naval squadron."

"Yes, First Citizen." The Foudre Rouge major snapped off a perfect salute, and then he spun around on his heels and marched out of the room.

Villieneuve let out a long sigh. He'd been operating on pure rage for the past month or more, and even for a man like him, such fury wore hard on one's psyche. He'd become obsessed with finding Ciara and convinced the only way she could have eluded his trackers for so long was with Confederation help. He was no fool, whether she'd tried to treat him as one or not. He'd developed a good sense of the resources deployed in the failed coup attempt, and it seemed unlikely she'd been able to assemble that level of funding herself. Where money was involved, he always thought of the Confederation, and the recollections of that enemy's vast wealth and the ways it had allowed them to best him so often, ratcheted the level of his anger ever higher.

He'd had the embassy monitored around the clock, both from outside, and using the surveillance assets still hidden in the structure itself. The orbital platforms had scanned Ambassador Kerevsky's ship without pause, and no shuttle had docked without first being thoroughly searched...officially for the purpose of ensuring the safety of Confederation personnel from renegade rebels who might do them harm. But all his efforts had come up blank. He'd even resorted to widespread searches, sending the Foudre Rouge out to break down doors throughout the city. His efforts had resulted in the capture of a few minor participants, but no sign at all of Sandrine Ciara. Even the captured plotters had failed to provide useful intelligence, despite...enthusiastic...interrogations. There had been a few vague mentions of Confederation involvement, but nothing sufficient to justify sending troops into the embassy...or turning the ambassador and his staff over to Sector Nine's Inquisitors. He would have done it anyway, without justification, but with the apparent Hegemony withdrawal from the Rim, he simply couldn't risk war with the Confederation. His forces weren't ready. Not yet, at least.

One day. I need a few more years, perhaps five...or a renewal of the war between the Confeds and the Hegemony. But the Union will have its revenge...and those rich and fat worlds of the Confederation will know obedience...

He looked down at the screen, at the document he'd just given the major to deliver. He might not be able to capture and interrogate the Confederation ambassador, but sending him, and all of his staff, offworld would leave Ciara on her own. She'd evaded him, remained at large, for far too long.

Let's see how well you can hide without your allies, Sandrine...

And when he finally found her, he would not only end the threat she represented with grim finality. Before he did, he would enjoy watching her broken, reduced to a whimpering wreck, sobbing and begging for death.

Chapter Twenty

Planet Calpharon
Sigma Nordlin IV
Year of Renewal 267 (322 AC)

"Admiral Barron is here at my invitation. He is to be treated with all appropriate respect, and Council debate is to proceed unimpeded while he is here." Akella spoke in a harsher tone than she'd shown in her talks with Barron, and he realized almost immediately that some of the men and women in the room were political rivals. That didn't make sense to him at first. Akella's genetic rating assured her the top seat, save only for certain extreme circumstances. But he quickly began to understand. Even in the Senate, power struggles raged over leadership positions and control over voting blocks. A Speaker only truly possessed authority if he controlled enough votes to pass the measures he desired. As much as Barron had come to see Akella as the leader of the Hegemony, he realized that was a gross oversimplification. She had considerable power, certainly, but she wasn't a dictator. Her control was far from absolute, and while she couldn't be removed from her seat absent proof of insanity, or some other significant impairment, she could be outvoted, even reduced to figurehead status.

And Tyler Barron had seen enough of the Senate's fouler

workings to realize that a removal for cause wouldn't require *actual* mental illness or any of the other specified situations, just enough votes aligned against her.

"Number One, with all due respect to our esteemed visitor, the Council is in session to review highly sensitive information from the battle lines. I am sure Admiral Barron would understand if we requested he leave this proceeding at some point. Of course, we will provide a reviewed and redacted transcript..."

"No." Akella's voice was cold, an anger there Barron hadn't heard before. He knew at once, there was bad blood between Akella the man who'd just spoken. *Thantor,* Barron reminded himself.

And Thantor is Number Two, her immediate successor.

Barron felt almost as though he was in the Senate on Megara. For all he'd hated the Hegemony as invaders and killers of so many of his comrades, he'd somehow imagined they were less beset by political bickering than the Confederation. Now, he wasn't so sure.

"Akella, be reasonable. The information..."

"Admiral Barron will not be asked to leave...and if this Council insists that he is, I will exercise my power to dissolve this meeting, and I will review the data from the Verification Force myself."

"You cannot do..."

"I can, and I will. Surely, you are familiar with the powers granted to the Number One of the Council. It is my place to preside over each meeting, and to determine the agenda. Admiral Barron has come a very long distance, in the aftermath of a bitter war between our nations. He is here to review the situation with the Others, and to decide whether to recommend to his government that they come to our aid. He must have all information we can provide to make his determination...and we must also earn his trust if we expect help from the Rim. Holding back information, excluding him from discussions about the situation, are inherently destructive to those aims."

Barron could hear a murmur moving around the able, and he could almost feel the shock at what Akella had said. There was arrogance on the Hegemony's Council, he realized without doubt, as much as he'd seen in the Senate's deliberations, more even, since the Hegemony was unmistakably the most powerful nation known…save perhaps for the Others.

"Enough nonsense. If no one has anything to add, perhaps we can begin." Akella's every word radiated a challenge, no something more. A dare.

No one responded.

"Very well. Megaron Ilius has come directly from the shuttle bay to address the Council." She turned toward the door where an officer stood wearing a dress uniform. "Megaron, the floor is yours."

Ilius stepped toward the center of the room. He turned and looked down the large table, where the highest-rated Masters in the Hegemony were seated. He was respectful, at least superficially, but Barron could sense the military commander harbored some resentments toward members of the Council. Barron knew little about the inner workings of the Hegemony, but he guessed that Ilius was firmly in the Akella-Chronos camp. Beyond the specifics of the political dynamics he was watching, he felt a strange sort of relief at seeing the Hegemony subject to many of the same problems that plagued the Confederation. For years, even as his hatred for the enemy grew, there had always been a kind of respect, almost an awe that a culture could move past the petty workings of politics and ascend to a higher level. Now, he realized, if such a civilization could exist, it was not the Hegemony, nor the revered old empire, which itself was torn apart by internecine conflict.

Perhaps that is mankind's curse, one we will never escape…

"Masters of the Council, it is an honor to once again stand before you. This time, amid the crisis we face, and the shadow cast across our future the news I bring is fractionally less dark and ominous than that we have endured in recent months. The vessels of the Verification Force, led by Commander Krellos, were able to categorically confirm the theory put forth by Commander Tragus of *Avia*. The Others' vessels do indeed emit detectable levels of Sigma-9 radiation…and Tragus's makeshift scanning routines allow effective fire locks on the enemy vessels. Hit rates in the encounter were considerably below levels we would consider normal battle standards, but we *were* able to verify a sufficient number of successful shots to conclude without reasonable doubt that the targeting program was effective." A short pause. "Further, we have scanner documentation of at least one enemy vessel exhibiting signs of significant damage, including secondary explosions and expulsion of internal materials through one or more hull breaches."

Akella had been watching her colleagues on the Council, but now she turned toward Ilius. "Thank you, Commander…both for your very welcome report, and for the great risk and effort you undertook to bring us this data."

Ilius nodded. "Thank you, Number One. Your words are a welcome addition to duty, which of course was all that was required." Ilius was silent for a moment. "With your indulgence, I would add that the entire Verification Force was lost…including Commander Krellos. We all know the commander's illustrious record, and though he is assured a place in Hegemony history, I would ask that this Council formally recognize his last efforts for the Hegemony…as well as the ultimate sacrifice he and his spacers made to aid us all in the fight we now face."

Akella stood up. "You are quite correct, Ilius. Commander Krellos deserves nothing less than the greatest honors this Council can bestow. I urge my colleagues to stand with me, in silent tribute, and then to vote as I do, to proclaim Master Krellos a Hero of the Hegemony and order that his likeness be carved into the Hall of Masters."

Ilius nodded, a silent acknowledgement, Barron guessed. He was a Master, and a protégé of Chronos, but his genetic ranking did not afford him a place on the Council...or a vote on Akella's motion.

"I stand with Akella. Krellos was a true hero, a Master of the Hegemony in every respect, and one deserving of all the honor we can provide." Thantor stood straight and erect, a little too much, Barron thought. He'd seen his share of insincere politicians, and they always overdid it. He also recognized that Akella had backed her rivals into a corner. She had sent Krellos, authorized the mission, and emphasizing its importance—and honoring those who had died carrying it out—could only strengthen her position. Her political adversaries could hardly make a stand refusing to honor an old man who'd performed one last desperate mission for the Hegemony, and died in the process.

He was even more impressed with Akella as he watched her. She'd seemed so...normal...when he'd spoken with her, like a real person and not the swamp creature he'd come to see in most politicians. But she could clearly play the political game as well, and with a considerable level of skill.

He watched as the other Council members spoke, each seeking to get on the record with some type of tribute to Krellos. For a few seconds, he almost imagined he was back home, on Megara, listening to the Senate prattle on about one pointless thing or another.

Finally, the showmanship—and the justifiable recognition of sacrifice—was over, and Akella spoke again. "We have extensive footage from the scanner reports of the exchange with the enemy. While much of the raw data is still being reviewed and analyzed, Commander Ilius has prepared a short sampling for us to see now. If you will all focus your attention on the large screen..." She turned and gestured toward a Kriegeri standing next to the room's main door. "Hectoron, dim the lights, please. And activate the display."

The room darkened, and the screen lit up, a blanket of dark space, and in the background, a sprinkling of stars. In the center of the screen, Barron saw...something. *A ship*, he thought...but like no vessel he'd ever seen. It was there, at least it seemed to be most of the time he stared at it. But there was something strange, as well, an eerie sensation. He couldn't quite lock his eyes on the ship. It didn't seem to be moving, not exactly, but it didn't appear to remain in the same place either.

Then, the image of the ship disappeared as the data shifted to a normal tactical scan. The ship was replaced by a standard scanner contact icon. The small oval lacked the strangeness the direct view of the vessel had exhibited, but it still wobbled strangely on the display, as the recording scanner clearly struggled to maintain contact. Barron began to understand why the Hegemony ships had so much trouble targeting their enemies. He couldn't explain what he was seeing, but it didn't take much to extrapolate the difficulties in establishing fire locks on ships whose locations you couldn't precisely pinpoint.

He sat quietly, watching as the battle unfolded. The mysterious ships—Barron still hadn't become accustomed to calling them the 'Others'—opened fire at a range that seemed almost impossible, especially for what appeared to be energy weapons of some kind. Barron had struggled to deal with the Hegemony railguns, and the Confederation had only recently partially closed that gap with its modified primaries. Even those great weapons, the pinnacle of Confederation science, had a range almost thirty thousand kilometers less than the Hegemony railguns.

And the ships on the display were firing at ranges close to one hundred fifty thousand kilometers greater than even the heaviest railguns.

Barron had moved past his unilateral disbelief in the Others, to a sort of acceptance that the Hegemony did, in fact, have another enemy. But he'd still been struggling to accept the premise that the Hegemony's adversary was a threat to the Rim. He'd even wondered if he should try somehow—and he had no idea how—to contact the Others. The Hegemony had invaded Rim space, killed Rim spacers...and the old adage floated around the edge of his mind.

The enemy of my enemy is my friend...

Barron was too cynical to believe some strange force from coreward of the Hegemony was a likely ally, but it still nagged at him. He had only Carmetia's impassioned pleas, and Akella's assurances, that the Others were indeed a deadly danger to the Rim as well as the Hegemony. Such claims were enormously self-serving for the parties involved...which didn't mean they weren't true.

It didn't mean they were, either.

As he watched the drama unfold on the screen, however, Barron began to believe what he'd been told. The images were no proof, of course, at least not of the Others' intentions with regard to the Rim, but what he was watching was so different, so *alien*, to all he'd seen before, he couldn't help but feel more closely aligned with the Hegemony. At least with the version of that polity represented by Akella's words and actions.

Don't forget...she authorized the invasion of the Rim. She may seem reasonable, even wise, but she is a believer in the Hegemony's destiny to rule all humanity...or at least she was.

The images on the screen told a story, of hope or of despair, depending on one's analysis. The Verification Force was scoring hits, proving the Hegemony had indeed discovered a way to track and target the enemy. But the hit rates were still abysmal, and for the forty or more vessels he knew were doomed as he watched, not one of the Others' ships had been destroyed...and only one had been damaged in any detectable way. That was undeniably an improvement over facing untrackable ships that couldn't be hit, but it was far from something offering the makings of victory. Tyler Barron had spent much of his adult life at war, and what time he hadn't been fighting had largely been spent preparing for the next struggle. His mind moved into action, adding up the numbers, applying them to a full-scale fleet battle. A Hegemony force might inflict some damage on the enemy—assuming Akella's people were able to refit all the scanner suites in their massive fleet before the next battle. They might even destroy a number of enemy ships. But there was no way they would win. No way they could win. Not without a vast increase in targeting effectiveness.

Or massive reinforcements.

Even as the playback continued, Barron's mind raced. He'd been suspicious of the Hegemony when he'd arrived, untrusting of the enemy his people had fought for six long years. He was still suspicious of them. But the threat he was watching, the almost effortless brutality of the enemy gunning down Hegemony ships, vessels his spacers had fought, bled, and died to match. He didn't doubt the Others existed, not anymore. A passing suspicion or two drifted by, imaginings that all he'd seen, all he was watching just then, had been staged to trick him. But he realized he was convinced. The Hegemony faced a dangerous and deadly enemy, one that quite possibly—if not probably—would destroy it.

Barron had imagined the Hegemony's defeat a thousand times, and in every instance, he'd felt nothing but satisfaction, grim joy at the fall of an enemy. Now that was all gone, replaced only by fear, by the realization that a power so great as that he was seeing, would very likely move on to the Rim, assert its dominance there as surely as it seemed intent on doing in the coreward space of the Hegemony.

He couldn't allow that. After two wars, millions dead, the

ghostly faces of lost comrades cried out to him to do something, to hold back the darkness, to preserve the Confederation and its Palatian allies.

To ensure that all the sacrifice and loss had not been for nothing.

Barron was convinced. He knew what he had to do. He just didn't know how to do it. He was forbidden to intervene without Senatorial permission, and even if he could convince that body to send the Confederation's fleets so far from home to fight alongside an enemy—former enemy?—he was far from sure it would make a difference.

Or that their consent—and reinforcements—would come in time.

He sat silently, his thoughts straying from the scene unfolding on the display, one side of his mind arguing with the other. For all the respect he'd gained for Akella, he'd have had no difficulty refusing her request, boarding his shuttle back toward *Dauntless* and heading home, leaving the Hegemony to face their struggle alone.

If he hadn't believed the enemy would turn its sights next on the Rim. On his own people.

He was still wrestling with his thoughts, the debate raging in his head, even as the scanner footage continued on the display. But in the deepest parts of his mind, he knew he'd reached a decision. The Others *were* a threat, not only to the Hegemony, but to the Rim as well.

More than a threat. They were death itself, at least to men and women like him and his spacers…and any others who wouldn't kneel down and surrender, beg to live their lives as slaves.

He would send word back to the Senate, his recommendation that the fleet fully mobilize and set out for Hegemony space at once. He would also send messages to those he trusted vastly more than the Confederation's governing body, to Clint Winters, Gary Holsten, and Vian Tulus.

And to Andi, as well, of course.

He felt a wave of sadness, and a touch of guilt. He missed his wife terribly, the pain digging into him like an open wound. But he had the solace, if that was the right word, of being focused on the danger and the looming struggle. Andi was back home, with nothing to do but wait for him to return. He felt relief that she was on Megara, safe for once, but that only inflamed the guilt. He'd considered giving her a softer version of the information he was sending the others, to ease her worry about him. But he discounted that immediately. She would soon discover the truth, and his foolish attempt to protect her would only end up hurting her.

He'd sincerely intended to return home after he'd met with the Hegemony officials, reviewed the data they had on the enemy. But the situation was too dire, the threat to the Rim—and by extension, to Andi herself—was far too imminent. He had to remain, at least for the time being. And if the Senate heeded his advice, most likely with an assist from Gary Holsten's machinations, he had no idea when he'd ever return home.

If he'd return.

He slammed a wall down in his mind, tried to ignore the pain, the cold fear that he might never see Andi again. He struggled with the effort, more than he had in the past. He'd been devoted to his duty with a singleminded focus his entire life. He'd been born into his role, and he'd never had a choice, not a real one. His career had been fulfilling, if also painful, and he looked back on it with pride. But the sacrifices had been great. Would Andi join that list? Would he fight and die far from home, without ever seeing her again, holding her in his arms?

His expression hardened, his will exerting itself. He would do what he had to do, as he'd always done. But first, he had to speak to Akella, alone.

He would do as she wanted, urge his people to come to

the Hegemony's aid. But he had his own demands. Total transparency, complete sharing of information. First, he wanted the scanning data the Hegemony had used to target the enemy ships...all of it, every detail.

And second, he wanted a technology team dispatched at once, back to Confederation space to aid Anya Fritz and her people in uncovering all of *Colossus*'s secrets. If Akella wanted the Rim to join the Hegemony's fight, she would have to do what he asked...beginning with trusting him as she wanted him to trust her.

Chapter Twenty-One

Highborn Flagship S'Argevon
Imperial System GH9-27C1
Year of the Firstborn 384 (322 AC)

The figure stepped onto the deck of the control room, tall, dark, casting a shadow that seemed more a manifestation of pure darkness than simply his massive form blocking one of the main illumination fixtures. Grand Admiral Tesserax was dressed all in red, a massive scarlet cape draped behind the darker red, almost black, of the robes he wore beneath. He was tall, two and a half meters, and broad, and his massive body appeared even larger for the implants, the bits and pieces of metal and machinery protruding from areas of his body.

The other forms in the control room, all save two who were as tall and imposing as Tesserax himself, leapt up from their seats, snapping to attention with an urgency that belied respect...and, even more intensely, fear. Then they all dropped to down to one knee, heads bowed. As one, the bridge crew spoke, almost hypnotically. "All hail the mighty Tesserax."

They remained in place for perhaps ten seconds, until the newly arrived figure waved his hand, a signal that they could rise. Again, almost in unison, they leapt up to attention and returned to their stations.

Tesserax walked across the deck, his heavy alloy boots clanging loudly on the polished surface. He stopped in front of a massive seat, surrounded on the floor, and above on the ceiling, by constructs that appeared to be retracted at present.

He sat, and he stared forward for a moment, totally still while the mechanisms of the chair activated. He could feel the small probe extending from behind his neck, slipping into the socket implant. An instant later, he felt the flow of information, the vast AI that powered vessel *S'Argevon*, pouring data through the now-connected circuit and into the thinking machine implanted in his neck and connected to his cortex. His personal AI interpreted and organized the data it received, feeding it into the biological sections of his greater brain complex at a manageable rate. The speed of thought and data analysis was far faster than any purely biological entity could match. Even the Highborn required implants to meet that maximum potential.

He considered the data on the system the fleet had just entered. There was one inhabited planet, notwithstanding smaller groupings of humans on research stations and mining outposts on three of the other worlds and moons. The populated world was old imperial, now possessed by those calling themselves the Hegemony. Tesserax's data suggested the leaders of that polity practiced a policy of genetic segregation, the highest among them called, 'Masters.' It was amusing, at least to the extent that Tesserax allowed himself time or thought for such superficialities as humor, to imagine such lower born creatures according themselves elite status for no more reason than they were surrounded by even more inferior animals. The humans served their purposes, of course, when properly controlled. The crew of *S'Argevon* consisted almost entirely of such creatures, harvested from former imperial worlds and modified to increase their abilities and usefulness...and to suitably pacify them.

The Highborn were never slow to utilize brutality when it served their purpose, but the need for thousands upon thousands of slaves to man the fleet's vessels was better served by simple cortex modification. The resulting Thralls were docile and obedient to the Highborn, who they worshipped as their gods, and savage and fierce in combat. The removal of the other detritus that plagued the minds of the humans made them quite useful, and allowed a great warship like *S'Argevon* to operate with only eleven of the Highborn aboard. If the vessel had not been a flagship, four or five would easily have sufficed. The humans still required sleep, of course, and their bodies were weak and fragile, but all resources had their drawbacks, and there were many advantages to using the primitive biologics as soldiers and ship crews. Even after the disasters that had destroyed the empire, billions of humans still survived, providing nearly endless new subjects to serve the Highborn.

Tesserax analyzed the data he had just received. The system had been fully scanned. The population of the primary world was estimated at seven hundred forty to seven hundred sixty million. That was a considerable density of human infestation, greater than any in the systems the fleet had passed to that point. He considered for a moment, evaluated the possibility of conducting harvesting operations. The Highborn needed more humans, to serve the fleet, to work in factories and mines. The return to the space claimed by the Hegemony had long been planned, and replenishing the inventory of human populations to serve was a primary purpose of the operation then underway.

Still, there would be time, and more than enough densely populated worlds to exploit. GH9-27C1 was adequate, with a sufficient infestation to justify harvesting, but perhaps it could better serve in another capacity, as had all the infested planets the fleet had passed through to date.

"The fleet will commence cleansing operations on the infested planet." He could have issued the command with a thought, directed the AI to issue the necessary verbal commands to the crew. But he'd given the order himself, something he often did, mostly for the benefit of the lesser creatures serving the ship and the Highborn. There had been many efforts to connect the humans into the neural net, but the few who survived the necessary implantation surgery had quickly gone insane. The primitive creatures were useful, to a surprising degree, but they definitely had their weaknesses.

"As you command, Highborn." The human, the highest ranked and rated then in the control room, spoke with awe and reverence.

Tesserax had deemed the planet not worth the trouble of commencing harvesting, but he had another reason for ordering the obliteration of three-quarters of a billion inhabitants.

To inflict terror on the humans.

The analysis of the engagement at Venta Traconis suggested strongly that at least one of the Hegemony vessels had been able to penetrate the phase shifting systems of the fleet and establish a usable target lock. There was no doubt that one of the vessels in the Highborn fleet had been hit, though the damage inflicted had been minimal. Nevertheless, it was a matter of some concern, even though many had suggested the single hit had been a fluke. That was weak-mindedness, of course, a victory of arrogance over analysis. The chance of a 'lucky' hit at the ranges of space combat was so remote, it was virtually indistinguishable from zero in mathematical terms.

Such failures of intellect were no longer relevant, of course. The subsequent engagement at GH9-24D8, the Upsilon Vega System, as the human referred to it, had left no doubt. In an unexpected display of initiative and analytical capacity, the humans had developed a way, crude and inefficient perhaps, but at least somewhat effective, to overcome the phase shifts of the Highborn's vessels. Nineteen hits had been recorded in that battle, and the utter destruction of the engaged enemy force had been little enough compensation for that shift in the tactical situation. One of the Highborn vessels had even suffered moderate damage and was still under repair. None of that changed the tactical situation, of course, but it did suggest a rather higher cost for the overall operation in terms of losses suffered.

Tesserax had only intended to exterminate the infestations on underpopulated worlds, quarantining the others until such time as pacification forces could suitably convert the raw masses into useful and docile servants of the Highborn. But he'd come to the conclusion it was best in the early stages of the invasion to make an ally of fear.

He focused on the data pouring into his cortex, and in his mind, he saw the surface of the planet, vast cultivated fields and hillsides, and, mostly along the coasts, more than thirty large metropolises. The construction was primitive, of course, but somewhat impressive in its own limited way, at least in terms of scale. For a moment, all seemed normal on the planet. But then, the sky was full of small metal objects. Warheads. Moving toward their targets.

The planet and its cities were protected, of course, first by orbital platforms, and then by ground-based interception systems. The space stations had been obliterated in an instant by the nearest fleet units, though three of the larger installations had required second hits to completely destroy them.

Then, the wave of missiles descended, arcing out in precisely targeted patterns, their number and courses perfectly plotted not simply to wreak havoc and destruction, but to utterly cleanse the planet.

The missiles rained down everywhere. Tesserax watched more than a dozen scanner feeds at once. In his mind, he could see what was happening, cities obliterated in firestorms of thermonuclear fury. Millions of the humans were dying, he knew, though that was a detail of no particular consequence. It was the strategy that interested him, the manipulation designed to break the Hegemony's fighting spirit. There was some waste, of course. The radiation-intensified blasts would aid in the total extermination of the current population, but they would also render the planet useless, at least before an expensive and time-consuming rehabilitation could be conducted. But that was of only slightly greater concern than the extermination itself. Old imperial space was full of habitable worlds, and heavily infested with humans suitable for modification. If it served to destroy ten or twenty worlds, and a few billion of the inhabitants, so be it.

The Hegemony Masters consider themselves advanced, capable. Now they will learn they are little more than animals.

Let them see the scorched, radiation scarred surfaces of worlds that had held millions of their kind. Let the fear march forward, before the Highborn fleet, doing its work, breaking the will of the humans.

Then, the survivors will learn their place. They will learn to serve us.

They will learn to worship us, the gods who reign over them.

Chapter Twenty-Two

Planet Calpharon
Sigma Nordlin IV
Year of Renewal 267 (322 AC)

"I don't really care, Akella. You can ask the Council's permission, or you can simply provide my people with the full data record on your own authority. But my condition is an absolute one. I will request that the Senate dispatch the rest of the fleet to Calpharon, and also direct my forces already present here to undertake hostilities against the Others as soon as I receive authorization...but only if you immediately turn over all scanning and targeting data on the enemy forces. Cooperation is a two-way street, Akella, and I will not even consider committing Confederation forces to battle unless we have all relevant data on effective tactics to engage the enemy." Barron had been arguing all morning with Akella—more debating, perhaps than arguing, but the fact remained, the Hegemony leader had been slow to consent to his two primary requests.

Demands.

He wanted the targeting data, including the most recent algorithms derived from it...and he wanted a Hegemony team dispatched at once, with orders to assist Commodore Fritz and her people in operating *Colossus*. They were demands difficult for any recent enemy to accept, but no more than coming to an adversary's aid, as Akella had bade him to do. He had come to see the threat of the Others, but if Akella wanted Confederation assistance, she was going to have to meet him halfway.

"Those are difficult conditions to meet, Tyler. The Council is unlikely to authorize the release of such sensitive military information, even if I strongly urge it...and they are absolutely never going to agree to train your people to operate *Colossus*. A large majority of the Council still supports every effort to reacquire the vessel. There was even a vote authorizing me to offer your government a large payment for *Colossus*'s return. I never followed up on that, of course. It is clear to me your people would never surrender the vessel...and I understand why they wouldn't. I do not see our efforts to absorb the Rim in quite the same terms you do, Tyler, but it is perfectly understandable to me how your people feel."

"Akella, I believe all you've said about the Others. I believe they are a threat to the Rim as well as the Hegemony. But I, too, have to convince my people to join yours, and that will *not* be easy. My first demand, I consider nothing less than essential. What is the point of sending Rim warships here if they are not able to target the enemy ships? If you really want help against your enemy, you have to show us you will do everything to enable us to provide that aid."

Akella didn't answer, but she nodded gently, a gesture that told Barron she understood, and that she agreed with him. Which, of course, didn't necessarily solve the problem.

"As for *Colossus*, my argument—my insistence—is based largely on the same premise. Clearly, the ship is a tremendous asset in any fight, at least if it is properly operated and supplied. If you are indeed serious about defeating the Others, you will also want *Colossus* in the battle line. And the only way you're going to get that—short of invading the Rim again—is to show my people how to operate it. We will get there ourselves, decipher its secrets, but that may be in five years, or ten. Longer than your people have, I suspect."

Akella nodded again, and then she said, "I am convinced, Tyler Barron. Indeed, I was before this last effort at persuasion. But *I* am not the problem. As you have no doubt realized, my position on the Council—and as Number One of the Hegemony—is not one of absolute power. There is much I can do on my own authority, but both of your...requests...fall beyond that purview. I can argue as emphatically as possible, use every political ploy I can conceive...but I still believe I would come up short of the required support." A pause. "Or, I can simply do as you ask...secretly. That would be risky, extremely so. Such an act is certainly sufficient for my rivals to initiate removal proceedings against me...with a considerable chance they would succeed. For most of my life, a good part of me would have welcomed such a result. I could return to my lab, and spend my life in quite research. But we face a terrible danger now, one we may not survive, despite all our best efforts. Political dissension would be the Others' ally now...as would Number Two's ascension to the top leadership post. He is a vain man, greedy and focused far more on his own pursuit of power than on leading the Hegemony through the coming ordeal."

"We have more than a few of those in the Confederation, too. You have my understanding, and my sympathy that you have to deal with such issues. I would help you if I could, if my demands were things I could live without. But they are not. Whatever you have to do, whatever risks are involved, if you want Rim military assistance—and understand, I cannot guarantee that no matter what you do—you will have to find a way."

Akella let out a long exhale. "Very well, Tyler Barron. You have come here at our request, and I can see how much effort it has taken for you to see beyond the understandable bad feelings from the war. I will do what I must, at whatever risk. I believe I can assemble a team of people I can trust to dispatch to *Colossus*. And I will see that the targeting information, and all supporting scanner readings are provided to you. I would order it uploaded to *Dauntless*'s data banks, but there is too much risk of detection, especially with a transmission of that size and duration. I will have data crystals prepared and brought to your shuttle…late tonight. Perhaps you can come up with some reason you must return to your ship, an illness, or perhaps some routine command business. That will offer us some cover, at least."

"Thank you, Akella…I truly mean that. I will not lie and tell you it is easy for me to imagine fighting alongside your people after everything that has happened. But I believe you…I am beginning to trust you. If you knew me better, you'd realize what a slow and rare thing that is for me."

"I feel as though I am beginning to know you as well, Tyler Barron…and also to understand you. Perhaps because, in many ways, I feel we are much alike."

Barron didn't say anything, but he agreed with her statement, more perhaps than he was ready to accept yet.

* * *

"You are young for your post, Lieutenant Simms. Your billet would normally have gone to a lieutenant commander, at least, and possibly a full commander, especially on a flagship like *Dauntless*. You are only here because Anya Fritz recommended you, so we expect that you will show your appreciation through the quality of your work." Atara Travis spoke to the officer, her tone imposing, not exactly hostile, but unrelenting in a way that Travis had long made her own.

Barron and his longtime comrade shared many traits with each other, but Atara had always had a harder edge than he did. She inspired loyalty in her spacers, almost as much as he did, but her approach had always been different, just a bit rougher.

He wondered if that was a natural result of her difficult childhood and her stubborn ascent from the impoverished ghettoes of her homeworld…or something she'd developed to stand out after so many years in his shadow.

Or both. That seemed the likeliest answer.

"Yes, Admiral. Certainly. Commodore Fritz's support is a source of immense pride. And, I will do my best, for you and Admiral Barron. For the Confederation."

Barron almost winced at the blinding earnestness of the youthful officer's response. *Was I ever that young?*

No, I wasn't, came the answer, from someplace deep inside him. Barron had been born into immense privilege and advantage, but he'd shouldered the attendant responsibilities for as long as he could remember.

"I am sure you will do that, Lieutenant." Barron spoke up, partially out of pity for the young officer. Atara seemed like she was ready to ride him hard—not even his trusted aide was immune from the stress building all around them all—and he decided to take a lighter approach. Anybody with Anya Fritz's full-throated support didn't need to be pushed to work hard…or to do his best. No one drove people harder than Fritz.

"There are petabytes of data, Lieutenant, all scanner readings from Hegemony ships facing the new invaders. You will immediately see the…irregularity…of the enemy contacts. We also have the results of Hegemony analysis, and the resulting theory of how to track these vessels with sufficient accuracy to establish fire locks. That method has been demonstrated to be at least moderately effective. Your job, and you can assemble any team you require, regardless of the ranks of the members, is to adapt the Hegemony algorithm to function with our own targeting networks. I don't know if we will become involved in this conflict,

Lieutenant, but I want us to be ready in case we do. Once you've ported the Hegemony routines to our own systems, and confirmed that they work, you will review the raw data in extreme detail. I don't mind borrowing from the Hegemony, Lieutenant, but I wouldn't object to us improving on their work as well...doing them one better, as we used to say back at the Academy. Do you understand what I'm saying?"

"Yes, sir!" The lieutenant still looked a bit intimidated—which seemed natural enough—but he was also enthusiastic, and clearly anxious to begin.

"I want you to get started immediately. If you have any trouble securing the personnel you need, just comm Admiral Travis or myself. This is our number one priority right now. I'm counting on you, Lieutenant. Don't let me down." Barron knew it was a little unfair dumping that on the kid...but he needed the scanner technician to work himself to exhaustion.

"Yes, Admiral!" The officer saluted crisply, and he turned and raced out of the room, looking a bit like he wasn't sure where to start.

"Are you sure about all this, Tyler?" Atara waited until the Simms had left, but then she looked at him with a concerned expression on her face. "I don't doubt these...Others...are a threat, and perhaps to us as well as the Heggies. But to ask the Senate to send the fleet, to dive right in alongside them, like they're trusted allies..." Atara Travis didn't often disagree with Barron, and truth be told, his own view wasn't far from hers. He didn't like the situation any more than she did, and he didn't trust the Hegemony, at least behind his fragile and tentative connection with Akella. But that didn't change reality. The Others *were* dangerous, and it seemed the wildest of wishful thinking to assume they would limit their hostilities to the Hegemony and stop short of the Rim.

"I have seen more of the Others than you have, Atara. I

don't like the situation any more than you do, but what if we'd allowed past incidents to keep us from allying with the Alliance, or with Denisov's people?"

"That's not the same situation, and you know it. I was there when we fought *Invictus*, and it was a bloody fight, one that still gives me nightmares. But it was two ships, on the edge of neutral space. The Hegemony invaded the Rim, occupied our capital."

"Then what about Denisov and his ships? How easy was it to trust a Union officer and his spacers? How many have died in the four wars we fought against them? Yet, if my memory is not faulty, Denisov's arrival pulled our asses out of the fire." Barron looked at Travis, and he reached out, putting his hand on her shoulder. "When was the last time we got to do something because we wanted to, because we were comfortable with it? Do we have a choice here? You've seen enough of the footage to know those ships are bad news. Can we risk facing them at Dannith, or Ulion? Do you think we could stop them at Megara? Or anywhere?"

She was silent for a moment, and finally, she just shook her head and said, "No...I know you're right. It's just hard."

"You bet your ass it's hard. Do you remember anything not being hard?"

"No, I guess not." A short paused, and then changed the subject slightly. "Who are you sending back?"

"Jon Riley." Barron didn't hesitate in his reply. He'd already decided who he was going to send to the Senate to make his case.

Travis looked surprised, for an instant. Then she just smiled and said, "Brilliant. Absolutely brilliant."

Chapter Twenty-Three

Confederation Embassy
Liberte City
Planet Montmirail, Ghassara IV
Union Year 225 (321 AC)

Sandrine Ciara walked down the street, trying to look as calm and unobtrusive as possible. She wore a disguise, a good one, a full-scale professional job, but she didn't fool herself. The AI scanners in the Hall of the People were leading edge. She *might* get past them if she went through the main entrance, but she doubted that chance was more than one in three...and a lot less if the paranoid Villieneuve still had the emergency protocols in place.

Paranoid? You're on your way to try to kill him, so is it really fair to call him paranoid right now?

She thought she saw movement toward her, and she tensed, turning to the side, her combat reflexes kicking into action. But it was nothing. She tried to relax her pose, ignoring the fact that a number of passersby were looking at her.

Do that again, and you might as well just walk up to Sector Nine headquarters and ask them to put you in a cell...

She moved down the street as quickly as she could without drawing further attention to herself. The Hall of the

People was just down the street. She'd decided against a run through the main entrance security, but she knew one or two other ways in that might avoid unwanted scrutiny.

Or, at least would have before Villieneuve got riled up by the coup attempt. There's no telling what changes he's made…

She couldn't be sure the security lapses she knew about were still in place, but it was her best bet…and if she did get in, she'd be better placed to reach the lower levels, where her true destination lay.

That wasn't where she was supposed to be going, at least not as far as Alexander Kerevsky was concerned. The Confed spy had sent her in to try to kill Villieneuve, but he'd intended her to target only the First Citizen, and perhaps his immediate advisors and guards who were present. But that was a fool's game, an effort far too direct, too audacious to succeed. She needed another way, one that rested more in the shadows. She wanted Villieneuve dead…and he would be just as out of the picture if he was killed alone, or along with a few thousand others.

Kerevsky wouldn't approve, she knew that. But as much as she had feelings for the Confed spy—and she did, real ones—she was an agent herself, and her Sector Nine training gave her a greater tolerance for collateral damage than Kerevsky would ever understand. She could take a wild chance, hoping against hope that she somehow got to Villieneuve and managed to kill him at close quarters, and then made good her own escape. Or she could sabotage the reactor under the Hall, obliterating the building—and a few square kilometers of central Liberte City. A lot of people would die, certainly, but if she could kill Villieneuve—and, with any luck more than a few of her potential rivals in the race to fill the power vacuum—she could avoid a renewed war against the Confederation. That was a fair trade for ten or twenty thousand of Liberte City's population. Preventing a future war alone would save millions.

That was the kind of thing the Confeds never

understood. They were fond of platitudes, of refusals to answer questions like, 'would you kill one to save ten?' But there was no question millions would be killed when Villieneuve completed his rebuilding of the fleet and invaded the Confederation. She would prevent that from happening if she secured power, and even if she didn't manage to gain the top position, any replacement for Villieneuve would be more concerned with consolidating power than provoking foreign wars.

She slipped around the corner, resisting the urge to look around her, to check if she was being observed or followed. She slipped to the side, down a small access road leading around to the back of the Hall. She looked along the blank gray masonry wall, her eyes searching for something she remembered. She'd almost given up hope, assumed Villieneuve had dealt with the security breach, when her eyes focused on it.

A small metal access door.

She walked over and pulled on it. It was locked. That wasn't a surprise. But now she faced one of the most dangerous moments in her mission. She knew the access code, at least what it had been, and in a moment, she was going to enter it on the small keypad half-obscured by tall weeds. When she did, one of several things would happen. The door would open, proving that the code was still good, that it hadn't been changed…or leading her into a trap, one triggered by the AI detecting an old and outdated code used for access.

Or nothing would happen. Or Foudre Rouge would come storming around the corner in a matter of second. She wouldn't know until she tried, or perhaps not until after. Until she reached the reactor.

Until she was back out of the Hall and in the safe house.

She paused and took a deep breath, and then she pushed herself forward. She'd gotten this far, but every wasted second was another chance of being detected. She leaned forward, shoving the tall grass aside and placing her hand on the keypad. She hesitated again, and a few seconds later, pushing against the fear, she punched in the code. She watched and waited, a time that seemed like hours, but she knew had been only a second or two. Then, the old door slid open, its old and corroded surface moving slowly, jerkily. But it did open, at least far enough for her to squeeze through.

She dropped down to the floor, her feet landing in a puddle, splashing water all around her. *Good. It's empty, not maintained. Just the way I remember it.*

She walked down the narrow hallway, pausing once or twice to look around, to confirm her memories the best she could. It had been years since she'd been in the sub-basement's largely abandoned corridors. She'd used the eerily quiet place for clandestine meetings she'd wanted to keep private, away from the prying eyes that scoured almost every square centimeter of the massive building.

She moved quickly—even down in the lower level, time wasn't on her side. She knew roughly the way to the reactor, though she had to stop several times and get her bearings. Unlike the empty basement corridors, the reactor *would* have security. Guards—at least two—plus surveillance systems, alarms. Once she got there, and took out the guards, she'd have at best a few minutes to do what she had to do.

And she wouldn't have much more time to escape after. Ideally, she'd give herself an hour or more to get out of the building and far enough away from the blast zone. But that wasn't remotely possible. Her sabotage would set off alarms, no matter how careful she was, and if she left enough time, someone would get down there and prevent the explosion. She could give herself ten minutes, at most…and she was far from sure that was long enough to get out of the kill zone.

But it was her best chance. Her only chance. Kerevsky had to leave in three days, and without her Confederation allies, she knew it was only a matter of time before Villieneuve's hunters caught up to her.

She stopped suddenly, her ears picking up something. Talk. Up ahead and around the corner.

She crept forward slowly, her hand moving around behind her, into the bag she'd hidden under her coat. There was a small pistol inside, and a knife.

She pulled the blade out. She had no idea where the guards would be in the room, and silence was still her ally, if only for a few more seconds.

She moved ahead, reaching the place she remembered, the hole in the wall, surrounded by crumbed masonry. It hadn't changed, not in all the time since she'd been there. She knew what lay beyond, a metal lined corridor, and less than five meters farther along, the entrance to the reactor room.

And the guards. Waiting.

She wasn't overly concerned about the sentries. They were dangerous, of course, but the posting was a dull and sleepy one, and she doubted they were expecting any trouble. If she kept her cool, remembered her training and experience, she could take down one of them, at least, before alerting the other one.

She tried to steel herself for the effort, to regain the confidence and the feeling of preparedness that had been so fleeting the past weeks in hiding. She'd felt more like a terrified animal, running from hunters than the cool and capable agent she was. Now she needed that strength back, she had to wash away the failure of the coup. The reactor sentries weren't from any crack team, but they could kill her easily enough if she gave them a chance.

She moved forward, feeling a familiar energy as she did, one that had been absent for weeks. Her hand gripped the knife tightly, and she continued down the corridor, almost gilding above the smooth metal floor. She took one final breath, slowly, quietly…and then she spun around the corner, moving quickly toward the door.

There *were* two guards, as she'd expected, flanking the doorway to the reactor. She moved up on one, reaching him an instant after he saw her. He started to turn, and his hand dropped to his sidearm. But he was too late. Her arm moved with blinding speed, and the razor-sharp edge of her blade whipped by along his throat. For an instant, he just stood where he was, and then a torrent of blood flowed out from the deep gash she'd left. He dropped to his knees, holding there for a second or two before he fell forward, landing face down on the floor.

But Ciara was already on the move. She'd covered half the distance to the other guard before the man managed to react. His hand was down to his waist, and then up, holding his pistol. Ciara's mind was racing, calculating, updating the situation with each passing fraction of a second. The doubts, the defeat, the fear…they were all gone in that brief instant. Only the stone-cold killer remained.

Her knife was out in front of her, its gleaming silvery alloy partially stained now with a sheen of bright crimson. Her eyes darted down, to her enemy's gun, and then back to his face. He was falling back slightly, trying to bring the weapon to bear, and she made a quick decision. A throat slash was too difficult, too easy to block. And it was probably what he expected. She angled her hand, bringing the point of the knife forward, and her eyes focused on her target. The chest could be difficult. The sternum could deflect a poorly aimed blow, as could the ribs. She'd killed before with blows to the chest, and she knew what to do. It was just a question of getting there before her opponent fired.

She figured she had two chances in three, which all things considered, wasn't too bad.

She held her breath as she lunged the last few centimeters, almost feeling the bullets she knew were coming. The knife was almost there, so close to the guard's chest she couldn't see the space between the two.

Then, she felt it. The weapon stopped for an instant, the point slicing through skin and muscle...and stopping on bone. But just for an instant. She felt the blade slide along the rib, and she pushed it with all the strength she could muster, shoving it to the side, directing it for the soldier's heart. The man was fighting her, his hand up, landing on her, a hard blow across her head that almost distracted her. But she was in a fight to the death, and she was a veteran killer. She hung on, her teeth grinding as she jammed the knife deeper...and the guard's body began to slide down. She shoved the blade one last time, and then she pulled it out hard, a fountain of blood erupting as she did.

The guard fell to the floor, landing with a lifeless thud.

Ciara's eyes darted around, checking for any other enemies. But there was nothing.

She slipped inside the reactor room, moving first to one panel and then to another. She didn't have much time, she knew that. If the surveillance systems hadn't sounded an alert yet, they would soon. She had no idea what reporting schedule the guards had been on, but when they didn't check in, that, too, would trigger an unwelcome intrusion.

She flopped down in one of the control chairs, her eyes scanning the screen in front of her as her fingers moved over the keyboard with blinding quickness. She wasn't supposed to have the control codes for the reactor, of course, not so much because her position hadn't been high enough as she'd never had a need to know. But Sector Nine had trained her well, and she knew all sorts of things she wasn't supposed to know.

She scanned the text scrolling down the screen, watching with her stomach in her throat at each step. Her codes to the outside entry had still been valid, but that was no guarantee her reactor passwords would work. But one after the other, the system accepted them and pushed her onto the next screen. She was pretty sure she could blow the whole reactor, but that would cause an explosion that would level half of Liberte City, likely including her safe house and the Confederation embassy. That option was pure suicide. Besides, if she truly intended to make a play for power after Villieneuve's death, it would help if she'd only killed thousands, and not millions, in her attack.

The ignition systems, on the other hand, used fission reactions, small and controlled…and vastly lower yield than the fusion that powered the entire complex and its defense net. She could trigger an overload in one of those. She wasn't sure what yield the resulting explosion would produce, but she guessed somewhere between ten and thirty kilotons. Enough to obliterate the Hall, and to kill Gaston Villieneuve and any of his closest allies who happened to be present…but with any luck, only those within five hundred or a thousand meters around the government structure would be killed or seriously injured.

The explosion would be a dirty one, especially since she didn't have time to properly shut down the main system, but it was the best she could do.

The radiation would add to the death toll, of course, and the cleanup would be expensive, but that was all incremental as far as she was concerned.

She typed quickly, holding her focus even as every few seconds she thought she heard something. It was just nerves, she knew…but she was also well aware that, eventually, someone *would* come, probably a whole platoon of Foudre Rouge with guns blazing. She knew she had to finish, and get the hell out, but she could only work her way through the security systems so quickly. One mistake could put the whole system into lockdown.

She pressed a series of keys, entering an authorization code, not hers, of course, but that of another highly placed Sector Nine official. She wasn't supposed to have it, but she'd used her…skills…to obtain it some time ago, along with a considerable amount of other useful information.

Finally, everything was ready. She set the countdown to ten minutes. Even as she did it, she told herself it wasn't enough time, that she couldn't get out of the building and far enough away so quickly. But any longer was just asking for someone to discover what she'd done and disarm the sequence. She didn't want to die in nuclear fire running away from the Hall, but she didn't want Villieneuve's thugs hunting her down either…and this was her only real chance to stop that.

She pressed a key, activating the countdown. Her eyes were glued to the screen, watching the first few seconds tick away. Then she typed another code, and locked the system down. Anyone who got there soon enough to realize what she'd done would have to spend two or three minutes, at least, trying to get into the system. That could be the difference of success or failure for her plan.

She leapt up from the seat and moved quickly out into the corridor, tracing her steps back to the old sub-basement. She hadn't brought a chronometer of any kind, so she didn't have an accurate measure of how much time she had left. Just the rough countdown echoing in her head.

She pulled her pistol from her bag, and tossed it aside as she climbed back out onto the small access street. She moved as quickly as she could out into the crowds on the main avenue. As she walked away from the Hall, she couldn't help but look all around her at the people.

People I am about to kill.

She'd rarely been plagued by guilt, even with the many—admittedly terrible—things she'd done, but something nagged at her as she made her escape. It seemed…wrong…to race away without warning the people all around her. But that was out of the question. It would only assure that she, herself, would not escape.

Besides, no one would have believed her anyway.

She couldn't save anyone else…or she wouldn't take the risks to try to save them. Whatever. It didn't matter. The only question that remained was, could she get far enough away in time.

She counted down, knowing her own estimate would get less and less accurate as the explosion approached. When she was close to the end, she would find someplace to hide, some kind of shelter that would provide a level of protection. But when to do that? At one minute? Or was her mental countdown off by more than that?

Ciara had her own sort of courage, different perhaps than that of a warrior in battle, but she'd always been able to keep her cool in dangerous situations, and this one was no exception. She felt as though she might projectile vomit, but she didn't. She just kept pressing forward, her pace gradually increasing, pushing herself as hard as she could.

Counting down as she ran.

* * *

"Wipe them…all of them. And after they're clean, throw them in the furnace. I've already taken care of the truly sensitive information, but there's no sense taking any chance of giving a gift to the Union authorities. They'll be in here thirty seconds after we leave, and they'll tear the place to the foundations looking for intel." Kerevsky hesitated, then he added, "For that matter, I want all these walls opened up and searched, and I wanted detectors run along the exterior. There've been a century of Confederation diplomats here, and who knows what any of those fools hid someplace. Anything like that's probably old and useless now, but we're not taking any chances. If an ambassador seventy years ago stashed a note he wrote to his Montmirailian mistress, I want it found and destroyed. Understood?"

"Yes, your Excellency." Kerevsky was always a bit put off by the form of address of a Confederation ambassador. It had always seemed pompous and out of place in a nation that called itself a republic. Besides, though he bore the full credentials of an ambassador, Kerevsky was really there as a spy.

And a rogue spy at that, one with no real authorization to do anything, who'd nevertheless first helped plan a coup, and then backed an assassination attempt on the Union head of state. Kerevsky had always been a bit of a loose cannon, but he'd never so blatantly exceeded his authority before. He wasn't sure if his feelings for Ciara were to blame, or simply his realization that the Union would always be a deadly threat to the Confederation, at least until something decisive changed all that. Perhaps that had become less tolerable in a time that included threats from coreward.

Decisive...like Villieneuve's death?

He knew the Union leader was insane, and also a genius, but that didn't mean whoever replaced him would be any easier to deal with. Though he couldn't imagine the First Citizen's successor could be much worse.

Still, he couldn't quite piece together how he'd gotten so deeply involved, so far into the machinations against the Union leadership. He was sure he'd covered his tracks, or almost sure. But the fact that the entire diplomatic mission was being expelled strongly suggested that Villieneuve suspected him of involvement. The First Citizen would no doubt have arrested him if he'd had real proof, but not even Villieneuve was likely to commit an act of war without ironclad evidence. Still, Kerevsky knew he was going to face the music when he got back. Gary Holsten would tear him apart, there was no doubt about that. The only question was, would he stop there, or would he issue a report to the Senate...and open the door to formal charges.

Perhaps even for treason. *I could have started a war here, so that might not be pushing things too far...*

His thoughts drifted back to Ciara. He wasn't sure what would happen if she succeeded, if she managed to put a bullet in Gaston Villieneuve's head. Would the word spread quickly? Or would some deputy slam a wall of silence over the whole thing and attempt to seize power himself, before anyone knew the First Citizen was dead?

Then, suddenly, the room shook, and a large panel attached to the far wall came loose and fell with a loud crash. Kerevsky turned and raced into the next room, and as he did, he could hear the thunderous explosion. It sounded like it was coming from just across town, near the Union government complexes.

It didn't make sense. *What could have caused such a massive…*

He stopped cold as his eyes moved toward the large window in the room. Or what had been a window. Now it was just an opening in the wall surrounded by shattered glass. And in the distance, a small, winding tower of smoke and flame, rising up and forming an all too familiar form.

A mushroom cloud.

Chapter Twenty-Four

Planet Calpharon
Sigma Nordlin IV
Year of Renewal 267 (322 AC)

"I know it will be some time, Admiral, until you hear from your government. While I remain hopeful that they will follow your urging and come to our aid, I have just received several disturbing reports." Akella was clearly upset, as visibly shaken as Barron had seen the Hegemony leader. He didn't know what she was about to tell him, but he was pretty sure he wouldn't like it.

"I sent a number of scoutships to try to sneak around the enemy forces and make contact with the inhabited planets we were forced to...abandon. It was foolish, perhaps, and the loss ratio among the ships sent in was horrific. But I just *had* to know."

Barron nodded. He still saw the Hegemony as enemies to an extent, and his sympathies were limited by that fact. But he suspected he would have done the same thing in Akella's place.

"I wanted to determine the occupation conditions, and if possible, get word to the populations that they hadn't been forgotten, that the fight has only just begun."

Yes...you would have done just what she did...

"Were the ships able to get communiques through the enemy occupation forces?"

"There were no enemy occupation forces. The scouts encountered vessels patrolling the enemy lines of communication, and many were destroyed in the resulting engagements. But there were no enemy ships around the occupied planets." Akella paused, clearly struggling with what she was trying to say. "There were no occupied planets, at least none with any enemy forces present. Or any populations left. Nothing but barren wastelands, radioactive graveyards. They bombarded the planets, Tyler. The exterminated the entire populations, at least on the three worlds the scouts were able to reach."

Barron stood still, stunned at what he'd heard. The Hegemony had behaved reasonably well as occupiers, one of the few things that helped him imagine fighting at their side instead of against them. Akella's people had compared well to the Foudre Rouge and Sector Nine. Life under Union occupation was far from pleasant for anyone.

But an enemy that would wipe out entire civilian populations *after* they had surrendered, to no military gain? That was evil on a level he could barely grasp. His mind drifted to the Rim, to all the Confederation planets he'd seen. Cities, expansive valleys filled with farms, billions of men and women working, playing, living.

Until the bombs came. Until death rained down on them all.

His thoughts were vivid, so real he had to remind himself it hadn't yet happened. But it *could* happen...unless the Others were defeated.

"I don't know what to say, Akella. Whatever happened in our past, neither of our people have ever engaged in that level of barbarity." Barron felt the need to comfort her somehow, but he was too experienced a veteran to think anything would lessen her pain. He carried the guilt for thousands of his spacers lost in the various combats they'd fought, men and women for whom he'd been responsible, who'd looked up to him to lead them through. But Akella was mourning *billions* dead, and she was the leader to every one of them, the ultimate authority that had pulled back her forces, declared, no, we will not defend this system this planet. He'd come to know her well enough in his weeks on Calpharon to have a pretty good feeling for how deeply the news had cut into her.

"It is war, Tyler. The realities of war against this enemy. I do not believe they intend to exterminate our entire population. They are here to enslave us, to force us to worship them as gods. At least, that is what the old records suggest. But it is clear now that they are more than prepared to commit genocide on worlds they deem to be inconvenient, or simply not worth the effort." There was a coldness in her voice. Barron could feel her coming to terms with just the kind of fight her people faced.

The fight we will face also…and, if the Senate doesn't send the fleet out here…

The room was silent for some time. Finally, Barron spoke, as much to break the eerie quiet as anything else. "You said '*several* disturbing reports?"

"Yes. We were also able to update our scouting data on the enemy's forces. They appear to be concentrating…and our analysis suggests a likely course."

Barron stood where he was, quiet, listening. But he already knew what she was going to say.

"They're on a direct line to Calpharon. They're coming here."

* * *

"I need to know the status of the scanner upgrades, and I want the absolute truth. Don't massage me, don't give me optimistic reports. Just tell be the hard facts." Barron was standing in his office on *Dauntless*, as much because he'd been too restless to sit since Akella had shared her news. The reports of entire populations being wiped out were horrifying enough, but it was the news that the enemy fleet was massing and heading for Calpharon that really had him on edge. There were more than ten billion people on the Hegemony capital. What would they face if the enemy reached the system?

He didn't know what the Hegemony forces would do, but he was pretty sure they'd offer battle somewhere before the enemy reached their capital. That's what he would have done in their place. And that fight was likely to happen well before he could hope for a response to his dispatches.

"One-third of the systems have been installed, Admiral." Atara Travis remained silent as Jarrod Simms gave his report to Barron. The young lieutenant had been given a big job, and a crucially important one, and he seemed to be handling it well...including perhaps the most daunting aspect of all. Standing in front of the legendary Admiral Barron and reporting in detail...and keep his shit together as he did.

"Lieutenant, I believe the Hegemony fleet will be setting out from Calpharon soon. This is not to leave the room, but the enemy forces are currently massing and heading this way. The Hegemony commanders don't discuss their strategy with me, but if I was in charge, I'd mount a defense somewhere along the enemy advance...well before they reach the capital." Barron paused for a moment. That's exactly what he'd done when the Hegemony fleet was approaching Megara. It had been his best effort, but it hadn't saved the Confederation's capital. He wasn't sure he believed the Hegemony forces would fare any better. But he knew they had to try.

"I want you to be ready to complete your work on the move. I know that will complicate things, but if the Hegemony high command consents, our fleet will move out with theirs. We are not authorized to conduct combat operations under our current rules of engagement, but we are here to gather information, and a chance to see the Hegemony and their enemy in battle is something we can't pass up. We are heavily reliant on secondhand information right now, and we need some direct observation to confirm just how great a threat we may face."

Simms held Barron's gaze, no small feat for an officer so young standing just half a meter from the great admiral. For an instant, uncertainty forced its way to his face. Barron ignored it. He'd put the officer in a spot, and he knew full well what he was asking was difficult, at least, if not almost impossible. He'd become used to Anya Fritz delivering on those impossible tasks for him, but it was no insult to say an officer wasn't Fritz.

No one was Anya Fritz...except Anya Fritz. The Confederation had never before seen an engineer like her, and Barron doubted very much it would soon see one again.

"Yes, Admiral. I will...make it work."

Barron found he believed the lieutenant's words, even though it was clear the officer wasn't quite sure *how* he'd deliver on his promise. He wasn't Anya Fritz, perhaps, but there was a similarity Barron recognized. And respected.

"Very well, Lieutenant. Of course, you will have access to any resource you require. Admiral Travis will make sure the fleet is at your disposal...and if you need anything we don't have, something we will have to request from the Hegemony authorities, you are to come directly to me. My aides will be advised you have immediate access to me, day or night.

"Yes, Admiral!" Simms hesitated for a few seconds, then he saluted and turned sharply, marching out the door to carry out his orders.

"Were we ever that young?" Barron waited until the door closed, and then he turned toward Travis.

"I wasn't...I'm not sure about you." Travis smiled. It was a lighthearted response, but one based in truth. Atara Travis came from a place much like Andi had, and she'd scraped and fought to survive from childhood. It sometimes seemed odd to Barron, the ultimate child of privilege—and obligation as well—that two of the people closest to him in the universe, his wife and his best friend, would come from such opposite backgrounds as his own. He tried to understand how difficult it had been to endure such deprivation, and he'd wondered frequently if either Andi or Atara had any real idea how difficult it had been for him, amid wealth and admiration, to shoulder the burdens, the expectations, not only of parents and family, but literally of the Confederation's billions. Barron had carried that weight since childhood, and he'd never known a moment's respite from it.

"He can handle it, Tyler. He knows his stuff...and he's a leader, too, at least one in the making. I've watched him with his teams. He drives them hard, but he's a little more...diplomatic...than Anya tends to be. At least as far as I've seen, they make up fewer nasty names to call him."

Barron laughed. Anya Fritz routinely drove herself to the point of utter exhaustion, and she expected the same from those working with her. Her almost pathological drive was in an emergency, but she didn't slack off in more routine situations...and that created a strange combination of awe and resentment in her subordinates.

"I believe he can handle it, too. Not that we'll need those scanners. We have no authority to engage in combat operations. All we can do is hang back at the transit point and watch...and run before any enemy can close on us."

Travis stared back, with a look that said something along the lines of, "You are the least likely person I've ever known to sit back and watch." But she remained silent.

"Still, let's make sure the fleet is at one hundred percent. I haven't heard anything official, but my guess is the Hegemony forces will be leaving soon, and since they're trying to get us into this fight, I doubt I'll have difficultly getting permission to go along. I want you to doublecheck everything yourself, Atara. We've got good people on this fleet, but this is a danger like none we've seen before, and we're as far from home as any Confederation force has ventured. I'll feel better knowing you're looking over everybody's shoulders."

"I'll see to it, Ty." Travis nodded, and she stood there with her commander—and her friend—a few seconds longer. Then, she left, as Simms had a few moments before, leaving Barron alone with his thoughts.

Barron stood where he was, and the silence and the removal of distractions allowed his thoughts to flow. He didn't want to be there. He wanted to be home, with Andi. He'd long been a creature of duty, but even his disciplined mind rebelled against the prospect of yet another war. He'd done his part, and then some, and his spacers had as well. Any fair assessment would state that they deserved to return to families and friends, to lives where they could wake up free of the stress of battle, of the ever-present fear of death.

But the universe wasn't fair. And Barron knew what was at stake, the deadly dangers facing not only his spacers, but those family members and loved ones as well. He lacked the authority he needed, and he had only had a contingent of the fleet with him. As decisive as he usually was, he had no idea what to do. It was an easy decision to follow the Hegemony forces, to get a firsthand look at the mysterious new enemy. But what would he do when he got there? What *could* he do?

He'd ventured coreward on the mission still mostly consumed by hatred for the Hegemony—and, as she stood there, he still carried a healthy pile of resentments—but his thoughts were more complex than they had been. Certainly, he'd seen admirable attributes in some of the Hegemony officials, Akella, of course, but also Chronos and Ilius, who'd sat in their command chairs facing him in so many battles. He knew they'd all been complicit in the aggression against the Rim...and yet, now he was beginning to know them as individuals. As people.

His thoughts were complicated, or they would have been if the situation had been normal. Under most circumstances, he might have learned to forgive and to accept the Hegemony as a neighbor, and perhaps one day, even an ally. But the situation was not normal. The clear threat of the Others made things much simpler for him, if more difficult to accept.

Though not, perhaps for the Senate...

He was concerned about the delay the long trip back to Megara would take, and the time the Senate would waste dickering and debating. He was worried about how long it would take to mass the fleet and outfit it for such a long journey.

But most of all, he was worried the Senate would refuse to commit additional forces, and deny his request to authorize intervention with the ships he had on hand. He was afraid they would delay and waste time until Confederation worlds were being bombed out of existence, just like the coreward Hegemony planets had been. It would be too late by then. The Hegemony, the most powerful of all the nations facing the Others would be defeated, and the Rim would stand alone.

We can't let that happen...

Chapter Twenty-Five

Confederation Naval HQ
Troyus City
Megara, Olyus III
Year 322 AC

"Jon, I am delighted to see you...though surprised. What are you doing back here? The fleet has not returned, has it? I've heard nothing to that effect." Prescott Riley was a Senator of middling seniority and power. He'd sent his son to the Naval Academy thinking a uniform and a few decorations—easily enough to arrange without actually subjecting the boy to any real danger—would serve well when it came time for the son to take the father's place in the halls of power. But the whole plan had backfired. Jon had bought into the navy mantra hook, line, and sinker, and worse, he'd ended up serving under Tyler Barron. The navy's famous admiral was an effective officer, if not a military genius, but he showed less respect to the Senate than might have been expected. And now the fifth Riley in line to represent Ventura in the Confederation's esteemed governing body showed no signs of any interest in politics, and often spoke recklessly of his intentions to pursue his naval career indefinitely.

"The admiral entrusted me with a message, father, one of grave importance."

"A message to the Senate?"

"Yes, sir…among others."

"Others?"

"Yes. He included dispatches for Minister Holsten and Admiral Winters as well…and also a private message to his wife."

"He entrusted all those to you? He must have great faith in your abilities and trustworthiness. That is a source of satisfaction and pride to me, Jon." The Senator paused. "I think it best that I have a look at those before they are delivered, however. It is always wise to avoid any surprises while the Senate is considering the admiral's proposals."

"They have already been delivered, Father. I sent officers to hand them directly to the recipients…just as the admiral ordered.

Prescott Riley felt a rumble inside, the roiling anger he'd spent a lifetime learning to control. Tyler Barron was a frustrating man to deal with…though as he considered the admiral's choice of his son as a messenger, his thoughts began to take shape. *No, this isn't a challenge to me. He's hoping I will side with him on…whatever is in these communiques.*

"You can give me the Senate dispatch now, Son."

The young officer hesitated.

"I will take that communiqué, Jon."

"Father, I believe my duty is to present it to the Senate body while it is in session."

Prescott Riley barely held back a wince at his son's almost unbearable naivety. His own father had educated him well in the political machinations that were the family's stock and trade. He had no idea where he'd gone wrong.

"Give that dispatch to me right now, son. Admiral Barron sent you here with it because he is expecting me to help him get…whatever it is he wants. Now, I can't do that unless I know what that is, can I?" He glared at his son with withering intensity. "Now!"

The officer stood still, looking for a moment as though he might defy his father. But he'd never been able to stand up to Prescott Riley's withering intensity, and after perhaps half a minute—enough time that he could tell himself he had resisted—he handed over the encrypted data chip.

The Senator knew his son was beating himself up, allowing self-recrimination to run wild over his inability to stand up to his father.

He wondered if Jon would ever realize he'd done exactly what Tyler Barron had wanted.

* * *

"Lieutenant, I need to speak with Commodore Eaton at once. Also, Fleet Captains Carruthers and Belvidere. They are all to report to my quarters as quickly as possible." He'd almost said his office, but he preferred the greater privacy of his personal suite. Tyler Barron's message hadn't directly requested anything of him, but he was comfortable enough interpreting the indirect language the two had so often exchanged.

"Yes, Admiral. At once." The officer's voice was sharp and crisp on the comm unit. Winters, like his friend and comrade, Tyler Barron, chose his people well, sub-commanders and aides alike.

He turned and looked at the screen. He'd set up the portable unit he always kept tucked away in a storage locker. His main comm unit was supposedly secure, though his status as naval second-in-command carried with it the feuding realities of top of the line security on his systems...and a lot of people who wanted to spy on his comm and data. Gary Holsten, at the very least, could tap into his main comm unit. That wasn't a problem, at least not most of the time. The head of Confederation Intelligence was an ally, and even if it angered Winters, Holsten's knowledge of his secret communiques was unlikely to cause harm.

But what one man could do, another could copy. He'd become accustomed to thinking of the Senators and their cronies as fools and imbeciles, but he knew that wasn't the case. Many of them were gifted in their own ways, and more than a few maintained staffs that could almost match the capabilities of Holsten's spies, especially when wading in the gray areas that powered most political careers.

Better to use the portable unit. It wasn't connected to anything else, and someone would have to gain physical access to tap into it. And, considering Winters's attitude and the orders he'd given to the guards that watched his door day and night, anyone trying that was likely to end up getting shot.

He slipped the data chip into the unit, and he sat down, his eyes focused on the screen. Barron's face appeared, and after a perfunctory greeting, the navy's C in C got right down to it.

Winters listened, and with each word he became more convinced. It tore at his insides to think of fighting alongside the Hegemony. His resentment toward the now-former enemy and their Masters was profound, and he doubted he could ever get past it. *Not after the losses we suffered…*

But reality had a way of asserting itself, and often brutal way. For all his hatred, he didn't deny that the Hegemony fleet was powerful, that their warriors were brave and well-trained. Any enemy that defeated them would be the direst threat to the Rim…and Winters wasn't the kind to believe that a hostile invader would stop after defeating one adversary. If the Hegemony fell, the Rim would be fighting for its life. He didn't have the slightest doubt about that.

And that meant helping the Hegemony, like it or not.

He watched the footage Barron had included, but as grim and convincing as it was, it hadn't been necessary. All

Winters needed was Tyler Barron's declaration that the new enemy was a danger. He was already thinking about force rosters and fleet deployments, deciding where to draw the ships to form the expeditionary force Barron stopped short of specifically requesting...but no doubt expected.

But there would be one battle first, one as fierce and dangerous as other, at least in its own way. One that would take place on the floor of the Senate.

The politicians had a way of waiting, of ignoring threats too long and then expecting their spacers and soldiers to bail them out. The Senators would argue the points, maneuver for position, prevaricate endlessly...until it was too late. Too late, at least, to help the Hegemony.

Clint Winters knew one thing for certain, a decision that formed in his head, and then slammed into place like a heavy metal door.

He was going to answer Barron's call, and he was going to bring the fleet with him. Even if he had to march a battalion of Marines into the Senate Compound to make it happen.

* * *

Gary Holsten sat and watched Tyler Barron's communiqué for the third time. He was usually someone who got the meaning from something on a first try. But Barron had clearly been concerned his messages might be intercepted, and he'd chosen his words carefully. It wasn't the first time Holsten had been compelled to interpret the true meaning in a message, but he'd realized almost instantly that this one was critically important. Worth all the extra care he could give it.

Tyler Barron was convinced. The Others, as the Hegemony somewhat mysteriously called this new enemy, were a threat to the Rim. A deadly threat.

There weren't many people whose opinions Holsten

believed immediately, without evidence, or his own analysis, but Tyler Barron was a member of that exclusive club. Barron had been on the front lines of the war with the Hegemony. He'd seen his spacers killed in vast numbers. He'd lost friends, too, longtime comrades like Sara Eaton. It had to be killing Barron somewhere deep inside to urge the Confederation authorities to intervene, to join forces with their recent enemy. And that's *exactly* what Barron was doing in the message, even if took a bit of interpretation to see it.

Barron's lack of directness—and the admiral was normally one of the most straightforward people the spymaster had ever known—meant only one thing. Barron was concerned about the Senate. There weren't many worlds in the Confederation clamoring for another war, of course, nor for the ruinous taxation that paid for it. The politicians would be extremely reluctant to vote for any commitment to a new conflict so soon after the truce with the Hegemony. He didn't even want to think about how the Senators would react to a request that they not only support a new war far from home, but that they do it to aid the hated Hegemony, still the enemy in the minds of most Confederation citizens.

They don't realize, it's also the last thing Tyler Barron wants to do. If he's suggesting it—and he is—it's a damned certainty there's no other choice. The situation coreward *had* to be critical, and the threat one that loomed over the Rim as well as the Hegemony.

Holsten didn't hesitate, didn't even think about it. Barron's word was enough for him. His contributions on the battlefront would be minimal. He didn't know anything about this new enemy, and he certainly didn't have intelligence assets placed to provide any useful information.

Except in the Senate. That was where he could help. Barron needed votes, he needed authorization to commit his forces…and for the rest of the fleet to be mobilized and sent to his aid.

That won't be easy...

But nothing worthwhile was easy.

Holsten turned toward his main workstation and began typing. It was time to pull up his Black Files again...all the dirt he had on the men and women of the Senate, the deepest and darkest secrets he'd gathered on the rogues and scoundrels who ran the Confederation.

It was time to use all of that. Time to speak in a language corrupt politicians understood.

Threats.

* * *

Andi stared at the screen, tears pouring down her cheeks. Tyler's message to her had been sweet, loving, and full of his best efforts to reassure her. And then he'd told her what was happening.

Another war.

She tried not to get ahead of herself. The Confederation wasn't at war again, not yet. But she was too experienced, too much a veteran to give credence to baseless optimism. Tyler had not gone coreward to find an excuse to aid the Hegemony. To the contrary, she was utterly certain he would have loved nothing more than watching the Confederation's recent enemy fall before some unstoppable foe. As long as he believed that force would stop there, that it would not continue on to the Rim.

Clearly, he *did* believe the Hegemony's enemy was a threat to the Confederation, and she trusted him enough to take his word as fact.

She'd had a kneejerk reaction, and she'd almost fired up the comm to call the shipyard and tell them to get *Pegasus* ready to go. Every fiber of her being cried out to her to go to Tyler, to stand at his side, to fight next to the only man she had ever loved.

Then reality struck hard. It wasn't possible. Travel

through transit points was dangerous to developing children, and she was past the point that allowed interstellar travel. She didn't have many choices just then. Staying behind, sitting and waiting...for news of victory or defeat. For that fateful communiqué that told her Tyler Barron's luck in battle had run out, that he'd been killed somewhere, almost unimaginably far from home. It was inconceivable for her to stay where she was, but anything else risked her child. Tyler's child. She could have disregarded any danger to herself to go to his side. But she couldn't risk their baby.

Her head pounded, and she put her face forward, cradling it in her hands. She was frustrated, scared...heartbroken. She was no fool, though sometimes she wondered if life as one wouldn't sometimes be easier.

She knew what the situation meant. Tyler was already there, hundreds of lightyears coreward, facing a deadly new danger. If the Senate did as he asked, if it committed the Confederation to a new war, sent the fleet to the front lines, it would be years before Tyler returned to Megara...if he ever did.

For an instant, against all logic, she hoped the Senate would refuse. But the solace only lasted a few seconds. *No,* she realized, *that would be worse...*

She knew Tyler too well. If he believed the enemy was a threat to the Rim, he would act, with whatever he had. And without the rest of the fleet, he would have only the task force he'd led to the Hegemony capital. It was a powerful force by any measure, save by comparison to the entire fleet. The thought of him fighting with such limited resources, facing an even greater chance of failure...of death...was too much.

There *had* to be something she could do, some way to help him.

But there wasn't. There was nothing at all.

She sat still, unmoving, and she lost all track of time. Then, the frustration overwhelmed her. She had no options, no way to help.

So, she did something she almost never did, something she would have ridiculed others for doing.

She sat there, and she cried.

Chapter Twenty-Six

Planet Calpharon
Sigma Nordlin IV
Year of Renewal 267 (322 AC)

"Chronos...I just wanted to say..." Akella's words, soft when she'd started, slipped into total silence.

"I know, Akella...I know." Chronos knew what she was trying to say, and he knew how difficult it was. The Hegemony was a society based on individualism above all things. Men and women could be friends, of course, or comrades, but each member of the ordered society, and especially the Masters at the top, were expected to exist on their own. They had duties, and all shared a stake in the sacred obligation to shepherd humanity, to guide it away from another decline—or pull it from the continued slide, depending on the theories to which one subscribed. But relationships were limited, based on shared interests or obligations, or on mutually satisfactory recreational sex. But mating decisions were expected to be purely rational, and Hegemony society had no equivalent of the pair bonding so common in other cultures.

Akella had conceived her first child with Thantor, a man she'd never much liked, and one who had become her greatest rival. But the pressure for the first and second highest rated human beings in the Hegemony to combine their DNA had been irresistible.

"I feel the same." It was as much as he would say, as much as he *could* say. He knew he'd allowed his affection for Akella to progress beyond what was allowed, especially for two top ten ranked Masters…and he was almost certain she shared his feelings. He didn't know what that meant, long term. If there even was a long term. But there was no time for it now, and no place for the controversy that would erupt if anyone else found out about it. He'd been able to disguise his visits to see Akella as trips to see the child the two of them shared, and that would have to hold for the time being.

"Be careful out there." Chronos could see from her expression, she felt foolish even as the words came out. They both knew the Hegemony was fighting for survival. There was no room for caution, no sacrifice too great to make in the pursuit of victory. Chronos had never been one to leave for war feeling he wouldn't return, but as he stood there and let his thoughts drift forward, there was only darkness. But he needed something better than that to tell Akella. If the words he was about to speak were to be the last between them, he would say something she could bear to remember, and not just warnings of grim darkness.

"Take care of yourself, Akella. Watch the Council. Without me here, you're one ally down…and Thantor is a snake. You're smarter than he is, but don't take your eyes off of him. Not for a second."

"I won't. I know what Thantor is."

He leaned forward and kissed her. He hadn't intended to do it, but his impulses took control…and he could feel her responding, her arms slipping around his back. He couldn't do anything so primitive as tell her he loved her, that they would be together when—if—he returned. He knew that wasn't possible, not for them. But for a few seconds, perhaps half a minute, he cast aside the obligations of a

Hegemony Master, the concerns of the supreme military commander. For those fleeting seconds, he felt only what he wanted to feel.

Then, he pulled slowly back, his eyes locked with hers for an instant, one last bit of silent communication. Then he turned slowly, and he was gone.

Off to face the Others…and, very likely, to his own death.

* * *

"All ships report ready, Admiral. The fleet is prepared to depart on your command."

Barron glanced over at Travis, acknowledging her report with a nod. His ships were ready, the morale of his crews better than he could possibly have expected. He knew his deeds had won him some of that, the respect and confidence of his spacers, and his grandfather's exploits contributed as well, the family name that carried so much weight with the Confederation's military.

It was also ignorance, he knew. The rank and file of the fleet no doubt seethed with resentment and anger toward the Hegemony, but they hadn't seen the footage he and the senior officers had, the scanner data showing the Others' vessels cutting through the Hegemony ships like cordwood. The vessels that had so battered their own ships, that had seemed so invincible when they had faced them in desperate combat. Barron didn't like hiding things from his crews, but his people were far from home and no doubt confused about why they had come so far into what they still regarded as enemy territory. He didn't need to test the limits of their endurance, not until there was no choice.

"Admiral, I have Commander Chronos on your line."

"Put him through." Barron tapped the side of his headset. "Commander."

"Admiral Barron, I wish to thank you for your decision

to join our forces in Pharsalon. Even if you are barred from combat, it will only serve to reinforce your conviction that we do indeed face a mutual and deadly adversary."

"That is my belief, Commander. I have already requested that my government authorize my forces to engage the Others, and that reinforcements be sent at once. While I am hopeful the Senate will heed my warning…" A lie, or close to it. Barron rarely expected anything but grief from the politicians. "…it can only help if I am able to send additional evidence, this time collected by my own people." Barron felt a brief concern about his words. He hadn't intended to suggest that *he* still doubted the Hegemony-provided data. But he suspected Chronos understood. He imagined his Hegemony counterpart would feel much the same about the Senate as he did, and completely understand the difficulties Barron faced dealing with them.

"I fear you will see more than you could wish for, Admiral. All reports suggest the enemy forces have massed and that a large fleet is advancing on Pharsalon even now. We should arrive before them, with luck, but not by long. You will very likely get a firsthand view of the enemy's combat power…as will I. This will be my first time facing the them myself."

"Good fortune to you, Commander Chronos. That is what my people wish to each other on the eve of battle."

"Good fortune to you as well, Admiral, in this campaign, and in whatever follows."

Barron cut the line. He was beginning to respect Chronos, even to like the Hegemony commander…and part of what lived inside hated himself for it, just as it did for his growing—friendship was the only word that came to mind—with Akella.

"Admiral Travis, our rules of engagement require us to avoid contact with the enemy, but our mission is to gather as much information as possible. So, while we will not be joining the Hegemony forces in their fight, I want every vessel ready for action at all times. That means rotating duty squadrons on alert, all systems maintained for combat operations, and scanners on full power at all times."

"Yes, Admiral. Understood."

Barron almost laughed. His order was for the benefit of the officers on the bridge. He and Atara had already discussed all of that, and she'd issued the necessary orders. If anything, his second in command was more hawkish than he was. In an odd contradiction, Atara both retained more animosity toward the Hegemony and exhibited more drive to engage the new enemy as well. She'd never been one for half-measures.

The fleet was ready...for whatever happened in the coming days.

But that readiness was largely wasted. Barron's rules of engagement shackled him, prevented him from intervening. He knew what he could do, and he was coldly aware of how inadequate it was.

Hold back and watch...and if the enemy approached, to run. The thought of fleeing sickened him, and if a small part of him still felt the Hegemony was only getting what it deserved, it went against everything that made him who he was to run and leave others to their doom.

He wasn't sure how he'd do it when the need came, which it almost certainly would. But he had a little time to find a way, to dig up the resolve to go against his every impulse and instinct.

* * *

"We're operating under restrictions that limit the admiral's options should he encounter any...enemy ships." Stockton had been fishing around for a way to refer to the Others. They weren't the Confederation's enemy, at least not officially, not yet. And though he knew the truce had been signed and ratified by all nations involved in the recent war, his instinct was still to think of the Hegemony as 'the enemy.' "That is a reality Admiral Barron will have to deal with, but for us it is far simpler. All we have to do is follow whatever orders he gives us. That brings me to my point. We must be ready to do whatever we are ordered to do, up to and including defending the fleet against an enemy about which we know almost nothing. That means full wartime footing, maximum patrols, exercises whenever the fleet stops or maintains constant thrust levels long enough. I know you've just gotten used to the idea of peace, but from the looks of things, you can forget that right now. I've let you all loosen up a little, figured you'd earned it after the last six years. But that's officially over right now, so consider my foot back on all of your necks, effective immediately."

Stockton was standing on *Dauntless*'s flight deck, addressing the flagship's combined fighter wing. Behind the pilots, in serried ranks, lay their fighters, neat and clean and perfectly aligned in parallel rows. The deck, and the Lightning fighters stowed down its length, looked better than he could remember, cleaner and neater than they ever had during the war. The pilots, and their flight crews, had enjoyed a year without combats, without klaxons sounding and scramble orders reverberating from the comm speakers down in fighter country. The maintenance crews had used that free time to reorder their domain, and the flight deck looked almost like new.

The pilots, to Stockton's dismay, if not his surprise—*you would have done no differently when you were their age*—had gone the other way. The razor-sharp instrument he'd created had dulled a bit, and it needed to be re-honed, restored to the deadly weapon of war it had been not long ago.

Stockton stared out at the eighty-six officers assembled, seventy-four fighter jocks and a dozen shuttle pilots. But even as his eyes panned over them, he knew the squadrons on the other battleships were similarly formed up, watching on their comm displays as the fleet's flight commander handed down the new realities. The message left no room for doubt, and no one who had come up under Stockton's leadership—almost everyone present—had the slightest doubt he *meant what he said*. They'd heard stories, of course, of the wild young pilot, with a loose interpretation of what following orders meant. They'd probably even heard a few of the old veterans, the handful who'd survived so many years of war, tell stories…of desperate fights in the depths of space, and poker games in the officer's clubs of the fleet. But all the younger pilots knew was the grim legend they saw before them, a man forged by loss and pain from the clay of that wild and talented young pilot into the hardened alloy of an admiral who had led the squadrons to victory over the Hegemony invaders.

Stockton stood for a moment, silent, mildly amused at the collective, as a partially restrained groan went up from *Dauntless*'s pilots. They'd gotten used to fewer flight hours and less intense discipline, and they were beginning to realize that was all over. Stockton didn't know if his pilots were going to war again. That wasn't his call. It was his job to make sure they were ready, ready for whatever Admiral Barron needed of them.

And nothing was going to stand in the way of that.

Nothing that didn't want to be obliterated by his unstoppable stubbornness and determination.

* * *

Ilius sat in his Sanctum, relishing the silence, and even more, the solitude. He'd always enjoyed his time alone, and he often sat for hours, thinking, meditating. But this was different. It wasn't the allure of silent hours of unobstructed thought that had pulled him from the bridge into his private domain. He wasn't escaping noise or the beehive of activity of the ship's main control center. He was hiding.

Ilius had long prided himself on his honesty, above all

with himself. He'd always been able to keenly analyze his own weaknesses and work to improve on them. It had been some years into his adulthood before he'd realized just how rare a trait that was. But now, it was failing him. He was in his Sanctum because he was afraid…and he was trying to hide that from his staff and his crew.

Ilius was a combat veteran, with a flawless record. He'd been decorated for both skill and bravery multiple times, and he was a Master of high—if not Council level—rating. But since he'd returned from his second encounter with the Others, something had been different. The grim and relentless power that drove him seemed stalled, and every thought of engaging the enemy again—what would be his third encounter with the Others—shook him ever more deeply. He'd managed to disguise it while he was on the bridge, but he'd come back to the Sanctum to focus, to meditate and open the depths of his mind. To regain his power over the fear that was gradually taking control of him.

He'd always considered himself a creature of logic, of rational thought, and that had carried him through the many dangers he'd faced in his military career. But there was something…different…about the Others, something that overcame his reason, that reached down to a place deep inside, where his darkest fears lived. He was determined to drive the force from within him, to regain his cold and analytical view of things.

The Others are only an enemy, like many you have fought. Stronger, perhaps, more advanced. But only an enemy, nevertheless.

He continued the mantra, in almost silent speech as well as thought, repeating it again and again, willing his mind to accept his reassertion of control. He pushed away the doubts, though they quickly returned, as some enemy throwing itself at his defenses.

You are above this. You control your emotions, your thoughts…your fear. This is the fight you were born for, the battle you have been training to fight all your life. You will not be defeated by fear, crushed before the final fight even begins.

He believed all that he was telling himself, some of the time. And then the doubts and terror renewed their seemingly relentless assaults.

Chapter Twenty-Seven

Senate Compound
Troyus City
Megara, Olyus III
Year 322 AC

"With all due respect to our esteemed Admiral Barron, I strongly urge caution on any action of this sort. It has been barely a year since we signed the truce ending the war with the Hegemony, and the admiral would now have us rush to their aid? Not just provide financial support or limited military intervention, but to mobilize the entire fleet, to send it dozens of jumps from Confederation territory to the barely known coreward depths? Tyler Barron is a hero of the Confederation, and no one can take that from him. But he is not a diplomat, and he does not have the experience to negotiate alliances with former enemies. I move that we send a blue ribbon task force to Calpharon to examine the situation firsthand, and to negotiate directly with the Hegemony leaders before reporting back to this body."

Kettle Vaughn was the leader of the Greens, one of the two political parties dominating politics on the worlds of the Iron Belt. The Greens, and their counterparts, the Reds, agreed almost universally in their support for strong industrial policy...and on virtually nothing else.

"With all due respect to my esteemed colleague..." Cyn Avaria stood up and glared across the Senate floor at Vaughn. Avaria was the leader of the Reds, the longtime controlling party in the Iron Belt, but currently the Opposition from those industrial powerhouse worlds by the razor slim margin of a single seat. "...it is not only foolish and ignorant, but also an astonishing display of ingratitude to so easily disregard the admiral's warning and his requests. No one wants war, of course, but few citizens have worked and fought and bled as much to protect the Confederation as Tyler Barron has. I demand we debate the merits of his request here and now and not simply defer the matter to a group of appointees chosen from Senator Vaughn's cronies."

The Senate erupted into shouts and sharp arguments, back and forth between individuals and small groups. Andi looked on, watching, getting angrier with every passing moment. She could feel Gary Holsten's hand on her arm, his grip tightening. Next to Tyler, and of course her old crew from *Pegasus*, no one knew her better than the Confederation spymaster...or had a better read on when she was about to lose her temper.

She'd had to tell Holsten about the pregnancy, and now that she'd ventured out in public, showing beyond her ability to hide it, there was little doubt the word would spread. Andi had spent her life in the shadows, prowling around the Badlands and selling her wares mostly in black markets hidden in dingy rooms behind taverns and stores that served as fronts. Her contacts and associates in those days had been even more averse to publicity than she was.

That had all changed. She'd gathered considerable fame herself in recent years, courtesy of her exploits, but her marriage to the Confederation's greatest hero had thrust her into a level of scrutiny that made her skin crawl. She'd have walked into hell if that was the only way to stay by Tyler's side, and standing along the gallery over the Senate floor, that's about where she felt like she was.

Andi wasn't sure who made her angrier, Vaughn arguing that Barron was a fool or a liar, and not to be believed when he warned about the threat he'd discovered, or Avaria, playing the role of his ally, when she was more concerned about feeding fresh military orders to the idled factories all around the Belt and enriching the already grotesquely wealthy oligarchs who backed—and ran—the Red party.

"What are we going to do, Gary? I don't care what these fools say, we've got to get help to Tyler. If he says there's a threat, I believe him. We can't just leave him out there with no support."

"I believe him, too, Andi, but if you mean what I think you mean, the Senate Compound is absolutely worst place to discuss it. Let's wait and see. The Senate is far from dependable, but Tyler and the navy do have allies down there, and there are others who will want to assume the role of defenders of the Confederation. Tyler is a hero. His name is known everywhere, from Megara to the dustiest mining colony on the Fringe. If they do not vote to send the fleet, we have options…some of them far less extreme than others. I know you're worried about him, Andi, and your…condition…isn't helping your nerves. But we can't rush this. The last thing Tyler would want was for us to try to…" He looked around and then lowered his voice. "…do what you're thinking. At least not while we have other options."

Andi knew Holsten was right, at least about what Tyler would want. In spite of all he'd seen, the corruption, the pure foulness of the Confederation's government so often displayed, he remained, at heart, a believer. He'd been forced to challenge the Senate before, to take things to the verge of armed mutiny. But he bore terrible guilt for those actions, and he'd tried every way possible to avoid a repeat of anything of the sort.

Andi felt differently. Completely. She had no respect for

the Senate, none whatsoever, nor, for that matter, any segment of the government. She'd made payoffs, bought her way out of inspections and out of trouble, seen the putrid underside of the whole creaking machine. She was prepared to line every Senator against a wall if that's what it took to help Tyler...and she was ready to bet she could find the Marines ready to do it. All she'd have to do was show them Tyler's message...and maybe add a few tears.

"We'll talk later in more detail, but remember, I have some influence in the chamber. My files are a bit thinner than they once were, perhaps, but there are quite a number of things some of our esteemed Senators would prefer remained under a Top Secret ban. Such things have a way of leaking sometimes, especially when people are...uncooperative." Holsten's voice sounded calm and pleasant, but Andi could hear the sinister tone, hidden to most, but clear to her ears.

And she loved every bit of it.

* * *

"Fleet exercises? By whose command?"

"By *my* command, Captain. Do you have a problem with that?" Clint Winters voice, his very tone defied anyone to answer that question in the affirmative.

"No, Admiral...of course not. It's just that, well, so soon after the war. I just thought..."

"You thought the lesson of the conflict we just fought— and barely survived—was to allow our forces' readiness to atrophy?"

"No, Admiral, of course not. But we still have a large number of people on extended leave, and..."

"All leaves are canceled, Captain. Effective immediately. We may be at peace again, but the navy is still a military organization, and discipline is paramount. You will issue the orders I have given you, and you will personally see that all personnel on leave are recalled to their posts without further delay. Or I will find someone else to do it. Your chief aide, perhaps."

"That will not be necessary, Admiral." A pause. "But this list of ships, it's almost eighty percent of the entire fleet. Are you sure it is wise to commit such a large percentage of our available strength to wargames? We'll be pulling forces in from everywhere, even the units stationed to defend *Colossus*."

"Do you think I would have ordered it if I didn't believe it was wise? Do you think I am a fool, Captain?"

"No, Admiral, certainly not. I will see to this at once. But, at the very least, we will need Senatorial approval to redeploy the new Home Fleet units to…Dannith? The games are to be held around Dannith? It would be much easier to assemble the forces someplace closer to the Core, or even the Iron Belt."

"Do I seem like 'ease' is my primary consideration, Captain? Perhaps the decay is worse than I thought. Where did the Hegemony come from? Where is our next conflict likely to arise? We live in a changed reality now, with billions of humans living far coreward, where we long believed no one had survived. What location could be better for military preparation exercises than the location most likely to be attacked one day?

"You're right, of course, Admiral. I will dispatch the fleet orders immediately…except for the specified Home Fleet units, of course. I will see to those personally as soon as we have authorization from the Senate."

"Very well, Captain." Winters almost argued further, but it would be too suspicious if he ordered the officer to disregard Senate directives, to, in effect, commit treason. And the last thing he needed was to make a lot of noise about the whole thing. He needed the Senate watching what he was doing like he needed two heads.

Or two of a few other things.

Besides, maybe Gary Holsten can help with this...a bit more quietly than you can.

* * *

Anya Fritz stared at the screen, her face emotionless for a few seconds, before a wide grin spread across her cheeks...and a laugh even escaped her lips. There were those in the Confederation service—a good number of them—who would have sworn the normally grim and serious engineer had never shown the slightest sign of amusement at anything. But those who knew her well, like Tyler Barron, realized she had quite a strong sense of humor, if a sophisticated one with somewhat of a slow burn.

Barron's words still floated in her mind. "I know the last thing you want or think you need is a group of Hegemony technicians telling you what to do...but I went to a lot of trouble to get them sent to you, so I would consider it a personal favor if you would be nice and diplomatic while you're draining them dry of any useful information. Also, by all means, please try to send them back whole, with none of them having seen the business end of an airlock."

Fritz nodded at how well Barron knew her, how he'd seen her reaction weeks before she'd had it. Still, it was hard to hold back the resentment, to accept that anyone could help her, speed her efforts to get *Colossus* up and running with a Confederation crew.

At least until she heard Barron's next words.

"Anya...I'm afraid I'm in big trouble out here. This new enemy is real, and from what I've seen—and my gut—I think we're going to have to join the fight, however much it sickens us to stand alongside the Hegemony. I don't know if we can defeat the enemy, even if the Senate does as I ask and send the entire fleet. We need *Colossus*, Anya. *I* need *Colossus*. You know I have absolute confidence in you and your work, but, on your own, you'll need to discover all kinds of things the Hegemony techs already know. Bleed them for information, use them to get what you need—for *Colossus*, and for our overall technological development—and know you're doing it for the Confederation…and because I asked you, because I need you to do it."

Fritz felt her doubts and resentments slip away, and she suddenly realized, the threat Barron had gone to investigate was real. Another war was coming, more death and destruction, and Barron needed her help as he had so many times before, no less at that moment than in all those other instances, when he'd been on the bridge and she down in engineering, frantically struggling to restore power or get engines back online.

She watched the rest of the message, and then she tapped at the comm unit, calling up Eric Kalmut.

"Yes, Commodore?"

"Eric, I know it's one of your all too rare off-duty periods, but I'm afraid I need you now. Assemble the rest of the department heads and meet me down in landing bay twelve. We've got visitors coming…important visitors."

"Yes, Commodore. I'll take care of it immediately."

"And, Eric…"

"Yes, Commodore?"

"Advise the others I expect the very best behavior from every one of them, no matter what they see or hear. These guests will be…controversial…but no one will be anything but utterly courteous and respectful. Is that understood?"

"Understood, Commodore." The officer's voice was close to normal, but Fritz could pick up something different, a combination of concern and curiosity. She almost explained, but then she held her tongue.

Let them all find out together…

"And, Eric…tell them all, if they've ever been scared of me, now is the time they *should* be, if any of them acts like

anything   other   than   exemplary   officers   of   the
Confederation."

Chapter Twenty-Eight

HWS Leonidor
Orbiting Planet Pharsalon
Ettara-Mordlin III
Year of Renewal 267 (322 AC)

The Battle of Pharsalon – Prelude

Chronos stared at the display, at the large blue and white sphere covering more than half of the screen. Pharsalon was the third planet in the system, a pleasant enough world, one covered almost ninety percent by a single massive ocean. Its inhabitants lived on two small continents, each surrounded by archipelagoes of hundreds of tiny islands. Its population was small for a world this far into Hegemony space, just under three hundred million. It produced a number of valuable products, and was, by all reasonable standards, a prosperous world.

It was also irrelevant, and neither its quarter billion people, nor the bounty of its seas had played any part at all in the tactical decision to attempt to hold the line there. Ettara-Mordlin III would have been sacrificed without hesitation—though Chronos would have added the guilt for its hundreds of millions to the stockpile building in the back of his mind.

The fleet was there for another reason, one far more material, but also more important than a few hundred million lives, at least in the context of the war effort.

Ettara-Nordlin VII was nothing like Pharsalon. Its dark and pitted surface was ugly, its atmosphere thick and caustic. It was hot, a raging inferno, despite its significant distance from the star it orbited. The planet was a textbook demonstration of out of control volcanic activity, and all across its scarred surface, rivers of molten rock flowed almost like water. Poisonous steam billowed out of cracks in the ground, and the shifting of its unstable continental plates caused tremors a hundred times more severe than the most catastrophic quakes seen on a more typical world.

It was a manifestation of hell, an image close to that depicted by artists of some fiery pit for the doomed. But it was one of the most valuable places in the Hegemony.

Ettara-Nordlin VII, it had a number of informal names, but nothing official, save the military designation, 'AM-1,' had the distinction of being one of the two places in the Hegemony where antimatter was produced in militarily useful quantities.

The rare and precious substance had been one of the foundations of the old imperial economy, but the secrets of its production—its economical production at least—had been lost in the Great Death. The Hegemony had rediscovered the techniques, after a sort, and it had begun to adopt antimatter technology in its battlefleets, most specifically in its railgun primary batteries, which used the substance to accelerate the projectiles to the required velocities.

The recovery of technology and technique had only been a partial one, however, and antimatter production was vastly more expensive than it had been in imperial times. The expense of supplying the warships engaged with the Rim powers had been heavy, and the need to fuel up *Colossus* had come a hair's breadth from toppling the entire economy.

The fact that the great ship—and its staggeringly expensive fuel—had been lost, surrendered to the Confederation, only made the whole thing seem like a staggering waste.

If the fleet couldn't hold, if the Others took Ettara-Nordlin, the Hegemony would lose half its antimatter production, and with it, a substantial part of whatever chance it had of holding on, of driving the enemy back.

Pharsalon had a few defensive orbital stations. They would be useful if the fighting came near enough for them to engage. More importantly, planet seven was ringed with massive fortresses, a contrast that evidenced Chronos was not the first to realize Pharsalon's inhabitants were far from the most precious resource in the system.

He'd brought his flagship into orbit around Pharsalon. He owed that much to the planetary administrator, and the millions looking on with what had to be growing terror. He would address them all, massage the truth enough to make them believe the fleet had come to protect them.

He would lie.

Then he would join the rest of his forces farther out in the system. The battle line would be drawn up around planet seven, just within the range of the massive orbital railguns. The greatest force the Hegemony had ever massed in one place, with the exception, perhaps, of *Colossus* and its supporting fleet, would be waiting for the enemy.

Even as he discharged his duties to the doomed masses of Pharsalon, his engineering teams were updating the scanner suites on the orbital forts, keying in the most recent targeting routines. The battle would be the first large scale test of the new programming, the first time massive Hegemony firepower would face the Others' vessels with at least a chance to hit. Chronos wasn't optimistic, but in a seemingly contradiction, he was determined. He didn't know if he could stop the Others in Ettara-Mordlin, but he was damned sure about one thing.

The enemy would get one hell of a fight.

* * *

"Admiral, it appears the en...the Hegemony have completed their scanner update to the orbital fortresses."

"Very well, Lieutenant." Barron almost admonished the officer for still thinking of the Hegemony as 'the enemy.' It was understandable, even reasonable, but it was also unacceptable given the circumstances. The best chance for the Confederation, the entire Rim, to survive was very likely to fight alongside the Hegemony. That meant learning to cooperate...and it damned sure meant getting past calling them 'the enemy.'

But Barron let it go. He would push his people, but he wasn't going to be unreasonable. And truth be told, *he* still thought of the Hegemony as the enemy often enough himself. That was something time would change...but he had no idea how long it would take.

Or, for that matter, how long any of them had.

He turned back and stared at the ugly gray and black sphere on the display. The seventh planet was so hideous, it almost hurt his eyes to look at it. But he'd instantly known there was something valuable about it when he set eyes on the defense network. Over one hundred orbital forts, each one massive and bristling with weapons. The array made the old Megara defenses look like a tiny picket line. Barron had fought before the Confederation's capital, and he had assaulted the legendary defenses of Palatia during the Alliance civil war. But he'd never seen anything like the massive display of power and might before him.

The fixed defenses alone made the system the logical choice to mount a defense...at least if the enemy could be drawn close enough to engage.

Then Barron realized that wouldn't be a problem. His mind had raced since he'd first spotted the defenses. Rare minerals, helium-3, tritium...there had to be something on that planet, something valuable enough to justify what had to be an unimaginable cost.

Then, suddenly, he knew. He didn't have the slightest doubt, but he'd ordered a full scanner sweep anyway, just to confirm it. And his sensors and probes told him exactly what he already knew. Massive energy readings all across the planet.

Ettara-Mordlin VII was an antimatter factory. And that made it incalculably, almost unimaginably valuable.

That's why we're here. The enemy has to go toward the fixed defenses...they can't ignore an antimatter production center. And Chronos can't give it up, either. Not without one hell of a fight.

Barron felt the resentment again as he realized the antimatter that powered every railgun shot that had torn apart one of his battleships might have come from there. Part of him almost wanted to see the Others blast that planetwide production facility to atoms.

But we're going to need that antimatter. Those railguns aren't pointed at your people anymore, and you're going to need antimatter from the Hegemony to refuel Colossus. *It would take a thousand years production at Confederation levels to replenish that monster.*

"Admiral...*Leonidor* and its escorts have rejoined the main Hegemony fleet."

Barron's eyes darted back to the display, but it was a pointless gesture. Between his ships and the massive Hegemony fleet, there were more than seven hundred contacts, all represented by symbols so small, the tiny labels next to them were unreadable. It was impossible to pick out Chronos's flagship, at least until the AI highlighted it with a large white star.

Barron wasn't sure why Chronos had left the main formation and gone to the inhabited planet, but he had a guess, and he'd have bet a fair amount he was right. There was a decent-sized population on that planet, a couple hundred million or more, Barron suspected...and all together, they weren't a fraction of the strategic asset planet seven was. Chronos had gone to reassure the people, to tell them the fleet was there to fight, and he'd done it to assuage the guilt and the feeling of failure he'd feel if there were heavy casualties on the planet.

He wondered if it had worked for the Hegemony commander. Such things never had for him.

"Admiral, I've got Admiral Travis on your line."

Barron activated the comm unit. *Dauntless*'s bridge felt naked without his aide, his comrade, the warrior who had stood at his side almost as long as he could remember. He'd sent her out on an inspection tour, to follow up on Jarrod Simms's work. The lieutenant had reported that all but twelve of the fleet's hulls had been updated, but as much as Barron liked the brilliant young engineer, he'd feel better after Atara confirmed those facts.

"Atara?"

"Yes, Admiral...I'm on *Formidable*. It looks like Simms lived up to his billing. I've run *Formidable*—and *Vincennes* and *Valiant*, too—through some pretty deep fire drills. Without actual enemy ships to target, it's hard to be completely sure, but I'm convinced enough. If and when we get the authorization to engage, we'll be ready. As ready as we can be."

"That's good to hear."

"Admiral Barron, we're picking up massive energy readings at the fourth transit point." The officer's voice pulled his mind back to *Dauntless*'s bridge.

The entry point Chronos said the enemy would be using...

"Scanners on full, and all capital ships, prepare to launch a spread of long-range probes. We may not be allowed to fire on whatever comes through there, but we can gather as much information as possible." Barron's head angled forward, and he spoke into the comm unit. "Looks like the party's about to get started, Atara. Get back here right away. We may just be spectators, but I'll still feel better with you on *Dauntless*'s bridge.

"On my way, Admiral."

Barron cut the line. He sat where he was, twitching in his chair. His stomach was tied up in knots. He'd experienced the fear of battle many times, and he'd never imagined anything else could be as unsettling. But sitting there, his hands tied, watching as a new enemy advanced…it was worse than being in the fight.

His mind was racing, tactical analysis, battle plans…but in the end, there was just one thought that was even remotely useful.

Good luck, Chronos…

* * *

Ilius stood on *Anthrocles'* bridge. He'd come from his Sanctum, the hard servant of duty that lived inside him overcoming the doubt and fear that had come close to paralyzing him. He could hide in his private space while the fleet was hurtling from one system to another, but the instant he'd heard the report of enemy ships pouring through the tube, he'd leapt to his feet. He knew his place, where he had to be. With any luck, none of the bridge crew would be able to see just how close he'd come to breaking.

He'd attacked the fear the way he did every problem, applying his considerable intellect to analyzing the cause. He'd faced death before, and however powerful the Others might be, however mysterious their technology and motives, dying was dying. There was no cause to fear meeting his end from the Others' mysterious blue beams any more than a Confederation bomber assault.

Then, he'd realized. It wasn't fear of death, at least no more than he'd felt before in other combat situations. He was struggling with being outclassed, outmatched, and outgunned by the enemy. Ilius had long sided with Chronos, and the rest of the fringe minority of the Hegemony's Master class, warning about the dangers of arrogance. But only then did he truly understand how much he himself had fallen prey to that deadly hubris. He'd never been in a battle where the Hegemony wasn't the superior force, and he found it difficult, if not impossible, to adapt his thinking, to accept that his people were the underdogs in this fight. It was fear, after a fashion, but it was more complex than just simple terror. The realization of what was haunting him had been the first step to purging himself of it, or at least gaining control over it. Still, he knew it would be a long struggle to adapt, to become the best warrior he could be in the changed dynamic.

Unless the Others killed him in the next hours. There would be a twisted sort of mercy in that.

"All fleet units report full combat readiness, Commander."

"Very well." Ilius commanded the force unceremoniously dubbed, Fleet Beta. He and Chronos had divided the available vessels—all together, better than two-thirds of all the Hegemony's forces—and each commanded one component. Chronos had the larger force, the equally casually named Fleet Alpha. The ships of Alpha, just over sixty percent of the Hegemony vessels in the system, were deployed forward. Chronos, facing the Others for the first time, would bear the brunt of the initial assault.

Ilius, supposedly with more experience facing the enemy, was positioned behind, with orders to move forward on whatever vector he believed best. It was a straightforward battle plan, and one that made perfect sense...at least against any other enemy. But Ilius knew just how hard the enemy would hit Chronos's ships. He wouldn't really have time to wait for an opportunity, to play for time until he could manage a flanking maneuver. In the black pit of his mind, he knew he would be compelled to push forward in a desperate attempt to support Chrono's beleaguered fleet, sooner rather than later, and that his ships would follow their comrades into the maelstrom.

Ilius had never gone into a battle so certain of defeat.

"Fighter command…I want all squadrons ready for immediate launch."

"Yes, Commander."

Ilius had all of the fourteen battleships in the fleet that had been retrofitted to carry small attack craft. The Hegemony's program of fighter deployment had been a response to the devastating effects of the Rim squadrons…and it had been heavily based on *Colossus*. The handful of battleships carried two squadrons each, a minute force compared to the massive wings the Rim dwellers had sent in on their desperate attacks. Worse, perhaps, the Hegemony forces had been designed to face Rim bombers, so they were outfitted as interceptors. The Hegemony ships lacked the modular designs that allowed the Rim craft to convert to bomber kits. The Hegemony engineers, working hastily in the time since the Others had appeared, had managed to come up with externally-mounted torpedoes—but they were far less accurate than their Rim equivalents, and they carried smaller payloads as well. The Kriegeri flyers piloting them had been trained to take their ships in close—very close—and a culture of self-sacrifice had grown up around the fledgling corps, at least in theory. None of the pilots had actually been compelled to make good on that mantra.

Ilius would send them out when he judged the time to be right…and he wondered how many, if any, would return.

He wondered with even greater urgency if the minuscule force would make a difference, if the small craft would prove as useful an asset to the Hegemony as they had been a threat out on the Rim. He'd seen relatively modest Confed bomber wings do devastating damage to Hegemony ships of the line.

But those were bombers, not fighters carrying a jury-rigged torpedo. And the Rim has a long tradition of small craft operations.

The Kriegeri learned quickly, but Ilius knew it was

unreasonable to expect them to perform at the same level as their former enemies. And the fledgling Hegemony fighter corps had yet to produce a standout leader...and certainly no one remotely comparable to the Confederation's Jake Stockton.

"Commander, the enemy are..."

"Yes, Kiloron, I see." Ilius stared straight ahead, watching as the huge screen in the forward of the control center lit up, dozens of flashes moving across the empty space.

The enemy had opened fire on Chronos's line.

Chapter Twenty-Nine

Sector Nine Safe House
Just Outside the Lethal Zone
Liberte City
Planet Montmirail, Ghassara IV
Union Year 225 (321 AC)

"I don't care how severe his injuries are, Doctor. This is the First Citizen. His life is the most important thing in the Union right now." Gravis Steves narrowed his eyes, and his voice deepened. "Important enough that yours now depends on his."

The doctor stared back, a look of pure fear on his face. The day had been a difficult one all around, and Steves knew the doctor had been working since the night before, trying to aid the thousands of wounded staggering around in the streets.

There was no explanation as to what happened, not yet at least, no public announcements—or secret communiques to which he was privy. All he was sure of was that it had been unauthorized. It wasn't that Villieneuve wouldn't order a nuclear detonation in the city if it served his purposes, but the First Citizen damned sure would have made arrangements to be out of the blast radius.

As it was, the only reason Villieneuve was alive was that

he'd decided to leave early and return to his villa. He'd had a headache or something...a minor malady that had saved his life.

Maybe.

That left what had happened firmly in the category of unsolved mysteries. Steves spent a lot of time analyzing threats to the Union, and to the First Citizen in particular, but he was at a loss for what had caused a fission explosion in the middle of Liberte City.

Steves had been on alert for months now, ever since the failed coup attempt. He'd played a central role in the particularly effective bit of espionage and security work that had warned the First Citizen just in time, and Gaston Villieneuve had proven his gratitude, both in promotions and power...and in vast awards of currency as well.

Steves's loyalty to his superior was based somewhat on that, but truth be told, he was as much a product of the Union's system as Villieneuve himself. His first though had been to let the First Citizen die, to open up a power vacuum and try to seize a higher position for himself. His true concern for Villieneuve only came after he'd determined that he wasn't high enough yet, not to make a play for the First Citizen's chair. And if anyone else took that sought-after seat, his future would depend almost solely on how the new dictator decided to treat the key aides of the former one.

History did not offer many signs of hope in that regard.

So, his future was best served, best secured, by Villieneuve's continued control over the government. He'd done all he could to keep things from getting out of hand, sent out dispatches that the First Citizen had been injured, but not badly, that he would be back at his desk in a day or two. Lies like that could buy time, a little. But now, he had to see that Villieneuve actually survived. And one look at his battered form, the clearly broken bones and dislocated shoulder, the hideous burns down one side of his body, didn't give him all that much cause for hope.

And that doesn't even factor in radiation...for yourself either. Steves had escaped major injury—he'd almost forgotten the dozen or so painful cuts and scrapes covering his body— but he knew that wasn't his only concern. Both he and Villieneuve had gotten heavy hits of radiation. He didn't have much doubt about that. He hadn't felt any symptoms yet, somewhat to his surprise, but he was sure t was only a matter of time.

It was probably nothing a good cleanse couldn't clear out, but that required a major medical center, and he hadn't come up with a way to get Villieneuve there in secret. He had half a dozen guards with him, all of whom he considered reliable, but he needed to round up more force, and he had to get Villieneuve to a hospital.

And he had to keep things quiet. If word got out about the First Citizen's true condition, the knives would be drawn in hours, and high-level functionaries all over Montmirail would begin making their moves to seize power. Fear of Villieneuve was a potent deterrent, but it only worked if people believed the man was alert and in charge.

And if the power struggle began in earnest, every prime mover would send assassins to finish Villieneuve off.

That would be the end for Steves, too. Loyalty in the Union was a strange beast, usually self-serving and not very idealistic. But it worked much the same as it did anywhere, and regardless of his reasons, Gravis Steves would protect the First Citizen.

With all his strength...whatever it took.

He pressed his hand against his jacket, feeling the holstered sidearm under his shoulder. The coat was torn in half a dozen places, but it was still hiding the pistol Steves had grabbed the weapon on his way out, almost on instinct, but that reflexive move hadn't extended to grabbing any reloads. The weapon held twenty shots, and if and when he'd gone through those—and sooner or later, he knew, looking at the chaos all around, he *would* use them—he'd be reduced to fending off enemies with a rock or a club.

That's a problem for later. I've got twenty shots before I get to that.

He turned and looked back, watching the doctor—in effect his hostage—working feverishly to save Gaston Villieneuve.

And probably to save Gravis Steves, as well.

* * *

"What the hell happened?" Kerevsky heard the words— he'd heard almost nothing but questions of that sort since the explosion had shattered every window in the embassy, and fried a fair amount of its electronic systems as well. He had the defensive contingent—all of thirty-four Marines— positioned all around, keeping watch on the mobs growing throughout the city with alarming speed. It was mostly a gesture, something to keep the embassy staff as calm as possible. There were hundreds of thousands in the streets, perhaps millions. If they got fired up to storm the compound, a handful of Marines weren't going to stop them…even if Kerevsky authorized them to gun down Union citizens.

He'd wondered what had happened himself, for a few minutes, at least. If the explosion had occurred anywhere else, he might still be trying to figure it out. But he knew Sandrine Ciara well enough not to underestimate her. She'd played him, at least with regard to her intent to try to shoot Gaston Villieneuve. She'd done what he'd asked, after a fashion. He didn't know for sure if Villieneuve was alive or dead, but there was a damned good chance the Union dictator had died in the blast. Ciara had just changed the plan they'd discussed, tried something that offered rather more chance of success, albeit at a considerable cost in collateral damage.

Was she really willing to kill so many people just to...

His mind stopped cold. No, it wasn't just a high percentage way to strike at Villieneuve. She wanted more than her enemy's death. She wanted the chaos, the mad fury in the streets.

She was making another play for power...and this time she was moving into a void, one of her own creation, and not up against an entrenched dictator who was waiting for her.

If she survived the explosion...

He'd done the math half a dozen times. He'd been estimating—guessing—how long it took her to reach her objective.

The reactor under the Hall of the People...that has to be it...

Then the time to sabotage the system, and to escape. He'd analyzed it every way he could, and the best he could come up with was a very narrow escape...if everything had gone perfectly.

If something—anything—had delayed her, she was mostly likely dead out there on the street, one of thousands of corpses still lying ungathered.

He'd felt the urge to go looking for her...but he quickly realized that was impossible. He'd never get close, and if he tried to move out in any force, he'd almost certainly trigger a violent attack from the mob. As much as he was concerned for her—despite the fact that she'd lied to him—the last thing he could do was tie the Confederation to an assassination attempt, and worse, to a calamity that had claimed thousands of lives.

He turned abruptly. He had to find out what had happened...and if Ciara was still alive. But first, he had duties as the Confederation ambassador. "Kyle..." He called for his aide.

"Sir?" The diplomatic assistant—and, in his lesser known role, Confederation agent—poked his head around the corner.

"We have to put together a statement of sympathy…and offer the Union government any assistance we are able to provide." *And try to find out if there* is *a Union government right now.*

"Yes, Ambassador. I will draft something immediately and bring it to you for approval."

"Very well." A pause. "Make it sound heartfelt." He wasn't sure it would matter, but from the looks of the crowd, anything that might defuse anger against the Confederation was worth a try.

* * *

The air was thick with dust, and every breath triggered a fresh coughing fit. Ciara stumbled forward, gritting her teeth against the pain. Her arm was broken, she was sure of that, but she hadn't managed to pinpoint the pain in her back. She'd almost panicked, in those first, terrifying moments when she'd awakened. She'd been afraid she'd broken her spine but, somehow, she'd managed to get up and move around, slowly and painfully, but without significant impairment.

In the end, her timing had been close to spot on. She'd gotten as far as she could, and when she guessed the countdown was under one minute, she frantically searched for some kind of shelter. She was far enough away, she bet, that whatever building she was in wouldn't come down on her, so she chose the sturdiest structure close to her and dove inside. Her guess had proven partially correct. The building as whole still stood, but a large section of wall had caved in, coming perilously close to burying her under the rubble. She'd crawled out and made her way into the street, and something that felt like two hours of walking had gotten her out of the fringes of the blast zone, though not away from the chaos, which seemed to have spread throughout the city.

All she wanted was to rest, to close her eyes and sleep. But that wasn't a possibility. First, she needed some medical assistance. Her arm was an inconvenience, a painful one, but the worst problem, she suspected, was radiation. She had no idea how much protection the building had offered her, but the growing turmoil in her stomach suggested she hadn't entirely escaped the unseen effects of the dirty explosion.

Even more importantly, she had a very limited time to make her bid for power. She was assuming Villieneuve was dead, of course, though she had no way to verify it. Still, even without her primary adversary in the picture, she knew she had to get a foothold before word got out that the First Citizen was dead. Once the secret spread, every fleet admiral and high government official would be evaluating his or her chances to seize the top position. Ciara wasn't scared of a good fight, not usually, but her own resources were scarce at the moment, and she had almost no preparations in place. Too many of her contacts, her potential allies, had been rounded up after the coup attempt, and many of them had died for their involvement in her plot. She could entice new ones, of course, gather confused mid-level officials to support her efforts, but it wouldn't be easy. She would gain those the old-fashioned way. She would promise them more than her rivals did...and she would convince them she had a chance at success.

That last bit would be the hardest part. Giving away prospective offices and cash awards were simple enough things to do. But presenting her dirty, disheveled, injured self as a real contender for power was going to be a challenge.

She thought about Kerevsky, wondered how angry he would be that she'd deviated from the plan so aggressively. She thought she could probably entice him back to her corner—though she was in no shape for a seduction, so that couldn't be part of the plan. Perhaps more enthusiastic assurances of a lasting peace between the Confederation and the Union. Villieneuve had been nearly obsessed with defeating the Union's neighbor, but Ciara was more than willing to enforce a peace—and even ally with—the Confederation…if that was the price of the help she needed.

But there were other problems. The embassy would be the center of attention. It was too dangerous to go there, at least while things were in so much turmoil. She was on her own for the moment. Fortunately, she still had some resources of her own. Not too many, but some.

Those would have to be enough. She was desperate, more desperate than any of her potential rivals. And that was a weakness she could turn to a strength, if she could make determination and a refusal to lose work for her.

Of such things, power was born.

Chapter Thirty

HWS Leonidor
Orbiting Planet Pharsalon
Ettara-Mordlin III
Year of Renewal 267 (322 AC)

The Battle of Pharsalon – The Attack of the Highborn

"Second division, increase thrust to thirty percent. Fourth division, alter vector plus forty, minus ten, plus forty. Get those ships around, and into range." Chronos was snapping out orders, almost without pause. He had enough aides, enough communications officers to relay his commands however quickly he spat them out, but even so, the sweating Kriegeri all around the control room showed the exhaustion they were feeling, the desperate fatigue from keeping up with their commander's frantic pace.

Chronos was facing the Others for the first time. Perhaps that was why he was so driven, why he defied the sense of hopelessness already working its way through the fleet. He'd turned off his analytical mind—at least with regard to the force matchups. He didn't need despair. He didn't need to determine his forces had no chance of victory.

He had to *make* a chance, somehow. He had to stop the Others stone cold, before another three hundred million citizens—and half the antimatter production in the entire Hegemony—were lost.

His demeanor defied the sense of order and intellect that had driven him his entire life, and it released the warrior within, the savage fighter who paid no heed to odds, to technology. That spirit had lived inside him his entire life. It was, no doubt, what had pushed him toward a military life, when, at his lofty ranking, he could have chosen any profession, or none at all. But what had strengthened it, truly released it, were his experiences on the Rim. The Confeds and their allies had fought without pause, without regard for the odds so heavily stacked against them. They had lost battles, lost worlds, including their capital, but they'd continued the fight. Had they analyzed the odds, followed a logical course, they would have surrendered. But they didn't, and they'd become the first known humans to escape absorption.

Even in the face of *Colossus*, they'd stood firm, without any detectable signs they had ever considered yielding. That almost instinctive, animalist determination to fight without regard to the losses they endured suggested a lower order of thinking. But that logic had been wrong. The Rim fighters had learned from the Hegemony even as they'd battled fiercely. Their engineers had certainly gleaned technological advancements from watching the battles and analyzing what they saw.

Chronos had learned some things as well, and first and foremost among those was never to give up. He'd also come to understand that the warrior's urges that lived in him were not antithetical to his ordered mind, that he could release them, draw strength from their power without surrendering his judgment, his incisive thought.

He'd never been the underdog before, never faced a superior enemy, and he wondered how he would have handled it if he'd hadn't witnessed the insane will and courage of the Rim warriors.

"*Farizar* and *Kirizon* have been destroyed, Commander."

Two battleships. Chronos stared out, at the space where the icons representing the two lost ships had been seconds before. He had his battleships out in front, pressing forward against the enemy, but also acting as a kind of bait. The Others mostly disregarded his cruisers and escorts, but they targeted the big battleships moving toward them at high velocities. That was bad, in every context save one. It allowed the even larger, more powerful monitors to move forward, to escape fire while they closed to their own firing ranges. It was a coldblooded tactic, one he'd never had to employ before against mostly overmatched enemies. But the idea of sacrificing battleships to serve as cover chilled his blood, even in his agitated, aggressive state. It was insane, each of the vessels lost representing years of construction and millions of Hegemony credits…not to mention over a thousand trained Kriegeri. But Chronos was certain of one thing, a fact his analytical mind and the warrior side then in control agreed upon. Whatever chance there was of victory, of defeating the Others, the cost would be horrendous, like nothing he had seen before, even in the deadly battles on the Rim.

"All divisions, continue thrust and vectors. All units are to follow the tactical plan, regardless of losses." His voice was like ice.

He glanced to the side of the display, to the large cluster of small ovals a million kilometers behind his fleet. Ilius's ships.

Chronos had developed the plan, ordered his second-in-command to remain behind, to wait for an opening to intervene, one he knew might never come. But as he saw more of his ships destroyed, and no small number badly damaged, he began to wonder if he'd made the right choice. Could he really afford to keep almost half his strength out of the fight for any amount of time?

Out of the fight now, but they'll be up soon enough. Running into a head to head brawl isn't going to work. Not against the Others. Ilius knows what he is doing.

He thought about slowing his ships down, about drawing the enemy farther forward. That might help Ilius's fleet gain a positional advantage.

No...it's not possible. You have to close, get your people in this fight, too. If you stay back, let the enemy blast the fleet while you can't shoot back, you're finished.

Chronos realized in an instant just how the Confeds, how Tyler Barron had felt, enduring railgun fire as they raced forward to bring their own primary beams into play.

And they got through that war...

It was a meaningless comparison, of course, but it still helped him.

A little.

"The forward line will prepare to open fire." His first twenty battleships would enter range in less than a minute.

First nineteen...

He stared straight ahead, eyes fixed on that thin line of ships, and right on the spot where one had been seconds before. He had more strength coming up, the might of the Hegemony, massed as it had never been before, but he didn't know if it would be enough. One side of his brain said yes, the other no. But none of that mattered. At the very least, the one-sided phase of the battle would soon be over. His ships and people would continue to die...but in a moment, they would start killing as well.

"Forward line entering range, Commander."

Chronos looked ahead, his eyes cold and focused.

"Open fire."

*   *   *

"I want those railguns double shotted, Hectoron, and I

mean now!" Helas sat calmly on her bridge, ignoring the danger from the withering enemy fire, brushing away the dark cloud of despair even then eroding the morale of her spacers. They could take it, she knew. Kriegeri were raised for military service, and often committed to their units at young ages. They were tough to break.

But the carnage unfolding all around was wearing them down.

"Yes, Commander." The officer sounded just a bit uncertain. Most of Helas's people were veterans from the Rim War, and they'd all seen the Confeds and their allies exceeding the recommended energy levels, overpowering their guns to increase effectiveness in battle.

But loading two antimatter canisters into a railgun designed to take one was something else entirely. As far as Helas knew, it had never been tried. She'd made an effort at analysis, tried to do some quick calculations to determine if the weapons—or the ships that carried them—could stand the strain. But then she looked up at the display, saw her ships being blasted to scrap, she gave the order anyway. They were all going to die if she did nothing, and if there was no escape, she damned sure intended to drag some of the Others down to hell with her.

She'd volunteered to command the advance force. Hell, she'd begged Chronos to give it to her. He'd been hesitant, no doubt knowing just what the loss rates were likely to be, but he'd given in. He probably hadn't had much choice. Her role in pulling the forces back from Venta Traconis had made her somewhat of a hero. Chronos had asked her if she was sure one last time…and then he'd approved her request.

She regretted it, a little and on some deep and submerged level. But even as she sat there, watching her ships destroyed all around her and resorting to increasingly desperate actions, she knew she would do it all over again if she had the chance. This wasn't an absorption attempt like the Rim War had been, not a typical conflict…it was a fight to the finish. And there was no other place she could be except in the leading wave.

"Gunnery reports double-loaded batteries ready to fire. *Omaliar* and *Wallisia* are also ready."

She looked straight ahead. Her ships had been firing for ten minutes, and they'd scored a number of hits. There were two enemy vessels showing signs of significant damage. That was something, and better than anything she'd seen in Venta Traconis, but it wasn't enough. Not even close Even with Chronos's main force coming into the battle, adding their fire to that of her ships, she had to do better...

"Hectoron...fire."

* * *

What the hell was that?

Chronos had been moving his eyes across the display, alternating between watching Helas's ships get blasted to scrap and turning away when he couldn't take it anymore. But something had just happened, something *different*, and though he'd seen it, he couldn't bring himself to believe it. He needed to be sure.

A few seconds later, he was.

"Enemy vessel destroyed, Commander. We have multiple confirmations."

Chronos heard the words, and he'd seen the ship disappear from the display with his own eyes. But he still had trouble acknowledging what had just happened. Somehow, it didn't seem quite real.

Several Hegemony forces had faced the Others before the current fight, with no confirmed kills to show for the losses they suffered. He'd come to Ettara-Mordlin with the intention of ending that streak, of destroying many enemy ships. Now, he realized, some part of him, at least, hadn't really expected to achieve that goal. In spite of all his bravado and confidence, he found himself surprised his people had scored a kill.

However close the Others were to untouchable, it was not clear that was the one thing they were not. Helas had just proven that. One ship destroyed was far from decisive, or even tactically important, but it was first blood, and in a situation where real doubt had existed about the enemy's vulnerability, that was everything. It was hope. It was a reason to fight on, to pour everything into the struggle.

The loss ratios were still abysmal, over forty Hegemony ships crippled or destroyed so far, for the one vessel Helas's task force had just become destroyed. But it wasn't about ratios, not in this instance. Helas had proven again the targeting revisions worked. But, for all of that, there was something else, something Chronos couldn't quite place...

That enemy ship was destroyed too quickly...

"Commander, the scanner readings are very confusing. We tracked two shots that struck the enemy ship, and..."

"And?" Chronos's tone was sharp, demanding. It was no time for his aides to sit in stunned silence. He needed information.

"According to our scanner replays, both *Hysarius* and *Volkom* scored railgun hits...but their projectiles appear to have inflicted damage far beyond any projections. Data reviews of the inbound paths indicate the weapons' velocities significantly exceeded standard levels.

"Exceeded? How do you explain that, Hectoron?"

"I...I cannot, Commander. I apologize."

Chronos didn't respond, not right away. The Kriegeri were admirable in most cases, at least to his sensibilities, but they could sometimes become a bit obsequious, especially around high-level Masters when they didn't have information that was requested. Or demanded. Some Masters were less patient with their subordinates that Chronos considered appropriate. He didn't tolerate it in his command, at least when he saw it. But he knew it happened.

Chronos also knew he couldn't expect the officer to have

the answers. He didn't have them himself yet.

"No apology necessary, Hectoron. Let us work the problem. Divert all data flow from the scanner array and the replays to the main AI. I want answers, and I want them now."

"Yes, Commander." The officer turned and leaned over his station, carrying out Chronos's command to the letter. Perhaps half a minute later, he had an answer. At almost the same moment, the solution suddenly appeared in his own mind. And it all made sense. A terrifying, dangerous kind of sense.

"Commander, the AI theorizes that Commander Helas's ships are..."

"Yes, Hectoron, I know...I know exactly what they are doing..."

And God help them. God help us all...

* * *

Barron watched the battle unfold on the display, his attention riveted, even as he marshaled every bit of the strength inside him to stay where he was, to keep his fleet back at the transit point. It went against everything he believed to hold back and watch an ally's ships being savaged, even when that ally still seemed half like an enemy. He had his orders, and they'd been given to him in clear and precise terms, written skillfully enough to deny him any possible justification for 'misunderstanding.'

One by one, the ships of the Hegemony advance force were obliterated, even as they stayed grimly in the fight, inflicting their own damage on the deadly enemy. Then, something changed. The impacts from the Hegemony railguns increased in intensity. The energy readings were tentative, certainly at the distance from Barron's ships to the battle underway, but the spike was sharp and noticeable. The Hegemony railguns were somehow hitting harder.

Barron was confused, at least until he saw the data on the projectiles heading toward the enemy fleet.

The velocities were enormous, almost 0.03c. That was far greater than any of his ships had faced during the war, a difference he found inexplicable. Had the Hegemony made a breakthrough of some kind, an advance in their weapons technology? One Akella had kept secret?

No, that doesn't make sense. She would know we'd see the increased capability, so why hide something...

His thought stopped cold as realization set in.

They're overpowering their guns...

Barron knew the concept well. He'd used it multiple times, usually to good effect, though not without consequences, burned and scarred crew, even destroyed ships. Weapons were rated for maximum power outputs, and moving beyond those levels increased the risk of burnouts, and even catastrophic malfunctions.

But Barron's experiences had been limited to running increased energy levels through conduits into his primaries and lasers. Hegemony railguns were powered by antimatter, and...

They're increasing the antimatter loads...

It suddenly made sense. And it didn't. Feeding more juice into a particle accelerator was one thing, but the railguns blasted chunks of superhard metal out into space. The basic system was already hard on the surrounding structure, one reason only Hegemony capital ships carried the great weapons.

How much more can those hulls take?

As if in answer to his thought, one of the forward Hegemony ships disappeared, but not from enemy fire this time. A few seconds later, another one blinked off the large screen.

He watched, shocked on one level at the recklessness of such tactics, but realizing on another, he would almost certainly have done the same thing. The results, at least, were clear. The Hegemony forward line was drawing blood, though it was bleeding itself to do it, and much more quickly.

He didn't know the technology that powered the enemy railguns, not all of it, at least. But he knew enough to realize the only thing the Hegemony vessels could have done was to jam more antimatter into their guns.

That *had* to be dangerous.

Antimatter was the most powerful—and volatile—fuel known to human science, and Chronos's people were taking wild chances with it.

Barron's insides froze. He wanted to wonder how the Hegemony warriors had become so desperate. But he knew already...he knew because he'd been there.

He remembered making similar decisions, watching ships destroyed and crews killed because they'd followed his orders, tore up their safety manuals, and done as he'd told them to do. His people had destroyed countless more Hegemony vessels through such tactics than they might have otherwise, but they'd paid for it as well.

Paid dearly.

Now, it was the Hegemony's turn to learn what that felt like. Part of Barron experienced a grim satisfaction at seeing his old enemy driven to the desperate kind of tactics his own spacers had been compelled to employ. He knew that was pointless, that such kinds of gratification always carried a terrible cost.

He was watching his old enemy struggling to survive, but his eyes were clear enough to see the future as well as the present, the inevitable vision of his own people fighting this same new enemy, struggling to find their own ways to battle them, at whatever cost.

Just as they'd done before. But he knew it would be even worse this time.

* * *

"Damage control teams to gunnery. All ships, I want engineering parties posted at all railguns. I expect those weapons to keep firing, whatever it takes." Helas felt a rush, a burst of excitement. Her makeshift tactic was working, at least where it wasn't blasting her ships to plasma. She would be in the history texts now.

If there are any history texts...

Her forces had become the first to destroy one of the Others' ships. It was noteworthy, and she and her people would be feted for their achievement.

If any of them made it out of the current fight, which seemed like a shaky prospect.

"Commander, we've got multiple reports coming in. Damage to railguns, casualties among the crews. We can't..."

"Maintain full fire...all shots with double loads." Helas wasn't oblivious to the hell she was inflicting on her gunners. Several of the task force's batteries had been destroyed by the overpowered shots, their crews wiped out before any had even had a chance to escape. Others were damaged, some knocked out of action for the duration, others with some hope of quick repair. And two ships were gone, destroyed outright as the overloaded antimatter canisters lost containment and annihilated.

Damage or no damage, she also knew all of her crews had been bathed in radiation as they'd worked feverishly in the raging heat of the contaminated gunnery stations. The shielding around the railguns was thick enough to offer protection against normal shots, but her double-powered blasts were almost certainly pushing hard gamma rays into her ships.

But the tactic—deadly, dangerous, costly—was also working. The double-shotted railgun rounds had better than half again the velocity of normal shots. They ripped through space that much faster, confounding the enemy's evasive routines, and scoring hits at better than double the rate of unmodified weapons.

The shots hit harder, too, the kinetic energy imparted to the target almost twice as great. Even the enemy ships, for all their technological superiority, suffered when one of those deadly chunks of super-heavy metal struck. No physical construct ever known could absorb such a hit without buckling, melting. Vaporizing.

Helas's best guess was three of the enemy ships had been badly damaged—two of those so badly, they were no longer firing—in addition to the one vessel destroyed. Then, even as she sat there staring right at the display, a second enemy ship winked out of existence.

She felt a rush of exhilaration, one that almost sent her leaping from her chair. But the joy was short-lived. Less than thirty seconds later, two more of her own ships were destroyed...and a third was close, its broken hull bleeding atmosphere, even as its crew frantically tried to restore basic power and maneuver.

Still, however grim the situation, it couldn't dampen the satisfaction of seeing enemy ships destroyed. What she had done, others could do. And that meant, whether she survived the battle or not, the war wasn't over. The Hegemony would fight on, with some chance at least, some way to hurt the enemy.

She heard the distant rattle as *Vegalitor*'s railguns fired again, and seconds later, she saw the impact, as a thousand kilograms of high-density metal slammed into an enemy ship. The mysterious vessel shuddered, and then it just hung there, looking very much like it was dead in space.

She clenched her fists in silent celebration, even as she turned toward her damage control screen, closing her eyes for an instant as she saw the sheer mass of warnings and red status icons scrolling down the page. That last shot had caused a deadly backblast of radiation, and a dozen systems had shorted out.

Vegalitor had led the first attack to destroy an enemy

vessel. But now the flagship itself was in trouble, the deep wound a self-inflicted one. Helas had known the risks of her reckless tactic, and they had struck home. She was still reading the reports and snapping out orders to her engineering teams when a deep explosion shook *Vegalitor*...and every light on the bridge went dark.

* * *

"Commander Helas is insane, Megaron. Three of her ships have been destroyed by railgun backfires. Her tactics are..."

"Her tactics are working. Commander Helas is showing us the way, Kiloron. *All* ships are to double load their railgun batteries. We will be in range in two minutes, and it's time we did some damage to the enemy. Some *real* damage." Chronos's tone was hard, his displeasure with the Kriegeri kiloron becoming clearer with every word.

But still, the officer continued.

"Megaron, we can't..."

"Was some part of my order unclear, Kiloron?" Chrono's voice was loud, booming, every bit of the pride and authority that went with his position as Number Eight of the Hegemony utterly apparent.

"No, Commander...certainly not." The officer sounded terrified...scared of Chronos now, even more than he was of the enemy. "Relaying your orders, Commander."

Chronos didn't respond. He just looked out, watching the shattered remnants of Helas's force fighting on grimly, even as his own line came up behind them. *Vegalitor* was along the front of the formation, but it was clear the battleship was badly damaged. Chronos had watched as the battered ship fired again, and scored a deadly hit. But it was the last shot *Vegalitor* managed. Helas's flagship had wounded itself, possibly mortally.

He had no idea how the ship was still there, or what had kept her main guns firing for so long. He'd almost have believed it was a manifestation of the pure stubbornness of his vanguard commander.

Helas had done more than he could have hoped, served with courage and distinction. She was a hero, even if she *had* lost sixty percent of her ships so far. But she'd drawn blood, four enemy ships destroyed outright, and at least a dozen others with measurable damage. That was still an uneven exchange…and yet it was better than Chronos had dared to imagine.

And he was leading more than one hundred battleships and monitors into the fight, throwing a massive portion of Hegemony power at the enemy. More than one hundred thousand Kriegeri, and two hundred Masters manned those capital ships, and thousands more the escorts accompanying them.

Helas *had* shown the way, desperate though it was.

Now, Chronos was going to put some real force behind it.

Chapter Thirty-One

Confederation Naval HQ
Troyus City
Megara, Olyus III
Year 322 AC

"Senator Flandry, I want to be sure there is no confusion between us, so I'm afraid I may be rather blunt. Tyler is out there, with a relatively small fleet. His reports leave little doubt this new incursion is a threat to the Confederation, and indeed the entire Rim, as well as the Hegemony. Yet, the Senate debates endlessly, with no vote in sight, and no certainty there will even *be* an authorization for the military to prepare to dispatch the fleet to Hegemony space, to Tyler's aid."

"Captain Lafarge, I am delighted to see you." The Senate Speaker addressed Andi by her naval rank, though she'd reverted to inactive status just after the end of the war with the Hegemony. The form of address was proper, and no doubt his effort to be as respectful as possible to her, but somehow, it just pissed her off. If she was being honest with herself, she'd have admitted that anything except a total and complete—and immediate—acceptance of all her requests, demands really, would have angered her. But she'd come to try to reason with the politician, somewhat of an ally of convenience to Tyler, at least before she took…other…measures.

"Before we get to the business you came to discuss, allow me to congratulate you. Another generation of Barrons is a cause for the entire Confederation to celebrate."

"Thank you, Speaker." It was a short, abrupt response, but it was the best she could manage. Andi was hiding multiple causes of annoyance. First, she'd have preferred that no one knew she was pregnant, and certainly not before she had the chance to tell Tyler. She tended to despise the sort of perfunctory well wishes commonly offered by people who simply were not a real part of her life. She considered every word she heard to be insincere, unless she had good reason to believe otherwise, and she found engaging in the choreographed dance of fake social interactions tiring. She wouldn't have ventured out at all, most likely, if Tyler hadn't needed her. But he did, and that being the case, there was no prison cell that could have held her, much less the palatial hotel suite that still served as home.

"Not to be rude, Speaker, but if possible, I would like to return to the matter at hand. Tyler led the mission to Hegemony space, as requested by the Senate. He has investigated, as he was sent to do, and he has sent back his report. It has been days now, and yet there has been no action." She was trying to keep her tone measured, her demeanor diplomatic, but the edge that always crept into her voice in tense situations was there. Andi looked as harmless as she ever had, a pregnant woman, unarmed and there expressing concern for her spouse. At least she appeared unarmed. The one weapon she carried—and it had been a very long time since Andi had gone *anywhere* completely unarmed—was very cleverly concealed.

Still, she could see beyond Flandry's reflexive charm. The Speaker was a bit intimidated. It didn't matter how harmless she looked, how pregnant she was…Andi was still the woman who'd killed Ricard Lille, and that reputation would follow her to her grave.

"Andi, I can assure you, I am Tyler's ally in all of this. Your ally." A pause, which Andi knew served as one massive 'but.' "There are problems, however. You can understand the reluctance of many to present their constituents with the prospect of a new war so soon after all the hardship and strife of the recently concluded conflict. I have made every effort to accede to Tyler's requests. I have not brought the matter to a vote yet for a simple reason. I do not, at this time, have enough support to guarantee approval. I can promise you, I will keep trying. Given time, I believe we can reach the desired result. I urge you to be patient."

Patient was the one thing Andi had *never* been, and she damned sure wasn't going to start while Tyler and his people were in danger so far from home. But ally or not—and she still wasn't sure—she realized she'd gotten everything she was going to get from Flandry.

She believed the Speaker had tried to gather the needed support...and that he'd failed.

Andi wasn't sure, of course. Flandry could just be full of shit. That was probably a coin toss, she figured, but it didn't matter. Refusal to try and failure were functionally the same thing in this case, and that only left her one choice. It was a sort of nuclear option, something that would cause the pompous politicians in the Senate to lose their minds. But it wasn't possible to express how little Andi cared what the Senators liked or hated.

It was time to press the button. Time to launch everything she had.

* * *

"No, Clint...not yet. Tyler wouldn't want that." Andi paused. Barron wouldn't want his friends taking crazy risks for him no matter how deeply he was in danger.

Andi was having none of that, of course. She was going to get him help one way or another, but before she let Winters bring the fleet to Megara and send Marines into the Senate Compound, she had another idea. "Get everything as ready as you can, just in case. But I think I have a plan, a less disruptive one."

Winters nodded slowly. "Okay, Andi. But don't wait too long. If I have to take action, I will need some time. And we don't know what is happening out at Calpharon…or how much trouble Tyler's facing." A pause. "Or, for that matter, how much of a threat is building against all of us."

Andi reached out and put her hand on Winters's shoulder. The admiral, Tyler's second-in-command, was one of the few people she considered a true friend. And his loyalty to Tyler was beyond question. It wasn't every day you found a friend ready to commit mutiny and treason to help you, after all.

But Andi knew what she was going to do. It wasn't much subtler, but it was a bit more elegant, and far less destructive. And it had the advantages of not requiring its participants to commit capital crimes and not risking an outbreak of civil war.

"I'm not going to wait. We have to get help to Tyler as quickly as possible, and I think my way will be quicker than yours." She paused and looked at Winters. "But what you're willing to do, Clint…I'll never forget it."

She stood there wordlessly for a few seconds. Then, she turned toward Gary Holsten. The spymaster had been standing there, quietly listening. His job description included stopping plots like the one Winters was prepared to attempt, but Holsten had always had his own interpretation of duty. Andi knew, without a doubt, if it came to armed action, Confederation Intelligence wouldn't interfere…and would probably help Winters's mutineers.

In addition to Holsten's recognition of the danger, and

his respect and admiration for Tyler Barron, he owed Andi. She knew the spymaster still carried guilt for sending her to Dannith, for the torture and interrogations she endured. She'd never held him to blame—when she agreed to do something, she took the responsibility herself—but she wasn't above using it to get what she wanted from him. If she had to work him, and she didn't think that would be necessary, the pregnancy would only add to her manipulation arsenal.

"Gary...I need your help." She hesitated, trying to get a read on what he was thinking. She was sure enough he would help her, but his expression was impassive. Holsten had just about the best poker face she'd ever seen. Tyler's was legendary, too, at least in the fleet...but it didn't work on her. She knew him too well.

And he was always just a little bit flustered around her. It was one of the first things that attracted her to him.

"If you've got some way to avoid the...other...option, I'm ready to do whatever I can." He'd carefully avoided any indication he would oppose outright mutiny, but he hadn't acknowledged support for it either.

"You've got some connections, both as head of Confederation Intelligence and through the Holsten family investments. We might be able to combine those to get what we need."

"Anyone I can reach—or pressure—you know I will, Andi. We can apply some considerable force, if needed, to secure cooperation, up to including a room full of agents shoving guns down people's throats."

"I don't even think that will be necessary, Gary. The people I need will be ecstatic about doing what I want them to do. It's the kind of thing they dream about. We just need to reach the decision makers. Quickly."

* * *

Andi walked down the corridor, deep in thought, ignoring the small cluster of people around her as she finalized in her mind just what she was going to say.

Her stomach was roiling, and it took a fair amount of effort to keep everything down. It wasn't nerves.

It wasn't *just* nerves.

Andi wasn't one prone to being badly affected by stress. She'd faced death numerous times without so much as a stomachache to show for it. But pregnancy was proving to be a...different...experience. She imagined laying guilt trips on her future son or daughter—she hadn't even taken the time to find out what she was carrying—recounting in excruciating detail every moment she spent doubled over, emptying her guts of what seemed like five times the volume she'd put in.

Andi was a warrior at heart, a killer. She was a Badlands prospector, an adventurer, and a quasi-criminal turned naval officer. But one thing she'd never imagined, not in all her days scavenging on the streets of her homeworld, nor deep in the bowels of some imperial artifact, was being a mother. It seemed almost an alien concept, and while, deep down there was happiness, it was held back by pain and worry over Tyler's absence.

And by the fact that she had no idea what to do with a child. She was as far from maternal by nature as anyone she'd ever known, and she doubted any of the things she was good at, the basics of knife-fighting, for example, would make for ideal mother-child bonding experiences.

What stories would she tell a child? Would she recount all the Badlands border scumbags she'd put into the ground? Try to describe the look of pure astonishment and terror in Ricard Lille's eyes when she killed him?

She pulled herself back into the present. She was standing in front of a door at the end of the hallway. It was time.

"Captain, this is the main broadcast center. When you

are inside and ready to begin, simply wave your hand, and the broadcast will begin. It will go live throughout Megara, and be immediately transmitted to the other planets of the system, as well as all space stations and ships in transit or port."

"It will go to other systems, as well, right?"

"Yes. Our broadcasts go to every planet in the Confederation. As soon as the signal reaches the telecom station positioned at each transit point, it will be recorded and sent through via drone. The transmission will then be sent across that system, to all worlds and other pockets of habitation...as well as to the telecom stations at the other transit points in that system. The time to receipt and rebroadcast varies. The transmission will reach orbital stations around Megara and nearby ships in a matter of seconds, and the outer planets and moons in just under six hours. Complete transmission to every inhabited world in the Confederation takes a little less than eight days."

Andi nodded. "Thank you." In other circumstances, she might have found a detailed description of the Confederation's communications lines interesting, but her mind was elsewhere at that moment.

She walked through the door, into a large room with a high ceiling. There were immense screens on each of the walls, larger even than the main display on *Dauntless*. And, in the middle of the room, there was a single podium.

She walked over to it, and stepped up onto a small raised dais. She took a deep breath, fighting off another wave of nausea as she did. Then she stood silently for a moment, gathering her thoughts. She'd faced the worst violence humanity could concoct, but the thought of speaking to the entire Confederation suddenly seemed daunting.

You hope you're speaking to the entire Confederation. The Senate could cut the broadcast...if they act fast enough. There was no way for the Senate—or any other authorities—to send orders to stop the transmission, at least none that could travel from system to system any faster than her signal. Quick action, getting word to the telecom station to stop the drone before it transited, would be the only chance.

That was why she'd scheduled it for this moment...when every Senator was in the Compound, debating the very issue that concerned her.

Why the head of Confederation Intelligence was going to create a power failure on the Compound grounds, plunging the politicians and their staffs into total darkness, and subjecting them to a short communications black out.

She wanted the Senators to hear what she had to say—in fact, she was counting on it. She just wanted a little delay, just long enough to eliminate the chance of any trickery, any efforts by the Senate to violate the free communications laws of the Confederation.

When they saw what she had to say, and realized that the hundreds of billions in the Confederation were going to see the same transmission, they would capitulate. She was as sure of that as she'd ever been of anything.

Either that, or they would face the wrath of voters for forsaking the Confederation's greatest military hero...and ignoring the pleas of his pregnant wife.

She waved her hand, and an instant later, she cleared her throat.

"Citizens of the Confederation, greetings. My name is Captain Andi Lafarge and, among other things, I am the wife of Admiral Tyler Barron. I am here now to tell you of the situation the admiral currently faces...and about delays in sending aid to him. And also of the malfeasance and incompetence of the Senate in ensuring the safety of the Confederation and the Rim..."

Chapter Thirty-Two

HWS Leonidor
Orbiting Planet Pharsalon
Ettara-Mordlin III
Year of Renewal 267 (322 AC)

The Battle of Pharsalon – The Inferno

Chronos had never seen carnage like that unfolding all around him, not even in the worst battles on the Rim. His ships were deep in the fight, all that remained of his battleships and monitors deep in range and returning the enemy fire. They were scoring hits, and killing enemy vessels. But the cost was almost beyond imagining.

The Kriegeri were fighting heroically, their skill and steadfastness a validation in Chronos's mind of the Hegemonic system. Those warriors were doing what they'd been born to do, what their natural skillsets allowed them to do. And for all the Rimdwellers considered the genetic rankings somehow evil, there was little or no resentment for the system among the Hegemony's residents. Society was well ordered, its residents funneled into roles they could handle, jobs and responsibilities within the range of their abilities.

And, of course, those who'd been absorbed during their

lifetimes knew another way, the barbarism and misery of so many worlds in the aftermath of the Great Death. Hegemonic rule brought structure, and if it curtailed some level of unrestrained freedom, it traded food and shelter and medicine for it, and allowed those absorbed to lives of plenty, supported by technology. Few in the history of the Hegemony had rebelled against such a trade.

At least before the Rimdwellers. But they didn't suffer as most of the others did. They may call the Great Death, the Cataclysm, but what they think of from that terrible time was nothing compared to what worlds coreward endured.

Chronos winced as another of his monitors blinked off the display. It was a rare expression of emotion, at least while he was on duty. Masters, too, were compelled to play their own role in the Hegemony, and as Number Eight and commander of the fleet, Chronos was barred from being human, from expressing fear or weakness. His people *had* to see him as a rock, unbreakable. They had to draw strength from him, power to face the mysterious and deadly enemy.

As he watched the battle raging, he could see his officers, his division commanders, developing their own tactics to fight the Others. The enemy was advanced, their might overpowering, but as he saw the ingenuity of his people, the creativity of their maneuvers, he felt something vaguely like hope the Hegemony could learn to defeat the enemy.

If we last long enough. And we can't do it alone.

He was more certain than ever that his people needed help. Even the wildly creative maneuvers he was watching were not things he could credit solely to the Kriegeri's training or the Masters' intellect. He believed in Hegemonic society, but he could see the weaknesses in it as well. Placing someone in a genetically predetermined role eliminated incentives to progress farther.

His commanders had learned the wild battle tactics he was viewing not on their own, but out on the Rim, from the Confeds and their allies. The societies on the Rim seemed bizarre to Chronos, but he couldn't argue that the wild scrum for position and prestige—one that was open to anyone with the drive and energy to pursue what he or she wanted—created a kind of…feral…energy, one that seemed to spur creativity.

We're better for our interaction with them, however unfortunate the circumstances.

His eyes moved to the extreme end of the display. There were roughly sixty small symbols there, clustered around the transit tube. Barron's Confed ships.

Chronos had done all he could to convince Barron the Confederation and its allies had to join the fight, but as he sat there, watching his unit commanders behaving a lot like Barron's subordinates, he suddenly knew with unexplained certainty.

We need each other. It's the only way we can win this war.

He saw the way the cultures complemented each other…and after six years of war against the Hegemony, no one knew how to face a technologically superior enemy like the Rimdwellers.

His hands tightened on the armrests, as *Leonidor* shook. For an instant, Chronos thought his flagship had been badly hit. But the damage control reports quickly put his mind at ease. One of the deadly enemy beams had grazed the vessel, slicing open some outer compartments, and overloading part of the scanner array.

That was close…

Chronos held his cold, impassive pose, but inside, he was shaken. If that shot had been a hundred meters or so toward the ship's insides, *Leonidor* could very well be a cloud of dust and plasma.

His people were hurting the enemy, but their losses were too high. They couldn't hold. He needed Ilius's forces.

Now.

He looked along the display, toward the large cluster of small circles, the three hundred ships he'd positioned behind. Ilius's command. It was time to call his second into the fight.

But his eyes stopped cold, just short of where he'd intended to look. The tiny dots were out of position.

Ilius was already on the move.

* * *

"Antoine, get your squadron together. We're running a preparedness drill." Jake Stockton stood out in the hall, speaking softly as he gave Blue squadron's current commander an order. His old command would always hold a special place in his heart, but even though the squadron remained *Dauntless*'s senior formation, it carried no resemblance to the pack of hungry wolves he'd commanded so long ago. That Blue squadron had been the creation of the young 'Raptor' Stockton, the pilot who had feared nothing, who defied an enemy to dare to take a shot at him. That kind of unrestrained bravado was the province of those younger than the current Stockton, of those who had seen a good deal less death and suffering.

"I don't understand, Admiral...you mean now? While the battle is going on? That's somewhat of a...a surprise, isn't it?"

"Do you understand what 'readiness' means, Lieutenant? How much warning do you expect when I am testing your ability to respond under difficult and surprise conditions?"

"But there was nothing on the comm, Admiral. No alert status or other orders."

"I just gave you your orders, Lieutenant...and unless you want to spend the next ten years hauling radioactive waste on a scut cargo shuttle, you will follow them. Without further questions."

"Yes, Admiral."

"Good. Now, see that you've got your people down in the bay and ready in fifteen minutes. And alert your flight crews. I want you all in place, and your fighters ready to go on a moment's notice. It's time we got past lazy celebrations and remembered we're all warriors."

"Yes, Admiral. At once."

But Stockton could barely hear the words. He'd turned around even as he was still speaking, and by the time the stunned officer replied, he was already back out in the corridor. He had five other squadron leaders to visit, and it was time-consuming doing it without the comm.

But if he used the regular lines, someone besides his pilots and flight crews might hear. He knew the rules of engagement, and what Admiral Barron was an wasn't allowed to do. But Stockton believed in being prepared...for whatever happened. And he'd seen nothing in the rules that prohibited some impromptu training exercises. It was of no matter if said drills left his fighters fueled and armed and ready to launch.

He'd managed to get the word to six of the other ships, via shuttles and trusted officers. That was far from the fleet's entire fighter strength, of course, but it was thirty-six squadrons, six full wings, that would be fully prepared, ready to launch on an instant's notice.

Just in case Tyler Barron decides to...interpret...his orders with a bit of creativity...

* * *

"All ships, this is Commander Ilius. You all know why we're here, and what is at stake. This system is vital to our defensive efforts, and it is also on a direct line to Calpharon. We *must* hold here. We must drive the enemy back. You can see the losses our comrades have suffered—and also the damage they have inflicted on the enemy. It is time...time for us to come to their aid. Time to drive the enemy back."

Ilius had never been one to give stirring speeches to his warriors. It had never really been the Hegemony way. But he'd listened to some of the rousing comments Tyler Barron and his comrades had made during the war. At first, he'd assumed such things worked in the chaotic atmosphere of the Rim nations and their armed forces, but that they'd be misplaced in the well-ordered Hegemony service. But now he was leading his Kriegeri into a battle he knew was almost hopeless. He'd almost been paralyzed by his own fear, and he'd taken a lesson from that. Kriegeri were chosen for their genetic suitability for battle, and they were flawlessly trained. But they were still human beings. If Ilius himself was not immune to fear, neither were his spacers. They needed his encouragement, the excitement he could rouse inside them.

They need me to lie to them, to tell them we have a chance to win the victory here…

He hid his own dark thoughts, and he held back the cold fear still pressing against his defenses. The fleet was drawing blood from the enemy, and that was good news. But it didn't take a Master level mathematician to see where the loss ratios would lead. The fleet couldn't win. The choice would come down to retreat or extermination.

He didn't know which he would choose if he commanded the fleet. His fear wanted him to run, to order the ships he led to make a mad dash for the transit tube, but some part of him saw the relief in a glorious death, in fighting to the end. He couldn't decide if that was the courageous option, or a coward's way out of a war he was sure his people would lose.

Fortunately, Chronos was in command. Ilius was grateful he had so few options himself. All that had been left to him was to choose his axis of advance…and he'd done that with all the skill and intellect he could muster. He was throwing all his ships against the enemy's extreme left wing. If his ships could get up to the line quickly enough, they just might enjoy local force superiority, at least for a little while.

He turned toward his chief aide. "All ships are to increase thrust to full power." He intended to minimize the time his ships were vulnerable to the enemy guns, while still outside their own firing range, even if that meant his ships would engage at high velocities and zip right past the enemy ships. That would make withdrawal more difficult, and risk trapping his entire force, but it exchanged a respite from almost certain heavy losses for possible future danger. That was a deal Ilius was prepared to accept.

He nodded as his aide passed on acknowledgements from the various sub-units of the fleet. Then he took a deep breath. His ships were entering the enemy's firing range. He'd done all he could to minimize the duration, to prepare his vessels for maximum evasive maneuvers. There was nothing left but to run the guns.

To blast forward at full until his ships were close enough to open fire and make the fight a truly two-sided one.

* * *

"The Hegemony fighters are exhibiting a greater degree of unpredictability than we projected. Our losses are considerably higher than even the most pessimistic forecasts." Tesserax sat at one end of a large polished metal table, his immense form casting a three-meter shadow across the floor as he addressed his comrades, the Supreme Council of the Pacification.

"I concur, Grand Admiral." Phazarax's voice was deeper even than Tesserax's. His position as head of the church gave him final authority on all matters dealing with the lower creatures of the Hegemony and the other former imperial sectors. "Our scouting mission of a century ago suggested no such flexibility of thought, and projections strongly indicated the Hegemonic society would have become less flexible, more calcified than what we are witnessing here. That assumption, for unknown reasons, has proven to be incorrect. They are still no threat, of course, to your forces, Grand Admiral, not in any real sense. Our losses, while unexpected, can be replaced, and I do not perceive any sequence of events in which they are able to make a real stand against our forces. My concern lies elsewhere, in the aftermath of conquest. We determined that the Hegemonic society was one well-ordered to produce new slaves to sustain our growth and expansion, one reason we allowed it to exist for so long, to develop on its existing course. We expected to find human beings with considerable drone-like characteristics, accustomed to close direction, and yet as the battle continues, we are witnessing no small degree of independent initiative. I had always expected we would have to terminate all or most of the Masters, but now I find myself speculating about what degree of harsh measures will be required to return the lower castes to a state of pure obedience."

"Your concerns are valid, of course, High Priest, and such decisions, when the time comes, will be largely yours to make. Yet, perhaps the problem is not as severe as it might appear. Analysis of the systems we have encountered to date suggests that Hegemony population levels exceed our estimates, perhaps by a considerable margin. Even if we are compelled to terminate larger numbers than expected to break any resistance, I am confident that more than enough will remain for our purposes. There may even be utility to it all in the end. A properly broken population may be more adeptly directed to their new purposes than one that is merely docile to start. As long as there is an excess of population, there is little real concern if termination levels are doubled or even tripled."

"I am inclined to concur, Tesserax, though I believe you were correct to call this assembly, that the matter was, at least, worthy of discussion. Are all present in agreement with the Grand Admiral's assessment? Its resolution that the Pacification proceed in accordance with the original plan."

A round of acknowledgements moved down the table, with almost perfect order and timing. It was unanimous.

"Very well then." Tesserax bowed his head to those gathered around him. "My thanks to each of you for this unscheduled meeting. I wanted to confirm that we were all in agreement before I proceeded to increase the intensity of operations in this system. Specifically, with the High Priest's agreement, I plan to launch an extermination assault against both the inhabited planet and also the seventh satellite of the star, which our scanners indicate contains a primitive antimatter production facility. It is now clear why the Hegemonic forces chose this system to make a stand, and my analysis is, the simultaneous destruction of a major population center and the elimination of what must be a significant percentage of their antimatter production can only serve to further unnerve and distract the forces now engaged with our fleet."

Everyone present gestured affirmatively. Then, a moment later, Phazarax spoke. "You indeed have my consent, Tesserax. Proceed as you see fit, with the full blessing of this Council."

The Grand Admiral rose, his immense form towering over the table. "Once again, my thanks to all of you. The enemy has called forth its reserves. All of its forces, save only for the small armada remaining at the jump point, are now committed and deep within the system. I have given the orders for the final phase. If fortune is with us, the bulk of the Hegemony fleet will be destroyed in this system in the next hours."

"We stand with you, Grand Admiral. Go with the support of all on this Council. The lower creatures in this system are expendable...and the destruction of enemy antimatter production is a first order priority."

Chapter Thirty-Three

Stallia Vente Hospital
Liberte City
Planet Montmirail, Ghassara IV
Union Year 225 (321 AC)

"First Citizen...can you hear me?"

The words were soft, distant. Villieneuve was floating, drifting along a cool breeze, lost, uncertain of where he was. He reached out, tried to follow the voice, to find his way back to...

To what? He didn't know. Or did he?

There was something else, something new. Anger? Was it new? Or was it old, just returning?

His view changed, morphing from a soft gauzy haze to a harsh, bright light. And beyond, faces, blurry at first, but slowly coming into focus.

"Where?" He croaked out the one-word question, his throat aching as he did.

"You're in the hospital, First Citizen."

"How...why?"

"There was an explosion...a nuclear accident. The Hall of the People is gone, First Citizen, and most of the surrounding buildings. You were leaving early...you were outside, close, but partially protected from the primary blast zone. I found you there, got you away."

"Who...are...you?" Then, before the man responded, "Steves?"

"Yes, First Citizen. It's Gravis Steves. I was able to contact your elite guards. There are fifty of them here. They are patrolling all around the hospital. You're safe."

"For...now...maybe..." Clarity was returning, and with it an irresistible urge, a yawning need to act, to take steps to preserve his power."

"Ciara?"

"As far as I've heard, she is still missing. She *must* be dead, sir."

"Can't assume that...who...is...running...government?"

"As far as anyone knows, you are, First Citizen. I put out word that you were in your bunker managing a response to this atrocity. So far it seems to be working."

"No...won't stop anyone...plots already...in works..." Villieneuve turned his head to the side...and the room flipped upside down. He could feel the vomit rising, and he tried to turn over before it came up, with limited success. He retched hard, and he felt the warm froth sliding down his neck and onto his shoulders.

"Please, First Citizen, you have to remain still. You've had a preliminary radiation cleanse, but I'm afraid you're still suffering from the effects of the contamination."

"Go...get out of here." The command was directed at the nurse trying to clean up the mess he'd made. Villieneuve was angry, not really at the nurse, or at Steves, whom he realized had probably saved his life, but at the situation, and at his own helplessness.

And at the realization that his political rivals were almost certainly plotting, if not already deep into efforts to unseat him, to seize power for themselves. He didn't have time to lay around in some hospital, but if he couldn't even turn his head without vomiting, he was stuck.

"No time...to stay...here..."

"First Citizen, you have six broken ribs, a partially repaired punctured lung, multiple internal injuries, second level radiation sickness. You *have* to stay here. Tell me what you need, and I'll take care of it."

"Steves...thank...you.   Help   me...now...and   you will...be...rewarded." Villieneuve detested being helpless, but he was a cold realist, and like it or not, he was completely dependent on Steves and on his guards. He'd managed to get a glimpse of one of the sentries outside his door. Steves had gotten his redshirts. The elite team was loyal, he was sure of that, though he realized an enemy only had to turn one of them to pull off a quick assassination. He wasn't exactly a hard target lying in bed.

"I did everything I could think of, but..."

"You did...well. Now, I...need my people. We need to...reassert...control. Lysien, Pepian, Velechaun...to start. Find them...and bring them...here..."

Steves was silent for a few seconds. "They're dead, First Citizen...all except for Velechaun. I couldn't find him. He's probably dead, too, but I haven't been able to confirm."

Villieneuve nodded, stopping the move halfway when his stomach rebelled again. He was alive, for the moment, but unless he could get back in control, he wasn't likely to stay that way. He had to find out which of his reliable people were still alive.

Assuming he could consider anyone reliable...

* * *

"Andre, thank you so much for coming. What happened was a nightmare, a terrible atrocity on our city." Ciara was sitting on a large couch, trying to look less weak and injured than she was. The townhouse belonged to Pierre Chantrel, and old ally...and a former lover. She'd gambled wildly, bet her life that Chantrel would help her, that he, too, would place a wager with monumental stakes. If she prevailed, and seized power, Chantrel would become her top industrial advisor...and no doubt shortly after that, the wealthiest man in the Union.

Contacting Andre Velechaun had been her second audacious bet, a far riskier one. Velechaun was one of Villieneuve's key people, a longtime ally of the First Citizen. But Ciara was well-versed in driving wedges between friends and comrades, and her overture to Velechaun had been accompanied by the daring claim that Villieneuve was in hiding somewhere, and that none other than the First Citizen himself had orchestrated the bombing in a fit of paranoia after the coup attempt, an effort to eliminate some of those close to him who might be tempted to emulate her actions. It was wild, hard to believe...but then Velechaun knew Villieneuve very well, and the whole fiction was something the First Citizen's ruthless mind just might conceive.

Anyway, Velechaun *had* come, and in a few minutes, she'd know if he was serious about listening to her proposal...or if he'd simply taken the chance to get close so he could kill her. The reports on the street proclaimed the First Citizen was fine and in total control of the government, but Velechaun's arrival told Ciara that wasn't true. Or, certainly, that it wasn't the whole story. Then, her guest hit her with a bombshell.

"Gaston Villieneuve was caught in the explosion...but he is alive." Velechaun's tone was neutral. She was usually good at reading people, but this time she had nothing. She figured it was about fifty-fifty whether he was there to discuss backing her efforts to seize power...or to put her down and collect his reward from Villieneuve. The odds had been better a few seconds before, when she hadn't known for sure the First Citizen had survived. She'd heard the media reports, of course, about Villieneuve being unharmed, but she hadn't believed them for an instant. If he'd been 'unharmed' he'd have been all over the broadcast nets.

He must be injured at least…

"That is unfortunate." She glanced up at Velechaun, and in that moment, she let her guard down and prepared to accept her fate, whatever it was. "So, did you come to talk? Or are there a hundred Foudre Rouge surrounding the house?"

"I imagine, from your perspective, that may seem the likelier option, and very probably, it would have been, save for one fact. I have known Gaston Villieneuve for a long time, and I have seen him during crises. I was by his side after the collapse of the Presidium, when he seized sole power. I watched him execute thousands as he solidified his base, including many loyal Sector Nine operatives, sacrificed because it was politically expedient for him to represent himself as new and separate from the old regime. That was all a fraud, of course, but I haven't forgotten. I think he was truly friends with Ricard Lille, but I don't believe the man has ever had a relationship with anyone else that wasn't based on expediency, or anyone he wouldn't expend if it served his purposes. Now, with your—and I assume *you* were behind the explosion—move against him, he is likely to continue to react very violently. Especially, as I believe he is wounded, and somewhere in hiding. It is a dangerous time to be his ally or confidante, and that is why I am here, Sandrine. I will not waste time telling you I believe in what you're doing, or that I feel you will be a better First Citizen than Villieneuve. But I believe I can make a deal with you, and that you will be less likely to suddenly order my execution if we are successful. I considered making my own play for power, but I lack the resources and preparation that you clearly have…even after the failure of your coup and the damage caused to your network." A pause. "I will settle for the number two position. If I support you, and we succeed, you will name me Chancellor. Those are my terms."

Ciara was surprised—a little that she wasn't being

gunned down by Foudre Rouge or Sector Nine thugs, but mostly at what Velechaun had said. She'd been prepared to do her best to persuade him to support her openly, or at least, covertly. She hadn't expected one so close to Villieneuve to be ready to throw in with her completely.

Or to have his price so carefully determined.

She was edgy about offering him the number two spot in her government, assuming she survived long enough to establish one. She knew Velechaun well enough, and his decision to hold back from a play on the top spot was in no way a guarantee against future treachery. All things considered, she'd have preferred someone less ambitious—and less capable—in the Chancellor's post.

But she needed allies, and Velechaun was a powerful one, all the more useful because Villieneuve probably expected his support.

"Very well, Andre. Support me fully, with all your resources and capabilities, and I will appoint you Chancellor."

Her new ally nodded. "Then it is done...First Citizen. My first advice, paramount above all things right now is simple in theory, though likely difficult in fact. Before we make any kind of overt move on the First Citizen's chair, we have to kill Gaston Villieneuve."

*　*　*

"She *has* to be dead, Ambassador. There can't be much doubt she was behind the explosion. It was a...higher magnitude...option than we'd anticipated, but for all the collateral damage, perhaps one with a higher likelihood of success. The real question is, did Gaston Villieneuve really escape as the media reports claim, or did she actually manage to get him?" Kyle Corbin had been sitting with Kerevsky for hours, going through every report, every news broadcast, trying to get some idea what was going on.

What was *actually* going on.

They had no real idea of the situation, but the one thing they both knew for certain was they couldn't trust anything the Union media said.

They'd sweated things out for the first couple days, the enraged mob outside worked up by early reports suggesting the Confederation had been responsible for the bombing, and looking as though they'd storm the embassy at any moment. Kerevsky hadn't relished the thought of the fallout from Confederation Marines gunning down Union civilians…and even less, the idea of being literally torn to pieces by that same enraged mob.

"I'm not so sure, Kyle. She's pretty…resourceful." Kerevsky wondered if his analysis of Ciara was impartial, or if it was colored by his affection for her. He *wanted* to believe she was still alive, but he'd never allowed desires to distort his analysis before. There wasn't any question, though. the more important mystery was Gaston Villieneuve's fate. If the dictator had been killed, the Union would likely slip into chaos as multiple parties struggled to take his place. Whatever happened, and whoever prevailed, it was almost certain to be a positive for the Confederation. Villieneuve's hatred for the Union's longtime enemy bordered on pathological, and while Kerevsky didn't doubt the Confederation could handle any Union aggression, with the discovery of the Hegemony, the situation had become far more complex. If the Confederation ever had to face both nations at the same time, not even considering what else might lurk out there, farther coreward, the results would be disastrous.

He didn't fool himself that any change in the Union would usher in more freedom for its people, but almost anyone would be less of a danger to the Confederation than Villieneuve.

And, if Sandrine still is alive, and if she somehow manages to seize control after all…we might just be able to work something out. He didn't have any doubt Ciara would sign a long-term treaty with the Confederation, in return for aid to prop up the Union's ever-teetering economy and her new and fragile regime.

"We *have* to know, Kyle. Send out some agents. Tell them to be careful...but we need to know if Villieneuve is alive or dead." He paused. "And we need to know about Sandrine Ciara as well."

At least, I need to know.

Chapter Thirty-Four

Highborn Flagship S'Argevon
Imperial System GH8-14F3
Year of the Firstborn 384 (322 AC)

The Battle of Pharsalon – "The Kill"

"All delivery vehicles fully armed and prepared to launch on your command, Grand Admiral."

Tesserax didn't move, didn't look over at the Thrall at the tactical station. The ship's crew, the technicians and specialists who operated the vast craft, were as nothing to him, expendable supplicants drawn from the vast hordes of worshippers. Simply serving the Highborn in such close proximity was an honor, one worth any danger, any death.

"You may launch on both targets."

Tesserax wasn't sure what effect the bombardments would have on the actions of the Hegemony fleet. He saw very little value in a world of some hundreds of millions of the lower creatures, though no doubt the enemy combatants, also of such lesser stature, might feel differently. Indeed, Tesserax was confident they would. Any distraction, any diversion of resources in an attempt to intercept the delivery vehicles, would only speed the destruction of the enemy fleet. Then, once their military assets were destroyed, the Hegemony would lay helpless before his forces. The reordering of the human society could begin in earnest, and those billions of inhabitants who survived would learn to take their places as supplicants and worshippers. Their obedience would be forged in the blood of those who resisted, their worship in the growing recognition that the Highborn were their superiors, as Gods destined to rule over them...and to shepherd them into the future.

S'Argevon shook, a slight vibration that Tesserax's superior senses detected. He very much doubted any of the Thralls had felt the delivery vehicles launching. The missiles were massive, equipped with all manner of electronic countermeasures to thwart interception. They carried multiple antimatter warheads, over a thousand in each. Three, perhaps four, of the giant missiles could wipe a world completely clean of its population and artificial structures. And over two hundred of them were now heading toward the target planets.

So much for distraction as a tactic. Now, it was time to unleash the final blow, to trap the enemy fleet, to turn a victory into extermination.

"It is time." His voice was deep, booming across the vast space of the ship's control center. "Initiate phase four."

"As you command." A moment later: "Phase four initiated, Grand Admiral. All commands confirm."

Tesserax stared straight ahead, his demeanor cold, unreadable, as it always was. But in his thoughts, deep within his exceedingly capable and complex Highborn mind, he prepared to savor his favorite part of such operations.

The kill.

* * *

"Commander Chronos, we're detecting multiple launches from the enemy fleet. They appear to be physical constructs...the AI's best projection is they are delivery vehicles for planetary bombardment warheads."

Chronos had already written off the population of Pharsalon, though the immediacy of the danger to the people there still jabbed at him, wearing down his resolve. Could he really sit there and make no effort to save them, however unlikely success might be?

Then he glanced at the display, and he froze.

The giant missiles were not just heading for Pharsalon. They were also targeting planet seven.

"All ships in quadrant nine...commence interception operations at once. I want those missiles destroyed." He knew he was drawing strength away from the main fight, reducing his fleet's already slim chances of prevailing in the battle raging all around. And a few seconds later, he saw more waves of missiles, and he knew the chances of intercepting them all were slim.

But planet seven represented forty years of work, trillions upon trillions of Hegemony credits, and thousands of Arbeiter killed during construction operations on its inhospitable surface. It was almost irreplaceable, and critically important to the war effort. The loss of three hundred million civilians, after all those lost already, would hurt, but an inability to keep the fleet supplied with antimatter would dash any hopes of saving the seven hundred billion citizens of the Hegemony.

Chronos watched as the ships in the designated division executed his orders, veering off from their courses, at least as quickly as thrust and existing velocities allowed. Almost immediately, he saw a missile targeted and destroyed, and then another. But he knew the calculus of the situation. Those missiles were big, and the warheads they carried were almost certainly enormously powerful, probably antimatter armed. His people could destroy half of the vehicles, or three-quarters. Or even ninety-five percent. But enough would get through to devastate the two planets.

Chronos looked away from planet seven, his eyes

moving back to the main battle area. Just in time to see a pair of his battleships wink off the screen. The fight was still raging all around, and his people were drawing blood themselves. But it was becoming clearer with every passing moment that his forces weren't going to prevail. But in that moment, he saw Ilius's ships moving up, driving right through the enemy fire, losing four of their big ships in the process. But then the reserves moved into their own range, and over a hundred ships opened up with railgun batteries…every one of the double loaded, their super-heavy metal projectiles streaking through space at unimaginable velocities.

And when one of those shots struck, even the nearly invulnerable hulls of the Others' ships gave way. One of the enemy ships in the forward group was struck by three shots in rapid succession. The vessel shook hard, and then split open like an egg. Two more of the Others' vessels followed, in explosions of such magnitude, Chronos could only imagine what the scanner readings would have said.

He felt a moment's satisfaction, and his hands clenched reflexively into fists as he silently urged Ilius and his warriors forward.

Then he saw the price they were paying.

No fewer than ten capital ships, two monitors and eight battleships were gone. Just gone. And two dozen other vessels had suffered some degree of damage. Some of that had happened during the early stages of the advance, when the enemy could fire and Ilius's ships could not. Things had moved closer to even…but not close enough.

Chronos watched as another of the black-speckled blue beams of energy tore through one of the already damaged monitors. The massive vessel shuddered, and then nothing. For a few seconds, Chronos thought the ship might survive. Then, it vanished in a searing blast of pure energy, and when the miniature sun was gone, nothing remained except for a cloud of extremely hard radiation.

But the rest of Ilius's ships were plunging into the battle, looking very much like they intended to fight to the bitter end.

Unless he called them off…gave the order to run.

* * *

"Admiral, the Heggies…I mean, the Hegemony forces…are fighting well, better than we could have expected. But they're still going to lose." Atara had walked the three meters from her post to Barron's command chair. She stood next to him, leaning over, her lips millimeters from his ear. Her words were for him only, and for all of *Dauntless's* technology and equipment, the quickest and easiest way to deliver them was still to walk over and whisper to him.

"I know, Atara." Barron had turned his head slightly, his voice almost as soft as hers. "But there's nothing we can do about that."

"Are you sure, Tyler? We could…"

"We have been expressly forbidden to intervene, to even engage the enemy in any situation absent a direct and intentional attack against us. There is nothing we can do." Barron paused, almost consumed by frustration. The urge to order his ships forward, to disregard his orders, was overwhelming. Duty held him back, discipline…and the realization that simply leading his ships forward, into the already wild melee would achieve nothing except the destruction of his entire force. The enemy was simply too powerful, too concentrated in the center.

He knew what he had to do. His fleet had collected enough data, more than it could ever use. The rules of engagement were clear. His decision had been made for him months before on the Senate floor.

"Admiral Travis…" He turned his head, and he looked right at Atara, his eyes no more than four or five centimeters from her own. "…the fleet will prepare to withdraw. The rear line will begin transiting as soon as the ships are in position."

He could see the hesitation, feel the pain and tension almost radiating off his friend and comrade. She had been almost inveterately hostile to the Hegemony, against any chance of siding with them. Now, she wanted to dash forward, to plunge into the battle.

But she didn't argue. She just nodded her head and turned back toward her own seat.

Barron knew she understood as well as he did. They had no other choice.

* * *

The engineer looked through the clear hyperpolycarbonate of the dome, up into the fiery red sky, streaked, as usual, with gray-white trails of toxic gasses. The planet was a nightmare, a vision of hell itself, but it was one of the most important places in the Hegemony. And, according to the scanner reports, it was about to be bombarded by waves of enemy missiles.

Much of the vast antimatter production facility was underground, bored deep into the planet's bedrock. It would take an enormous amount of destructive energy to knock it out entirely, though smaller, targeted impacts could cause significant damage to transmission lines and other critical systems.

Vigius was a Hegemony Master, and the head of engineering at the sprawling antimatter foundry, but at that moment, all he could do was look up into the planet's impenetrable haze, his eyes squinting, trying to detect some sign of warheads descending toward the surface. That was foolish, he knew, a pointless effort in more ways than one. But the reports had also confirmed the destruction of the orbital fortresses. All of them. The planet's defenses were gone, the ships posted around it destroyed. There were no options left, no modes of defense remaining available.

Nothing but to gaze up at the sky, searching for signs of approaching death.

Vigius was somewhat typical of his exalted caste in Hegemony society. He'd been cocky as a young man, arrogant, overly proud of the genes inside him, an advantage for which he could claim no personal credit. Much of that had mellowed with age, as the cumulative effects of his own misjudgments, mixed with some examples of clearly brilliant work by many of the high-level Arbeiter on his staff, had given him cause to think. He still believed in the Hegemonic system. There was simply too much proof, far too many clear correlations between strong genetics and intelligence, ability. But it was far less an exact science than he'd once believed.

His thoughts were strangely philosophical for a man facing imminent death. *Or maybe not*, he thought. *What else is there to fill these last moments?*

He wasn't a warrior, though he knew enough about the current military situation to entertain the thought that he was actually fortunate. If there were antimatter warheads even then descending from orbit, his end would come quickly, as it would for all of his people. For the rest of the Hegemony, from the Kriegeri in the warships fighting all around the system to the billions living on planets across a vast swath of space, there would be continued terror and anguish. Some would also die quickly when their times came, and others in agony, screaming in pain and uncontrolled fear.

How is this possible? We are—were—the pinnacle, the society destined to rebuild humanity, to restore the glory of the empire…while avoiding its terrible mistakes. He'd always believed that, supported the Hegemony's sacred purpose with all his heart. Now, all he saw was the hubris, the uncontrolled arrogance.

Why do we always think we know more than we do? In our way, while speaking so boldly of the need to avoid the empire's course, what have we done but emulated it, taking from them the unshakeable belief that we are always right.

Now, we will pay the price. As the empire did before us.

He heard the klaxons in the background, the alarm system calling the staff to the underground bunkers. Vigius twitched, his body's reflexes trying to respond to the warning call. But his intellect was still in charge, and he knew there was no point. No need to spend the final seconds of his life crawling into a doomed hole in the ground.

He took a breath, sucking in a lungful of the station's sterile, artificial air. But in his mind, it was the spring breeze of his homeworld. *How many things did I ignore, fail to appreciate? How many things I planned to do were left undone? We think so highly of ourselves, yet we are so fragile, we have so little time.*

As he continued his thoughts, his eye caught something, a trail of light, of flaming sparks as one of the warheads came down through the planet's dense atmosphere.

Some of those warheads will be set for airburst, others for burrowing mode. It was a realization of no real value, and yet it was worth all he had left, the difference between dying in minutes, or dying in seconds.

His mind raced, every person in his life to whom he still had something to say staring at him from the dark reaches, every decision he regretted, pushing its way to the forefront of his thoughts.

He could hear his heart pounding, and as he wiped the sweat from his forehead, he could feel that his hands, too, were wet with perspiration. He was afraid, as scared as he'd ever been.

And yet, there was peace there, too, a strange calm. He ached not for himself, nor for his people on the planet, but for the others, still doomed to fight a hopeless war, to endure just long enough to see all they knew, all they'd lived for and cared about destroyed.

His thoughts slipped back, wondering if the incoming

bombs were set to burrow, or...

He never completed that thought.

In an instant, it was all gone, Vigius, the building he was in, every surface structure in any direction for kilometers upon kilometers, obliterated in the unimaginable fury of matter-antimatter annihilation.

Chapter Thirty-Five

Senate Compound
Troyus City
Megara, Olyus III
Year 322 AC

"What you did was outrageous, Captain. I will see that you are clapped in irons. You can deliver that brat you're carrying in the deepest, darkest cell in the detention center." Kettle Vaughn was apoplectic. Andi had considered ignoring the Senate's demand that she appear, but she knew her work wasn't done, not until the politicians voted to authorize the fleet to go to Tyler's aid. She'd backed them into a corner with her broadcast, maneuvered them to the edge of the precipice.

Now, it was time to push them over.

Vaughn's words came at her, almost like a fuel stoking her own volatile rage. Andi was not the kind to take abuse, to stand helplessly while some miserable fool threatened her.

Not even when that fool was a Confederation Senator.

She'd killed men for less. Far less. And she wouldn't have lost a night's sleep for putting Vaughn in his grave either. But killing a Senator in the middle of the Compound would have a lot of...complications. And it wouldn't do anything for Tyler.

So, she just took it, or at least what Andi Lafarge considered 'taking it.' But that was only going to go so far.

"Senator Vaughn, you can threaten me all you want, but I've faced some *really* intimidating people in my life and lived to tell about it. If you think a pompous buffoon of a politician from some industrial shithole—especially one with such…unfortunate…taste in suits—is going to make the grade, you're sorely mistaken. You are too stupid to realize it, of course, but you're actually in my debt. My solution was more elegant, and probably a lot less unpleasant for you than the others you might have faced. I realize that your particular breed of Elventian boreworm doesn't understand loyalty, Senator, but do you really think the navy, the Marines, were going to let you ignore Tyler's request for aid? Did you think they would allow you to dicker and debate endlessly while the danger grew ever more dire? You're too stupid and too arrogant to realize that your Senate rank does not make you invulnerable, regardless of what you tell yourself in the mirror when you're shaving. Now, do you want to keep threatening me, and pretending that you've got enough inside your entire worthless sack of blood and guts to scare me? Or do you want to do what you already know you have to do? Because if we don't resolve this today, and exactly the way I want it, I swear to God, you worthless maggot, I will go from one end of the Confederation to the other, and tell the people exactly how the Senate abandoned their great hero…and tried to manhandle his pregnant wife."

Vaughn stepped back a bit, his face a mask of astonishment. Andi knew he was accustomed to people pandering to him and kissing his ass, and she wondered if anybody had ever spoken to him quite the way she just had.

Or had enjoyed it as much.

Or if he was capable of understanding that what he'd just heard was her holding back and 'taking it.' Anything that didn't end with a blade deep in his chest cavity pretty much qualified as that.

There was a tense quiet for a moment, and then a voice cut through the quiet. "Senator Vaughn...whatever your feelings about Captain Lafarge's actions...I daresay she had left us with few options. Senator Avaria has already promised her support for the measure to send reinforcements to Admiral Barron, and to authorize him to negotiate an alliance with the Hegemony and deploy his forces to battle however he deems appropriate. If you join us, the matter will pass by a large margin, and perhaps the other factions will yield to the inevitable, and allow us to pass the authorization unanimously. I don't like the thought of another war any more than you do, but I can't imagine Admiral Barron does either. If he sees a threat, it is very likely a real one, best faced hundreds of lightyears from here before it ends up on our doorstep."

Andi watched as Speaker Flandry spoke to his colleague. Flandry was somewhat of an ally, though she suspected he, too, was secretly enraged at the way she'd gone around them, boxed them in.

She also didn't care.

Flandry was enough of a realist to know he didn't have a choice, but she couldn't imagine the politician, no less arrogant in his own way than Vaughn, if somewhat smarter, was happy with her either. She just didn't care. She was slightly more disposed to the Speaker than she was to vermin like Vaughn, but all things considered, she wouldn't shed a tear if the whole Senate fell into a volcano somewhere.

At least after they gave her the vote she needed.

"Senators...I understand you all work on a different schedule than productive elements of society, but can we move this along, please. Admiral Winters is waiting to hear from me, and if there is a problem, I feel duty bound to make another address and tell the people of the

Confederation what is happening here."

So, I guess now we'll see if any of you have the guts to actually try to arrest me and try to get me to recant what I said.

You don't have a hole deep or dark enough for that...

* * *

"Thank you, Clint. It's far from ideal, but it's the best I can manage." Andi was usually extremely adept at hiding weaknesses, but she knew that wall was crumbling, that her sadness was fully on display to her friend.

She handed the data chip to Winters. It was just about the last way she wanted to tell Tyler he was going to be a father, but it was her only choice. She couldn't go with the fleet, not without exposing the baby she carried to terrible hazards in the transit points. She'd thought about not telling him, of waiting until they were together again, whenever that would be. She told herself that would be a mercy, that it would spare him pain, prevent distraction while he was leading his forces.

But too many people in the fleet already knew, and the idea of him finding out by accident was even more upsetting than delivering the news by recorded message.

"Andi...I know this is difficult for you, not only because the prospect of a new conflict is a grim development for all of us, but because you are not the kind to stay behind, out of the fight. But there's no other way, not now, and you know it. So, take care of yourself and try to think positively. That's what Tyler would want, and you know it."

Andi winced slightly. Winters's last comment had been well-meaning, but it had also been somewhat of a low blow.

"I know that, Clint. It is hard to stay back, to sit here while everyone I know and care about is going off to fight. But it's more than that. Another war? So soon after the last one? Won't we ever have peace, some time just to *live*?"

Andi had spent most of her life pursuing what she

wanted. That had mostly been about surviving in her days back in the Gut, and then it had become a pursuit for success, for wealth. Now, she had everything she'd ever wanted...and a good number of things she'd never imagined. She was enormously wealthy, she had Tyler, she was even about to have a baby, something she'd hardly ever imagined. Everything about her life was good just then, save for the one thing that destroyed it all, cut across her happiness like a jagged blade.

War.

She'd always been a fighter, a warrior in her own right, if not exactly a disciplined soldier or spacer. But she was tired now, and all she wanted was peace, to live with her small but growing family, and the few true friends she'd acquired along her way.

But as she sat there, that seemed an impossible goal. Everyone close to her was a warrior of one kind or another, and now they would all face hardship and danger. Again.

She looked up at Winters, and despite her best efforts, she couldn't hold back the tears. "Please, Clint...tell Tyler I'm okay. Don't let him know I'm...so weak."

"You are the farthest thing I know from weak, Andi. Let me tell you a secret, one thing I've come to learn from a lifetime in service. Fighting is hard on us, the pain, the loss, the stress...but it's harder on those we leave behind. We think of our comrades, those we lost, and those wounded, hurt, but it is too easy to forget spouses and children and parents back home. They suffer as we do, perhaps even more so. And for you, one so used to being in the fight, I can't imagine what you're feeling." Winters paused, and Andi felt a wave of appreciation, for his words, and even more, for his obvious but welcome effort to pretend he didn't notice she was crying.

"Thank you, Clint." A pause. "I mean it."

"Ease up on yourself, Andi. What you did was incredible. You've done more for the Confederation with that maneuver than anyone else in any of this…and even more for Tyler. Even here, kept away from the front, you fought the fight. And you won."

She leaned forward and hugged the admiral, planting a kiss on his cheek. "Thank you," she said again, as she pulled slowly back. Then, a moment later: "So, when do you leave?"

"Tomorrow." He managed something like a smile. "I…ah…I took some steps before I had authorization to make sure the fleet was provisioned and ready, just in case. I guess that was forward thinking of me."

Andi, against every expectation, matched his tentative grin. "Well, I guess that *was* handy, wasn't it?" Her face slipped back into a nondescript expression. "Take care of yourself, my friend. Come back. All of you. Please."

But even as she said it, she knew not all of them would come back.

She just hoped some of them would.

Chapter Thirty-Six

Highborn Vessel E'Septalon
Imperial System GH8-14F3
Year of the Firstborn 384 (322 AC)

The Battle of Pharsalon – "The Flank Attack"

"We are underway, Grand Admiral. Your orders are understood and will be obeyed." Hellerax sat in his chair, his massive stature greater even than Tesserax's. Even among the Highborn, the self-styled gods of the galaxy, he was an impressive sight. His implants seemed perfect, well-located, with their exo portions polished to a bright sheen. He was younger than Tesserax, not one of the Firstborn, but his abilities had powered his advancement, and placed him in command of his own attack force.

He'd received his orders, and he'd acknowledged, though it would be almost an hour before the message reached Tesserax's flagship. For all the technology of the Highborn, aside from carrying messages through jump points, the speed of light remained the upper limit on communications.

Hellerax's ships were tasked with the final phase of the battle, the maneuver that would turn the Hegemony's defeat into annihilation. The orders were clear. Emerge from the deep outer system where his ships had been hiding, and proceed toward the enemy's jump point, cutting them off, trapping their survivors in the system where they could be attacked from multiple vectors and exterminated. The command of the flanking force was an honor, a high posting for one not of the Firstborn, and Hellerax was determined to make full use of it.

He'd run the calculations three times—just in his head, of course, it was nothing more than basic third-level differential vector calculus—and the results had been the same. His ships would arrive before the enemy could reach the jump point. There was no chance the Hegemony fleet would escape. Only a single variable had remained, the force that had remained out of the fight, sitting just inside the jump point while the battle raged.

Those ships would have been close enough to intervene, but the scanners confirmed the data he'd received a few minutes earlier. They were already retreating through the jump point. Indeed, most of them had already gone. Perhaps the Hegemony forces had detected his flanking force, realized that their main fleet was doomed. The vessels that had departed were few relative to the size of the force that would be destroyed, but Hellerax was relieved to be rid of them. Their positioning had placed them well to interfere with his flank attack, even to threaten his entire force.

It was a pity that even such a small force should escape, but once those vessels were gone, and his own ships were firmly position, the die would be cast. The cream of the Hegemony's strength would be destroyed, leaving only scattered forces to defend over four hundred inhabited planets.

The Highborn would move forward to victory, and the humans, the vast masses of genetically inferior animals, would learn the new reality. They would learn to serve and worship the Highborn.

For eternity.

* * *

"All ships, maintain fire, double loads on all shots." Ilius had lost thirty-one ships. Twenty-eight of them had fallen to enemy fire, and three to the breathtakingly dangerous practice of jamming in double-strength antimatter loads before firing his railguns. He'd counted at least six different ways the reckless tactic had backfired, sometimes causing moderate damage…and others total disaster.

But he'd also seen the effects on the targeted enemy ships. The Others' ships were enormously powerful, far more advanced than the Hegemony's own. But when one of those railgun shots slammed into the hull at twice the normal velocity, even the hardened, shielded alloy of the enemy warships shattered and vaporized.

The hit rates were up, too, in addition to the higher damage inflicted by each impact. The Others' ships had seemed almost like something untouchable, otherworldly, but his people had gunned down enough of them to put that particular view to rest. They were superior, far stronger than his own ships. They had massive advantages in combat.

But they could be killed.

"*Knicherus*, *Lovenus*, and *Trangus* report railguns out of action, Commander. *Trangus* indicates a possibility of restoration. The other two ships will require several months in spacedock to repair their weapons systems."

Ilius didn't respond, and he took mercy on himself and didn't try to calculate the odds on any of his damaged ships reaching a spacedock. He was about to order all ships whose railguns were down to advance and engage with secondary weapons systems, but a glance at the display told him they were already doing just that.

Advance, for his ships, actually meant deceleration first, and then acceleration in the opposite direction, back toward the transit tube. His fleet had reached the enemy position at high speed, and zipped right by. Now all his ships were blasting their engines, working down their velocities along the vector leading in-system...and his ships without railguns were in the lead, diverting all available energy to engines, struggling to close with the enemy and stay in the fight, somehow.

Ilius had always felt pride in his Kriegeri, but now that swelled beyond what he'd experienced before. He'd wondered how his warriors, always brave, but also always the stronger combatant, would handle facing a superior enemy. He'd been concerned, that their resolve would crumble, that they would not be able to match the grim endurance the Rimdwellers had shown in similar circumstances.

That doubt was gone. Utterly. Facing overwhelming odds had brought something out from deep within his Kriegeri fighters, a strength he'd never seen before.

No, not 'never.' You saw it in Barron's warriors...

His people had done their best, better than he'd dared to expect. But, as he looked out across the display, a conclusion solidified in his mind.

It's not going to matter. The battle is lost.

His people had blooded the enemy. No, more than that, they had hit the invaders hard. But they'd paid a staggering price for that. And his ships were too badly damaged, his crews too exhausted to continue much longer. He *had* to pull out. He had to get his fleet back where he could reorder his formations and repair at least some of the damage suffered.

But he did nothing. He just sat and watched his ships continue the fight. They were too far in, with no real chance to escape.

His only choice was to die running or die fighting.

And that was no choice at all.

* * *

Chronos knew the battle was over. All that remained was to determine what remained of Hegemony military power. If he lost his entire fleet, his people were doomed, whatever dim hopes remained extinguished utterly. The forces that remained, back at Calpharon, and scattered through all the inhabited systems of the Hegemony, were too few, too weak to mount a reasonable defense. At least without a core of the fleet he now commanded.

His people had fought hard, and in many ways, they had done better than he'd dared to hope. Now, it was time to save as many of them as he could. The dash back to the transit tube would be costly and dangerous, but he was sure he could get a good number of ships out. If he gave the order immediately.

But Ilius's ships were the problem. His friend's ships had moved deeper in-system than any other Hegemony forces, carried past the enemy line by their high velocities. He would order Ilius to withdraw as his own forces did, but he knew as he gazed at the positions of those ships, they would suffer terribly on their journey back to the jump point.

It was even possible they would be wiped out.

But there is no other choice. It is time to order the retreat...

"Commander! Scanners are picking up enemy ships inbound from the outer system." A pause, then, in an even more emotional tone, "They're heading toward the transit tube, Commander. They're positioning themselves between us and our line of retreat."

Chronos's head swung around wildly, his eyes moving to the end of the display and focusing on the new contacts. It was a sizable force, not as large as the main fleet units he was facing, but big enough to blast his worn and damaged ships to bits as they raced toward it...and past it to the tube. And they wouldn't be alone. The main enemy fleet would be on his tail, pursuing his fleeing ships. His forces would be trapped between the ships on their tails and the flanking force.

He'd be lucky if a dozen ships made it out of the system. *It was a trap, and you fell right into it. Fool!*

His thoughts were dark, his self-recriminations merciless. He'd lost the fleet in a single battle. He'd destroyed the Hegemony.

He watched as the last of Barron's ships moved through the tube. He didn't blame the Confederation commander. He'd exceeded an order or two himself in his time, but he'd never committed treason. He felt a spark of resentment at the Confeds for leaving his people to their deaths, but it didn't last. His warriors in the system, very likely about to die, had been the enemies of Barron and his spacers, killed their friends and comrades. The Rimdwellers might have agreed to help, and they might have made a difference. But there wasn't time to get over the past, to find a way forward.

Chronos turned back to the main section of the display. He almost ordered his forces to stand where they were, to fight until the very end. But even without significant hope, he *had* to make a run for the tube. If he could get twenty ships out, or ten…or even one, it was better than nothing.

Some way to keep the fight going, even without hope of victory.

*   *   *

"Admiral, all main fleet units have transited. Only *Dauntless*, *Repulse*, and *Indomitable* remain in the system."

Barron could hear the frustration in Atara's voice, the unspoken message screaming somehow from her perfectly on point words. *We should not be running.*

Barron agreed, almost more than he could endure. But now wasn't the time for treason, if there ever was such a time. The Confederation faced a new enemy—there wasn't any doubt in his mind about that—and strife between the fleet and the Senate could only hamper the war effort. When they saw all the data he had collected, even the most recalcitrant Senators would have to acknowledge the danger. He'd always believed he best way to handle politicians was to scare the hell out of them. That wouldn't be hard. He was a combat veteran of two decades' service, and *he* was scared to death.

"Advise *Repulse* and *Indomitable* they may transit when ready." There was no particular reason to hold *Dauntless* back, but somehow it helped him being the last to transit, the last to abandon the old enemy, the Hegemony warriors he was rapidly coming to think of more as allies.

Chronos is no fool. He's done some real damage to the enemy, convinced his warriors they can hurt the Others. They'll do better next time. He'll pull back…my guess is any time now. He'll make a run for the transit point, pull his fleet out, battered, but still a force in being. There would be another fight, Barron was sure of it, and with any luck, his forces and the rest of the Confederation fleet would take their places in the battle line.

Atara relayed the order to the two other battleships herself. Her tone was deadpan, totally without emotion. He'd served at her side in multiple battles, victories and defeats alike, but he'd never seen her look so…beaten.

Barron took a deep breath, and he looked one last time at the display, at the Hegemony fleet, for so long a feared and hated enemy, fighting with all the spirit and courage anyone could ask of veteran warriors. There was still resentment—he suspected some of that would remain all his life—but his respect was continuing to grow.

He held his gaze as one more enemy ship, and four of Chronos's battleships, vanished from the screen in the continuing melee. Then, his eyes dropped to the deck.

"Atara…bring us around in line behind *Repulse*. We'll transit immediately after…"

"Admiral!"

Barron's head swung around, trying to determine where the voice came from. His eyes settled on Ensign Caravelle, the most junior officer on *Dauntless*'s bridge.

"Enemy ships, sir...at least I'd bet they're enemy ships. Coming in from the deep outer system."

Barron looked back at the display, and he saw it. At least forty contacts, looking very much like the Others' ships.

"I think you're right, Ensign." He turned toward Atara. His first impulse was to order his last three ships to accelerate, to expedite their transit. But the words that came out were completely different.

"*Repulse* and *Indomitable* are to abort transit and decelerate to station-keeping velocity."

"Yes, Admiral." There was an energy in Atara's voice, one that hadn't been there a few seconds before. One Barron understood, but also thought misplaced. He knew she wanted to engage, to come to the aid of the Hegemony fleet—something he thought amusing considering the rage she'd still nursed when they'd first arrived—but three Confederation ships moving against more than three dozen enemy vessels was no cause for celebration.

"All ships are to launch full spreads of probes. I want all the data we can get on those ships."

But even without the enhanced scans, the reams of analysis the AIs would pump out, Barron already knew what was happening.

The enemy *had* beaten the Hegemony fleet to the system, at least an advance force. And they'd hidden deep beyond the farthest planet, out among the comets and deep space debris surrounding the star in the vast zone between the system and interstellar space.

It was a trap. The whole thing was a trap all along. And Chronos fell right into it.

You would have fallen into it as well...

His mind was racing, analyzing, trying to sort the information coming in too quickly to assimilate. But behind the uncertainty, the frantic confusion, a single conclusion was forming, one that struck Barron like and iron fist to the gut.

The Others were going to position themselves in front of the transit point. Chronos's ships would be forced to run right into the waiting guns of massed enemy ships...and they would have the rest of the Others' fleet hot on their tails, firing all the way.

His one assumption, the belief he'd used to justify his withdrawal, to convince himself he wasn't *really* abandoning his new allies, was gone, replaced by one unassailable fact.

None of Chronos's ships were going to escape. At least not many. Hegemony military might would be broken right in the Ettara-Mordlin system.

The war would be as good as over before he even heard back from the Senate, before a Confederation vessel fired a single shot.

Chapter Thirty-Seven

Temporary Government Headquarters
Liberte City
Planet Montmirail, Ghassara IV
Union Year 225 (321 AC)

"I want to thank you both, for your support. Gaston Villieneuve has been at the very pinnacle of the Union government for more than thirty years, and I do not dispute that he has exhibited enormous drive during that time, nor that he has some accomplishments to his name. But he has caused considerable harm as well, with his unrestrained paranoia, and his inveterate hostility toward the Confederation. A century of wars has stunted our economic growth, and defeat in the last of those conflicts brought us to the brink of ruin. I promise you both, and all those who support my term as First Citizen, there will be no more pointless war. I offer a future of prosperity, of growth in our economy that will rival that of the Confederation. I will see that we finally exploit long under-utilized resources. I will bring nothing less than cooperation with our former enemy, and even financial support from the Confederation that enables us to grow, to create wealth, to calm a restive population."

One of the men facing Ciara looked back, somewhat unconvinced from the look on his face. "There is much in what you say that is cause for satisfaction, Minister Ciara, yet I question how much of it is possible. Help from the Confederation? That seems a difficult proposition. Four wars and millions dead has created considerable enmity on their side of the border as well as on ours. You are very persuasive, Sandrine. Our presence here attests to that fact. But much of what you offer seems dangerously tentative." The general stopped short of according her the First Citizen's title she'd given herself. She felt her stomach tense slightly, and she reminded herself, the support she was thanking her guests for had not yet been fully given.

Simply put, she still had to close the deal.

She'd gained a shaky kind of control over Liberte City, and an even more tentative hold over the planet as a whole. But she was ahead of herself with the 'First Citizen' title, and she knew it.

"General, I understand your concerns. These are uncertain times, and yet, I believe we must rely on our trust for each other. I take you at your word that you can deliver the Liberte City garrisons, and effective control of all vital military bases on the planet...as well as the orbital defense forces, which are not even under your direct command. What is served by my doubting you, by my insisting on proof you cannot provide? I know you, I understand your stature among those you claim to represent. And I take you at your word."

She paused a few seconds, her eyes fixed on the general's. He looked a bit uncomfortable, and she waited until he was about to speak before she continued.

"But I *will* offer you proof, General, at least of my ability to deliver peace with the Confederation, and to obtain financial aid from them as part of an expanded and ongoing relationship."

The general's tension level eased slightly, his look of

skepticism replaced by one of curiosity. "How can you do that, Minister?"

"Allow me to introduce you to another of my allies. Ambassador?"

Alexander Kerevsky walked into the room from the small antechamber. Despite the dust and debris that seemed to be everywhere in the capital, the Union representative was dressed in his finest, looking as though he was about to meet the highest authorities.

Which, as far as Sandrine and her supporters were concerned, he was.

"General Riennes, Minister Chromas, it is a pleasure to meet you both. I believe we've crossed paths before, General, though we were never formally introduced." Kerevsky turned his head slightly, toward the third person standing around Ciara, and he nodded. "Minister Velechaun, it is a pleasure to see you again."

"The pleasure is mine, Ambassador." Velechaun was the first to respond, but the others followed almost immediately.

"Ambassador Kerevsky, it is a surprise, and a great pleasure to see you here." Riennes looked for an instant as if he might extend a hand, or bow slightly, or something. But in the end, he just managed a tense smile. The proper greeting for ambassadors in the middle of a coup was a matter of some question, especially when it appeared the diplomat was somehow involved in the change of government underway.

"Ambassador, I have heard much about you, and I am pleased to finally meet you in person." Adrienne Chromas was an exceedingly charming woman, who exhibited an aura of kindness and moderation. It was all fake, of course. Ciara found Chromas a bit offputting, though she knew in many ways the Sector Nine supervisor was almost a mirror image of herself.

There was a short, awkward silence, and then Riennes

spoke. "Ambassador, I apologize for the directness of what I am about to say, but I do not believe time and circumstances offer us any useful alternatives. Minister Ciara has suggested...no, I'd say rather more than *suggested*, that the Confederation would provide material assistance to her new government. Is this the case?"

Kerevsky looked back at Riennes. "General, I hope you will appreciate that I am going to answer you as honestly and completely as I can. I am a diplomat, and in my position, I have certain powers, certain discretionary assets I can employ on my own authority. I have—and I trust you will keep what I am about to say in the strictest confidence—advanced approximately one million Confederation credits to First Citizen Ciara for use in...securing the new government. I have prepared a dispatch to Megara, which I will send as soon as I am able to ensure a safe passage, recommending that the Confederation government authorize me to negotiate a new treaty with the Union, one that provides for a lasting peace between our two nations, and also for ongoing financial support, both in the form of direct subsidies and also in promoting investment in the Union by private Confederation industry. My people have never wanted to be an enemy of yours, General, and a Union government seeking peaceful coexistence and cooperation has always been our fondest wish."

Riennes didn't answer immediately. Ciara watched, trying not to let her nerves show. Kerevsky hadn't offered anything truly substantive—save for revealing that he'd provided moderate funding to her operations—but she hoped it would be enough. After all, if the ambassador had promised anything more substantive, it wouldn't have been believable anyway.

"Very well, Ambassador, your honesty is...refreshing. And it enhances your credibility in my view. If you are prepared to offer your personal assurance that you will pursue your stated requests with all your power and influence…" He turned toward Ciara. "…I believe I am prepared to offer my full support."

"As am I," Chromas added, before Kerevsky could respond.

The Confederation ambassador stood where he was, looking a bit uncomfortable, but otherwise completely steady. "I offer you my full assurance, General…and Minister, that I will do everything in my power to see that the Union receives all the economic support it needs to revitalize its economy."

Ciara was relieved as she heard Kerevsky's words. She'd managed to tape the proceedings, of course, despite her strictest assurances to both the Confed ambassador and her prospective Union allies that all surveillance systems had been deactivated. She vastly preferred persuading Riennes and Chromas to throw in with her…but she also believed in backup plans. The tapes would be more than enough to ensure both of her guests met an unpleasant end if Villieneuve retained power and saw them. She hoped to avoid blackmail, but it didn't hurt to have a little something close to the vest.

Kerevsky would be angry, too, if he found out. He'd been extremely reluctant to get so involved, but she'd managed to persuade him. She liked the idea of extorting her ally and lover even less than she did her other two guests, but she knew she would do what she had to do. She was close, so close, to absolute power. It was like a drug, and irresistible addiction. She would do anything to attain it, to feel its warm embrace.

Even sacrifice those closest to her.

General Riennes bowed his head forward and removed his hat. "First Citizen…I am yours to command."

* * *

"Fleet Admiral...your loyalty will not be forgotten. Montmirail is in the hands of madmen, the planet infested with traitors, and we must do whatever is necessary to cleanse our beloved Union." Gaston Villieneuve turned toward the other figure in the small group of three. He was still weak, and he'd given up trying to count the number of separate places on his body that hurt. But he had more important things to deal with just them...like holding on to his power. "Yours as well, Tia. I am quite impressed by the number of Sector Nine agents you have brought under your wing, especially when many at the highest ranks of the agency have descended to disloyalty and treason. You will both find me most appreciative and grateful."

"You are the rightful First Citizen of the Union. If we allow failed revolutionaries to seize power, killing thousands of innocent civilians in the process, what are we? Not a government, certainly. You have my loyalty, First Citizen, as always, but I must ask one thing of you, your solemn assurance that when we have defeated the traitors, you will do all that is necessary to clean house, to root out every disloyal official, every would be rebel. The rot must be ripped out, root and branch to ensure the future." Tia Salamanca was particularly vicious, even for a career Sector Nine enforcer, and it showed in her tone. Villieneuve had already promised her the top position in the agency once the coup was crushed, but he'd also made a mental footnote to get rid of her once he didn't need her anymore. She was too brutal, too smart...she could be a threat one day. And Gaston Villieneuve had promised himself, once the current crisis was over, he could cut off potential dangers at the root.

Villieneuve stared back at the Salamanca, his eyes narrow, his look one as frozen as space. "I can promise you, Tia, with absolute sincerity, that when this is all over, every conspirator, every sympathizer, every Union citizen that has failed to do his or her duty to deter and defeat the traitors, will rue the day they were born.

The word 'justice' had never had a darker, more threatening sound.

"Very well, First Citizen." The admiral spoke before Salamanca could respond. "I wish my first suggestion could be to blockade Montmirail now, to trap the treachery there, and to begin the cleansing at once. But I'm afraid that is impossible."

Villieneuve knew that already, but hearing it from his cohort truly made it hit home. He had a disadvantage in the capital system, at least at that moment. Ciara had surprised him with her resilience, and her pure audacity...though he was sure Kerevsky had also been involved somehow. It had taken all he could muster not to order the admiral to blast the Confed ambassador's ship to atoms, but the last thing he needed was trouble with the Confeds, at least while he was dealing with the insurrection.

Besides, the ship was sitting under the guns of the orbital forts...and Villieneuve didn't control those.

But once he'd crushed Ciara and her followers and reestablished himself in uncontested control of the government, he would see the Confeds were repaid for their interference...not matter how long it took.

"I am inclined to agree with you, Admiral, that the intelligent move now is to pull back and organize. We must rally support among the military and on the other worlds."

"We will have to leave the system at once, First Citizen. It is shameful, perhaps, but that traitor, Riennes, has managed to gain control over the system defenses, both the fortresses and the patrol fleet. Our forces here are inadequate to guarantee your safety, much less to attack and destroy the traitors, as I would like. The future of the Union is in our hands, and there is no room for carelessness, for unnecessary chances. We must go and rally the battle fleets, ensure that none of the heavy units, or as few as possible, fall into the hands of the conspirators."

"Indeed, Admiral. I agree entirely." It galled Villieneuve to be chased away from his capital, but his instincts had rarely betrayed him before. He didn't have enough strength in the Ghassara system, at least not enough to be sure of victory. He had to move first, and quickly. The struggle for power would ultimately hinge on who secured control of more military assets.

He liked to think he would easily secure all the fleet's heavy battle units, but he stopped himself. He couldn't underestimate Ciara again...and General Riennes had contacts throughout the navy. Some unit commanders would likely declare for the new government.

His first thoughts had been of quick fixes, of crushing the rebels, exterminating any who supported them. But the fight before him would be longer, more difficult than that. The situation had gone beyond a coup, beyond the machinations of groups of plotters and troops moving about in the dark. Things were about to get ugly. Very, very ugly.

The Union was about to erupt into civil war.

Chapter Thirty-Eight

CFS Dauntless
Ettara-Mordlin System
Year 322 AC

The Battle of Pharsalon – "Barron's Choice"

Barron stared at the display, unmoving, his eyes fixed on the enemy ships approaching his position. He could see Chronos's forces as well, clearly beginning a run for the transit point. If it hadn't been for the flanking force, a good number of them would have made it out, Barron was sure of that. They would have paid—heavily—but they'd have salvaged a force in being, lived to fight another day.

But now they were doomed. A few ships might make it through, but the fleet as a fighting unit would be destroyed, and with it, any hope the Hegemony had of resisting the enemy invasion.

Any hope the Rim had, too. There's no way we can face this enemy alone...

His head ached, a pounding pain, like a drum behind his temples. He'd saved his own force, all except the three ships remaining in the system. There was time to pull them out as well. He could leave Ettara-Mordlin without losses, and while part of him rejoiced at the lack of casualties, it made him feel somehow...dirty...to flee without harm when the cream of the Hegemony fleet was about to be obliterated.

He watched the enemy forces, analyzed their vectors. They'd been coming in on a line toward his ships, but they'd adjusted their course as his forces had withdrawn, and now they were moving several light minutes in-system from the point. Barron felt a surge of anger, a resentment that his force had been dismissed as a threat. Admittedly, his ships *had* run, and only three remained in Ettara-Mordlin. His trio of battleships was hardly a threat to the enemy, at least by any conventional standards...though pride surged out from the depths of his thoughts and asserted that three of the best battleships in the Confederation navy were a threat to *anyone*.

His mind rehashed the rules of engagement, the orders the Senate had given him. Clearly, the situation warranted action. His ships were on the flank of the enemy flanking force, and though the bulk of his force had transited, they'd gone through at minimal velocities. They could reverse their vectors very quickly and return...if Barron sent for them.

But he was forbidden to engage. There was no leeway, no latitude. If he attacked the enemy flanking force, he would do so in direct violation of the Senate's orders. Worse, the officers who obeyed his commands would be equally guilty. The rules of engagement had been published throughout the fleet, and every ship commander, every bridge officer, would know any order to attack was mutinous. Barron might throw his career away to do what he believed was right. He might even risk spending the rest of his life in a military stockade...or worse. But how could he do that to his people? They were loyal, devoted. If he ordered them in, if he asked them to follow him, he doubted one in a thousand would refuse. He told himself their actions would be their choice, that they had their own free will, but he didn't believe that was really true. Not in this case.

And yet, would he be serving them by allowing the Hegemony to be defeated? He had no doubt now, the Rim would be next...and that it would fall. The families, the loved ones of all his spacers, they would die, or become slaves. If anything was worth fighting for, wasn't preventing such a fate?

He was silent, deep in his own tortured mind. And then he made his choice.

"Atara...*Repulse* is closest to the transit point. They are to send a shuttle through with orders for the fleet to return at once at maximum possible speed...fully prepared for battle."

"Yes, sir!" He could hear the energy and excitement in her voice. There was no mistake, at least, that Admiral Atara Travis was a willing participant in the mutiny about to take place.

He turned and looked at the approaching enemy ships. If he plotted the right vector, he could catch them just as they were forming up to meet Chronos's escaping ships. The enemy was vastly superior in technology, but Barron's ships would have the positional advantage, at least at first.

And he would make it count.

There was only one problem. He'd have some real force when the rest of the fleet returned, but until then, he had to make three ships count.

"Atara, *Dauntless*, *Repulse*, and *Indomitable* are to set a course for 135.208.360, maximum thrust."

"Yes, sir!" Travis repeated the command into the comm with withering assertiveness. She was in her battle zone, the place he'd seen her so many times. She was ready to fight.

And so was he.

"*Repulse* reports shuttle away. Forty seconds until transit. All ships are on the specified heading at full thrust.

Barron felt the feral side of him taking control, pushing away the warning signs, even as the intellectual part of his brain screamed about the absurdity of leading three ships forward, unsupported. The rest of the fleet would be close behind, of course, and his tiny advance guard *would* have some surprise on its side. But it was still a wild risk.

Fighters, I need to get squadrons into space. Assuming they can scramble in time.

"Atara, scramble…"

"Admiral, I've got Jake Stockton on your line. He reports his fighter drill is underway on all three ships remaining in the system. All squadrons are in the bays and ready for launch."

"A what? What drill?" But even as he spoke the words, understanding dawned.

Barron was stunned, although he realized almost immediately that perhaps he shouldn't be. He was violating orders himself, and he'd never known an officer to be as liberal on interpretations of commands as Jake Stockton.

Though, technically, running a drill isn't a violation of anything…

And it meant he had over two hundred fighters ready to go.

He felt a wave of relief, gratitude that he had officers like Stockton serving under him, men and women who thought for themselves, showed initiative. Eighteen squadrons of bombers would vastly amplify the combat power he had available until the rest of the fleet returned. It wasn't enough force to meaningfully hurt the enemy either. But just *maybe*, it was enough to buy the time he needed until the rest of his ships could return.

He turned toward Atara, and he said, "All squadrons…launch. Their orders are to attack."

He took a deep breath, and he repeated the command.

"All squadrons…attack!"

* * *

"High Commander Hellerax…we're picking up three ships inbound from the jump point. The force that remained there during the battle has mostly withdrawn, but now the remaining vessels appear to be moving toward our flanking force."

The Highborn commander turned, glaring across the control room toward the Thrall officer. "That is absurd. What could three of the human vessels possibly hope to accomplish?" But even as he spoke, he saw the ships coming on himself...and, seconds later, small clouds of dots appearing in front of each.

His first thought was to turn to face the approaching ships, to destroy them and then come about to engage the enemy's main force even then approaching. But there wasn't time. If he turned, he would sacrifice the advantage of his longer-ranged weapons, and he would give the enemy main fleet time to make a run through his line, to get more ships out of the system.

And he was there to ensure the Hegemony fleet died where it was.

"Three ships, and whatever cluster of miniscule craft appear to be launching from them, cannot possiblely be a threat to the flanking force. All ships are to continue as per the existing plan, and to prepare to engage the small enemy force with rear batteries if it continues to close."

"As you command, Highborn." The Thrall, highly-ranked among his slave comrades, bowed no less obsequiously than those of lower positions. Then he returned to his station, snapping out his own orders to the other humans present in the control room.

Hellerax turned toward the display, watching himself as the new contacts moved forward, directing his thoughts to the ship's AI, commanding it to modify the scanning protocols. He remained committed to his directive, to interposing his force between the enemy fleet and its escape path. But he was troubled nevertheless about the strange behavior of the small group of enemy vessels. He reviewed the scans, analyzed the new information flowing in from the sensor arrays. For an instant, he imagined they weren't ships at all, but instead some kind of massive missiles, placed as a trap to move against his ships as they passed by. But the readings all suggested standard vessel similar to the others deployed in the system. If anything, the newer contacts were less advanced, their energy readings weaker than the other ships in the system.

He couldn't make any case to himself to alter the plan, to interrupt his fleet's flanking maneuver. If the three ships continued to approach, his fleet had more than enough firepower to destroy them, without deviating from the plan.

But what are those smaller contacts?

He watched as the clouds moved forward, advancing in front of the ships that had launched them. His first thought had been missiles, but scanner reports confirmed they carried no detectable quantities of antimatter. It was possible they were nuclear warheads of some sort, but he was confident his fleet's defensive batteries could handle them if they approached.

His conclusions made sense, and he believed they were correct. But he was still concerned.

Then, he pulled his attention away. His ships were approaching their appointed positions…and the enemy fleet, now in wholesale retreat, was approaching.

It was time to finish them. Time to make the victory complete.

* * *

"It's been a year, but I know none of you have forgotten the fighting around *Colossus*. I know what you can do, what you have done, so I won't waste words now. You are the best, the most elite squadrons in the fleet, and by extension, in all of human-occupied space. We're outnumbered here, and outgunned, but I've been watching this whole fight, and beyond the handful of Hegemony fighters, I haven't seen any other small craft. These bastards have savaged the Hegemony fleet, and they're going to do the same to our own ships...unless we do something about it. You've all got full bomber hits, and double-warhead plasma torpedoes, so make them count. These ships are tough as hell, there's no question about that. But, by God, so are we! So, follow me once again. Follow me into the fight!"

Stockton pulled back on the throttle, feeding power to his engines. He had no idea what kind of point defense to expect, whether the way toward the approaching ships would be wide open...or if one order from the enemy fleet commander would unleashed a wave of deadly fire that wiped space clean of his squadrons. He thought about it for a second, and then he put it out of his mind. It didn't matter. There was no choice. His people were going in anyway, and they'd know what they faced soon enough.

He stared at his combat display, at the lines of enemy ships ahead of his wings. They hadn't changed their alignment to react to Barron's approaching attack.

They probably don't consider three ships a major threat.

And that means, they haven't seen Lightnings, or at least they don't know what a few determined squadrons can do.

He felt his blood rising, the heat of battle flowing through his body. He was older, wiser than he'd been years before, and he'd come to appreciate the tragic cost of battle. But deep in his soul, he was still an animal, a predator.

A hunter.

"We don't know much about these ships, but we fought the Hegemony enough, and we saw how much trouble they've had here. This is a new enemy, the most powerful one we've ever faced. So, we're going to do just what we do best. We're going to take our Lightnings in, all the way in, and we're going to plant these torpedoes into the guts of those ships. There's something about them, something that throws off the scanners, so, let's see how that works at a thousand kilometers, or five hundred. Or less. Because when I say close, I mean *close*."

Stockton wasn't even sure what he was asking of his people was possible. But that had never stopped him before, and it damned sure wasn't going to here, hundreds of lightyears from home. He didn't know what kind of defenses the enemy had, but he hadn't seen them launch any fighters in the battle, so he was willing to bet his squadrons would come as a surprise to them.

Two hundred bombers weren't a lot, not against the fleet looming ahead...but he had another eight hundred on the way, and two hundred of those were sitting in the bays, courtesy of his staged drill, just as *Dauntless*'s, *Repulse*'s, and *Indomitable*'s squadrons had been.

He reached down, grabbed the throttle...and he blasted his ship at full thrust, knowing every one of his pilots would follow his lead. He looked again at his screen and then out of the front of the cockpit into the blackness of space.

Stockton knew what was happening, where he was leading his pilots. Into another war, against a new enemy, one even darker, more powerful than the ones they had faced before. Barely a year of peace, and now it was gone, and along with it, the hopes of so many of his people.

And the lives of the thousands who would almost certainly die in the war his attack was about to start.

Even his own thoughts, of time with Stara, of living a life without wondering if each day would be his last, and seeing that same fear in her eyes...they were shattered as well.

There was a part of him mourning, despondent over what was happening all around, but mostly, he found himself wishing he felt differently than he did, wondering what was wrong with him, what disconnect inside him drove the inexplicable thoughts taking control of him as his ship blasted hard toward the enemy, toward combat.

He felt like he was back home.

Chapter Thirty-Nine

Colossus
Lyra System
Year 322 AC

"You can't be serious, Admiral." Sonya Eaton stared back at Winters with an expression that suggested she was looking at a man with two heads. "There must be someone else, someone senior to me...someone better qualified."

"No one I trust as much as I do you, Sonya." Winters stood a meter from the flustered officer. He was telling the truth. He did trust her, and she'd proven her abilities again and again. But Winters was trying to make his point without mentioning that the fleet's pool of senior officers had been badly depleted by years of war. That was an unpleasant enough topic under any circumstances, but the last promising member of the high command to be killed had been her sister.

Sara Eaton had been the navy's rising star, the officer in the group just under Barron and Winters most likely to succeed one day to the top command. But the last war had claimed her, as it had Van Striker and so many others, and now it fell to her younger sister to fill her shoes.

"But, Admiral..."

"The decision's been made, Captain...though it's no

longer Fleet Captain Eaton, I'm afraid. Admiral Barron and I discussed this even before he left, and I'm afraid your command of something like Colossus makes it a virtual necessity. Your stars will be delivered to your quarters tomorrow, but for now, you'll have to take my word for it, Commodore Eaton." Winters extended his hand, and a stunned Sonya Eaton just stared at it for a good ten seconds before reaching out and grasping it.

"I don't know what to say, Admiral. I'm…"

"Don't say anything. You earned this position, and even more, you earned the trust Admiral Barron and I have in you. This feels like a reward now, but you may feel differently when we're fifty systems coreward, and you're sitting in the middle of the biggest target in the fleet. I only have limited information, but based on what Tyler sent me, this war is going to be nasty, far worse than any we've fought before, if you can wrap your head around that. We're going to need the best every one of us has to give…and not all of us are going to make it back. If any of us do. And you'll be commanding the one ship we don't really know how to operate. So, hold back the thanks, at least for now. You'll have Anya Fritz, and the team the Hegemony sent out to offer technical support, but you're still going to have one hell of a job on your hands."

"I'll do everything I can, Admiral. I won't let you down."

"I know you won't, and so does Admiral Barron. That's why you got this command. Just do your best, it's all any of us has to offer."

"Yes, Admiral. I will."

Winters nodded, and then he managed to smile, a skinny, haunting sort of grin. "One year of peace, Sonya. One year. We've barely licked our wounds, and we're not even close to replacing our losses…and it looks like another war has found us. Another enemy. One we know almost nothing about."

"That's okay, Admiral. We'll do what we have to do, as

we've always done." There was defiance in her tone, strength. But Winters knew it was almost certainly fake.

As fake as his own.

*   *   *

"I just wanted to tell you, we're all proud to have you in command, Commodore. We couldn't have a more worthy officer in charge...especially with us heading coreward, and possibly into battle." Anya Fritz stood in front of Eaton, and her words dripped with sincerity, even though the engineer was also a commodore, and one whose commission bore the earlier date. Frtiz technically outranked Eaton, at least when they were off *Colossus*. But the sparkling new commodore held the ship command, and with it, domain over everyone onboard. The official status of such an interpretation was a fact of no particular significance, however. Anya Fritz's rank was symbolic of her status, of all she'd done. But it was largely superfluous. The engineer had never expressed the slightest interest in commanding anything except her teams of sweating technicians.

"Thank you, Commodore Fritz. I'm hoping you can bring me up to speed on developments onboard. From what I've heard, you've made considerable progress." Eaton could see the power in Fritz's expression, the strength in her posture. The engineer almost radiated an aura of pure determination.

Eaton knew Fritz was unlikely to do anything besides work her magic to keep *Colossus* operating, and Eaton was grateful for that fact. But if Fritz ever stepped out of her bounds as head of the engineering team, Eaton doubted she could face down the legendary officer. Eaton was tough, herself, one who'd served alongside some of the Confederation's very best, but Anya Fritz was a force of nature.

Eaton was grateful they were on the same side. And

there was no one in the Confederation she'd rather have crawling around the almost endless guts of the massive warship, conflicting ranks or not.

"We have made progress, Commodore Eaton." A pause, and a sour look on Fritz's face. "The Hegemony team has been of…considerable…assistance."

Eaton didn't imagine the sentence she'd just uttered was the most difficult thing Fritz had ever done. But it sounded very much like it was close.

"That is not surprising, Anya…who even knows how many years they spent restoring it, and the newer tech in it is theirs, not ours. I have no doubt you'd have managed everything yourself, but right now, we need every shortcut we can get. Admiral Winters is already out at Dannith with the fleet, and we've got to follow as quickly as possible. I think our fleet is going to need everything it can get to win this fight.

Or even to survive it…

"I think you're right, Sonya…and there's no question, *Colossus* is the strongest thing we've got. The strongest thing the Hegemony's got, too." A pause. "With any luck, we'll be able to set out for the Badlands in a month, maybe a bit sooner."

Eaton had been hoping to get started more quickly, but she realized that had never been realistic. She just nodded.

Fritz stood quietly for a moment, and then she said, "It did help having the Hegemony team here, but we're going to need even more from them. If *Colossus* is going to fight a war for us, Admiral Barron's going to have to get more from our new…allies…than a few engineers. We can fly out there on fusion power, but when this thing goes into battle, we're going to start burning through antimatter…and if we don't want to turn this massive warship into a toothless floating hull, the Hegemony is going to have to give us more."

Fritz was silent for a moment before she continued.

"A lot more."

*   *   *

"The fleet will move out at once, Commander. All ships, full thrust to the number two transit point." Winters sat in *Victory*'s command chair, looking out over the flagship's staff. The battleship was the newest in the fleet, the largest and most powerful vessel ever launched from a Confederation shipyard. It was also one of the small number of active ships that was not a veteran of the recent war. Her launch had been barely three months before, and her workstations and corridors were still almost blindingly new and bright.

The ship had enhanced primaries built into her hull from scratch, weapons considerably more powerful than the patch jobs that had been crammed into the fleet's existing line ships. She carried an extra reactor as well, a triple fusion unit larger than anything the Confederation had built before on a movable hull, and a resource that cut a full thirty seconds from the recharge time of her main batteries. She was the best in the fleet—save, of course, for *Colossus*—and the natural choice for a flagship. Winters hadn't really thought twice about using her as such, though he'd thought for a passing moment that he would turn the ship over to Barron when the fleet linked up with the admiral's advance force.

Then he realized, with a bit of a grin, he probably couldn't pry Barron out of *Dauntless* with a crowbar.

And she's not even the real Dauntless, *at least not as far as he sees it...*

Winters was still a little surprised the Senate had approved a new war, that they had sent him coreward with broad new powers for Barron. That had all been Andi, of course, and he couldn't help but be relieved—and amused—at how thoroughly she'd outpaced both him and

Gary Holsten in efficiency. Winters had been ready to engage in outright mutiny, even to send Marines into the Senate chambers to force a vote at gunpoint. And he could only imagine the threats and blackmail that had spawned from Gary Holsten's dirty little collection of files.

But in the end, it had only taken one pregnant woman with the audacity to address the entire Confederation, to rouse the people behind one of their own, one of the few revered as a genuine hero on every planet in every system. Tyler Barron had inherited a beloved old name, and his own actions had only polished it further. Andi had recognized that, and she'd gone to the people, not as one of the most dangerous women alive, not as the warrior who'd killed Ricard Lille, but looking sad and desperate, asking for the men and women of the Confederation to rise up behind their hero, to leave the Senate no choice, no room for dirty political wrangling.

And she'd made sure the camera angles left no doubt she was carrying Tyler's child.

Winters imagined the general consensus was that Andi had been lucky to marry into a dynasty like the Barrons. She'd come from nothing, less than nothing, and most of her career had been disreputable to a certain extent at least, and obscured in the shadows.

But Clint Winters knew the more complex truth. Tyler Barron was pretty damned lucky, too, and Winters himself was fortunate to have them both as his friends.

He sat quietly, and thought about Andi, stuck home, out of the action for once, probably for the first time in her life. For all the dangers she'd faced, all the enemies she'd fought, he knew this would be her greatest challenge in many ways.

There wasn't much he could do about any of that, about the deadly dangers all his people faced, or the frustrations Andi would have to endure. But he promised himself one thing.

He would make sure Barron survived the war, see that he

made it back to his wife, to the child he didn't even know was on the way. He would do that whatever it took. Somehow.

Whatever the cost to him.

Chapter Forty

CFS Dauntless
Ettara-Mordlin System
Year 322 AC

The Battle of Pharsalon – "To Forge an Alliance"

Barron stared straight ahead, trying to decide who was crazier, him or Jake Stockton. He was leading three battleships in a reckless charge against a whole enemy fleet.

But Stockton was out in front, taking just over two hundred bombers into the teeth of that same fleet, with no idea whatsoever what kind of defenses the enemy had against small craft.

The only excuse either of them had was that they were well positioned to take the enemy ships from the rear. It was an advantage, but a fleeting one, and if Barron waited for the rest of the fleet to transit back, it would be lost.

Besides, the best he could figure, the rest of his ships would reach engagement range just about the same time as Chrono's retreating forces did on the other end. Atara and *Dauntless*'s AI agreed with his calculations as well. Without help, the Hegemony fleet would be torn apart, hit from two directions as they fled, and the only thing he could do to mitigate that was throw what he did have into the fight.

Immediately.

He slid around in his seat, his shirt matted to his back by sweat. It had only been a year since he'd been in battle, and he'd spent the last several months planning and expecting a fight. But now that it had come, he felt rusty, a little uncomfortable. How much of that was normal nerves before a battle, and how much concern over the consequences of his completely unauthorized and illegal actions, he had no idea.

"Admiral, *Conqueror* and *Endeavor* have just transited."

Barron felt himself exhaling, a bit harder than normal. He hadn't really doubted his fleet would return when they received the orders—though every command officer in the force was effectively abetting treason—but it was still reassuring to see they begin to appear.

Still, Atara's report, and the reality it represented, didn't change the calculus for the next twenty minutes or so—the returning vessels were well behind his tiny vanguard, and the ships had low intrinsic velocities as they came through. But it still gave him a boost...and he suspected it was good for morale all around.

"That's good to hear, Admiral Travis. This may be extraneous, but advise the new arrivals they are to proceed after us at full thrust and engage the enemy the instant they are in range. And I want full evasive protocols in effect. Those enemy weapons are no damned joke, and they'll open up long before we get into range." Barron wanted to believe his ships would come up from behind and avoid any heavy enemy fire until their own primaries were in range. But he couldn't count on it. The enemy would still focus mostly on the far larger Hegemony fleet, but he knew *he* would order a few ships to spin around and fire at the new attackers coming in, if he was in their place, and he wasn't going to bet the enemy commander would do anything different.

"Yes, Admiral."

An instant later, Barron added, "Advise Captain Devers

on *Conqueror*, she is to pass these orders on to the other ships as they arrive." That would save some time, a little at least. Conqueror was twenty light seconds closer to the transit point than *Dauntless* and her two companions. Not a big time savings, but Barron knew every second counted. Besides, he suspected he and Atara were going to get very busy, very soon.

"Yes, sir." A few seconds later. "Done."

Barron looked back at the display, watching as Stockton's squadrons closed. They were will within point defense range—at least what had been point defense range when facing Hegemony ships—but they hadn't been fired upon. Yet.

Barron let himself hope the enemy was baffled by his strike craft, that their immensely powerful ships were devoid of the precise weaponry needed to face bomber attacks.

It turned out, he was partially right.

* * *

"Commander, scanners show three of the Confederation vessels moving on the enemy flanking force. They appear to have launched bombers, and the strike force is moving into attack range."

Chronos heard the words, and he felt a strange mix of hope and confusion. He'd hoped Barron would find some way to intervene in the battle…but then he'd realized, it didn't really matter. The Confederation ships Barron commanded weren't enough to turn the tide anyway. Part of Chronos still wanted whatever help he could get, but he also cheered Barron's escape. It would serve little purpose, perhaps, save to allow the Confederation commander to die somewhere else, some other day. Chronos knew any hope of defeating the Others would die with his fleet, but he knew enough about Tyler Barron to bet he'd give the enemy a few surprises before he went down.

But now Barron was attacking with the last three of his ships that hadn't transited. That made no sense, none at all.

Not until Chronos saw the first two Confed hulls emerge from the tube.

He's bringing his ships back. He really is attacking.

He was confused, at first. He'd given up hope that Barron would violate his orders, throw his ships in to the hopeless fight. But then he understood.

Barron was hitting the flanking force, coming at them from behind.

He's outflanking the flanking force...

It made perfect sense. The enemy had been about to catch his fleet between two forces...but now their own flanking force was about to be hit from two sides.

Chronos stared for a moment, his mind racing, analyses flying wildly around in his thoughts. The enemy was tough, and they had enough strength in the system to crush both the Hegemony and Confederation forces.

But if we hit that flanking force hard enough...we just might do some real damage, and then get through the tube.

Live to fight another day.

"All ships, maintain full thrust. All targeting routines at maximum power. Ignore the ships on our tail. We're going to hit that force ahead of us...while the Confeds take them from behind." He felt a burst of energy, and an excitement that reinvigorated him, drove away the defeat that had lain on him like lead.

"All ships acknowledge, Commander. Except for Megaron Ilius's force. They are two light minutes behind us, and we are still awaiting a reply."

That was two minutes until Ilius got the command, and more than an hour before his battered force could reach the tube. Chronos had planned to rip through the enemy flanking force, make a dead run to escape the system. But if he did that, Ilius and his people were as good as dead.

Abandoning Ilius and his ships probably made sense,

despite the cost. Chronos's forces would remain a fleet in being; they would keep the war going. He knew his younger self would have pressed forward in an instant, gone with what the numbers and the cold analysis told him, despite the fact that Ilius was his friend.

But six years of war on the Rim had changed him.

Fighting against Tyler Barron and his warriors had changed him.

He wasn't going to leave his friend, and thousands upon thousands of Krieger, behind. Not without at least trying to buy them the time they needed.

"I want all railguns double loaded...and I want all secondary batteries online and firing as they come into range. We're going in...and we're going to blast that flanking force to radioactive scrap!"

* * *

Stockton's fingers tightened, and his ship lurched hard, loosing its payload toward the enemy ship right in front of him. He'd improvised on the way in, changed his tactics on the fly. He'd decelerated hard as he approached the enemy ship, something that seemed completely unnatural, but there hadn't been a choice. He wasn't able to get a solid target lock beyond a thousand kilometers.

And he wasn't able to get a *really* solid fix outside five hundred.

He'd let himself hope, for a few brief moments, that his bombers would be free from defensive fire as they approached. But that had been too much to hope for. The enemy batteries had opened up far closer in than he'd initially feared, and the weapons firing were cumbersome, clearly not designed for anti-fighter operations.

But they were deadly when they hit, and he'd lost over thirty of his ships since the batteries had opened up. And that number was almost certain to rise as his squadrons slowed almost to a standstill to deliver their torpedoes from a range so short, he didn't know what to call it. 'Point blank' and other terms of the sort had long applied to vastly larger distances. The concept of a bomber coming in less than five hundred kilometers was something new, something he'd just made up. At normal attack speeds that was less than a fifth of a second to the target ship, far too little time for an assaulting ship to pull away in time.

His ships *had* to decelerate hard and come in to knife-fighting range. It was the only way they could get effective targeting.

They'll probably call it the 'Stockton Maneuver.'

The thought of it made him sick to his stomach.

He watched his torpedo moving toward the enemy vessel. It was strange, as well, to see a warhead moving so slowly, but it had gone out with the intrinsic velocity of his almost stationary fighter. He hesitated for a few seconds, scolding himself for it as he pulled hard on the throttle and maxed out his engines.

You got lucky there, Raptor…someone was asleep at the switch. You were a sitting duck waiting to see if that torpedo hit.

He felt the g forces slamming into him, pressing him back into his acceleration couch. His ship began to move forward, and even as it did, he swung the throttle around, pulling away in as wild an evasive pattern as he could manage. He realized he was holding his breath, waiting for the fatal shot to come in. But it didn't, and as he sailed back past the target ship, he saw his torpedo slamming into the hull.

He didn't know how much damage, if any, he'd done…and he wouldn't have even had confirmation of the hit if he'd been quicker to make good his escape.

We're going to need some way to get decent scans and damage assessments…maybe a small probe or something to launch with the torpedo.

That was an issue, a problem that needed to be solved.

But not just then. Stockton had to get his people out after their runs, and get them back to base to rearm.

And he had to organize the squadrons he knew would be coming in next. First, a mirror image of the initial one, the wings from the other three ships that had run the fake drills. And, after that, the squadrons from the rest of the fleet, six hundred more ships, hopefully benefitting from what he'd learned so far on the first attack.

He looked down and winced as he saw that twenty more of his ships were gone, pilots who'd been less lucky than he was, who'd gotten blasted as they slowed to a crawl to commence their own attacks.

The feel of battle against the Others was entirely different than it had been against the Hegemony, but Stockton knew then and there, with a sickening certainty...the fights ahead would be no less costly than those of the last war.

"All squadrons, back to base. Refuel and rearm." But even as he gave the commands, he doubted there would be time for a second sortie. The mission was to get as much as possible of the Hegemony fleet out of the system...and then to run.

To run as quickly as possible, and then to regroup.

And to try to figure a way, *any* way, to stop the enemy next time.

*   *   *

"All ships, full thrust. Divert power from weapons, if necessary, but I want those engines at maximum output." Ilius hated running. It wasn't something he'd had to do very often, and he was finding the role as the underdog decidedly irritating. His first urge was to stay and fight, to fire his weapons with every last watt of power, to win where he was...or to die.

The problem with that plan was a simple one. The odds

of dying in such a scenario were close to one hundred percent. His ships were outmatched, and with Chronos's command heading toward the transit tube at maximum thrust, they were badly outnumbered, too. He was running for a simple reason. It was the only way to survive. The only chance to save even a portion of the Hegemony combat power he commanded.

The scene was a nightmare, the darkness of defeat coming down on him, the cold breath of death heavy on his neck. Ilius had overcome the fear he'd felt earlier, the vague and general panic at facing so mysterious an enemy. He'd regained control and the fear sitting in his gut now was more familiar, if it was also more severe than it had ever been. He was prepared to die, if that was his fate, but he couldn't lie to himself, couldn't ignore the fact that he was afraid.

He waved his hands at the various acknowledgements. His ships had all received the order. They would all fed what power they had into their engines. About half of his remaining force was still firing at least some of their weapons, but with every passing moment, every enemy hit, another ship's guns went silent. How many had sufficient engines and reactor power to make a good run at escaping was a guess.

Ilius leaned back, feeling the pressure as the g forces generated by *Anthrocles*'s massive thrust overwhelmed the dampeners. His ship had suffered damage in the battle, but providence had spared her engines and enough of her power generation to allow her to blast away at full thrust. That gave the ship a chance, at least, to make it to the tube. But it was still a long way. The massive velocity of Ilius's approach had plunged his ships deeper into the system than any other Hegemony forces, and that meant their route back out was just as long. He doubted any of his people would have made it out, but the intensity of Chronos's attack on the enemy flanking force, coupled with the apparent return of Tyler Barron's Confederation fleet, had distracted the enemy. Almost half the ships that had been bearing down on his battered and limping force had been diverted, sent to engage Chrono's ships before the enemy flanking force was overrun.

It was a welcome respite, though one he knew his comrades would pay for as the diverted ships closed on Chronos's command from yet another direction.

He turned to issue a new series of orders, but he never managed to get them out. *Anthrocles* suddenly shook hard, and the flagship spun wildly out of control. All around the bridge, and no doubt everywhere else on the ship, whole series of internal explosions erupted, one system's destruction setting off that of the next in showers of sparks and billowing eruptions of black and gray smoke. The bridge filled quickly with caustic fumes, and Ilius found himself choking and gasping for air along with his officers.

Then, an entire section of the ceiling and the support superstructure collapsed, burying half the bridge crew—and the fleet's second-in-command—under tons of metal and debris.

Ilius lay on the deck, feeling the pain of his broken body, gasping for a lungful of what passed for air on that tortured bridge, even as he wondered if his vessel had been mortally wounded.

If any of his ships would make it out. He didn't reach a conclusion.

Then everything went black.

Chapter Forty-One

CFS Dauntless
Ettara-Mordlin System
Year 322 AC

The Battle of Pharsalon – "Carry on the Fight!"

"All ships, commence deceleration now! All primary batteries, maintain maximum fire!" Barron's hands gripped the armrests tightly, sliding a bit on the sweat-covered leather. It was an affectation that had remained with him in battle, from his first desperate fight with the Alliance *battleship* Invictus, through all the wars he'd fought. It was harmless enough, though he could never explain exactly why he did it.

"Yes, Admiral. All units acknowledge. Deceleration full, primaries maintain fire."

Even as Atara spoke, *Dauntless*'s bridge lights flickered slightly, a sign the main guns had fired. Barron remembered when firing primaries knocked out almost all power to the rest of a ship for three, four, five seconds. Confederation reactors, and even more crucially, power transmission systems had advanced rapidly during the wars. For a brief few months, there had been no detectable signs of a ship's primaries firing, but then the enhanced guns were installed in the fleet's battleships, and the increased power drain caused the slightest return to the old dimming.

Barron watched as the particle accelerator beams lashed out, slicing through space toward their targets. *Dauntless*'s four shots all missed, the closest of the beams coming within two thousand kilometers of the target. His ships had all been upgraded with what was being called the '*Avia*' system, the advanced targeting routines Barron's stubbornness had extracted from his would-be Hegemony allies. But even with the Sigma-9 detection procedure, it was damned hard to hit the enemy ships. *Dauntless* had scored a single hit, on the battleship's first shot, but that early luck had not repeated itself. *Repulse* and *Indomitable* had also scored a single hit each.

That wasn't good enough. It wasn't going to get the job done, not unless the rest of the fleet got into range damned quickly. Barron had sent multiple communiques, urging the approaching units to push their engines to the max, and they'd responded by wildly abusing their power systems. Two ships, a battleship and a cruiser, had blown out their thrusters entirely. Barron had no idea if the damage was bad, or if the vessels had just ruptured a power line or something easily repairable. The answer to that question would determine if those vessels escaped with the fleet...or if fifteen hundred of his spacers were already effectively walking dead.

Barron was about to issue another order, or at least he was going to urge his gunners to focus harder, to do better. But before a word escaped his lips, he saw a flash on the display.

Indomitable was gone.

The battleship had taken a hit as the three ships approached the enemy line, a grazing shot, one that had inflicted significant but not critical damage. But the fatal shot had been dead on, a direct hit amidships, one that split the great vessel open, and tore its containment apart before its reactors could scrag. The explosion was cataclysmic, almost as though a small star had been born, and had lived a lifespan of perhaps thirty seconds before dissipating. There was nothing material left of the battleship, no matter at all larger than scattered atoms. Only a cloud of hard and dense radiation, where one of the greatest ships of the Confederation had been, with its eleven hundred crew.

Eleven hundred twenty-three, Barron's mind recalled, with unpleasant clarity.

He slapped his hand down on the comm unit, pulling up the direct line to *Dauntless*'s gunners. He had no place directing a single ship's operation, though for a few moments more his entire effective command consisted of only two vessels.

"Listen to me, all of you. This is Admiral Barron. We need to draw some blood. I know those things are hard to hit, but you have to make this Hegemony targeting system work. You have to give me what you've given me so many times before." Barron knew that wasn't entirely accurate, of course. A lot of spacers had been through the crew rosters of the two *Dauntless*'s. He tended to think of them as all one group, even though he knew that was inaccurate. His normally complete recollection of such details eluded him, though, and he had no idea how may of the gunners down there were veterans of the Hegemony War, and how many were fresh transferees from the brief peacetime restructurings.

He didn't even know if there was anyone in gunnery who'd served on the old *Dauntless* in the Union War, or even earlier, in the fight with *Invictus*, when his beloved ship had faced the Alliance flagship out on the Far Rim.

But he didn't care. If they were on *Dauntless* now, they were members of that family…and he expected them to act that way.

And that meant finding a way to hit those enemy ships.

"And increase the power flow on all weapons. Knock it

up to one thirty..." That wasn't aggressive...it was straight out reckless. But the situation was already desperate. "...and make your shots count."

"Yes, Admiral." The gunnery officer's response was shaky, edgy. Barron wasn't sure if the man was more scared of the enemy...or of him. He tried not to misuse the weight his name and record placed on his words...usually at least. But just then, he was willing to employ any manipulation to get what he needed from his people.

He watched as another shot went wide, and then, as *Repulse* fired a few seconds later and scored a hit. Barron's clenched his fist in satisfaction, but part of him was disappointed *Dauntless* hadn't connected first.

But his flagship, the namesake of his beloved old command, didn't let him down. Two minutes later, the recharged primaries fired again...and three of the four shots struck a damaged enemy ship just ahead. One of the hits cut a long gash in the outer hull, but the other two struck the vessel dead center.

The ship hovered in space for a few seconds, as Barron and every officer on *Dauntless*'s bridge watched in tense anticipation.

Then, a cheer went up as the enemy vessel exploded in the fury of matter-antimatter annihilation.

His people had drawn blood...and even as he watched and listened to his people celebrating, the volume rose to almost deafening levels.

The first line of the approaching fleet had moved into position, and almost as one, thirty Confederation battleships opened fire.

* * *

"Commander Chronos...the Confederation fleet is fully engaged. They caught the enemy flanking force from behind. The Others have begun to adjust their facings, and they're heavily engaging Admiral Barron's ships now. But the Confeds took out three of the Others' ships…and they did heavy damage to five more."

Chronos listened to the report, feeling a strange sense of relief that, for once, he wasn't on the receiving end of Tyler Barron's fury. The Confed ships were outmatched, of course, but at least they had the transit tube just to their rear. His own ships were under fire from behind now, the main enemy fleet closing hard, even as his force continued its fight against the flanking formation ahead of it.

As they tried to buy time for Ilius's ships to escape. At least some of them.

Chronos hadn't been able to contact his friend. *Anthrocles* had been badly hit, though through some miracle, the flagship had managed to maintain a reasonable amount of its thrust capacity. But repeated communiques to its bridge had gone unanswered.

Chronos wanted to hold his position, to give Ilius's people more time. But he knew he couldn't. He and Barron had bracketed the flanking force between them, and inflicted considerable damage. But now, his own ships faced the same treatment. He could make a run for it, dashing through the battered and disordered enemy task force that had intended to bar his route. But he had to do it without any delay. Every second lost brought the mass of the enemy fleet closer to the rear of his shattered formation.

He looked over at the display. Ilius's ships were coming on hard, most of them at least. There were a few lagging behind, vessels with damaged engines or compromised power generation. Chronos wanted to help them, but he knew there was nothing he could do. Every Master, every Kriegeri on the ships that couldn't keep up was going to die.

As more than a billion of our people have already…

"Kiloron, we're out of time. Commander Ilius's forces will have to follow us the best they can." He'd have felt better if he'd been able to reach Ilius, but it really didn't matter. He couldn't sacrifice the Hegemony's ability to fight on, not even in a direct exchange for this friend's life.

"All ships, full thrust forward...directly toward the Confeds on the other side...and the transit tube beyond."

* * *

"Go, go, go...all of you. Full deceleration as you approach. I don't want anybody firing from outside five hundred kilometers...so make sure you slow down enough to maneuver inside the envelope." Stockton had led his second strike in, just over two hundred bombers, the same as he had the first wave. Now he had six hundred coming in, every remaining fighter the ships of the fleet carried. There were rookies in there, mixed with veterans...and a few real aces in the mix. But they were all facing something new. A different enemy, and different tactics to engage that foe. They were learning as they went, and he was directing them, leading them, even though he had only an hour's more experience at it than they did.

But he was Jake Stockton, and as uncomfortable as it made him to acknowledge the effect that had on his pilots, the reality was undeniable. And useful. He could get more from the squadrons than anyone...and young pilots would die for him almost without hesitation. It was a heavy burden, one he knew he'd carry to his grave. But that didn't matter just then. He *needed* those pilots to fight for him, to do as he said.

To die for him.

He watched as eight Lightnings, all that remained of a squadron, moved in on an enemy ship, blasting their engines at overload levels, decelerating until they came almost to a halt in front of their target. The two closest were less than three hundred kilometers away, and all were inside the five hundred kilometer zone.

Two of them disappeared almost immediately, but the

other six managed to get their torpedoes off. The weapons moved toward the enemy ship, their engines burning furiously, accelerating them from the almost zero intrinsic velocity they'd launched with.

The enemy defensive fire took out two of them, but the other four slammed into the target in rapid succession. It was almost impossible to miss at such close range.

Barron's eyes darted back to the fighters, now only three...and then he watched as another vanished. He could imagine the frantic efforts as the last two pilots scrambled to blast their engines, to build up enough velocity to conduct some sort of evasive maneuvers.

And the fear...he imagined what those pilots were feeling, the last of twelve as they were, racing against time, against an enemy they didn't understand. Stockton was transfixed for a moment, hoping against hope they would make it.

But he knew they were dead, even before two sharp spears of energy finished them both, no more than ten seconds before the containment failed in their target ship, and that vessel disappeared in a billowing cloud of titanic fury.

Stockton mourned his lost pilots, a whole squadron wiped out, but one thing really hung there for him, like a dark cloud.

They didn't live long enough to realize they'd taken out their target...

That seemed like a small enough mercy, and yet one his lost pilots had been denied.

It was the kind of thing only one of his pilots could fully understand.

* * *

"All ships with damage to drive or power systems are to transit immediately, at maximum possible speed. And all escorts." The smaller ships existed to protect their larger cousins, but against the approaching enemy battle line, the cruisers and smaller vessels had nothing to offer, save for more dead spacers if they stayed. "Fully operable battleships are to remain in position, and prepare to receive returning bomber squadrons." Barron knew they were running out of time, but there was no way he was abandoning Stockton's fighters. The bomber wings had done their share—more than their share—yet again, and Barron was confident he could get them landed and make good his escape.

At least something close to confident.

Most of Chronos's ships had gone through the point already, and the survivors from Ilius's battered task force were going through now. Chronos had argued with Barron, insisting the Confederation ships transit first, but the Hegemony forces were the harder hit by far, and Barron's were in the best position. The Confed admiral had held his ground, and Chronos had finally yielded and sent his people through. But *Leonidor* remained, attaching itself to the Confederation line with the Hegemony's supreme military commander at the helm.

We'll make one of us out of him one of these days...

Lingering resentment clashed with newfound respect, but Barron was at last confident that he, and most of his people, could find the way forward, the way to stand beside their old enemies and face the new threat that endangered them all.

The Senate presented a worse problem than an old enemy turned ally.

"Admiral Stockton reports his lead squadrons will enter final approach range in two minutes, Admiral."

"Tell him his ships are to land anywhere they can reach. And all battleships are to make their run through the point as soon as their bays are full."

"Yes, Admiral."

Barron knew the landing would be a terrible, confused

mess…but he also knew Stockton would make it work. They could reorder the squadrons later, get the fighters back to their own motherships. All he cared about at that moment was getting his people out of there, the fastest way possible.

He felt satisfaction growing inside him, a warm glow at what his people had achieved, but he pushed back hard against it. They weren't out yet, and even if his forces made good their escape, they had paid a heavy price for their intervention. They'd saved Chronos's fleet, what was left of it anyway, but they'd lost more than twenty percent of their number, and even more of their bombers.

And that didn't even take into account the fact that Barron was much more likely to face a trial and imprisonment than a victory parade.

But at that moment, there was nothing in the universe that mattered, nothing save his spacers. The Senate could order him shot when he got out, but until then, he would do everything possible to bring out as many of the people who'd followed him in as he possibly could.

He watched as Stockton's lead units approached the waiting battleships. The formation was a disordered wreck, but the strike force commander was somehow keeping it all just enough in line, directing groups of fighters to waiting motherships, and nursing his wounded birds in, too. Barron couldn't understand how Stockton had any fuel left—he'd launched with the first strike, and both those ships and the entire second wave, had already landed. But no one knew how to fly that ship like Jake Stockton did. He'd land it, even if he was down to his last watt of power when he did it.

Barron saw a cluster of fighters heading toward *Dauntless*, bound for the flagship's waiting bays. He figured it would take another ten minutes, maybe twelve to get all the squadrons safely aboard…and fourteen or fifteen before the rest of the enemy force got close enough to open fire.

That was *close*, but it wouldn't be the first time he'd survived by a margin of two or three minutes.

Barron's and Chronos's ships had battered the enemy flanking force, inflicting heavy losses and forcing at least part of the line to pull back. There were sixteen of the deadly vessels still in position, and they continued to fire away at the retreating Confeds, a fact Barron recalled sharply as *Ardent*—and the forty-one fighters that had landed in her bays—blinked off the display, one more casualty near the end of a bloody day.

Another few shots ripped by close to his ships, but he'd trained his people well. Conducting evasive maneuvers while launching or recovering fighters was an impossibly difficult maneuver, probably something out of reach to any team that didn't have Barron in the command chair and Jake Stockton herding the squadrons in.

Barron watched as the last of the wings flew into the bays, and then as Stockton himself came into *Dauntless*'s bay, the last to land Then, he snapped out the order. "All remaining ships, maximum thrust for the transit point. And advise Commander Chronos that it's time to get the hell out of here."

Chapter Forty-Two

Planet Calpharon
Sigma Nordlin IV
Year of Renewal 267 (322 AC)

"I know Chronos has thanked you, Admiral Barron, multiple times I suspect, but now it is for me to do the same, to offer my sincere gratitude, both personally, and as Number One of the Council, on behalf of the entire Hegemony." Akella stood in front of Barron, wearing the strange robe and pants combination that seemed to be the Hegemony's incarnation of formal civilian dress.

He nodded, and he said, "Thank you, Akella. Perhaps, you will send an affidavit to the Senate on my behalf, requesting leniency at my court martial." He smiled thinly as he spoke the words. He'd meant it as a joke, but it had come out sounding serious. The truth was, he didn't think anything Akella said would make a difference. He fully expected the Senate to crucify him...but he didn't care. He was sure he'd done the right thing, and he knew he'd do the same thing again if he had the chance. And against the losses his people had suffered—27,544 casualties at last count, over seventeen thousand of them killed—he found it hard to care what the pompous fools on Megara did to him. What was a cell somewhere, compared to the sacrifices his spacers had made? The only thing that really tugged at him was leaving Andi behind. Had he married her so she could live in loneliness, while he spent the rest of his life in the stockade? He wished he could let her go, convince her to leave him, to start a new life somewhere else—with someone else, if that was what she wanted—but he knew her too well. She was even more stubborn than he was, and she would never leave his side, even if she could only remain there in a figurative sense while he rotted away in some cell.

He looked over at Akella, though, and through his own pain and uncertainty, his remembered an enemy turned ally, one he could imagine one day calling friend.

If he survived.

"Ilius...have you..."

"He's still alive, but that's about all I know. It's all anybody knows. The med teams have been working around the clock, but the only thing they've managed to come up with is that they're shocked he's still alive." A pause, as Akella looked down sadly. Chronos is there now. The two are very...close."

Barron felt the urge to go himself, but he held back. The Confederation and the Hegemony had fought alongside each other...once, in the closing moments of the battle. Barron knew they were tied together, that each owed any hope of survival to the other's aid and cooperation. But human beings were fragile and flawed creatures, and old hatreds died hard. He'd learned to work with Chronos and the Hegemony commanders, to fight with them. But he imagined how he would feel if Atara lay in a hospital bed, near death...if he would welcome Chronos in that stressful and painful moment.

No...not yet. I will wait, give them time. If this alliance is going to work, we need to learn to respect each other, to recognize the strengths of the other, as well as the weaknesses.

"Any word on the enemy fleet?"

"That's one bit of good news, or what passes for good news these days...amid a storm of bad news. They seem to have paused. The few scoutships we've managed to get in and out have collected some data. The Others inflicted far more damage than they sustained, of course, a loss ratio we cannot possibly sustain. But it appears our combined forces inflicted enough damage to delay the enemy offensive. Whether they've paused to make repairs or whether the fight in Ettara-Mordlin drained their supplies more quickly than they expected—or, most likely, both—we have gained a respite, probably a brief one."

"That is certainly good news." It *was*, by all military standards, but Barron knew, if enough time passed, word would reach Megara of what he'd done...and the Senate would send orders relieving him, demanding he return at once to be tried. He didn't know how he'd handle that when it happened. He'd probably ignore it if it came on some courier boat, without the force to impose the Senate's will on him. After all, how much worse could it get than treason?

But if the Senate sent a fleet, could he expect the spacers with him to resist, to fight their comrades? Or would he try to subvert whoever was sent for him? He didn't know...and he was sure he wouldn't know, not until the situation was upon him.

"You said bad news, Akella?"

"Yes...well, aside from the entire situation, of course. This is likely something you would have noticed immediately if you knew our stellar geography better...but there are no highly defensible systems between Ettara-Mordlin and here, no good place to mount another effort to stop the enemy fleet."

Barron stared back at her, feeling a coldness as he grasped where she was going. "So, the next battle will be..."

"Here." She paused. "That is right, Tyler Barron. In all likelihood, our next chance to stop the enemy, and very likely our last chance, will be right here. At Calpharon."

*   *   *

"Come on, old friend…you made it this far. No one on the medical staff can explain how you did. What's the point of surviving all the way back here just to die in the hospital? Besides, I'm going to need you. I can't win this fight alone." Chronos sat next to the pod holding Ilius's almost lifeless body. Somehow, *Anthrocles* had made it out of Ettara-Mordlin and all the way back to Calpharon, despite damage that had seemed desperately critical.

And inside the monitor's broken and battered hull, Ilius, the second in command of the fleet, lay in a deep coma, clinging somehow, even less explicably, to his own life.

Fewer than half of Ilius's ships had made it out of Ettara-Mordlin, and for all Chronos told himself the Hegemony fleet remained a battleworthy force, between the lost ships and the dozens and dozens of badly damaged hull in need or repairs, he wasn't really sure. Tyler Barron was a welcome addition, though it still remained to be seen how much Confederation power he could deliver. Chronos couldn't imagine the Rimdwellers turning on their great hero, ignoring his warnings.

But then he was often shocked and appalled at some of the petty nonsense that dominated the Council proceedings, and by all accounts, the Confederation Senate was worse.

Chronos had survived his first battle against the Others, and he had learned a great deal about the enemy. Some of that was useful, and he was beginning to understand how to fight them. But more of it simply sapped his strength, and filled him with a dread that told him his people were doomed, that they could never win the fight that lay ahead.

He was ready to do whatever was necessary. He would scrape up every ship in the Hegemony, every vessel stationed somewhere—anywhere, and he would bring that strength to the capital. When the Others came, he would be ready. Ad ready as he could be.

And just maybe, he'd have Confederation reinforcements at his side.

Tyler Barron at his side.

* * *

"*Victory*, this is *Dauntless*. Do you read?"

Barron listened to the comm officer repeating the communiqué, reaching out to the flagship of the enormous Confederation fleet still emerging from the transit point.

Barron had been surprised when the Hegemony scoutships had reported approaching Confederation vessels, and absolutely stunned at the size of the force as he watched it coming through. The ships had not answered any communications—not surprising considering they were deep in Hegemony territory, and at least somewhat concerned about whether it was hostile space or not—but then a signal came through from Victory. Whoever was in command of the massive force was almost certainly in the Confederation's largest and newest battleship, and Barron waited anxiously for the answer to the question eating away at his insides.

Are they here to join the fight...or to arrest me?

He'd been pessimistic at first. Despite his urgings, he simply could not imagine the Senate doing what he'd asked. But then he'd realized. There hadn't been time for word of his mutiny to get back to Megara, and much less, for a fleet sent in response to arrive.

Despite himself, he found optimism creeping in.

Then, the answer came back, and it was spoken by no comm officer, no sterile AI's. Just a voice he knew immediately, blaring through the speakers.

"Admiral Barron, you old wardog, your reinforcements are here. I just hope we didn't miss the party."

"Clint Winters, my God, are you a sight for sore eyes. Or, maybe no a sight, exactly, but damn, am I glad you're here." Barron paused. "But how...how the hell did you get those fools in the Senate to send the whole fleet?"

"It wasn't me, old friend...nor for that matter, Gary Holsten. We were still running around in circles, trying to figure out what to do, when that wife of yours stepped up and made those corrupt old fools behave like a bunch of trained lap dogs."

"Andi?" Barron sound surprised, but he wasn't. Not really. He'd known Andi too long for that. "What did she do?"

"I'll tell you when I see you, my friend. It's one hell of a story. Simple as hell...and yet brilliant."

Barron just smiled. 'Simple but brilliant.' That was Andi. Her way had always been a combination of directness...and her own form of vaguely twisted genius. It was part of what he loved about her.

"We can talk back on Calpharon. I've already cleared the fleet's approach authorization."

"If it's okay with you, I'd like to shuttle over to *Dauntless* now. I have some things to discuss that I don't think should wait. And one thing, I *know* shouldn't, a message from Andi for you. One you've got to see as soon as possible."

Barron wasn't sure what Andi would have to say, but any communication from her was good news as far as he was concerned.

"Come on over...it'll be good to see you again in flesh."

"I'm on my way, Ty...and sit down, and relax for a few minutes. This may be the last time you hear this for a long while, but I've got good news for you."

Blood on the Stars will Continue with
The Last Stand
Book 14

Appendix

Strata of the Hegemony

The Hegemony is an interstellar polity located far closer to the center of what had once been the old empire than Rimward nations such as the Confederation. The Rim nations and the Hegemony were unaware of each other's existence until the White Fleet arrived at Planet Zero and established contact.

Relatively little is known of the Hegemony, save that their technology appears to be significantly more advanced than the Confederation's in most areas, though still behind that of the old empire.

The culture of the Hegemony is based almost exclusively on genetics, with an individual's status being entirely dependent on an established method of evaluating genetic "quality." Generations of selective breeding have produced a caste of "Masters," who occupy an elite position above all others. There are several descending tiers below the Master class, all of which are categorized as "Inferiors."

The Hegemony's culture likely developed as a result of its location much closer to the center of hostilities during the Cataclysm. Many surviving inhabitants of the inward systems suffered from horrific mutations and damage to genetic materials, placing a premium on any bloodlines lacking such effects.

The Rimward nations find the Hegemony's society to be almost alien in nature, while its rulers consider the inhabitants of the Confederation and other nations to be just another strain of Inferiors, fit only to obey their commands without question.

Masters

The Masters are the descendants of those few humans spared genetic damage from the nuclear, chemical, and biological warfare that destroyed the old empire during the series of events known as the Cataclysm. The Masters sit at the top of the Hegemony's societal structure and, in a sense, are its only true full members or citizens.

The Masters' culture is based almost entirely on what they call "genetic purity and quality," and even their leadership and ranking structure is structured solely on genetic rankings. Every master is assigned a number based on his or her place in a population-wide chromosomal analysis. An individual's designation is thus subject to change once per year, to adjust for masters dying and for new adults being added into the database. The top ten thousand individuals in each year's ratings are referred to as "High Masters," and they are paired for breeding matchups far more frequently than the larger number of lower-rated Masters.

Masters reproduce by natural means, through strict genetic pairings based on an extensive study of ideal matches. The central goal of Master society is to steadily improve the human race by breeding the most perfect specimens available and relegating all others to a subservient status. The Masters consider any genetic manipulation or artificial processes like cloning to be grievously sinful, and all such practices are banned in the Hegemony on pain of death to all involved. This belief structure traces from the experiences of the Cataclysm, and the terrible damage inflicted on the populations of imperial worlds by genetically-engineered pathogens and cloned and genetically-engineered soldiers.

All humans not designated as Masters are referred to as Inferiors, and they serve the Masters in various capacities. All Masters have the power of life and death over Inferiors. It is not a crime for a Master to kill an Inferior who has injured or offended that Master in any way.

Kriegeri

The Kriegeri are the Hegemony's soldiers. They are drawn from the strongest and most physically capable specimens of the populations of Inferiors on Hegemony worlds. Kriegeri are not genetically-modified, though in most cases, Master supervisors enforce specific breeding arrangements in selected population groups to increase the quality of future generations of Kriegeri stock.

The Kriegeri are trained from infancy to serve as the Hegemony's soldiers and spaceship crews, and are divided in two categories, red and gray, named for the colors of their uniforms. The "red" Kriegeri serve aboard the Hegemony's ships, under the command of a small number of Master officers. They are surgically modified to increase their resistance to radiation and zero gravity.

The "gray" Kriegeri are the Hegemony's ground soldiers. They are selected from large and physically powerful specimens and are subject to extensive surgical enhancements to increase strength, endurance, and dexterity. They also receive significant artificial implants, including many components of their armor, which becomes a permanent partial exoskeleton of sorts. They are trained and conditioned from childhood to obey orders and to fight. The top several percent of Kriegeri surviving twenty years of service are retired to breeding colonies. Their offspring are Krieger-Edel, a pool of elite specimens serving as mid-level officers and filling a command role between the ruling Masters and the rank and file Kriegeri.

Arbeiter

Arbeiter are the workers and laborers of the Hegemony. They are drawn from populations on the Hegemony's many worlds, and typically either exhibit some level of genetic damage inherited from the original survivors or simply lack genetic ratings sufficient for Master status. Arbeiter are from the same general group as the Kriegeri, though the soldier class includes the very best candidates, and the Arbeiter pool consists of the remnants.

Arbeiter are assigned roles in the Hegemony based on rigid assessments of their genetic status and ability. These positions range from supervisory posts in production facilities and similar establishments to pure physical labor, often working in difficult and hazardous conditions.

Defekts

Defekts are individuals—often populations of entire worlds—exhibiting severe genetic damage. They are typically found on planets that suffered the most extensive bombardments and bacteriological attacks during the Cataclysm.

Defekts have no legal standing in the Hegemony, and they are considered completely expendable. On worlds inhabited by populations of Masters, Kriegeri, and Arbeiters, Defekts are typically assigned to the lowest level, forces, with senior officers of the rank sometimes directing combat units as large as twenty to fifty thousand. Kiloron is usually the highest level available to Kriegeri, though a small number have managed to reach Megaron status.

Megaron

The title suggests the command of one million combat soldiers or the equivalent power in tanks and other assets, however, in practice, Megarons exercise overall commands in combat theaters, with force sizes ranging from a few hundred thousand to many millions. Megarons are almost always of the Master class.

Blood on the Stars will Continue with

The Last Stand
Book 14